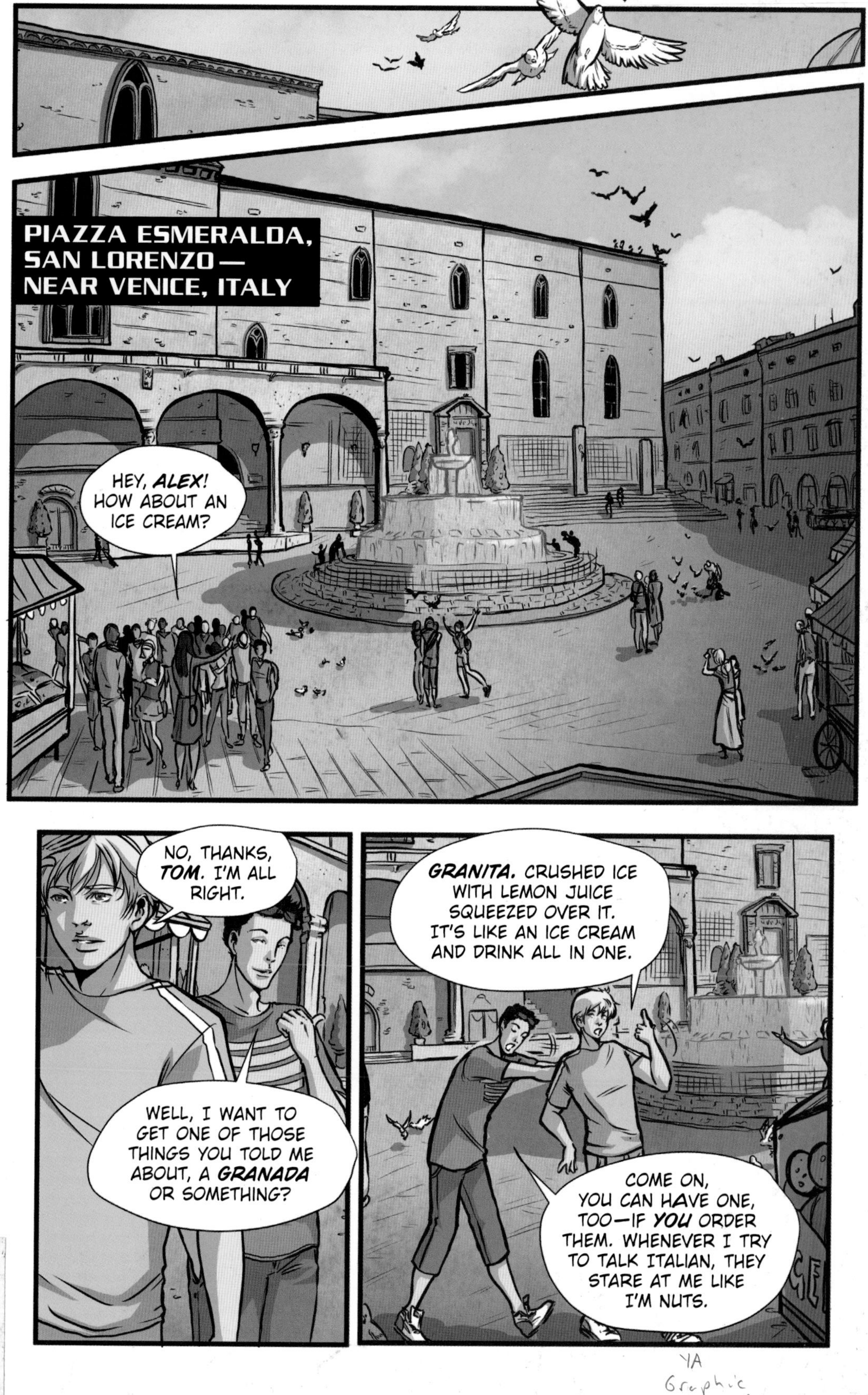
PIAZZA ESMERALDA, SAN LORENZO— NEAR VENICE, ITALY
HEY, ALEX! HOW ABOUT AN ICE CREAM?
NO, THANKS, TOM. I'M ALL RIGHT.
WELL, I WANT TO GET ONE OF THOSE THINGS YOU TOLD ME ABOUT, A GRANADA OR SOMETHING?
GRANITA. CRUSHED ICE WITH LEMON JUICE SQUEEZED OVER IT. IT'S LIKE AN ICE CREAM AND DRINK ALL IN ONE.
COME ON, YOU CAN HAVE ONE, TOO—IF YOU ORDER THEM. WHENEVER I TRY TO TALK ITALIAN, THEY STARE AT ME LIKE I'M NUTS.

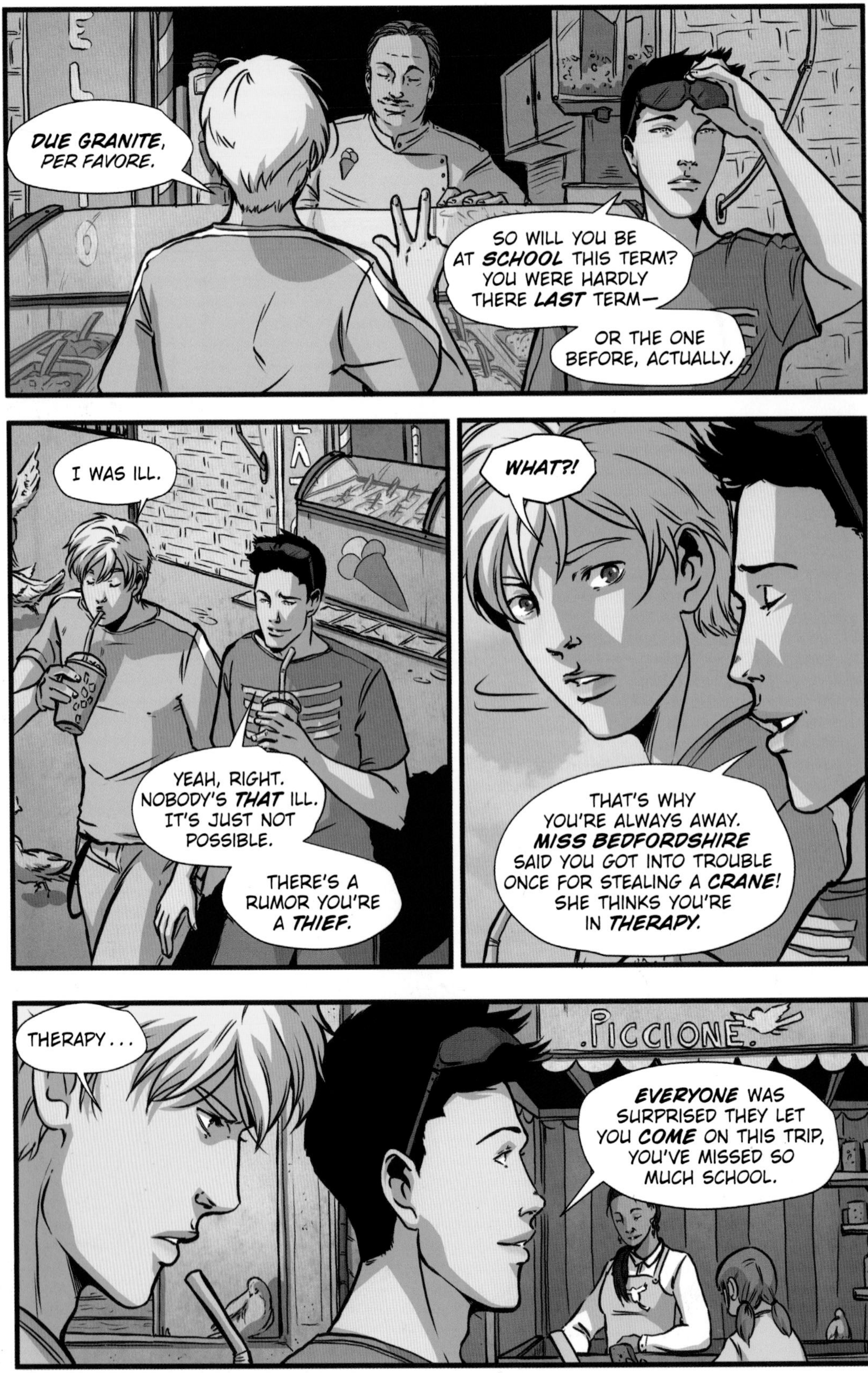

DUE GRANITE, PER FAVORE.
SO WILL YOU BE AT SCHOOL THIS TERM? YOU WERE HARDLY THERE LAST TERM—
OR THE ONE BEFORE, ACTUALLY.
I WAS ILL.
YEAH, RIGHT. NOBODY'S THAT ILL. IT'S JUST NOT POSSIBLE.
THERE'S A RUMOR YOU'RE A THIEF.
WHAT?!
THAT'S WHY YOU'RE ALWAYS AWAY. MISS BEDFORDSHIRE SAID YOU GOT INTO TROUBLE ONCE FOR STEALING A CRANE! SHE THINKS YOU'RE IN THERAPY.
THERAPY . . .
PICCIONE
EVERYONE WAS SURPRISED THEY LET YOU COME ON THIS TRIP, YOU'VE MISSED SO MUCH SCHOOL.

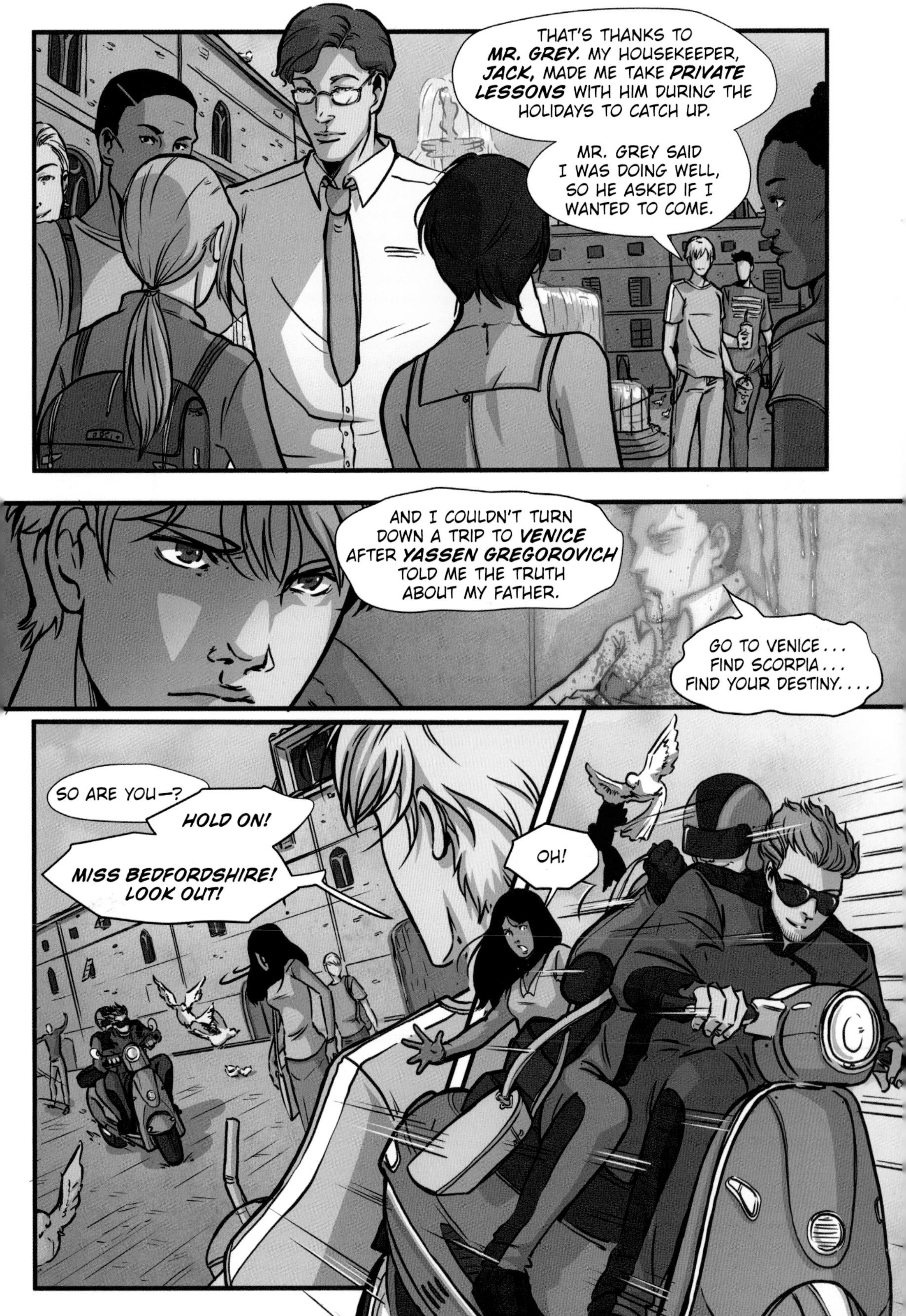
THAT'S THANKS TO **MR. GREY.** MY HOUSEKEEPER, **JACK,** MADE ME TAKE **PRIVATE LESSONS** WITH HIM DURING THE HOLIDAYS TO CATCH UP.
MR. GREY SAID I WAS DOING WELL, SO HE ASKED IF I WANTED TO COME.
AND I COULDN'T TURN DOWN A TRIP TO **VENICE** AFTER **YASSEN GREGOROVICH** TOLD ME THE TRUTH ABOUT MY FATHER.
GO TO VENICE . . . FIND SCORPIA . . . FIND YOUR DESTINY. . . .
SO ARE YOU—?
HOLD ON!
MISS BEDFORDSHIRE! LOOK OUT!
OH!

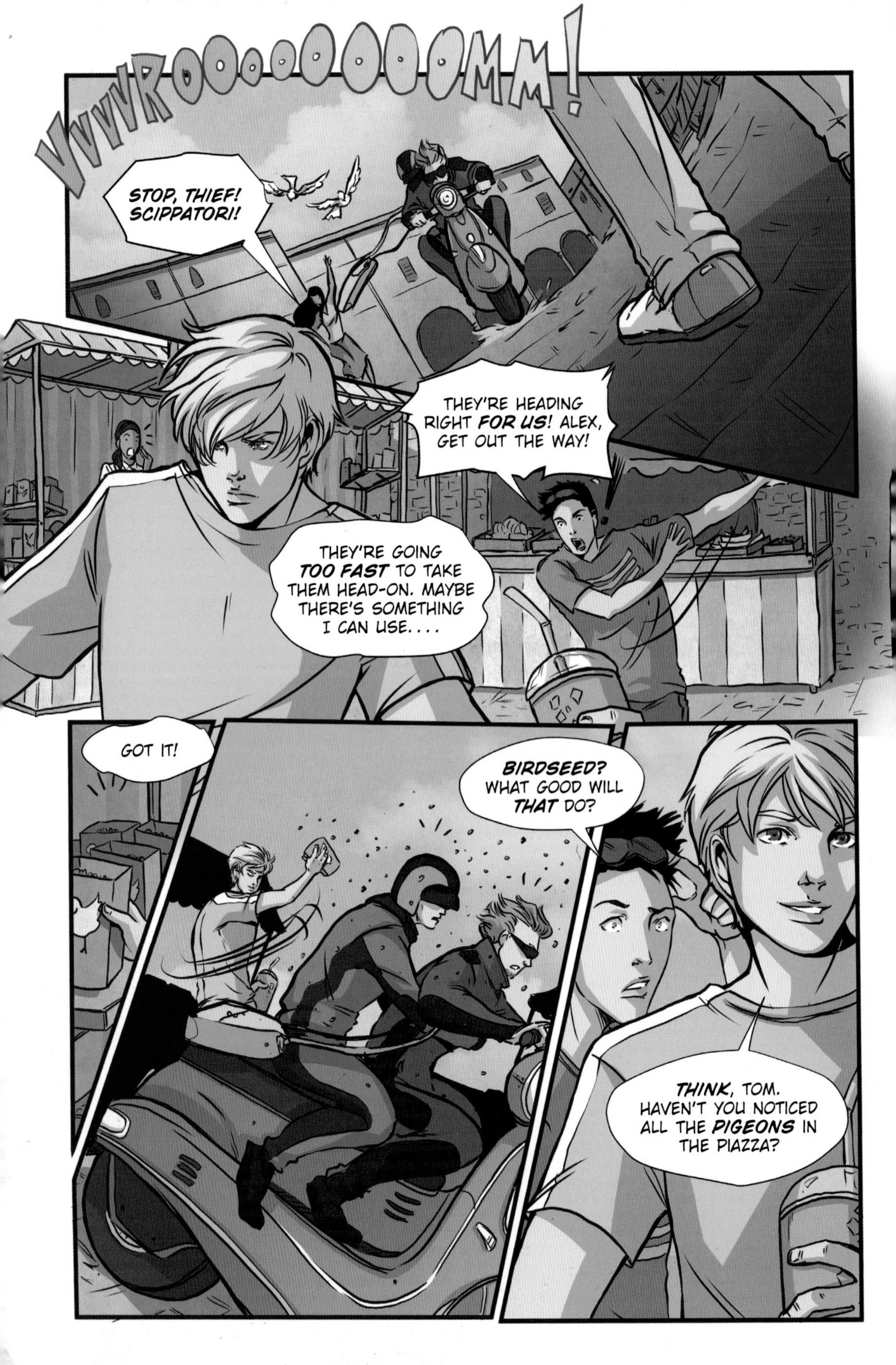
VVVVROOOOOOOOOMM!
STOP, THIEF! SCIPPATORI!
THEY'RE HEADING RIGHT FOR US! ALEX, GET OUT THE WAY!
THEY'RE GOING TOO FAST TO TAKE THEM HEAD-ON. MAYBE THERE'S SOMETHING I CAN USE. . . .
GOT IT!
BIRDSEED? WHAT GOOD WILL THAT DO?
THINK, TOM. HAVEN'T YOU NOTICED ALL THE PIGEONS IN THE PIAZZA?

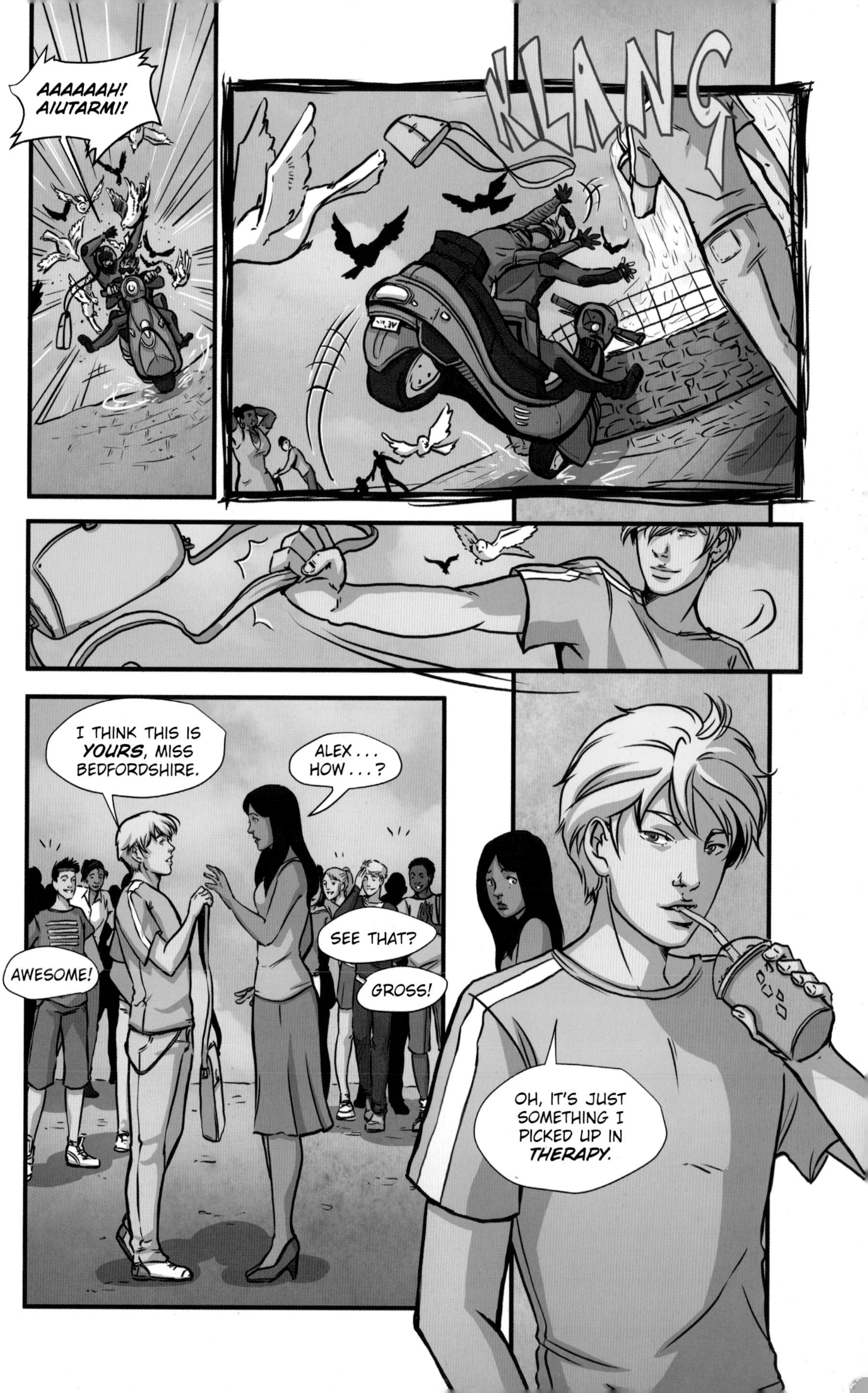
AAAAAAH! AIUTARMI!
KLANG
I THINK THIS IS *YOURS*, MISS BEDFORDSHIRE.
ALEX . . . HOW . . . ?
SEE THAT?
AWESOME!
GROSS!
OH, IT'S JUST SOMETHING I PICKED UP IN *THERAPY*.

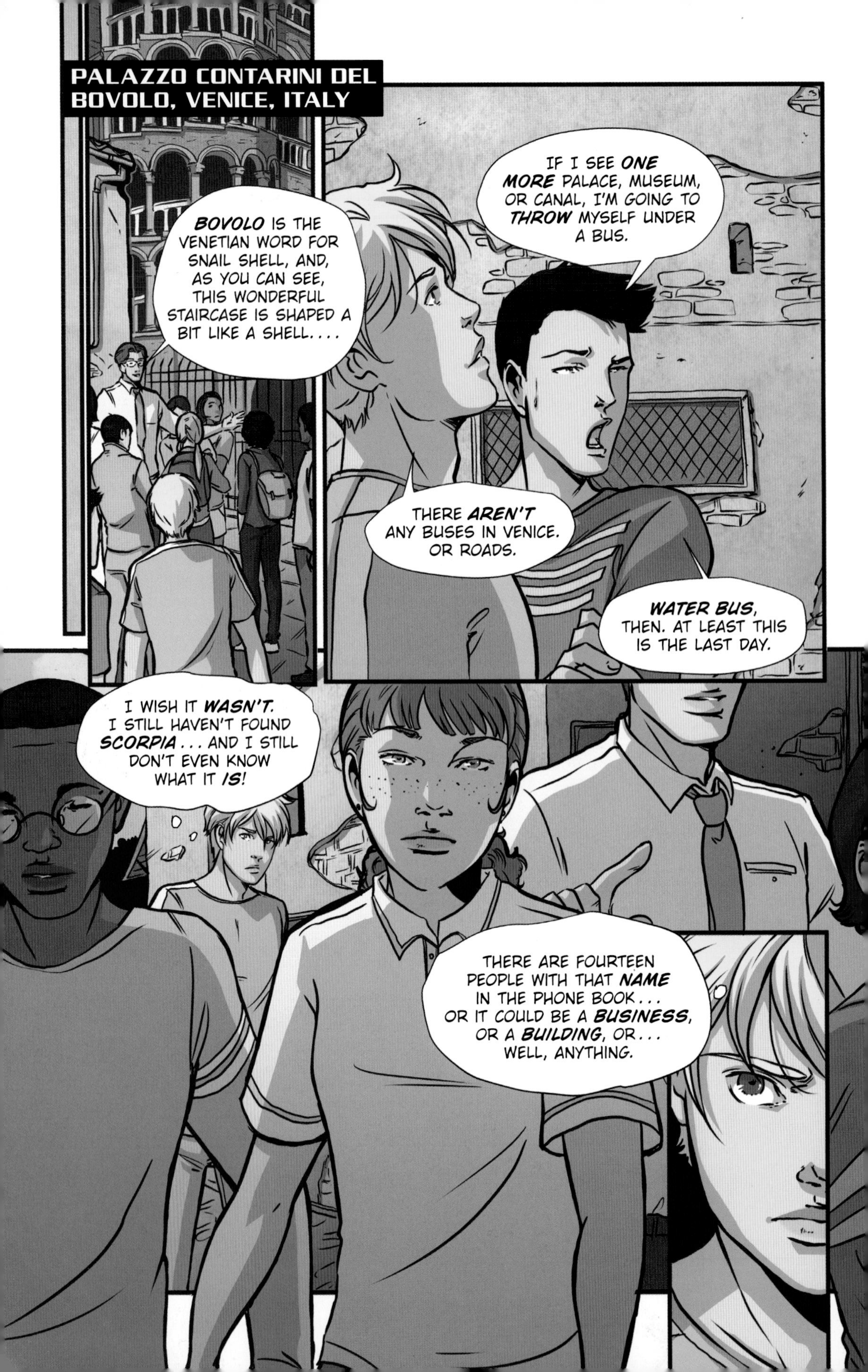
PALAZZO CONTARINI DEL BOVOLO, VENICE, ITALY
BOVOLO IS THE VENETIAN WORD FOR SNAIL SHELL, AND, AS YOU CAN SEE, THIS WONDERFUL STAIRCASE IS SHAPED A BIT LIKE A SHELL. . . .
IF I SEE ONE MORE PALACE, MUSEUM, OR CANAL, I'M GOING TO THROW MYSELF UNDER A BUS.
THERE AREN'T ANY BUSES IN VENICE. OR ROADS.
WATER BUS, THEN. AT LEAST THIS IS THE LAST DAY.
I WISH IT WASN'T. I STILL HAVEN'T FOUND SCORPIA . . . AND I STILL DON'T EVEN KNOW WHAT IT IS!
THERE ARE FOURTEEN PEOPLE WITH THAT NAME IN THE PHONE BOOK . . . OR IT COULD BE A BUSINESS, OR A BUILDING, OR . . . WELL, ANYTHING.

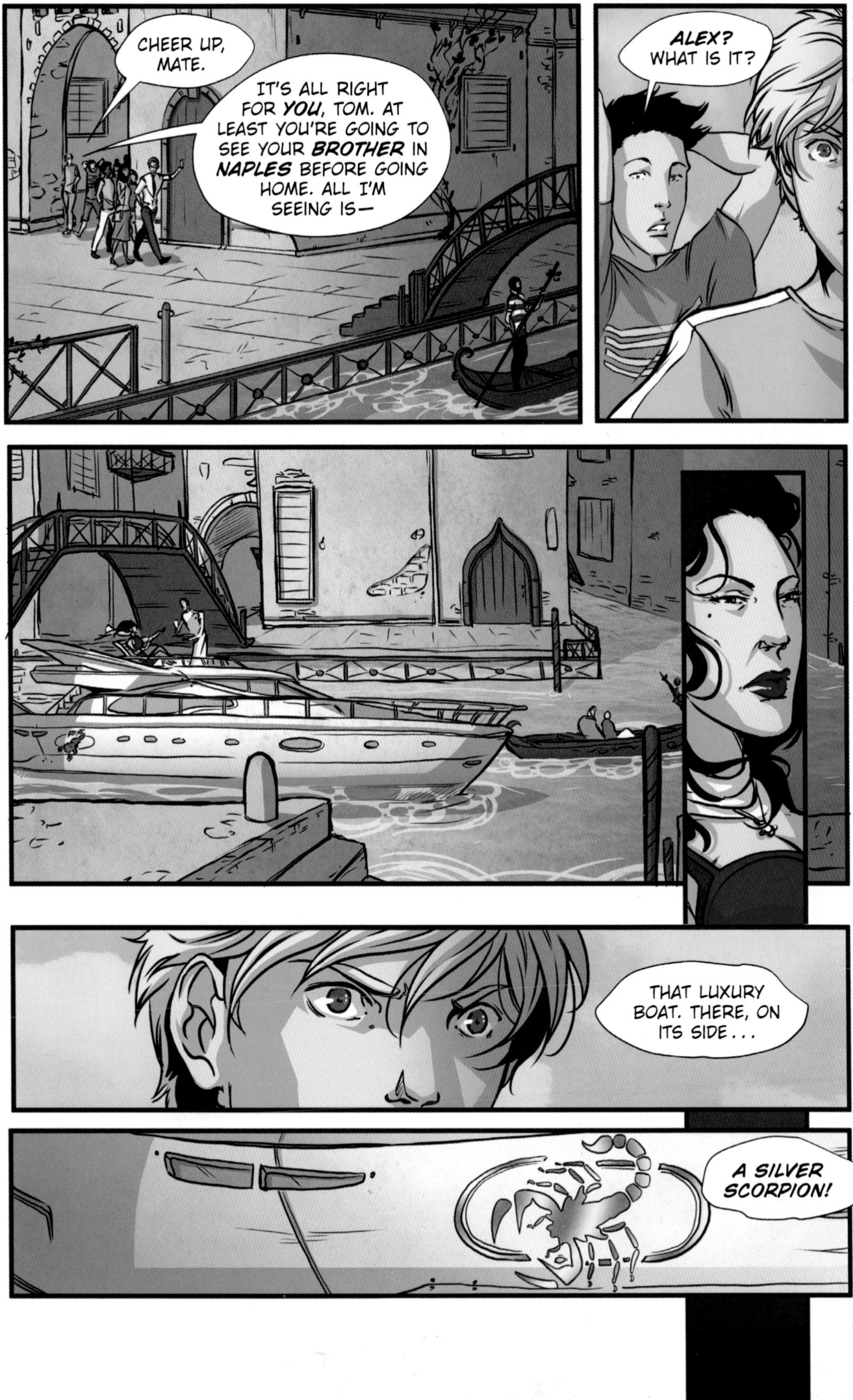
CHEER UP, MATE.
IT'S ALL RIGHT FOR YOU, TOM. AT LEAST YOU'RE GOING TO SEE YOUR BROTHER IN NAPLES BEFORE GOING HOME. ALL I'M SEEING IS—
ALEX? WHAT IS IT?
THAT LUXURY BOAT. THERE, ON ITS SIDE . . .
A SILVER SCORPION!

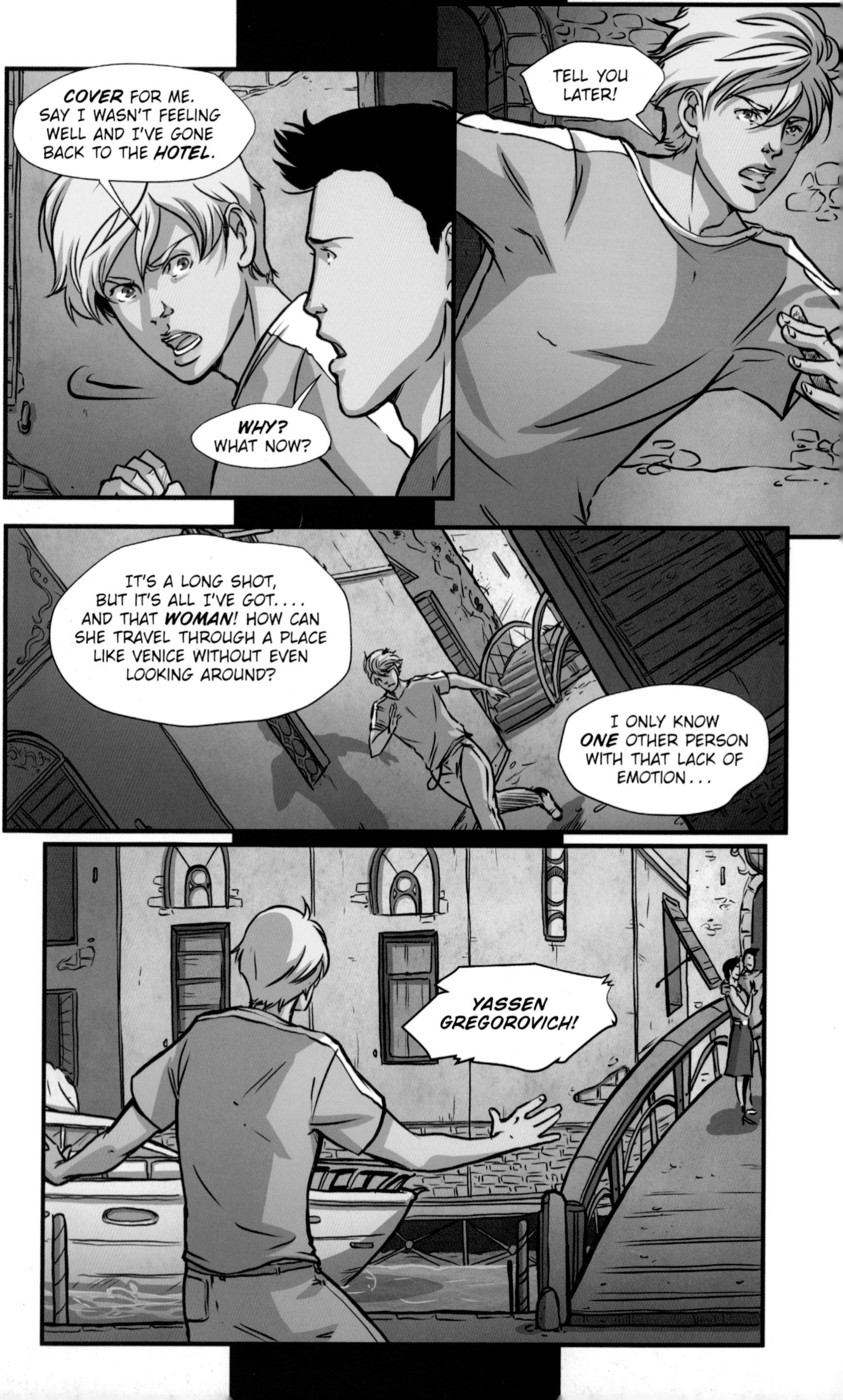
COVER FOR ME. SAY I WASN'T FEELING WELL AND I'VE GONE BACK TO THE HOTEL.
WHY? WHAT NOW?
TELL YOU LATER!
IT'S A LONG SHOT, BUT IT'S ALL I'VE GOT. . . . AND THAT WOMAN! HOW CAN SHE TRAVEL THROUGH A PLACE LIKE VENICE WITHOUT EVEN LOOKING AROUND?
I ONLY KNOW ONE OTHER PERSON WITH THAT LACK OF EMOTION . . .
YASSEN GREGOROVICH!

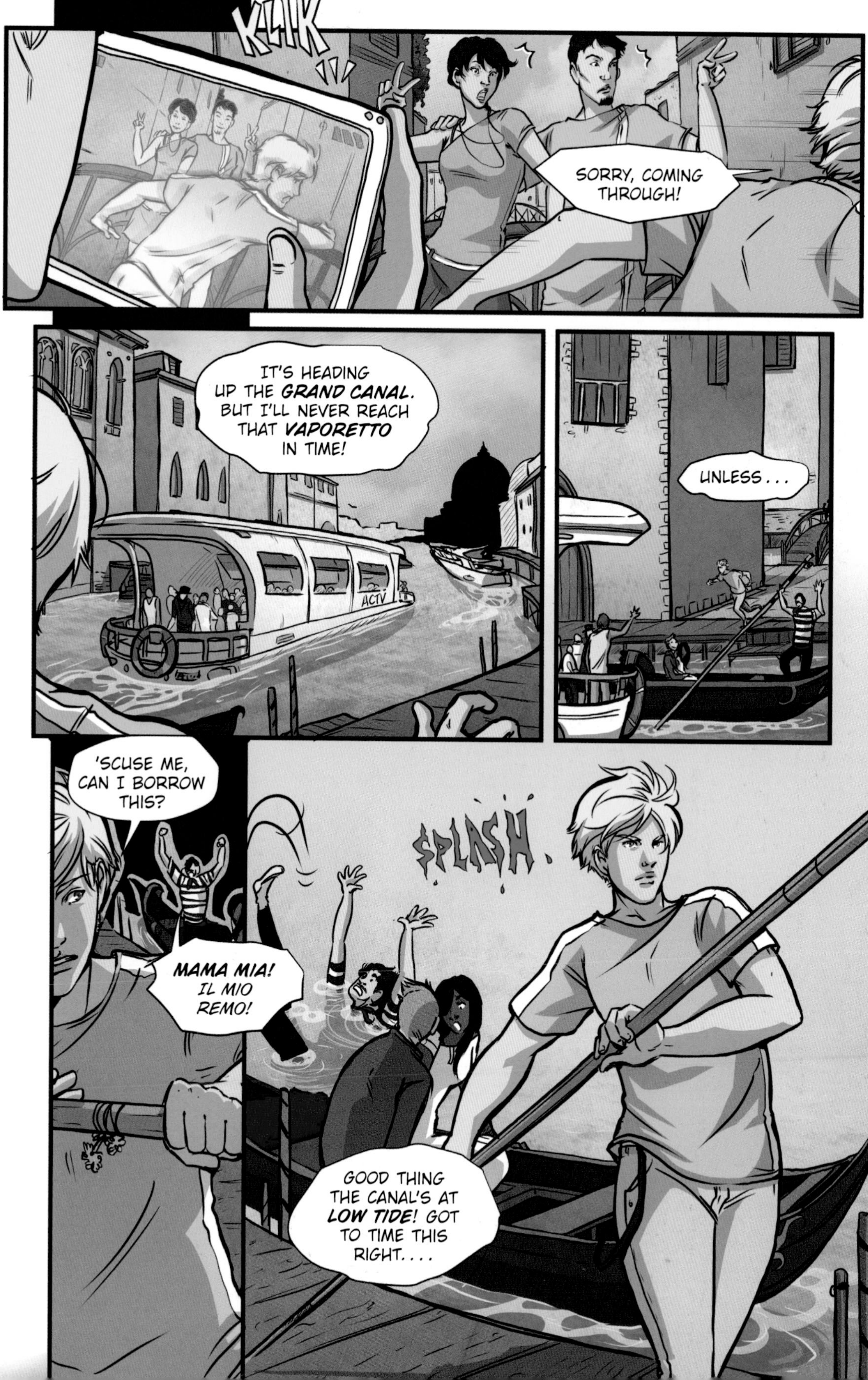
KLIK
SORRY, COMING THROUGH!
IT'S HEADING UP THE GRAND CANAL. BUT I'LL NEVER REACH THAT VAPORETTO IN TIME!
UNLESS . . .
'SCUSE ME, CAN I BORROW THIS?
SPLASH
MAMA MIA! IL MIO REMO!
GOOD THING THE CANAL'S AT LOW TIDE! GOT TO TIME THIS RIGHT. . . .

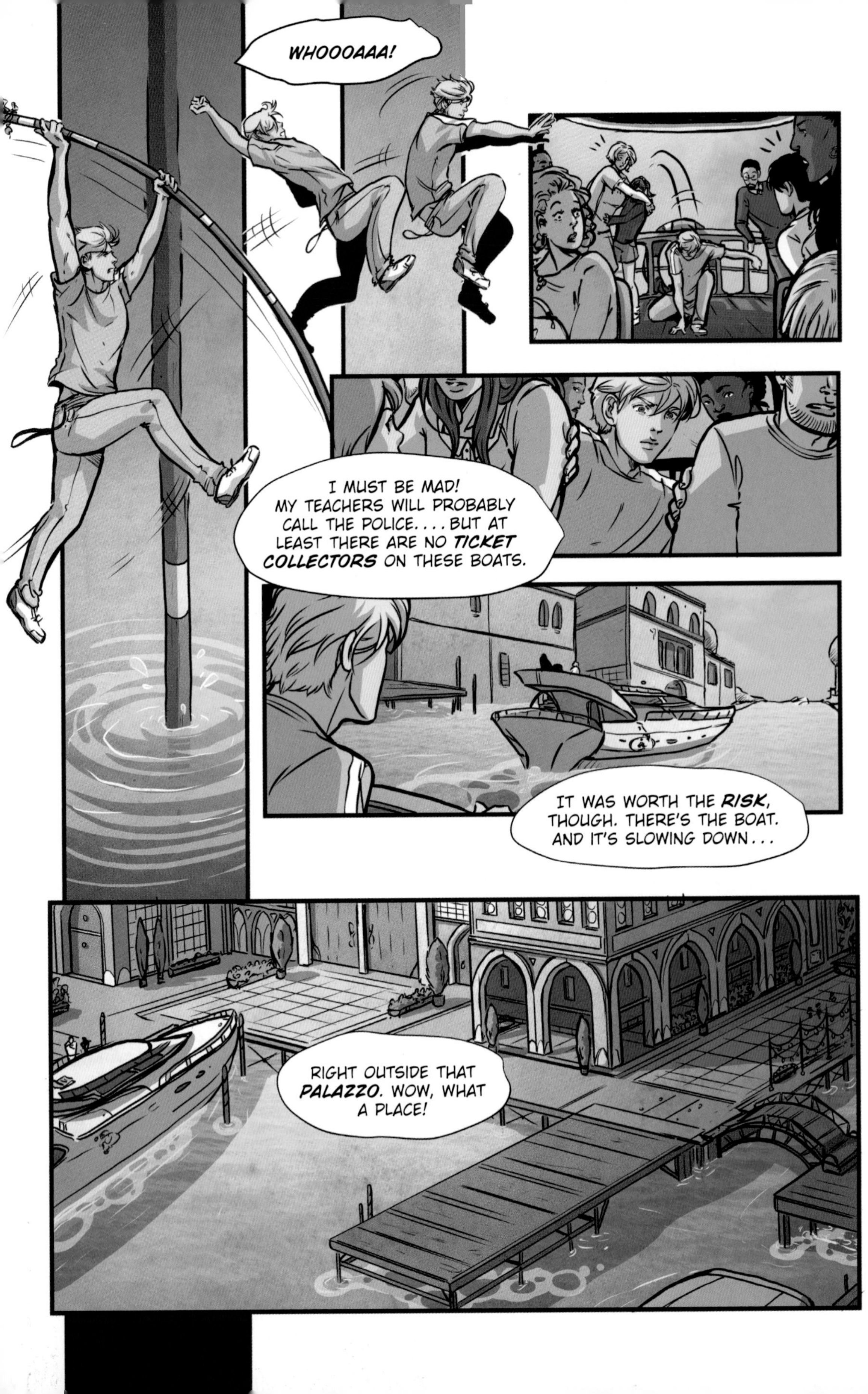
WHOOOAAA!
I MUST BE MAD! MY TEACHERS WILL PROBABLY CALL THE POLICE. . . . BUT AT LEAST THERE ARE NO *TICKET COLLECTORS* ON THESE BOATS.
IT WAS WORTH THE *RISK*, THOUGH. THERE'S THE BOAT. AND IT'S SLOWING DOWN . . .
RIGHT OUTSIDE THAT *PALAZZO*. WOW, WHAT A PLACE!

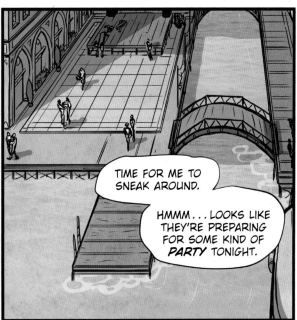

TIME FOR ME TO SNEAK AROUND.

HMMM... LOOKS LIKE THEY'RE PREPARING FOR SOME KIND OF *PARTY* TONIGHT.

SCUSATE, STO CERCANDO PER... *SCORPIA?*

CHE COSA VUOI DIRE? *VAI VIA!*

YOU, *ENGLISH.* YOU CANNOT BE HERE. *GO AWAY.*

SORRY, I WAS *LOST.* I'LL GO.

BUT I'LL BE *BACK.* THAT MAID NEARLY *FAINTED* WHEN I MENTIONED *SCORPIA.* THIS PLACE *MUST* BE CONNECTED SOMEHOW!

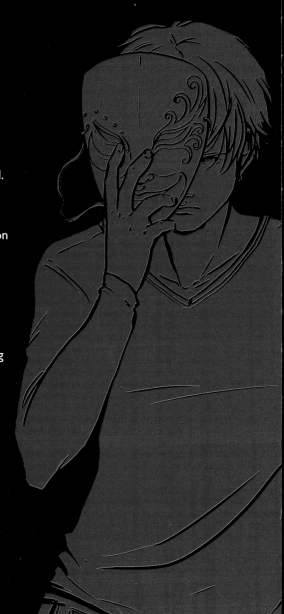

Copyright © 2016 by Walker Books Ltd.
Based on the original novel *Scorpia* copyright
© 2004 by Stormbreaker Productions Ltd.

Adapted by Antony Johnston
Inks by Emma Vieceli
Colors by Kate Brown
Flat colors by Nathan Ashworth
Trademarks © 2003 Stormbreaker Productions Ltd.
Alex Rider™, Boy with Torch Logo™, AR Logo™

First U.S. edition 2017

Library of Congress Catalog Card Number pending
ISBN 978-0-7636-9257-5

APS 22 21 20 19 18 17
10 9 8 7 6 5 4 3 2 1

Printed in Humen, Dongguan, China

This book was typeset in WildWords
and Serpentine Bold.

Candlewick Press
99 Dover Street
Somerville, Massachusetts 02144

visit us at www.candlewick.com

ALEX RIDER

**ACTION
ADRENALINE
ADVENTURE**

SCORPIA

THE GRAPHIC NOVEL

ANTHONY HOROWITZ

ANTONY JOHNSTON • EMMA VIECELI • KATE BROWN

CANDLEWICK PRESS

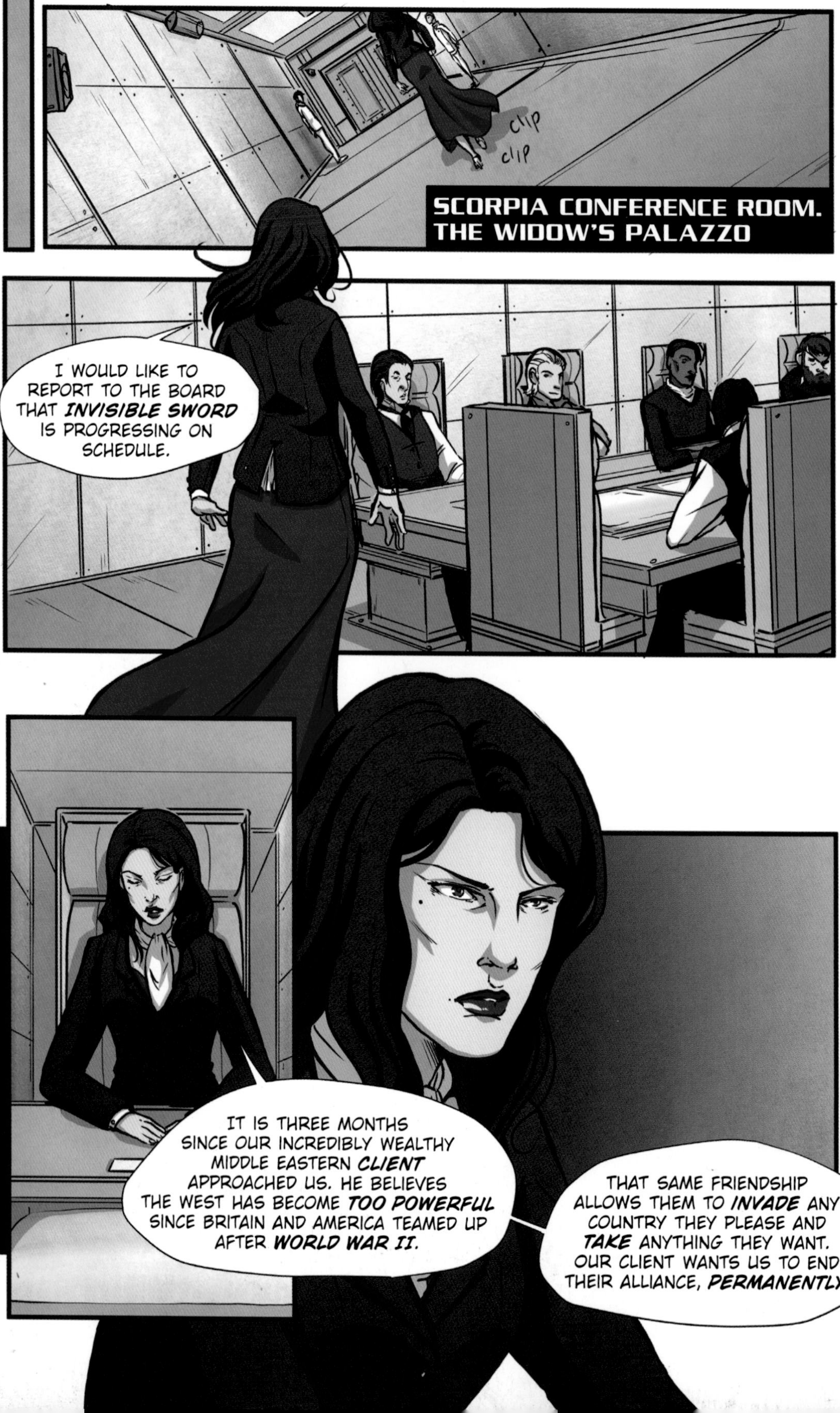
clip
clip
SCORPIA CONFERENCE ROOM. THE WIDOW'S PALAZZO
I WOULD LIKE TO REPORT TO THE BOARD THAT INVISIBLE SWORD IS PROGRESSING ON SCHEDULE.
IT IS THREE MONTHS SINCE OUR INCREDIBLY WEALTHY MIDDLE EASTERN CLIENT APPROACHED US. HE BELIEVES THE WEST HAS BECOME TOO POWERFUL SINCE BRITAIN AND AMERICA TEAMED UP AFTER WORLD WAR II.
THAT SAME FRIENDSHIP ALLOWS THEM TO INVADE ANY COUNTRY THEY PLEASE AND TAKE ANYTHING THEY WANT. OUR CLIENT WANTS US TO END THEIR ALLIANCE, PERMANENTLY.

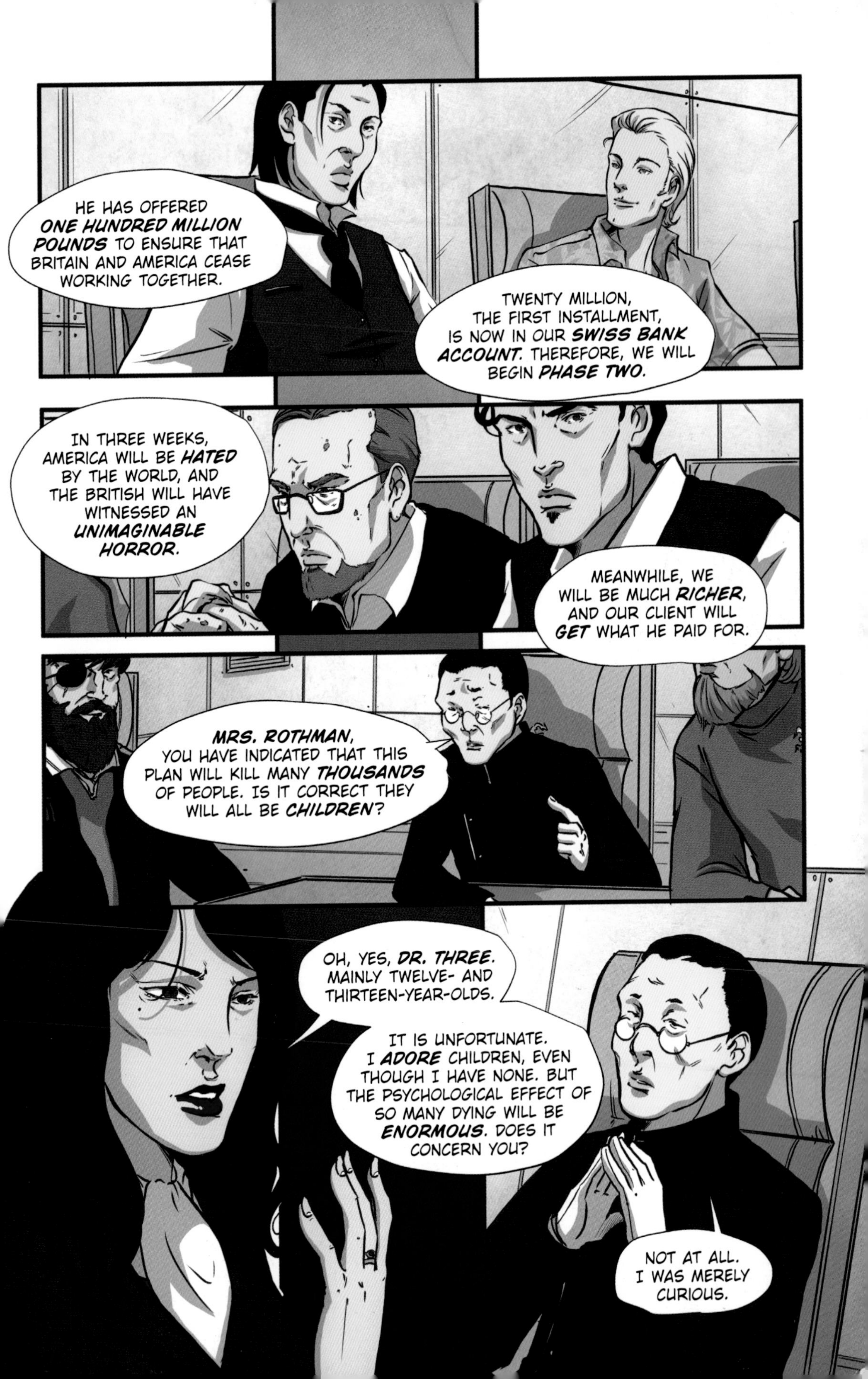
HE HAS OFFERED ONE HUNDRED MILLION POUNDS TO ENSURE THAT BRITAIN AND AMERICA CEASE WORKING TOGETHER.
TWENTY MILLION, THE FIRST INSTALLMENT, IS NOW IN OUR SWISS BANK ACCOUNT. THEREFORE, WE WILL BEGIN PHASE TWO.
IN THREE WEEKS, AMERICA WILL BE HATED BY THE WORLD, AND THE BRITISH WILL HAVE WITNESSED AN UNIMAGINABLE HORROR.
MEANWHILE, WE WILL BE MUCH RICHER, AND OUR CLIENT WILL GET WHAT HE PAID FOR.
MRS. ROTHMAN, YOU HAVE INDICATED THAT THIS PLAN WILL KILL MANY THOUSANDS OF PEOPLE. IS IT CORRECT THEY WILL ALL BE CHILDREN?
OH, YES, DR. THREE. MAINLY TWELVE- AND THIRTEEN-YEAR-OLDS.
IT IS UNFORTUNATE. I ADORE CHILDREN, EVEN THOUGH I HAVE NONE. BUT THE PSYCHOLOGICAL EFFECT OF SO MANY DYING WILL BE ENORMOUS. DOES IT CONCERN YOU?
NOT AT ALL. I WAS MERELY CURIOUS.

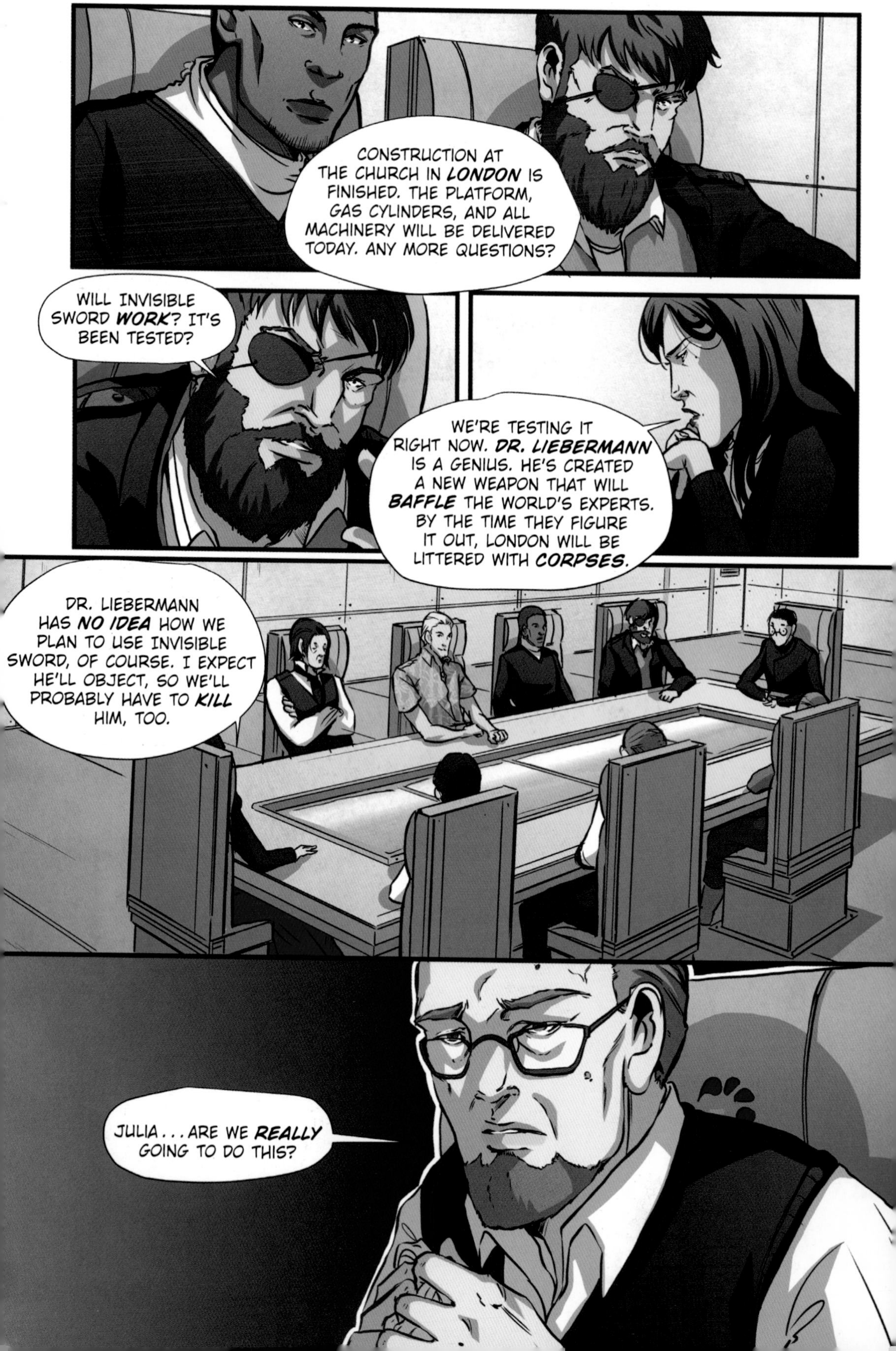
CONSTRUCTION AT THE CHURCH IN LONDON IS FINISHED. THE PLATFORM, GAS CYLINDERS, AND ALL MACHINERY WILL BE DELIVERED TODAY. ANY MORE QUESTIONS?
WILL INVISIBLE SWORD WORK? IT'S BEEN TESTED?
WE'RE TESTING IT RIGHT NOW. DR. LIEBERMANN IS A GENIUS. HE'S CREATED A NEW WEAPON THAT WILL BAFFLE THE WORLD'S EXPERTS. BY THE TIME THEY FIGURE IT OUT, LONDON WILL BE LITTERED WITH CORPSES.
DR. LIEBERMANN HAS NO IDEA HOW WE PLAN TO USE INVISIBLE SWORD, OF COURSE. I EXPECT HE'LL OBJECT, SO WE'LL PROBABLY HAVE TO KILL HIM, TOO.
JULIA . . . ARE WE REALLY GOING TO DO THIS?

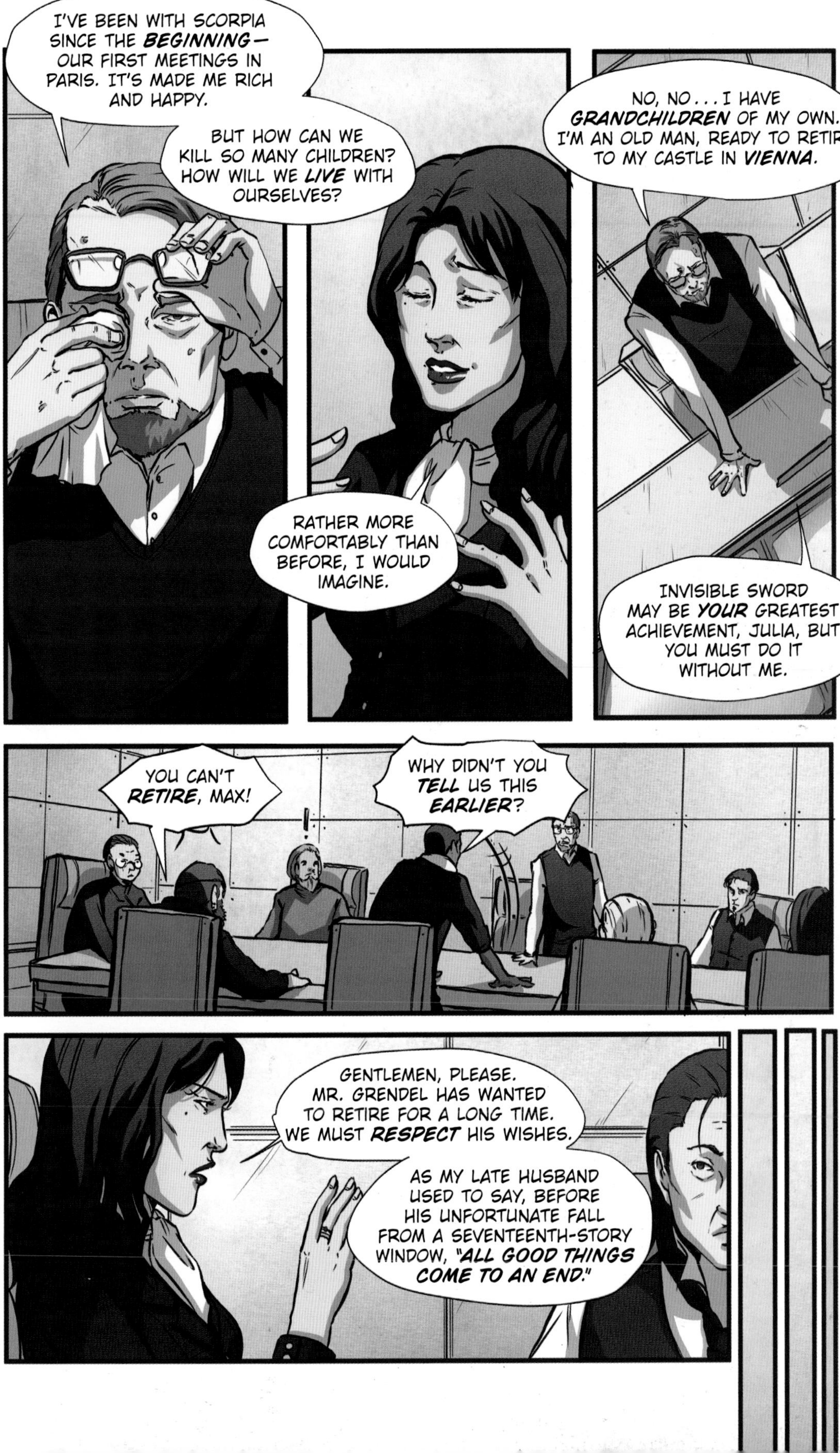
I'VE BEEN WITH SCORPIA SINCE THE BEGINNING— OUR FIRST MEETINGS IN PARIS. IT'S MADE ME RICH AND HAPPY.
BUT HOW CAN WE KILL SO MANY CHILDREN? HOW WILL WE LIVE WITH OURSELVES?
RATHER MORE COMFORTABLY THAN BEFORE, I WOULD IMAGINE.
NO, NO . . . I HAVE GRANDCHILDREN OF MY OWN. I'M AN OLD MAN, READY TO RETIRE TO MY CASTLE IN VIENNA.
INVISIBLE SWORD MAY BE YOUR GREATEST ACHIEVEMENT, JULIA, BUT YOU MUST DO IT WITHOUT ME.
YOU CAN'T RETIRE, MAX!
!
WHY DIDN'T YOU TELL US THIS EARLIER?
GENTLEMEN, PLEASE. MR. GRENDEL HAS WANTED TO RETIRE FOR A LONG TIME. WE MUST RESPECT HIS WISHES.
AS MY LATE HUSBAND USED TO SAY, BEFORE HIS UNFORTUNATE FALL FROM A SEVENTEENTH-STORY WINDOW, "ALL GOOD THINGS COME TO AN END."

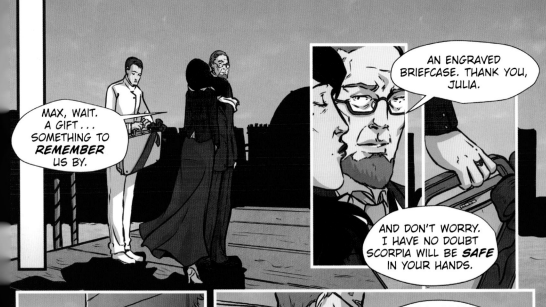

MAX, WAIT. A GIFT... SOMETHING TO *REMEMBER* US BY.

AN ENGRAVED BRIEFCASE. THANK YOU, JULIA.

AND DON'T WORRY. I HAVE NO DOUBT SCORPIA WILL BE *SAFE* IN YOUR HANDS.

OH, JULIA, YOU SHOULDN'T HAVE...

CLICK

AAAAAAAARGH!

GOOD-BYE, MAX.

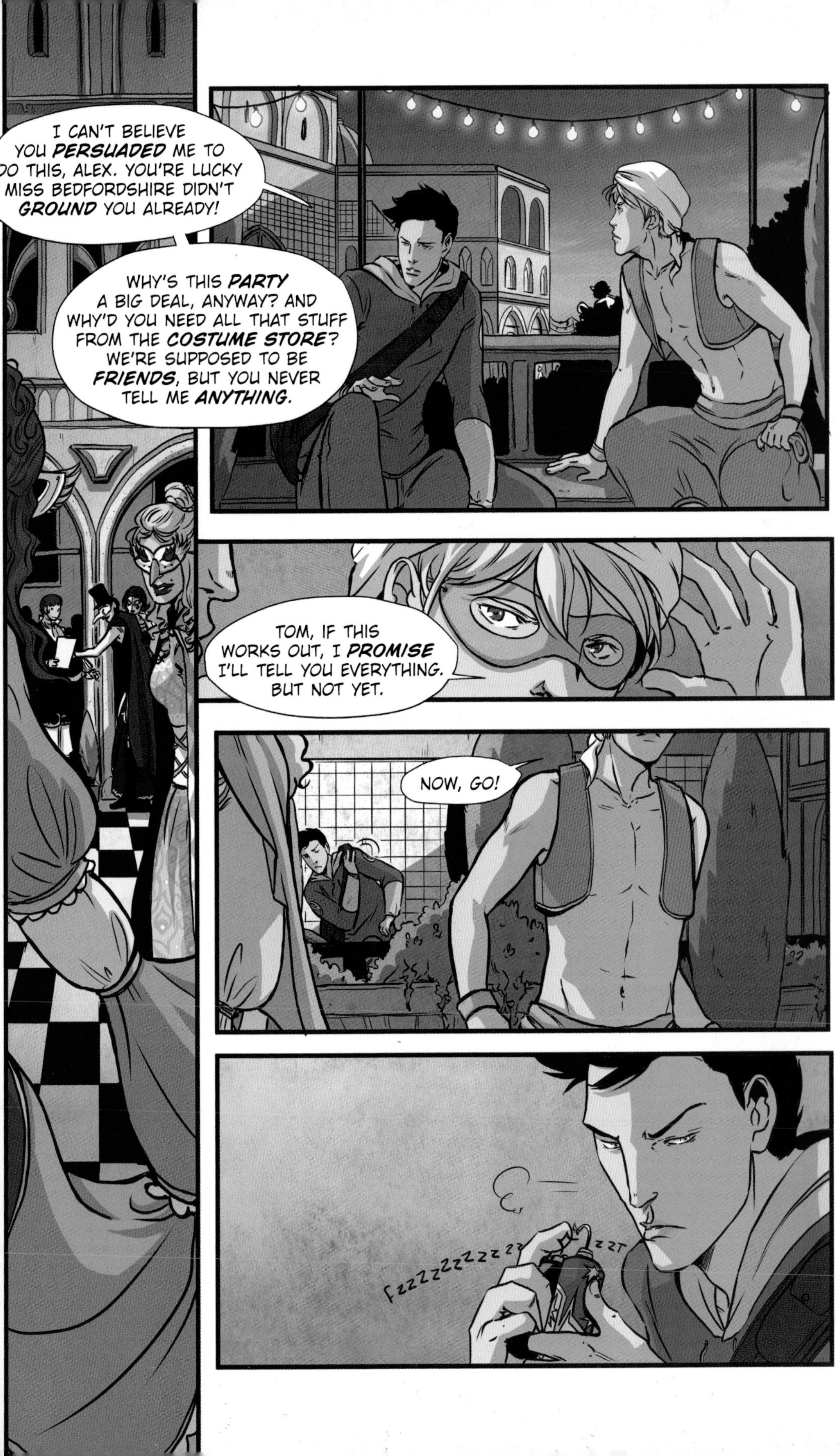
I CAN'T BELIEVE YOU PERSUADED ME TO DO THIS, ALEX. YOU'RE LUCKY MISS BEDFORDSHIRE DIDN'T GROUND YOU ALREADY!
WHY'S THIS PARTY A BIG DEAL, ANYWAY? AND WHY'D YOU NEED ALL THAT STUFF FROM THE COSTUME STORE? WE'RE SUPPOSED TO BE FRIENDS, BUT YOU NEVER TELL ME ANYTHING.
TOM, IF THIS WORKS OUT, I PROMISE I'LL TELL YOU EVERYTHING. BUT NOT YET.
NOW, GO!
FZZZZZZZZZZZ
ZZT

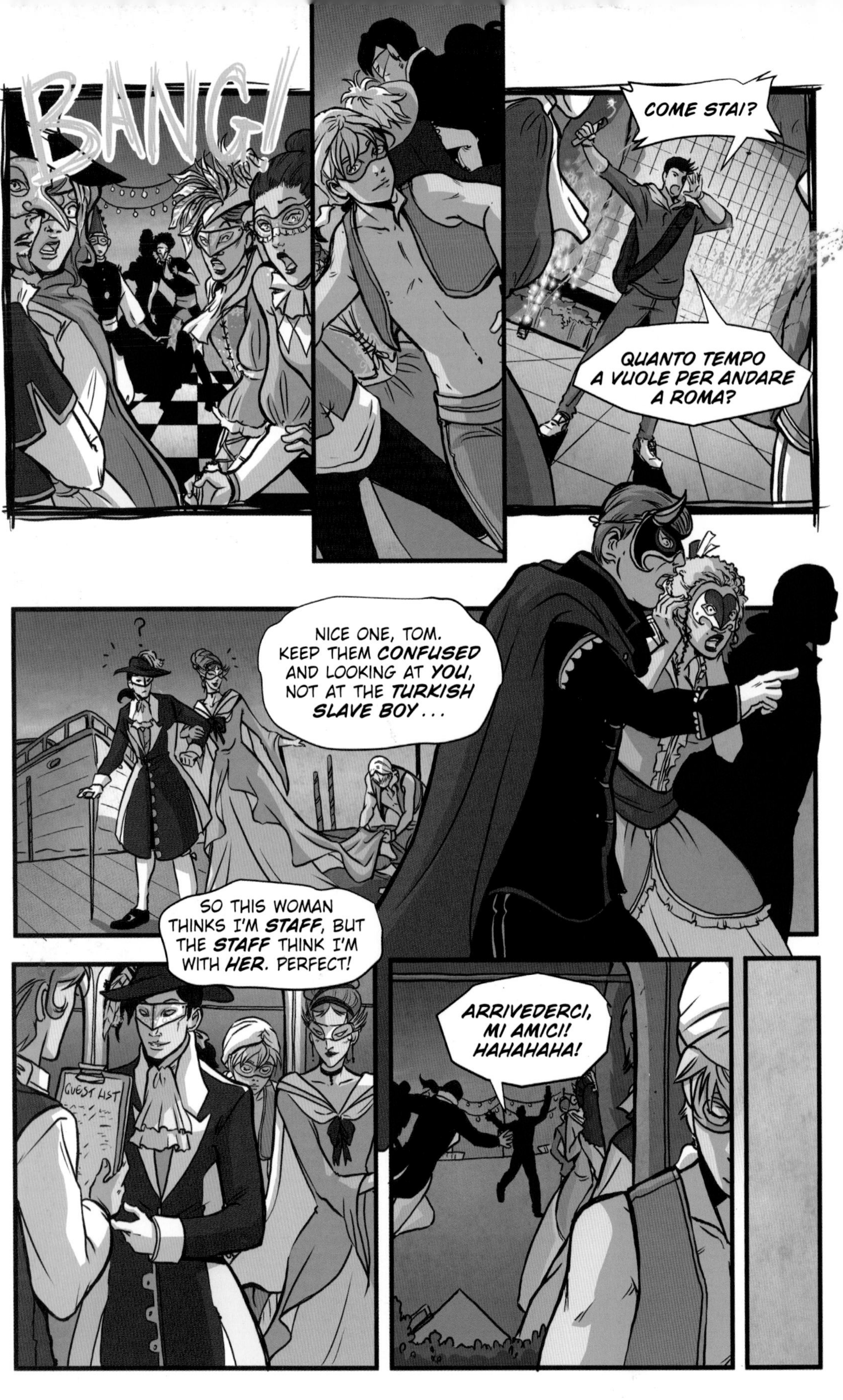
BANG!
COME STAI?
QUANTO TEMPO A VUOLE PER ANDARE A ROMA?
?
NICE ONE, TOM. KEEP THEM *CONFUSED* AND LOOKING AT *YOU*, NOT AT THE *TURKISH SLAVE BOY* . . .
SO THIS WOMAN THINKS I'M *STAFF*, BUT THE *STAFF* THINK I'M WITH *HER*. PERFECT!
GUEST LIST
ARRIVEDERCI, MI AMICI! HAHAHAHA!

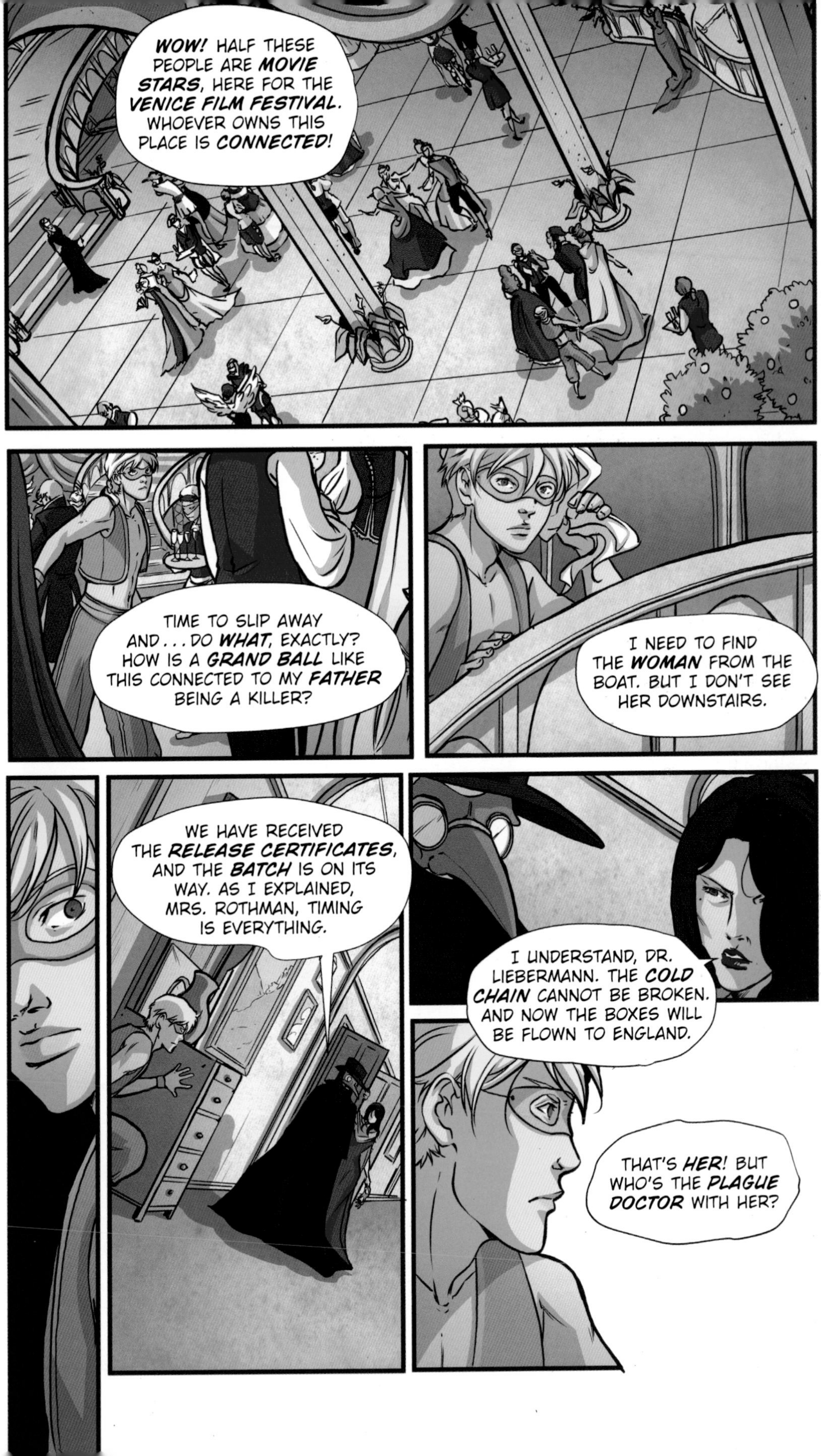

WOW! HALF THESE PEOPLE ARE MOVIE STARS, HERE FOR THE VENICE FILM FESTIVAL. WHOEVER OWNS THIS PLACE IS CONNECTED!
TIME TO SLIP AWAY AND . . . DO WHAT, EXACTLY? HOW IS A GRAND BALL LIKE THIS CONNECTED TO MY FATHER BEING A KILLER?
I NEED TO FIND THE WOMAN FROM THE BOAT. BUT I DON'T SEE HER DOWNSTAIRS.
WE HAVE RECEIVED THE RELEASE CERTIFICATES, AND THE BATCH IS ON ITS WAY. AS I EXPLAINED, MRS. ROTHMAN, TIMING IS EVERYTHING.
I UNDERSTAND, DR. LIEBERMANN. THE COLD CHAIN CANNOT BE BROKEN. AND NOW THE BOXES WILL BE FLOWN TO ENGLAND.
THAT'S HER! BUT WHO'S THE PLAGUE DOCTOR WITH HER?

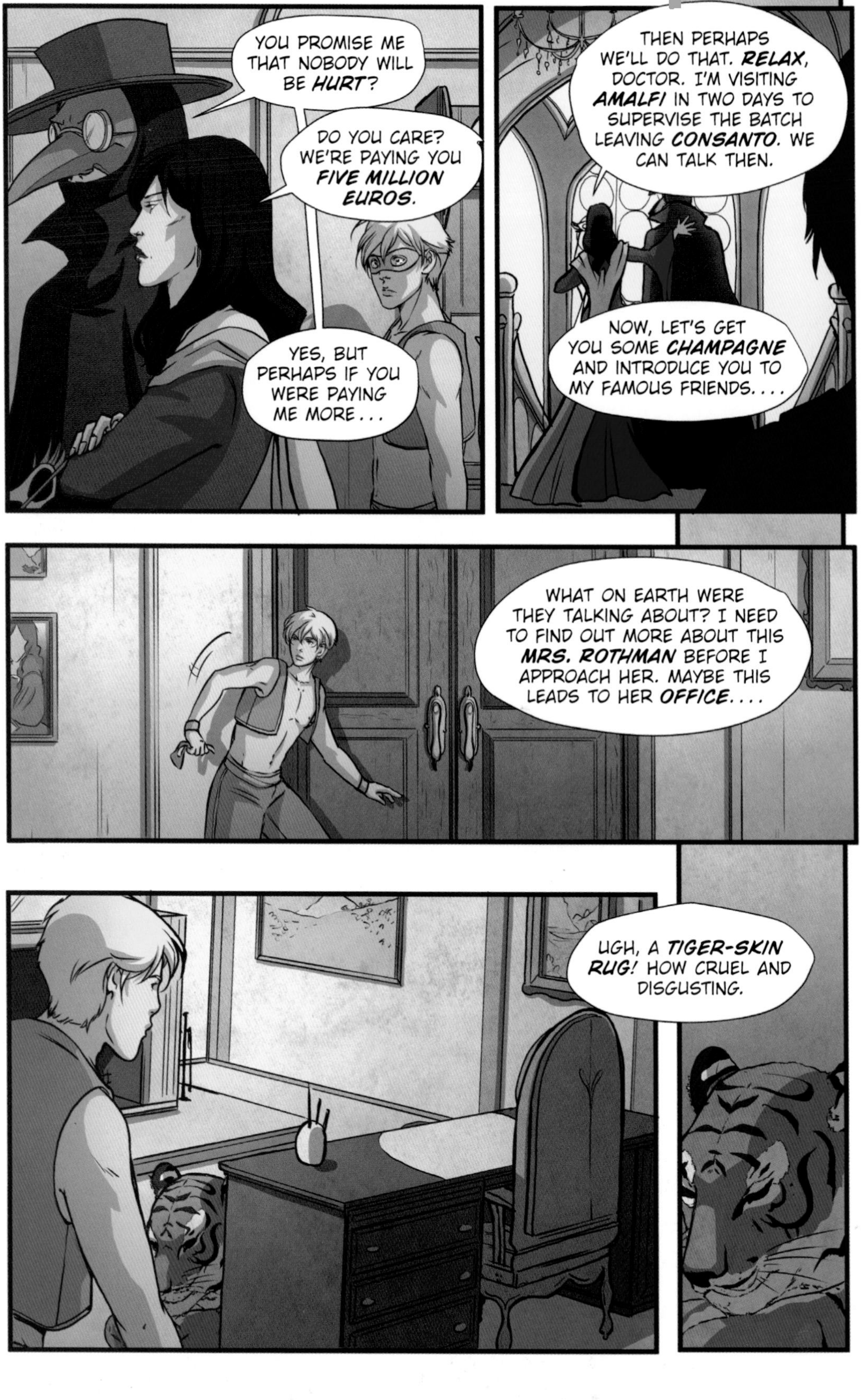
YOU PROMISE ME THAT NOBODY WILL BE HURT?
DO YOU CARE? WE'RE PAYING YOU FIVE MILLION EUROS.
YES, BUT PERHAPS IF YOU WERE PAYING ME MORE . . .
THEN PERHAPS WE'LL DO THAT. RELAX, DOCTOR. I'M VISITING AMALFI IN TWO DAYS TO SUPERVISE THE BATCH LEAVING CONSANTO. WE CAN TALK THEN.
NOW, LET'S GET YOU SOME CHAMPAGNE AND INTRODUCE YOU TO MY FAMOUS FRIENDS. . . .
WHAT ON EARTH WERE THEY TALKING ABOUT? I NEED TO FIND OUT MORE ABOUT THIS MRS. ROTHMAN BEFORE I APPROACH HER. MAYBE THIS LEADS TO HER OFFICE. . . .
UGH, A TIGER-SKIN RUG! HOW CRUEL AND DISGUSTING.

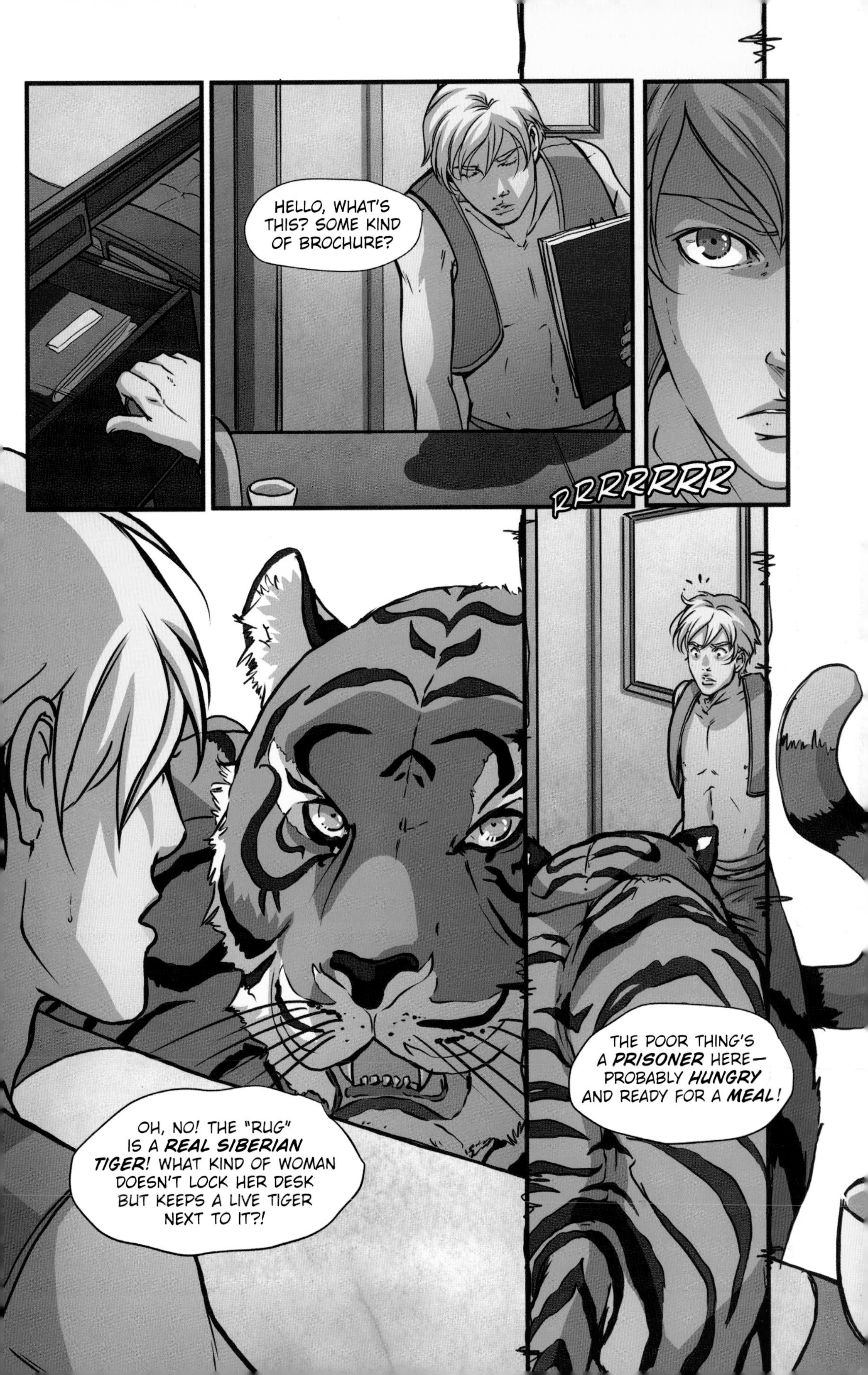
HELLO, WHAT'S THIS? SOME KIND OF BROCHURE?
RRRRRRR
OH, NO! THE "RUG" IS A ***REAL SIBERIAN TIGER!*** WHAT KIND OF WOMAN DOESN'T LOCK HER DESK BUT KEEPS A LIVE TIGER NEXT TO IT?!
THE POOR THING'S A ***PRISONER*** HERE— PROBABLY ***HUNGRY*** AND READY FOR A ***MEAL***!

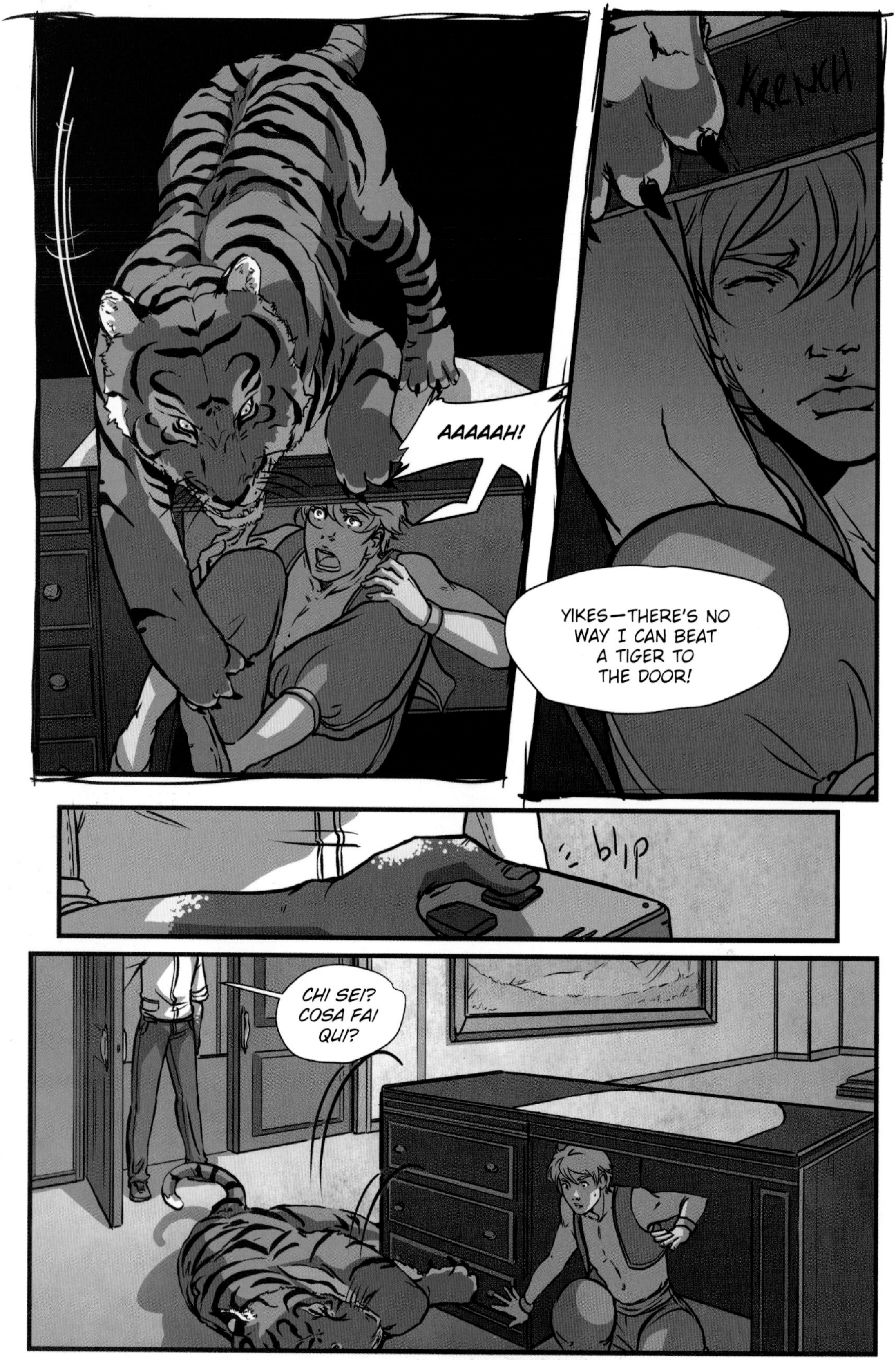
AAAAAH!
KRENCH
YIKES—THERE'S NO WAY I CAN BEAT A TIGER TO THE DOOR!
blip
CHI SEI? COSA FAI QUI?

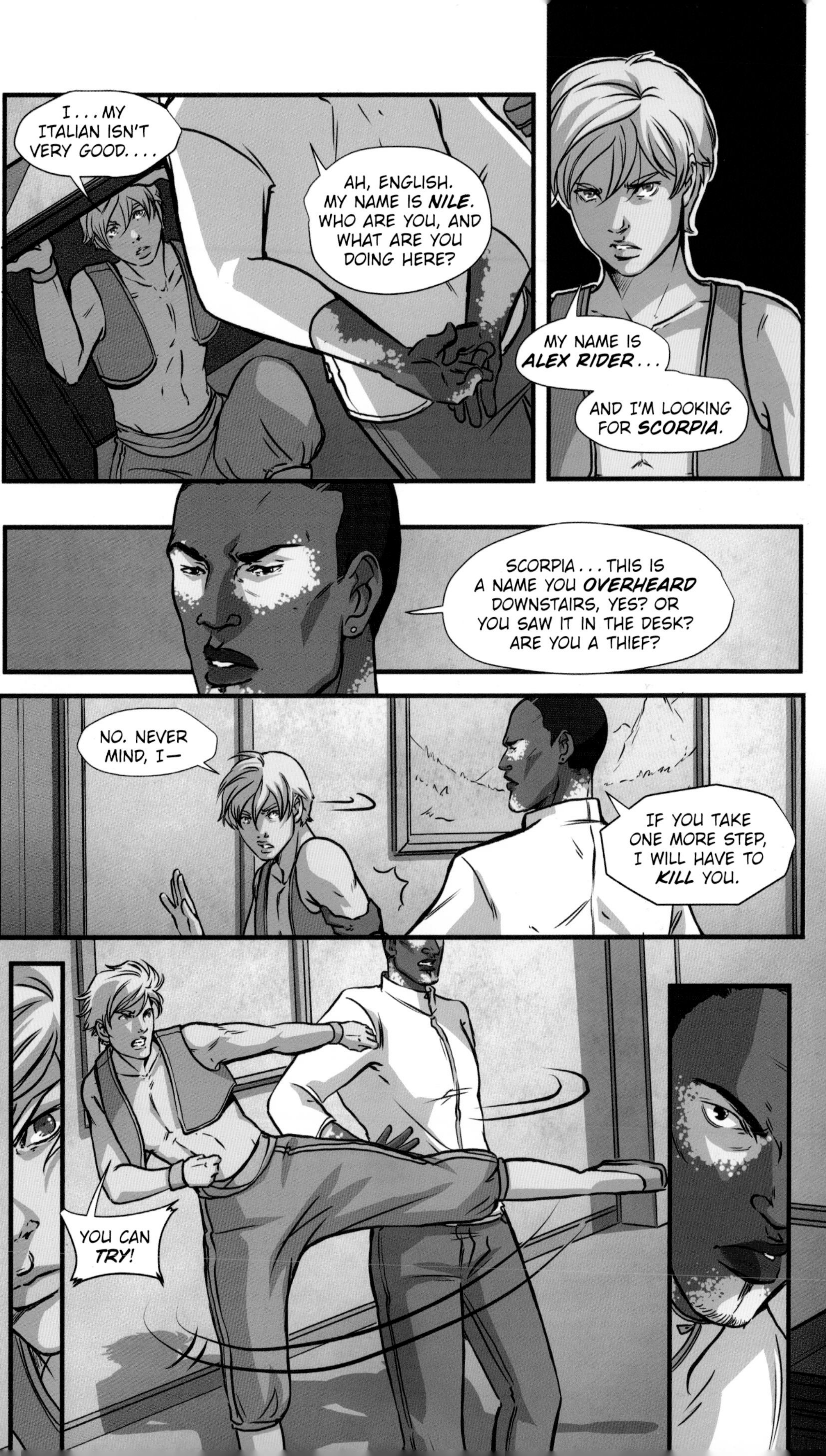
I . . . MY ITALIAN ISN'T VERY GOOD. . . .
AH, ENGLISH. MY NAME IS NILE. WHO ARE YOU, AND WHAT ARE YOU DOING HERE?
MY NAME IS ALEX RIDER . . .
AND I'M LOOKING FOR SCORPIA.
SCORPIA . . . THIS IS A NAME YOU OVERHEARD DOWNSTAIRS, YES? OR YOU SAW IT IN THE DESK? ARE YOU A THIEF?
NO. NEVER MIND, I—
IF YOU TAKE ONE MORE STEP, I WILL HAVE TO KILL YOU.
YOU CAN TRY!

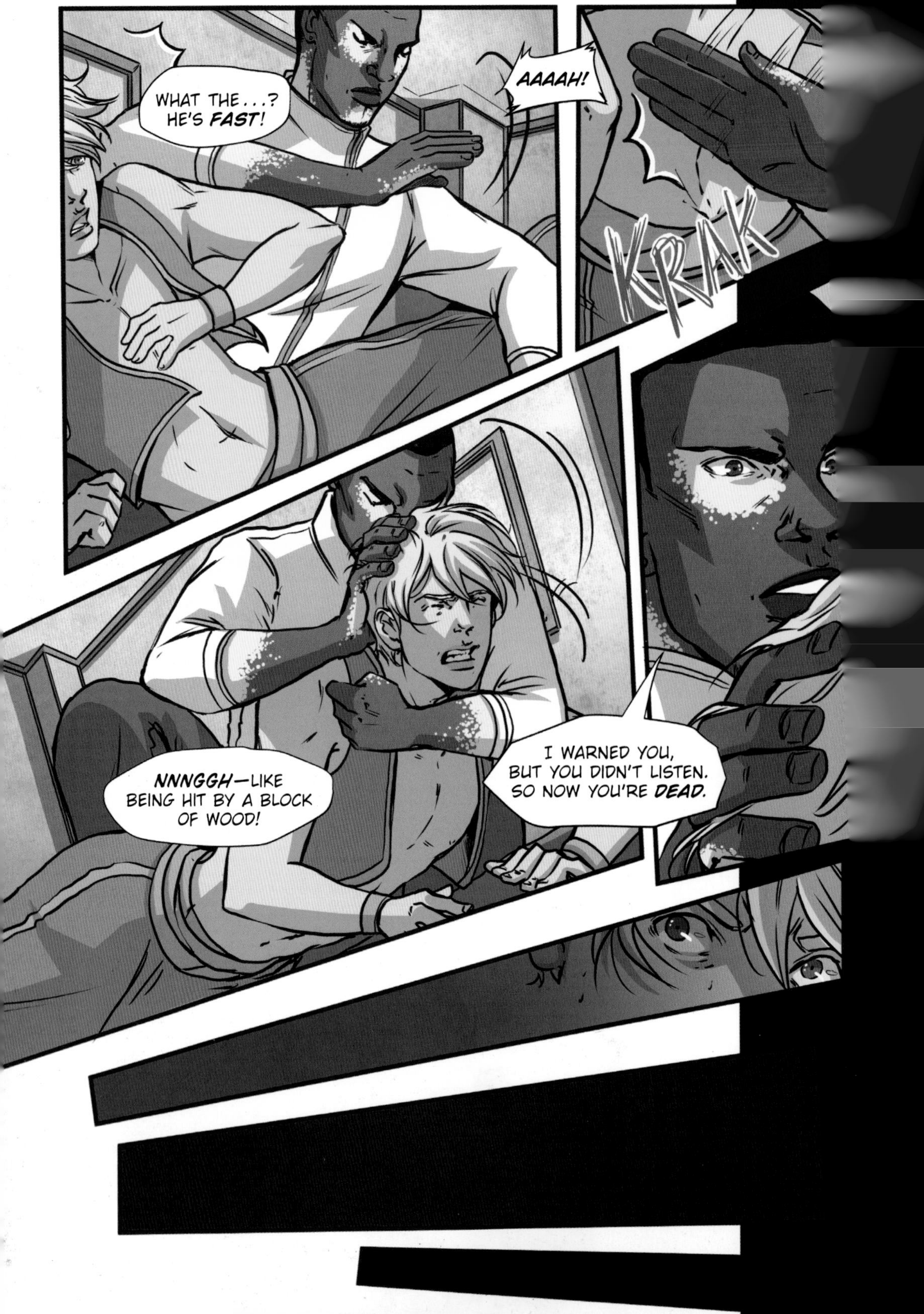
WHAT THE . . .? HE'S FAST!
AAAAH!
KRAK
NNNGGH—LIKE BEING HIT BY A BLOCK OF WOOD!
I WARNED YOU, BUT YOU DIDN'T LISTEN. SO NOW YOU'RE DEAD.

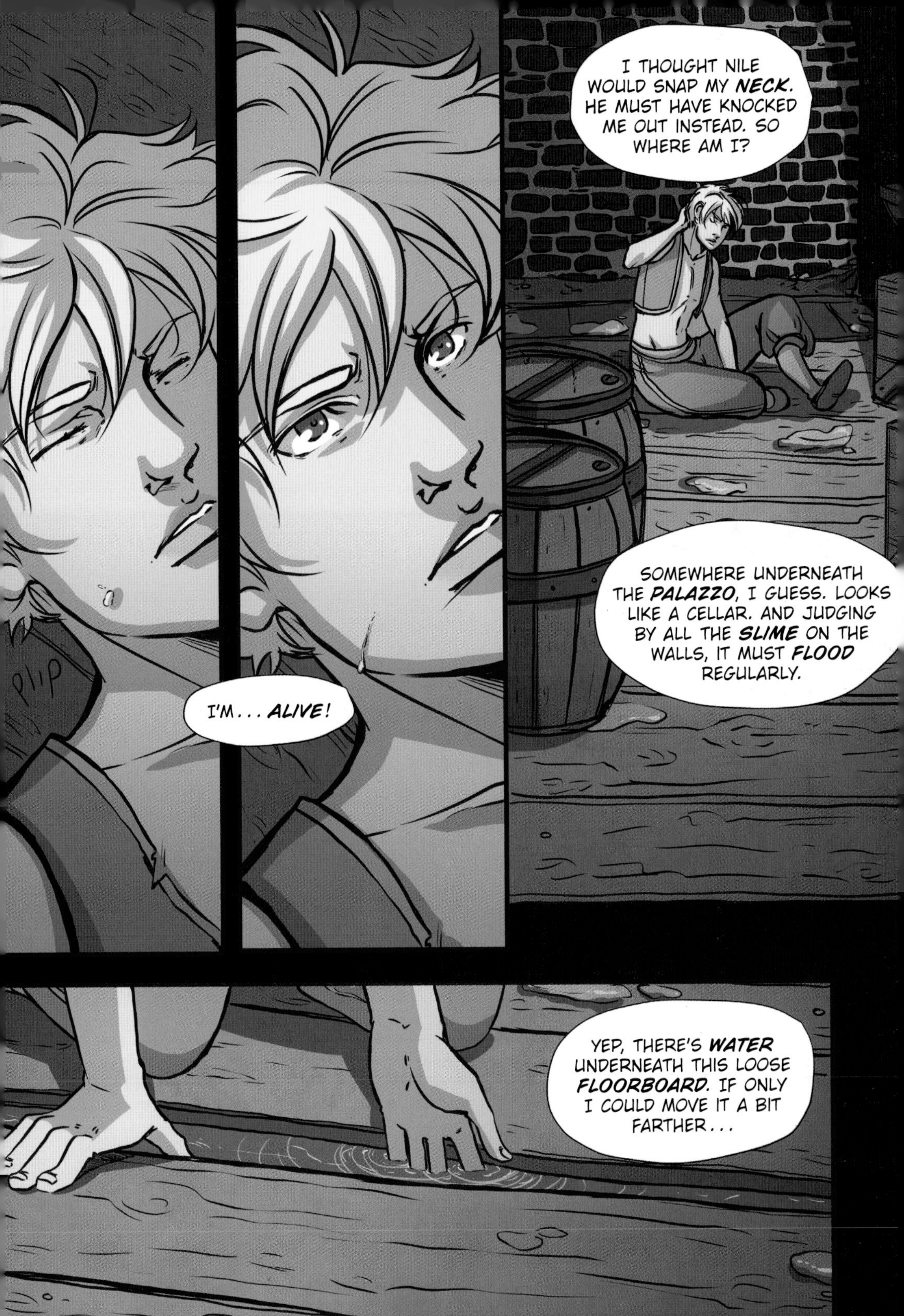
PLIP
I'M . . . ALIVE!
I THOUGHT NILE WOULD SNAP MY NECK. HE MUST HAVE KNOCKED ME OUT INSTEAD. SO WHERE AM I?
SOMEWHERE UNDERNEATH THE PALAZZO, I GUESS. LOOKS LIKE A CELLAR. AND JUDGING BY ALL THE SLIME ON THE WALLS, IT MUST FLOOD REGULARLY.
YEP, THERE'S WATER UNDERNEATH THIS LOOSE FLOORBOARD. IF ONLY I COULD MOVE IT A BIT FARTHER . . .

AND THE DOOR'S JAMMED TIGHT. GREAT.
THAT'S THE STORM SURGE SIREN! VENICE IS FLOODING . . . AND THIS ROOM WILL FILL UP! NILE PUT ME IN HERE TO DROWN!
THAT LOOSE FLOORBOARD IS MY ONLY CHANCE! IT'S AROUND HERE SOMEWHERE. . . .
KRUNCH
GOT IT! THERE'S A PIPE, AND WATER RUSHING IN . . . SO IT MUST ALSO BE THE WAY OUT! HOPE I CAN SQUEEZE THROUGH. . . .
NNNF! IT'S TIGHT! AND PITCH BLACK. I CAN'T SEE A THING!

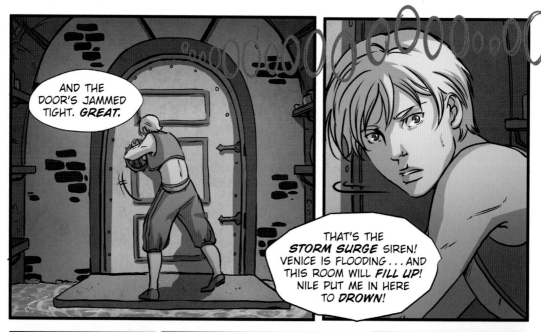

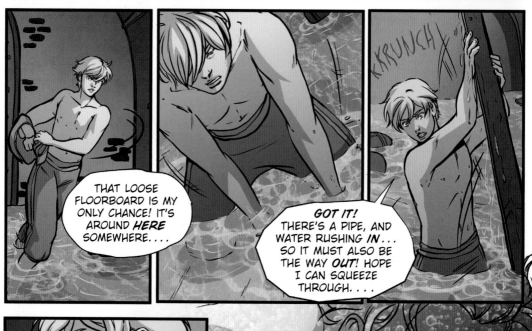

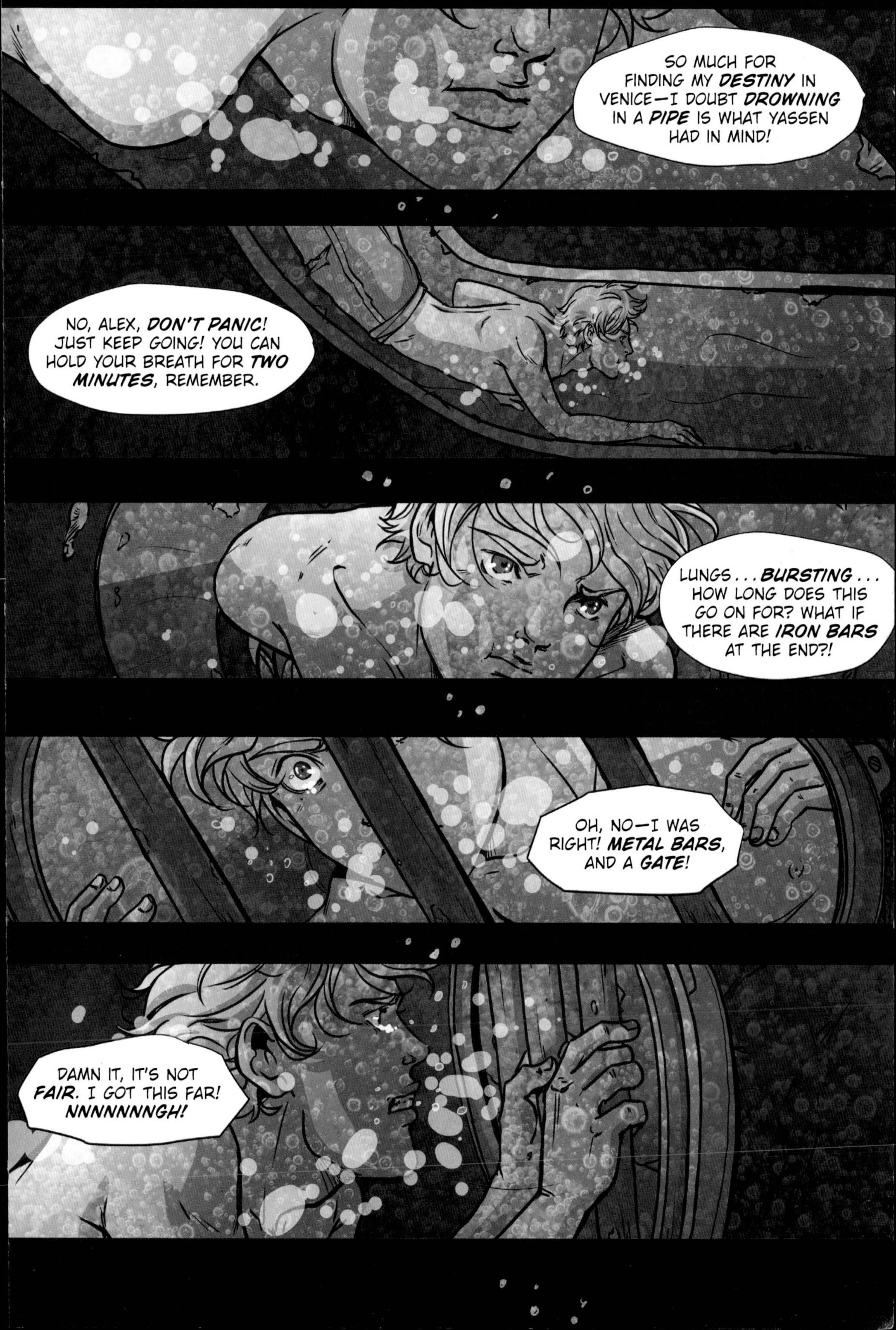
SO MUCH FOR FINDING MY DESTINY IN VENICE—I DOUBT DROWNING IN A PIPE IS WHAT YASSEN HAD IN MIND!
NO, ALEX, DON'T PANIC! JUST KEEP GOING! YOU CAN HOLD YOUR BREATH FOR TWO MINUTES, REMEMBER.
LUNGS . . . BURSTING . . . HOW LONG DOES THIS GO ON FOR? WHAT IF THERE ARE IRON BARS AT THE END?!
OH, NO—I WAS RIGHT! METAL BARS, AND A GATE!
DAMN IT, IT'S NOT FAIR. I GOT THIS FAR! NNNNNNNGH!

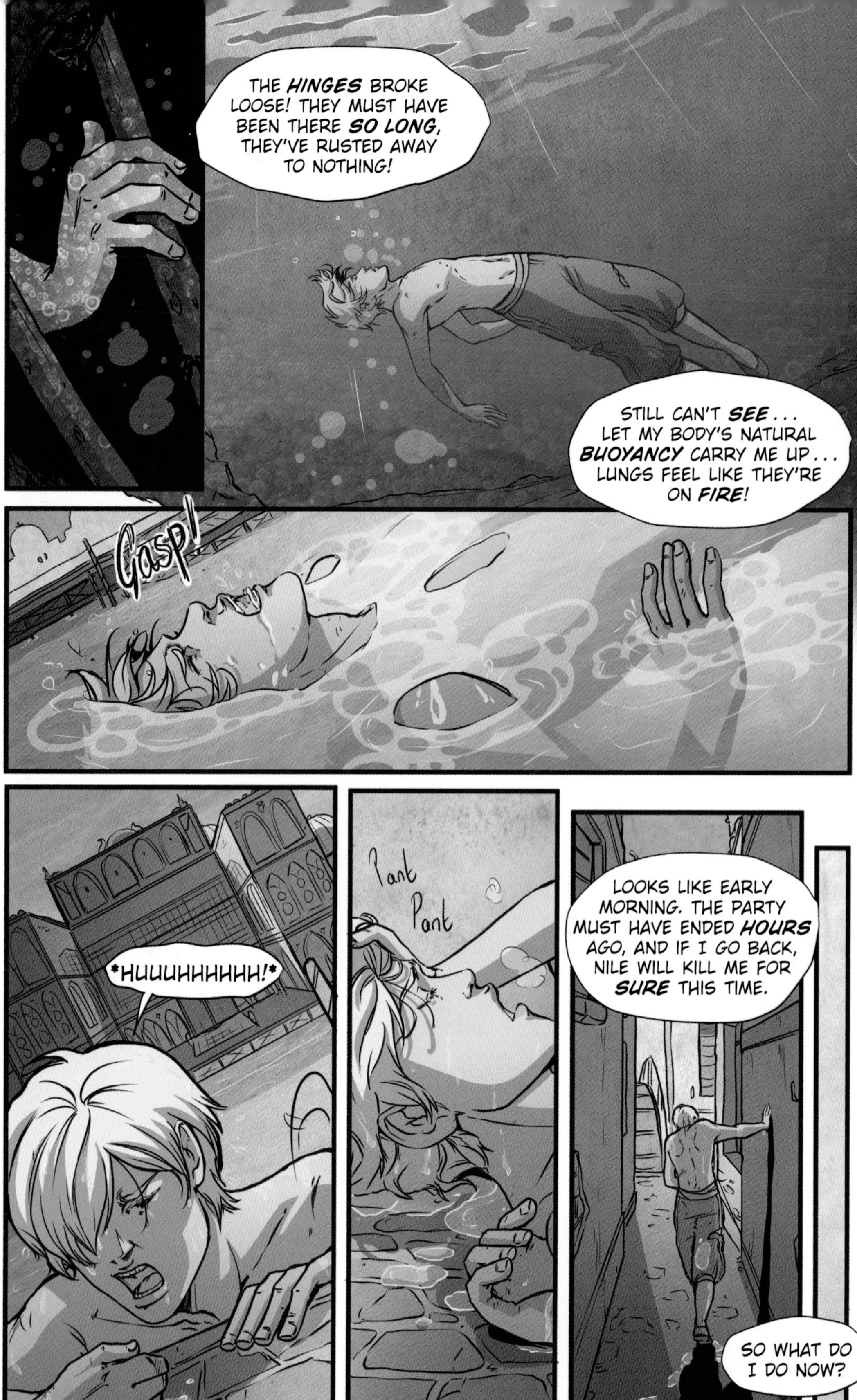
THE HINGES BROKE LOOSE! THEY MUST HAVE BEEN THERE SO LONG, THEY'VE RUSTED AWAY TO NOTHING!
STILL CAN'T SEE . . . LET MY BODY'S NATURAL BUOYANCY CARRY ME UP . . . LUNGS FEEL LIKE THEY'RE ON FIRE!
Gasp!
HUUUHHHHHH!
Pant
Pant
LOOKS LIKE EARLY MORNING. THE PARTY MUST HAVE ENDED HOURS AGO, AND IF I GO BACK, NILE WILL KILL ME FOR SURE THIS TIME.
SO WHAT DO I DO NOW?

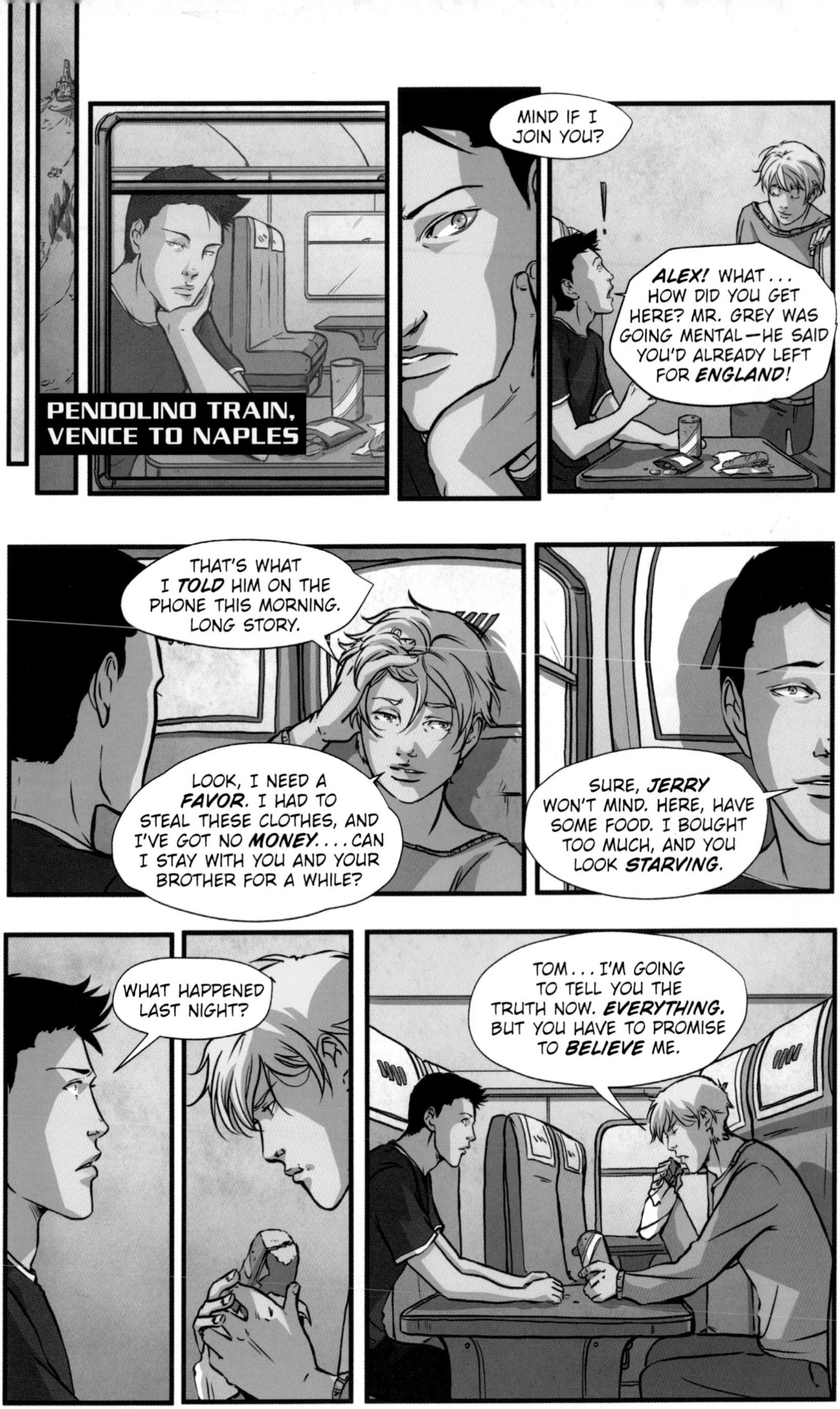

PENDOLINO TRAIN, VENICE TO NAPLES
MIND IF I JOIN YOU?
!
ALEX! WHAT . . . HOW DID YOU GET HERE? MR. GREY WAS GOING MENTAL—HE SAID YOU'D ALREADY LEFT FOR ENGLAND!
THAT'S WHAT I TOLD HIM ON THE PHONE THIS MORNING. LONG STORY.
LOOK, I NEED A FAVOR. I HAD TO STEAL THESE CLOTHES, AND I'VE GOT NO MONEY. . . . CAN I STAY WITH YOU AND YOUR BROTHER FOR A WHILE?
SURE, JERRY WON'T MIND. HERE, HAVE SOME FOOD. I BOUGHT TOO MUCH, AND YOU LOOK STARVING.
WHAT HAPPENED LAST NIGHT?
TOM . . . I'M GOING TO TELL YOU THE TRUTH NOW. EVERYTHING. BUT YOU HAVE TO PROMISE TO BELIEVE ME.

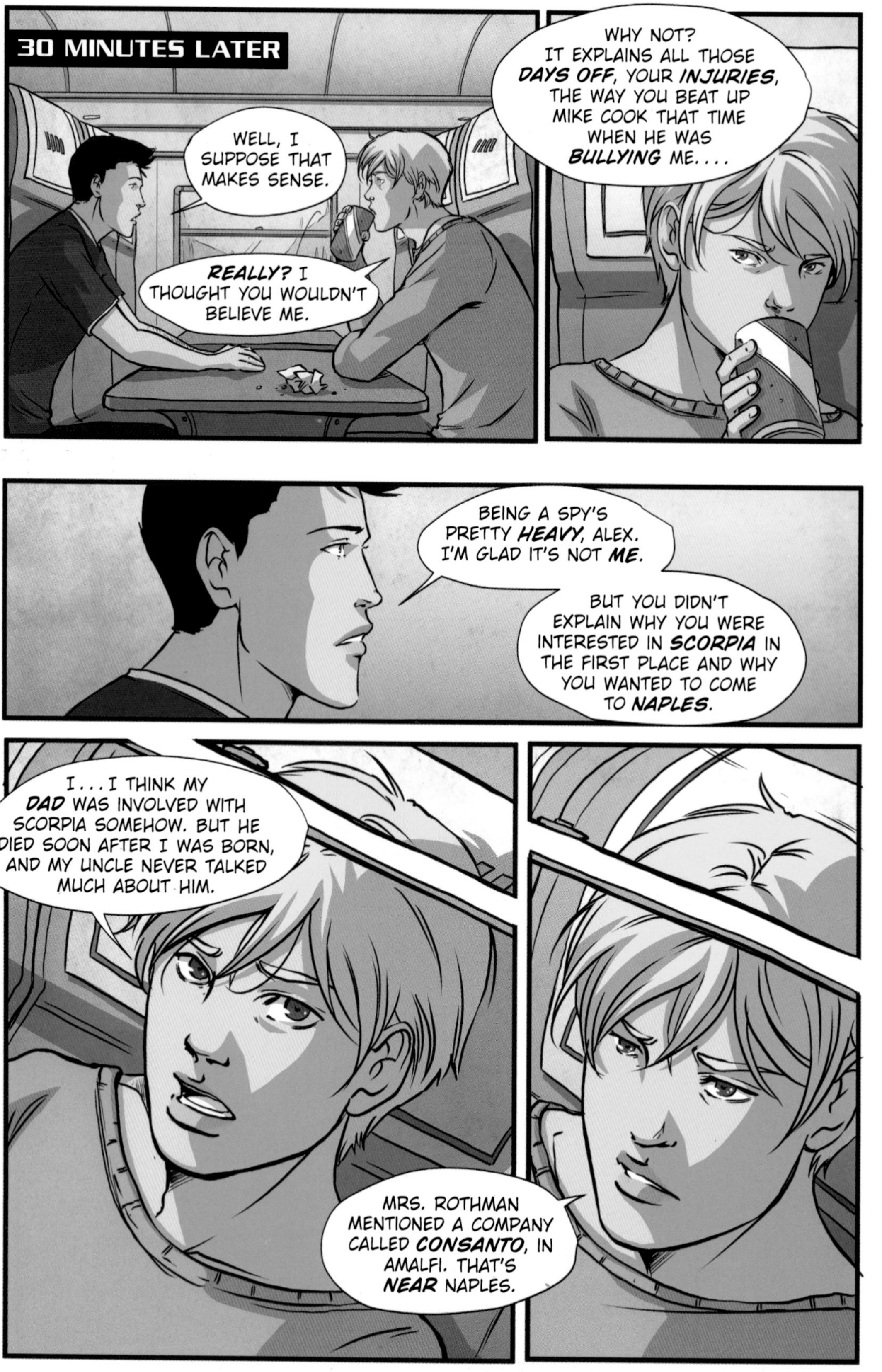
30 MINUTES LATER
WELL, I SUPPOSE THAT MAKES SENSE.
REALLY? I THOUGHT YOU WOULDN'T BELIEVE ME.
WHY NOT? IT EXPLAINS ALL THOSE DAYS OFF, YOUR INJURIES, THE WAY YOU BEAT UP MIKE COOK THAT TIME WHEN HE WAS BULLYING ME. . . .
BEING A SPY'S PRETTY HEAVY, ALEX. I'M GLAD IT'S NOT ME.
BUT YOU DIDN'T EXPLAIN WHY YOU WERE INTERESTED IN SCORPIA IN THE FIRST PLACE AND WHY YOU WANTED TO COME TO NAPLES.
I . . . I THINK MY DAD WAS INVOLVED WITH SCORPIA SOMEHOW. BUT HE DIED SOON AFTER I WAS BORN, AND MY UNCLE NEVER TALKED MUCH ABOUT HIM.
MRS. ROTHMAN MENTIONED A COMPANY CALLED CONSANTO, IN AMALFI. THAT'S NEAR NAPLES.

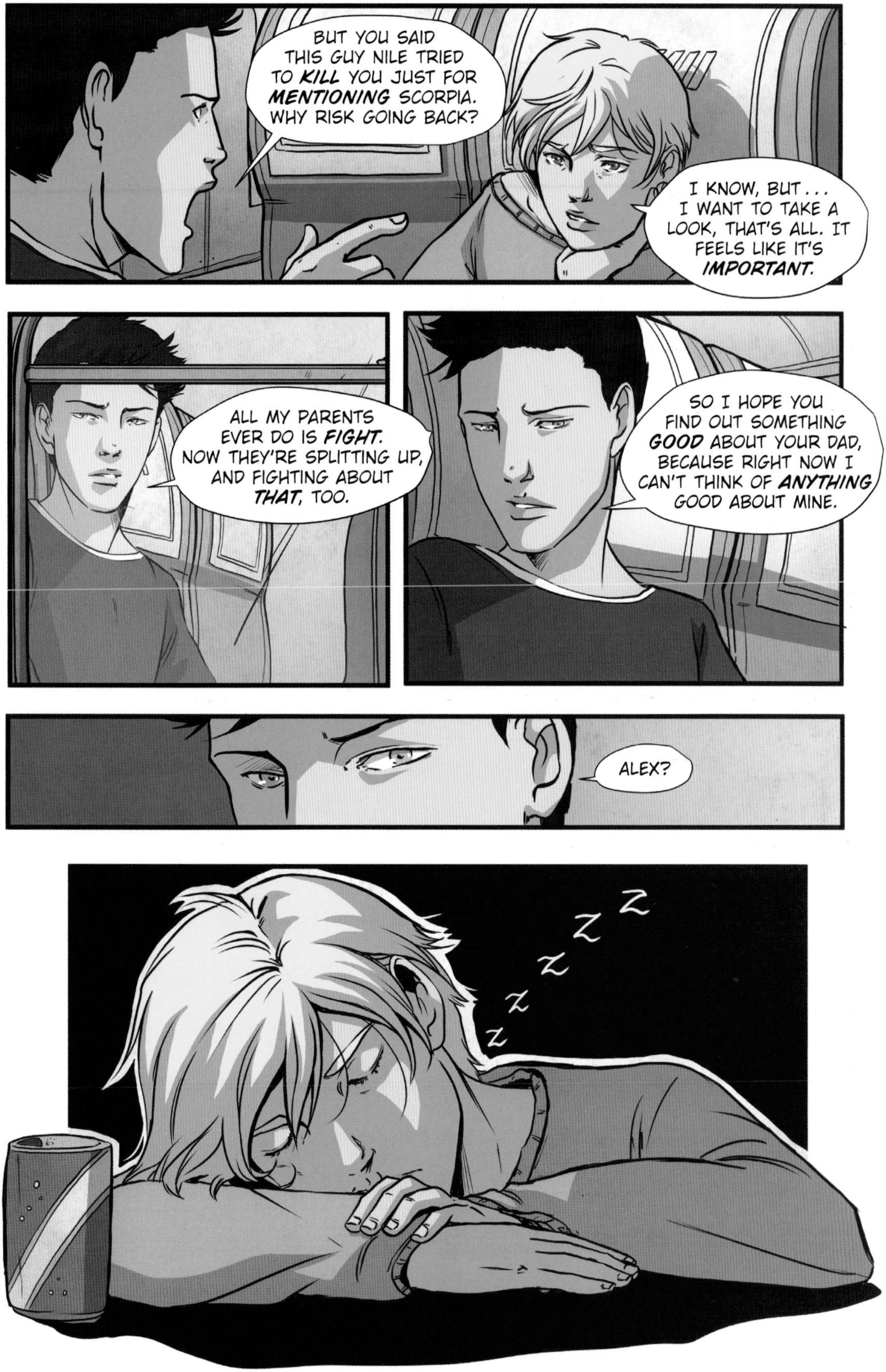
BUT YOU SAID THIS GUY NILE TRIED TO KILL YOU JUST FOR MENTIONING SCORPIA. WHY RISK GOING BACK?
I KNOW, BUT . . . I WANT TO TAKE A LOOK, THAT'S ALL. IT FEELS LIKE IT'S IMPORTANT.
ALL MY PARENTS EVER DO IS FIGHT. NOW THEY'RE SPLITTING UP, AND FIGHTING ABOUT THAT, TOO.
SO I HOPE YOU FIND OUT SOMETHING GOOD ABOUT YOUR DAD, BECAUSE RIGHT NOW I CAN'T THINK OF ANYTHING GOOD ABOUT MINE.
ALEX?
Z Z Z Z Z Z

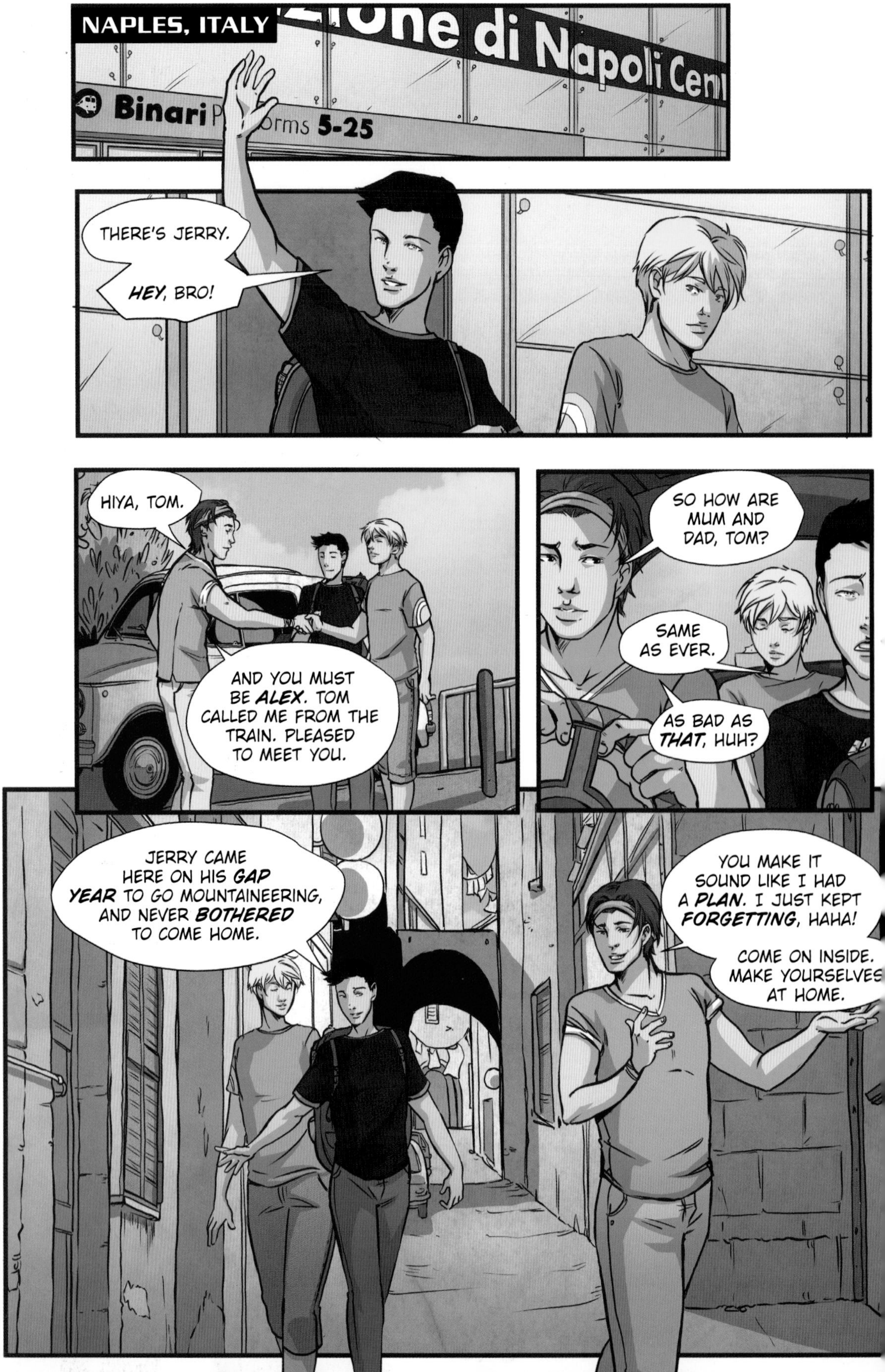
NAPLES, ITALY
zione di Napoli Cen
Binari Platforms 5-25
THERE'S JERRY.
HEY, BRO!
HIYA, TOM.
AND YOU MUST BE ALEX. TOM CALLED ME FROM THE TRAIN. PLEASED TO MEET YOU.
SO HOW ARE MUM AND DAD, TOM?
SAME AS EVER.
AS BAD AS THAT, HUH?
JERRY CAME HERE ON HIS GAP YEAR TO GO MOUNTAINEERING, AND NEVER BOTHERED TO COME HOME.
YOU MAKE IT SOUND LIKE I HAD A PLAN. I JUST KEPT FORGETTING, HAHA!
COME ON INSIDE. MAKE YOURSELVES AT HOME.

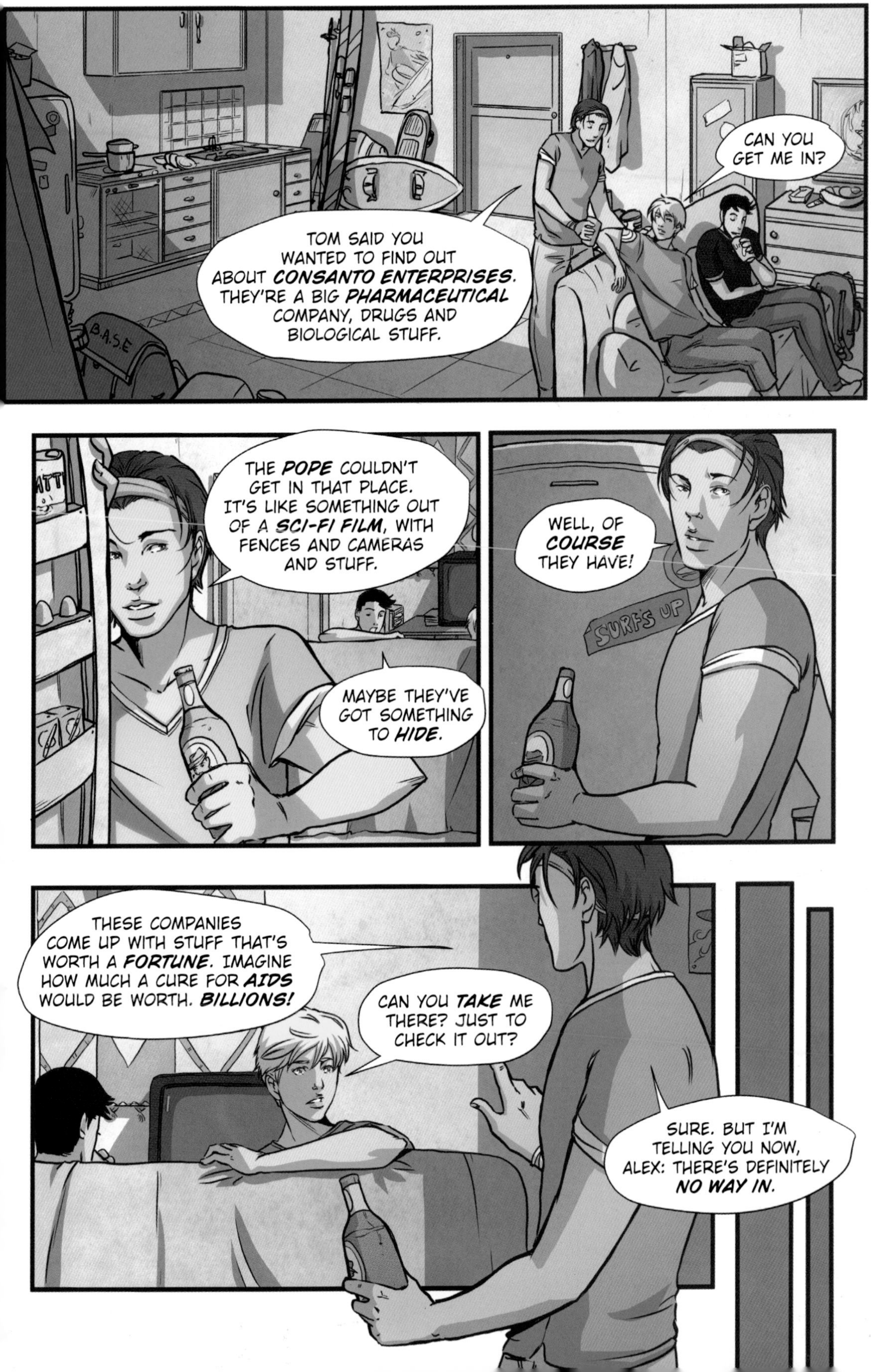
TOM SAID YOU WANTED TO FIND OUT ABOUT **CONSANTO ENTERPRISES**. THEY'RE A BIG **PHARMACEUTICAL** COMPANY, DRUGS AND BIOLOGICAL STUFF.
CAN YOU GET ME IN?
B.A.S.E
THE **POPE** COULDN'T GET IN THAT PLACE. IT'S LIKE SOMETHING OUT OF A **SCI-FI FILM**, WITH FENCES AND CAMERAS AND STUFF.
MAYBE THEY'VE GOT SOMETHING TO **HIDE**.
WELL, OF **COURSE** THEY HAVE!
SURFS UP
THESE COMPANIES COME UP WITH STUFF THAT'S WORTH A **FORTUNE**. IMAGINE HOW MUCH A CURE FOR **AIDS** WOULD BE WORTH. **BILLIONS!**
CAN YOU **TAKE** ME THERE? JUST TO CHECK IT OUT?
SURE. BUT I'M TELLING YOU NOW, ALEX: THERE'S DEFINITELY **NO WAY IN**.

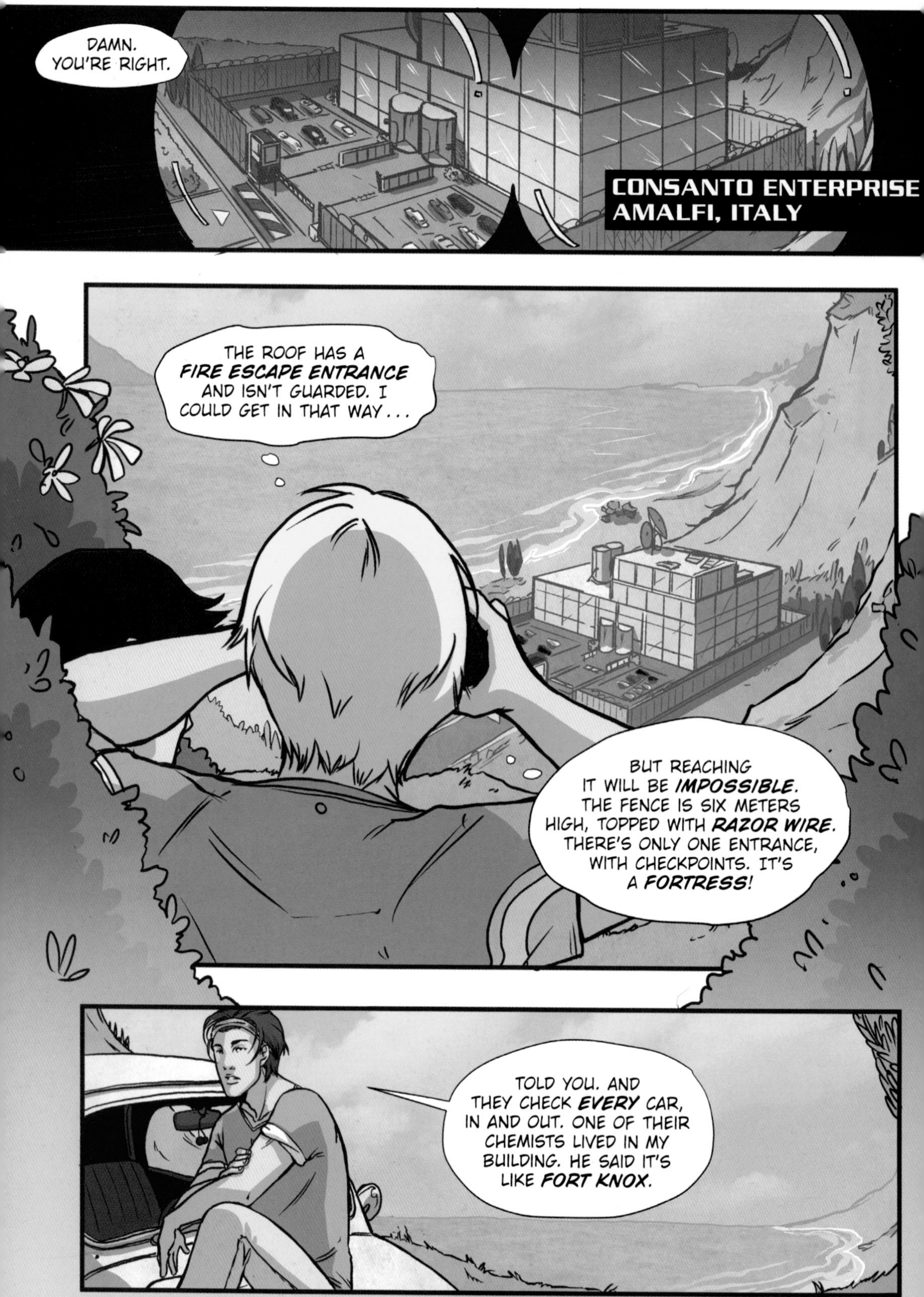
DAMN. YOU'RE RIGHT.
CONSANTO ENTERPRISE
AMALFI, ITALY
THE ROOF HAS A ***FIRE ESCAPE ENTRANCE*** AND ISN'T GUARDED. I COULD GET IN THAT WAY . . .
BUT REACHING IT WILL BE ***IMPOSSIBLE***. THE FENCE IS SIX METERS HIGH, TOPPED WITH ***RAZOR WIRE***. THERE'S ONLY ONE ENTRANCE, WITH CHECKPOINTS. IT'S A ***FORTRESS***!
TOLD YOU. AND THEY CHECK ***EVERY*** CAR, IN AND OUT. ONE OF THEIR CHEMISTS LIVED IN MY BUILDING. HE SAID IT'S LIKE ***FORT KNOX***.

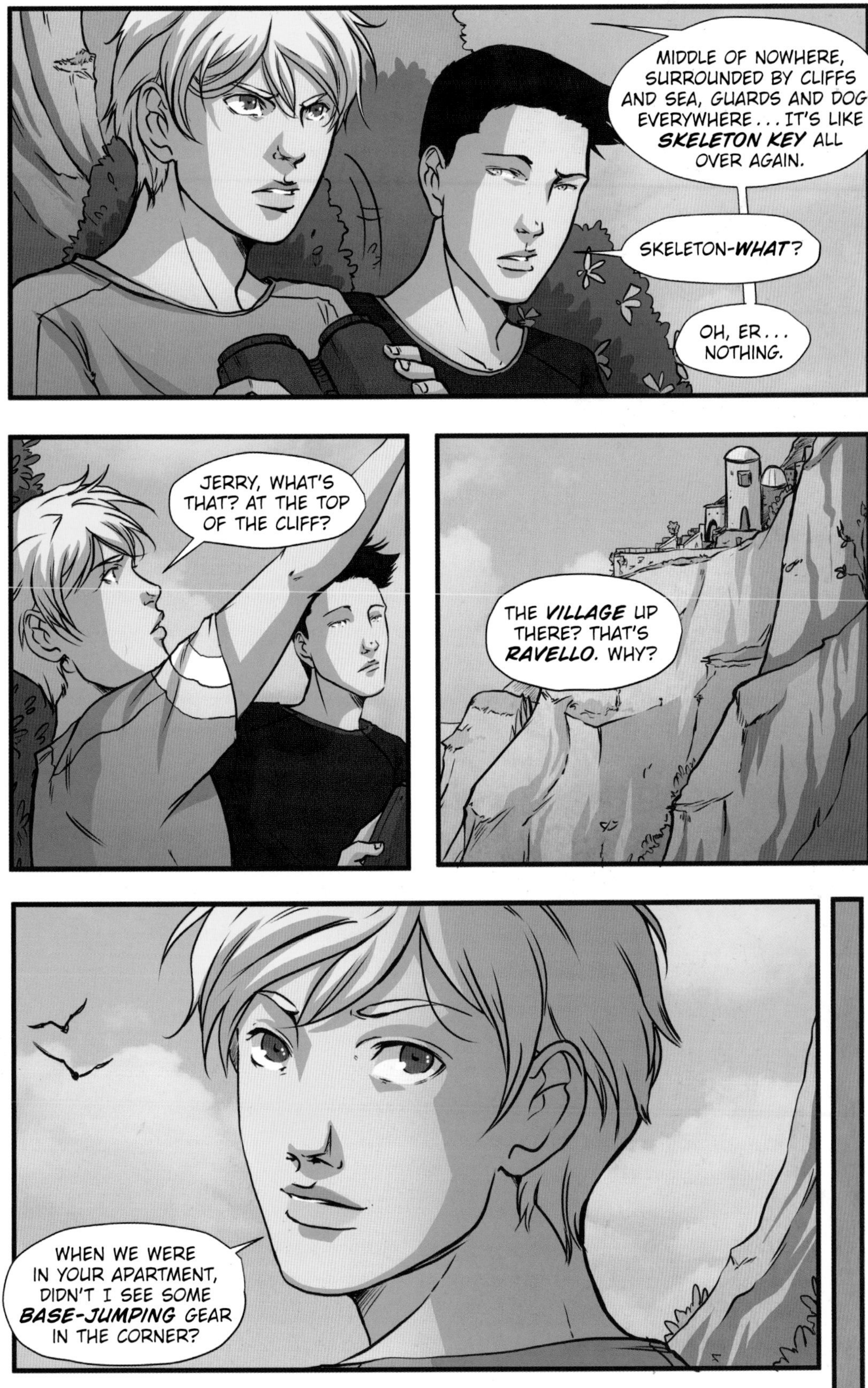
MIDDLE OF NOWHERE, SURROUNDED BY CLIFFS AND SEA, GUARDS AND DOGS EVERYWHERE . . . IT'S LIKE **SKELETON KEY** ALL OVER AGAIN.
SKELETON-***WHAT***?
OH, ER . . . NOTHING.
JERRY, WHAT'S THAT? AT THE TOP OF THE CLIFF?
THE ***VILLAGE*** UP THERE? THAT'S ***RAVELLO.*** WHY?
WHEN WE WERE IN YOUR APARTMENT, DIDN'T I SEE SOME ***BASE-JUMPING*** GEAR IN THE CORNER?

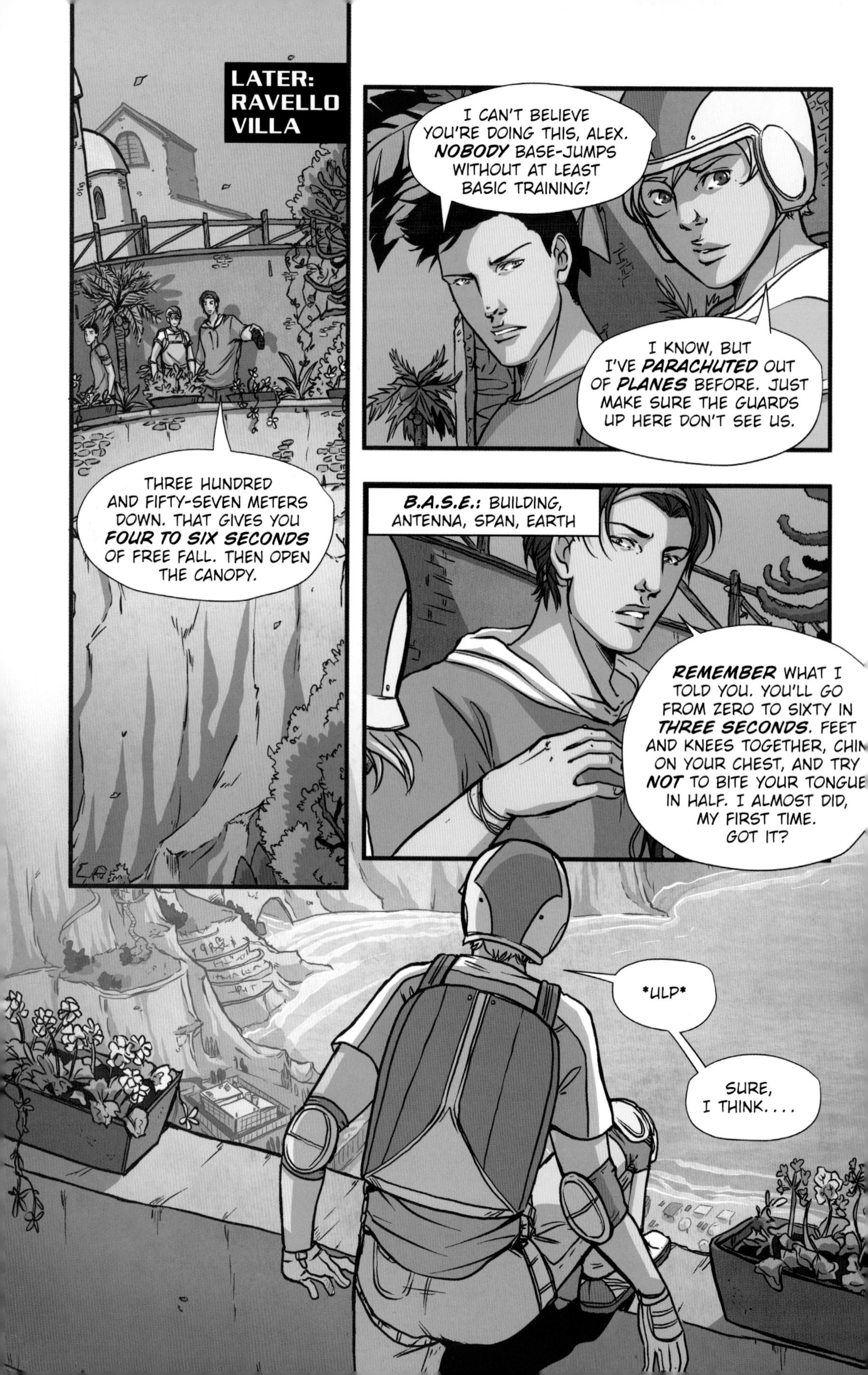
LATER: RAVELLO VILLA
THREE HUNDRED AND FIFTY-SEVEN METERS DOWN. THAT GIVES YOU FOUR TO SIX SECONDS OF FREE FALL. THEN OPEN THE CANOPY.
I CAN'T BELIEVE YOU'RE DOING THIS, ALEX. NOBODY BASE-JUMPS WITHOUT AT LEAST BASIC TRAINING!
I KNOW, BUT I'VE PARACHUTED OUT OF PLANES BEFORE. JUST MAKE SURE THE GUARDS UP HERE DON'T SEE US.
B.A.S.E.: BUILDING, ANTENNA, SPAN, EARTH
REMEMBER WHAT I TOLD YOU. YOU'LL GO FROM ZERO TO SIXTY IN THREE SECONDS. FEET AND KNEES TOGETHER, CHIN ON YOUR CHEST, AND TRY NOT TO BITE YOUR TONGUE IN HALF. I ALMOST DID, MY FIRST TIME. GOT IT?
ULP
SURE, I THINK. . . .

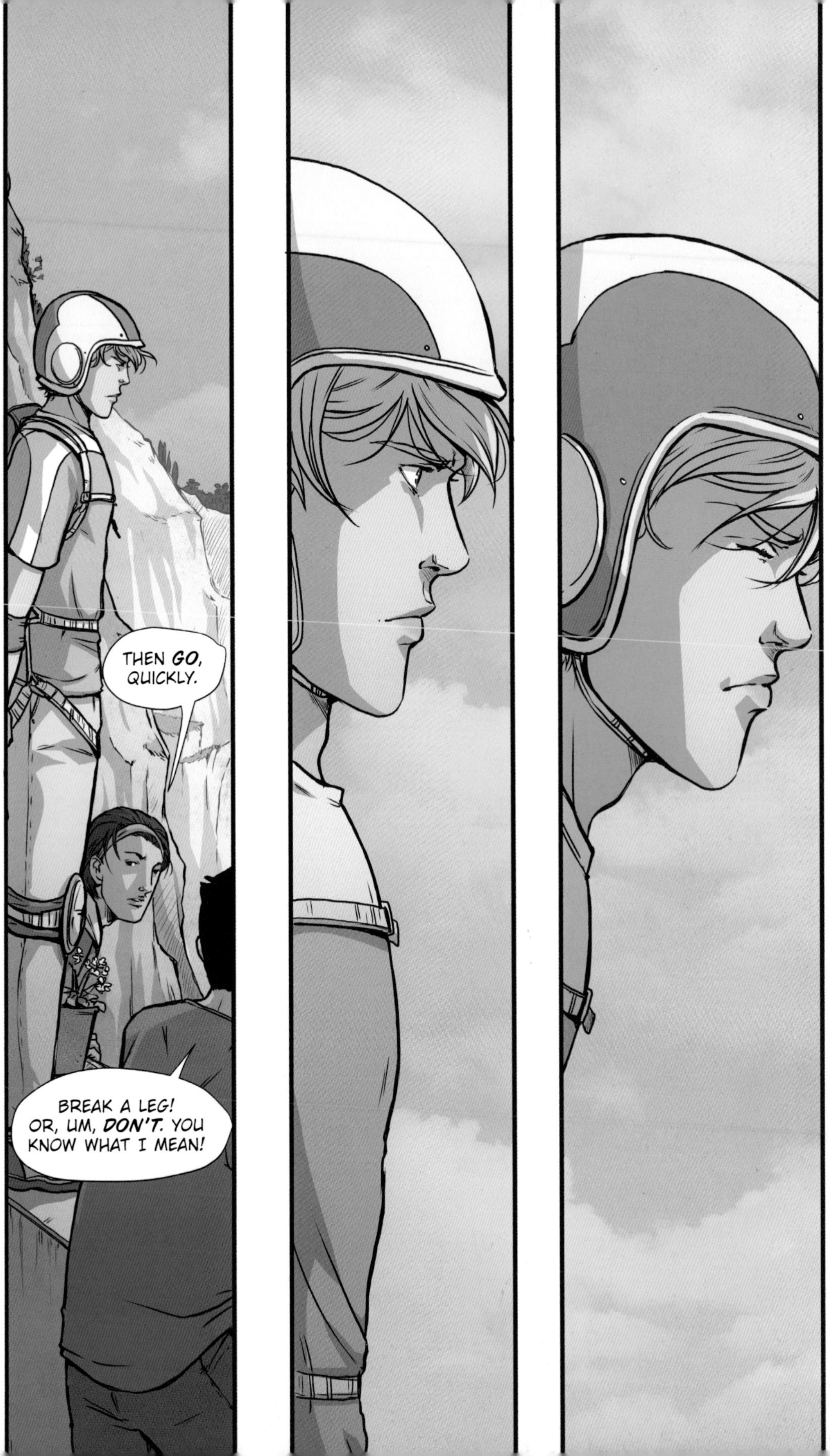
THEN GO, QUICKLY.
BREAK A LEG! OR, UM, DON'T. YOU KNOW WHAT I MEAN!

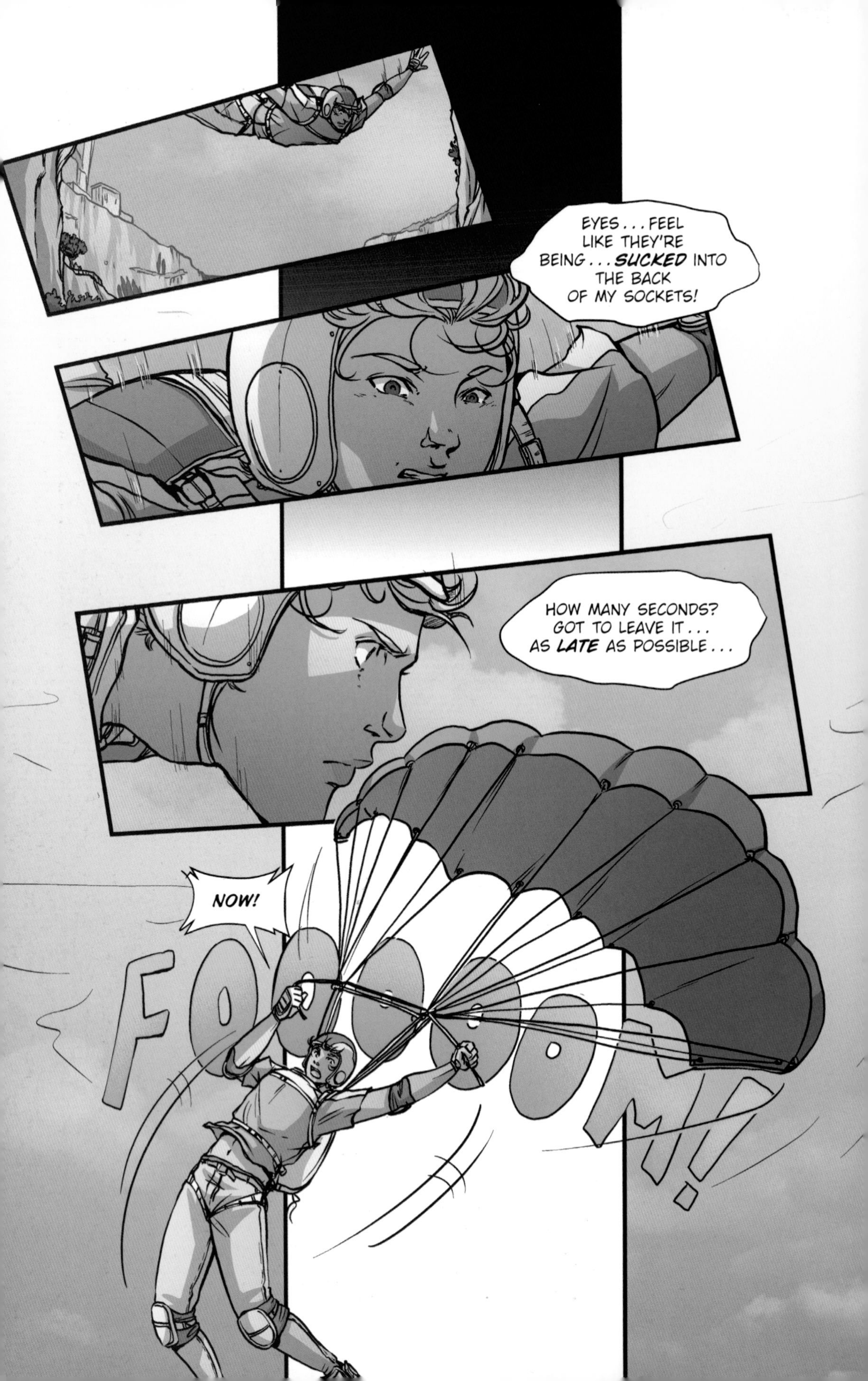
EYES . . . FEEL LIKE THEY'RE BEING . . . SUCKED INTO THE BACK OF MY SOCKETS!
HOW MANY SECONDS? GOT TO LEAVE IT . . . AS LATE AS POSSIBLE . . .
NOW!
FOOOOM!!

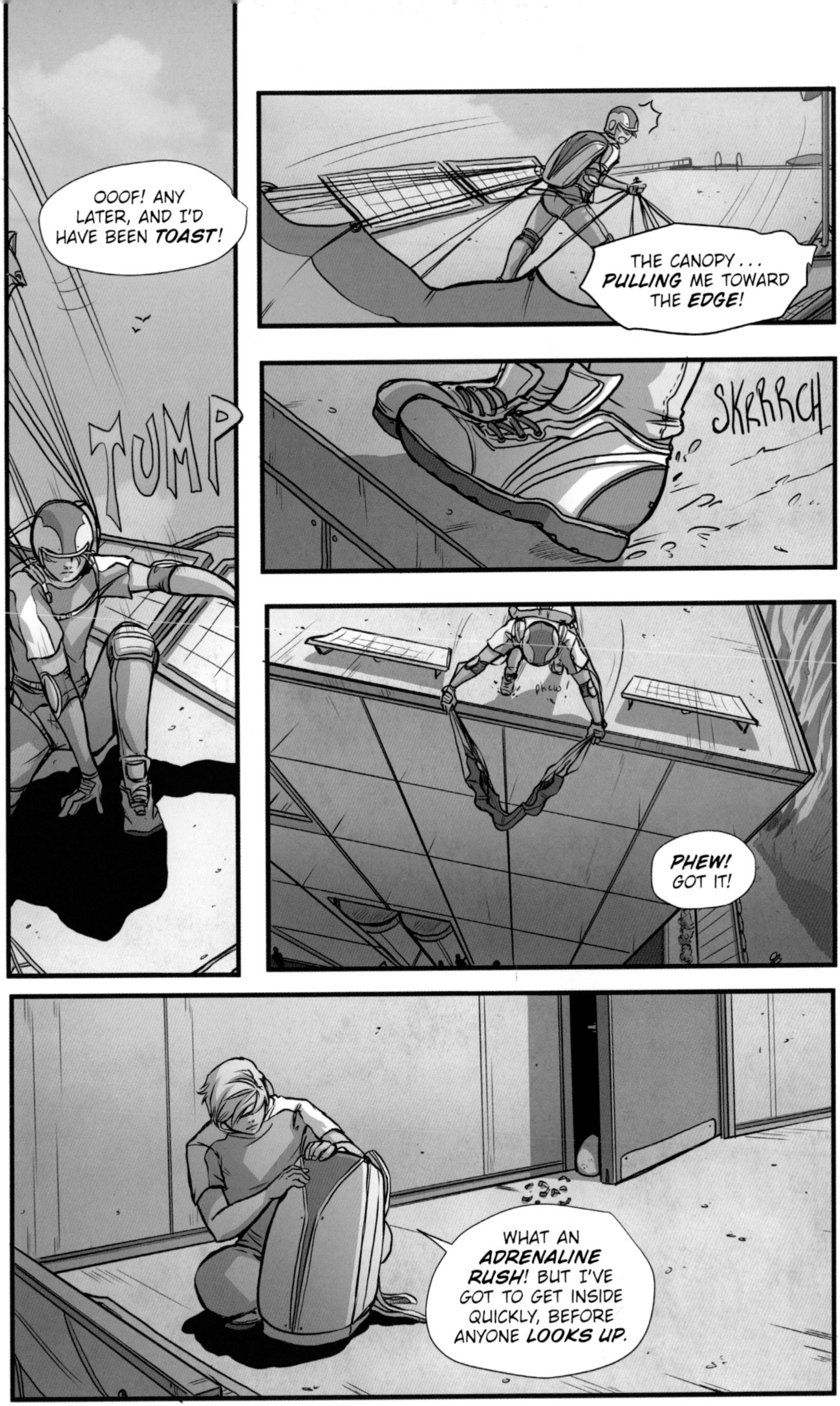
OOOF! ANY LATER, AND I'D HAVE BEEN TOAST!
TUMP
THE CANOPY . . . PULLING ME TOWARD THE EDGE!
SKRRRCH
PHEW! GOT IT!
WHAT AN ADRENALINE RUSH! BUT I'VE GOT TO GET INSIDE QUICKLY, BEFORE ANYONE LOOKS UP.

THE DOORS ARE AUTOMATIC FROM OUTSIDE, BUT THE **KEYPAD** CONTROLS THEM FROM INSIDE. I WON'T GET BACK OUT THAT WAY.

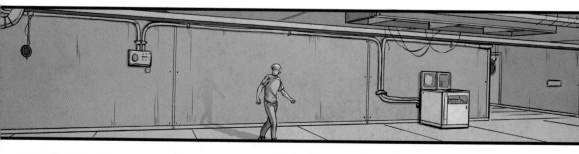

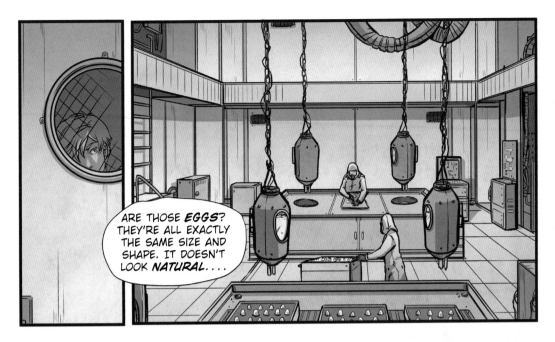

ARE THOSE *EGGS*? THEY'RE ALL EXACTLY THE SAME SIZE AND SHAPE. IT DOESN'T LOOK *NATURAL*....

WHAT ARE THEY MAKING IN HERE? *CHEMICAL WEAPONS*, PERHAPS?

YOU THERE!

WHO THE HELL ARE YOU? WHAT ARE YOU DOING HERE? THIS IS A *SECURE* AREA!

I...I'M LOST. MY NAME'S TOM. MY *DAD* WORKS HERE.

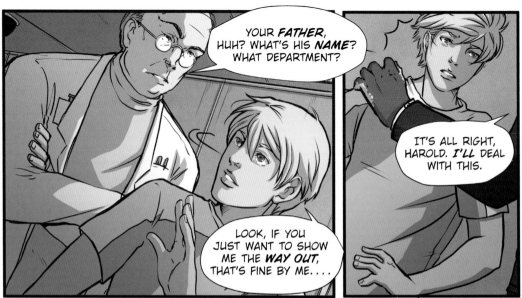

YOUR *FATHER*, HUH? WHAT'S HIS *NAME*? WHAT DEPARTMENT?

LOOK, IF YOU JUST WANT TO SHOW ME THE *WAY OUT*, THAT'S FINE BY ME. . . .

IT'S ALL RIGHT, HAROLD. *I'LL* DEAL WITH THIS.

OH, NO . . . NILE!

DIDN'T YOU JUST LEAVE?

AS YOU CAN SEE, DOCTOR, THERE'S BEEN A SERIOUS *SECURITY BREAKDOWN*. MRS. ROTHMAN SENT ME BACK TO DEAL WITH IT.

THIS BOY IS *ALEX RIDER*. HE'S A *SPY*.

WHAT?! WELL, WHAT ARE YOU GOING TO *DO*?

I JUST TOLD YOU. WE *CAN'T* HAVE SECURITY PROBLEMS ON THESE PREMISES . . .

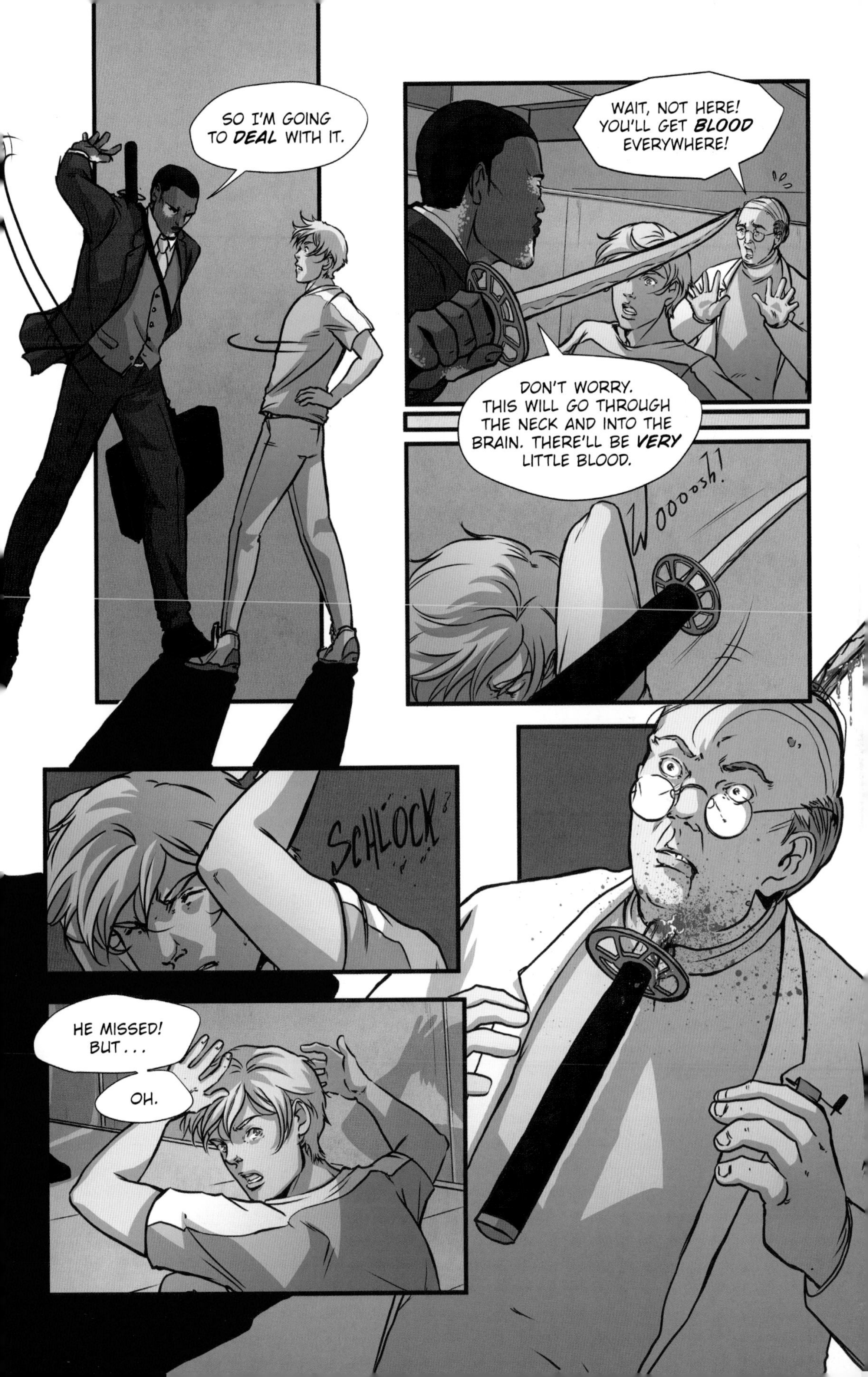
SO I'M GOING TO ***DEAL*** WITH IT.
WAIT, NOT HERE! YOU'LL GET ***BLOOD*** EVERYWHERE!
DON'T WORRY. THIS WILL GO THROUGH THE NECK AND INTO THE BRAIN. THERE'LL BE ***VERY*** LITTLE BLOOD.
Woooosh!
SCHLOCK
HE MISSED! BUT . . .
OH.

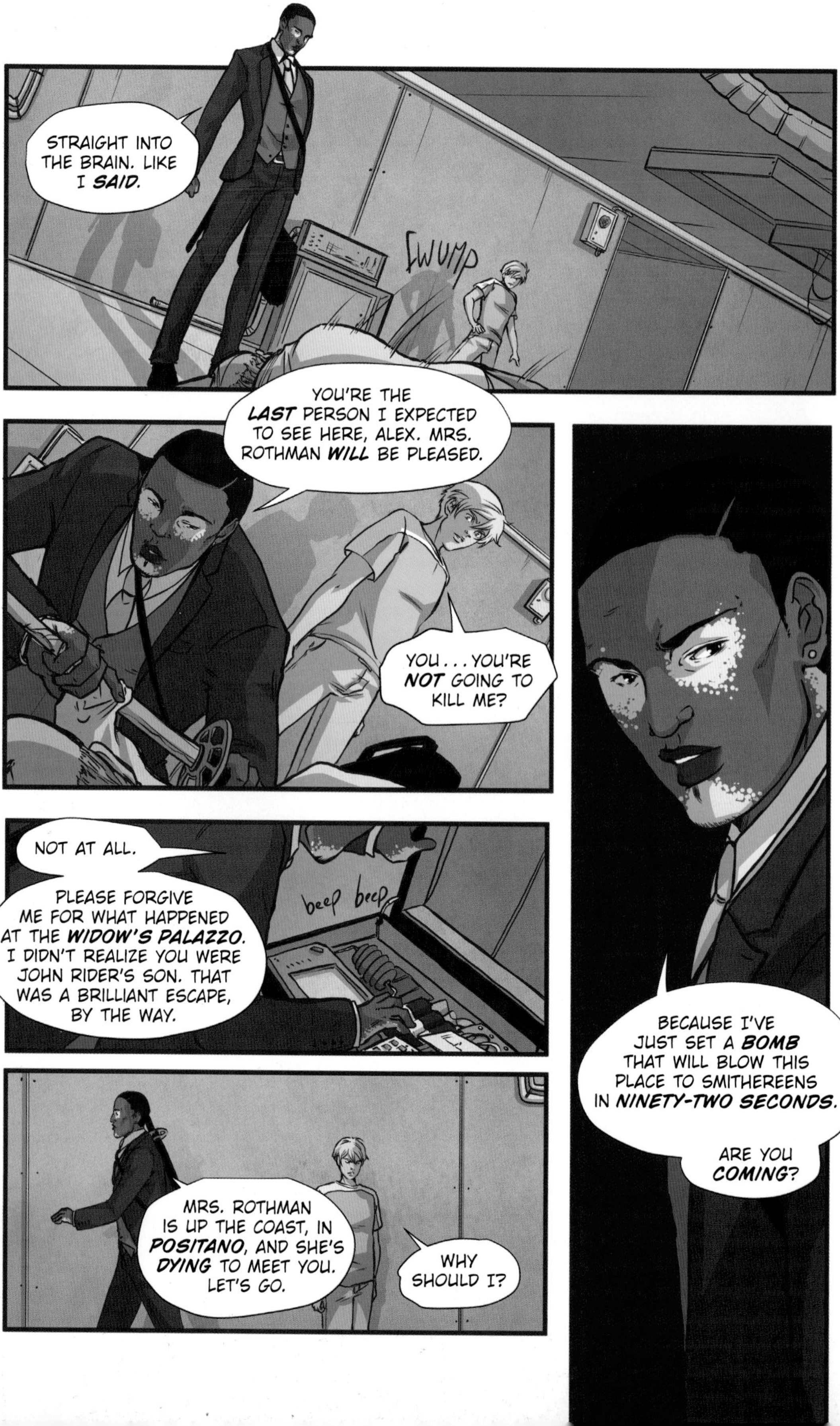
STRAIGHT INTO THE BRAIN. LIKE I SAID.
FWUMP
YOU'RE THE LAST PERSON I EXPECTED TO SEE HERE, ALEX. MRS. ROTHMAN WILL BE PLEASED.
YOU . . . YOU'RE NOT GOING TO KILL ME?
NOT AT ALL.
PLEASE FORGIVE ME FOR WHAT HAPPENED AT THE WIDOW'S PALAZZO. I DIDN'T REALIZE YOU WERE JOHN RIDER'S SON. THAT WAS A BRILLIANT ESCAPE, BY THE WAY.
beep beep
MRS. ROTHMAN IS UP THE COAST, IN POSITANO, AND SHE'S DYING TO MEET YOU. LET'S GO.
WHY SHOULD I?
BECAUSE I'VE JUST SET A BOMB THAT WILL BLOW THIS PLACE TO SMITHEREENS IN NINETY-TWO SECONDS.
ARE YOU COMING?

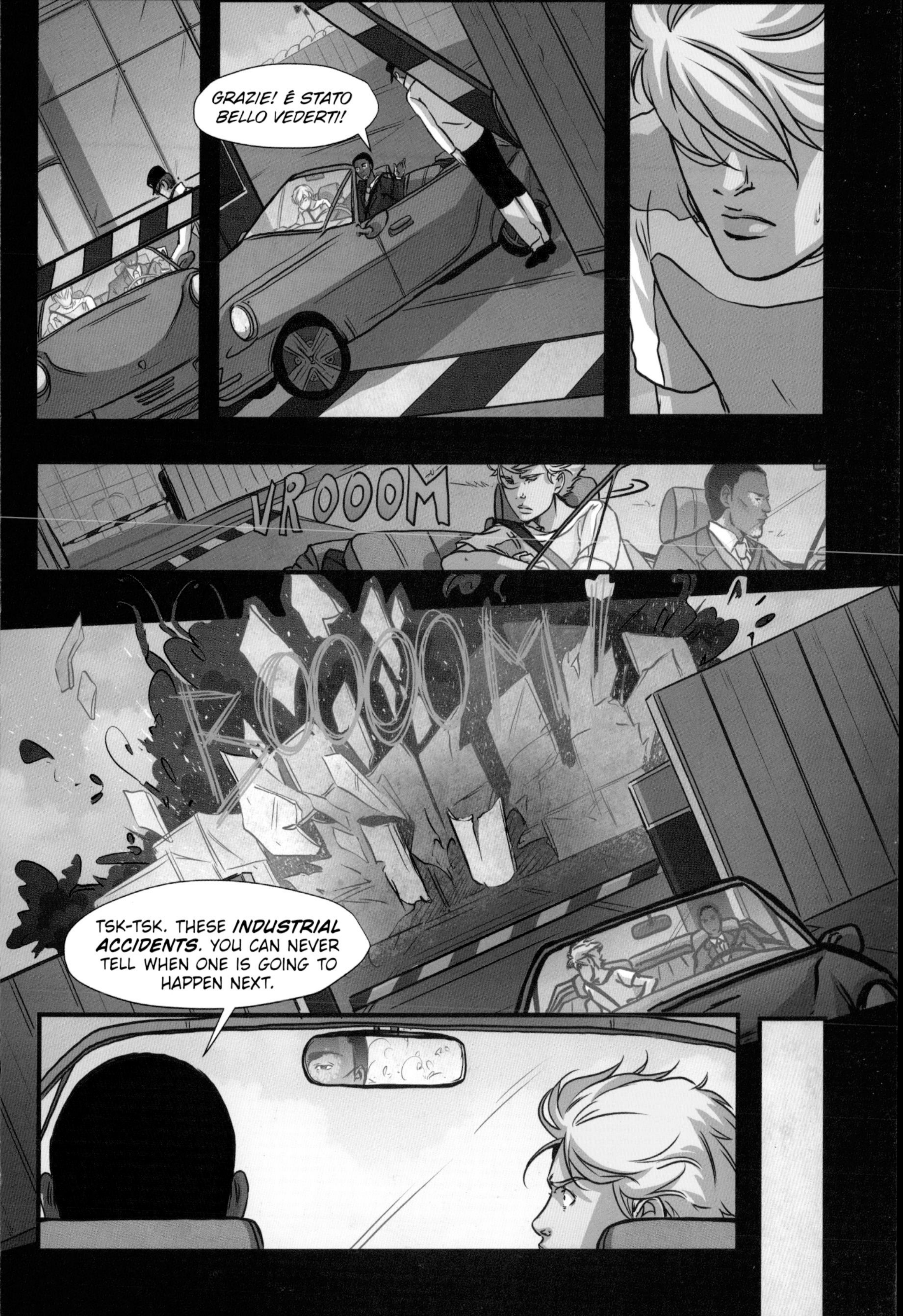
GRAZIE! È STATO BELLO VEDERTI!
VROOOM
ROOOOOM!
TSK-TSK. THESE *INDUSTRIAL ACCIDENTS*. YOU CAN NEVER TELL WHEN ONE IS GOING TO HAPPEN NEXT.

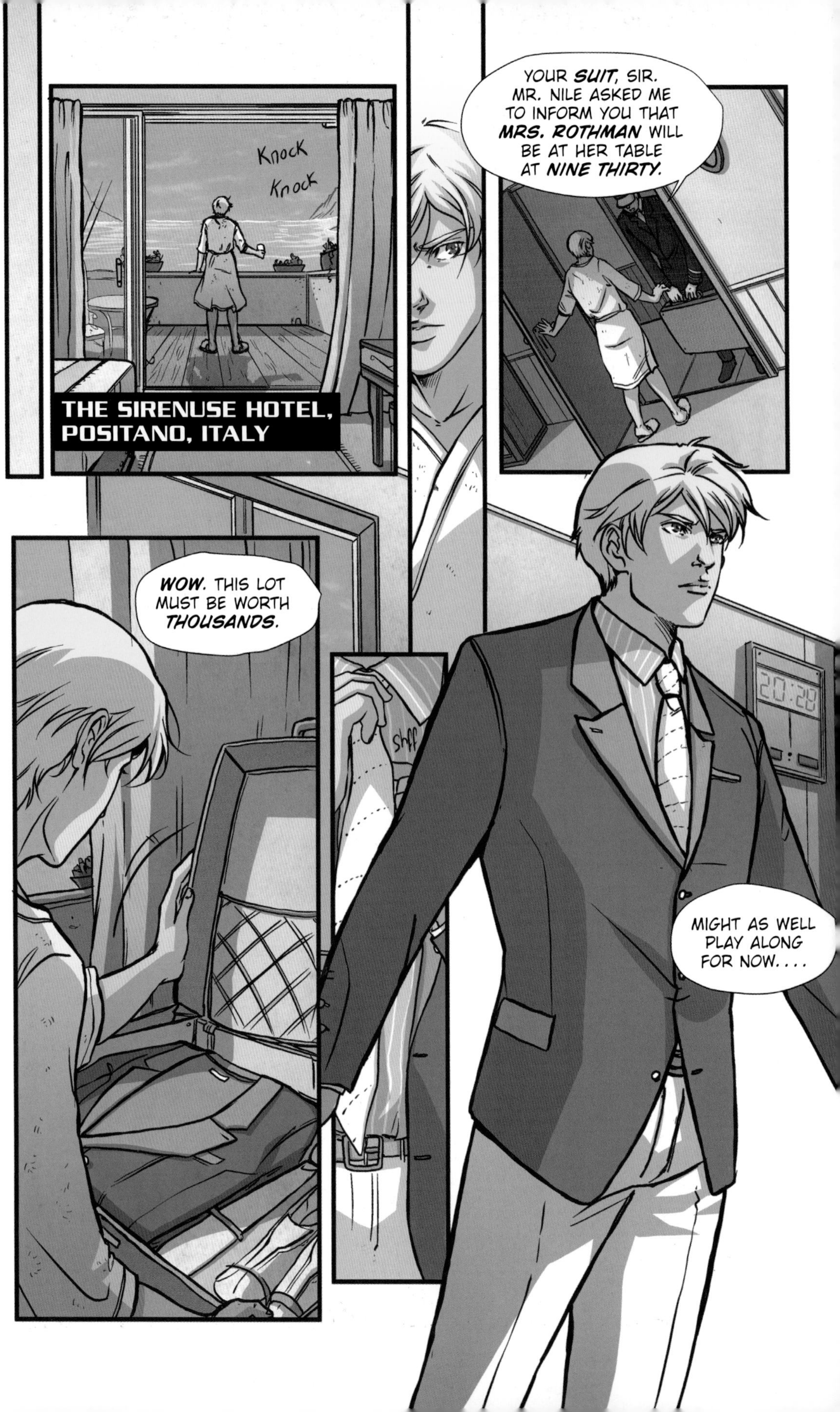
Knock
Knock
THE SIRENUSE HOTEL, POSITANO, ITALY
YOUR SUIT, SIR. MR. NILE ASKED ME TO INFORM YOU THAT MRS. ROTHMAN WILL BE AT HER TABLE AT NINE THIRTY.
WOW. THIS LOT MUST BE WORTH THOUSANDS.
Shff
MIGHT AS WELL PLAY ALONG FOR NOW. . . .

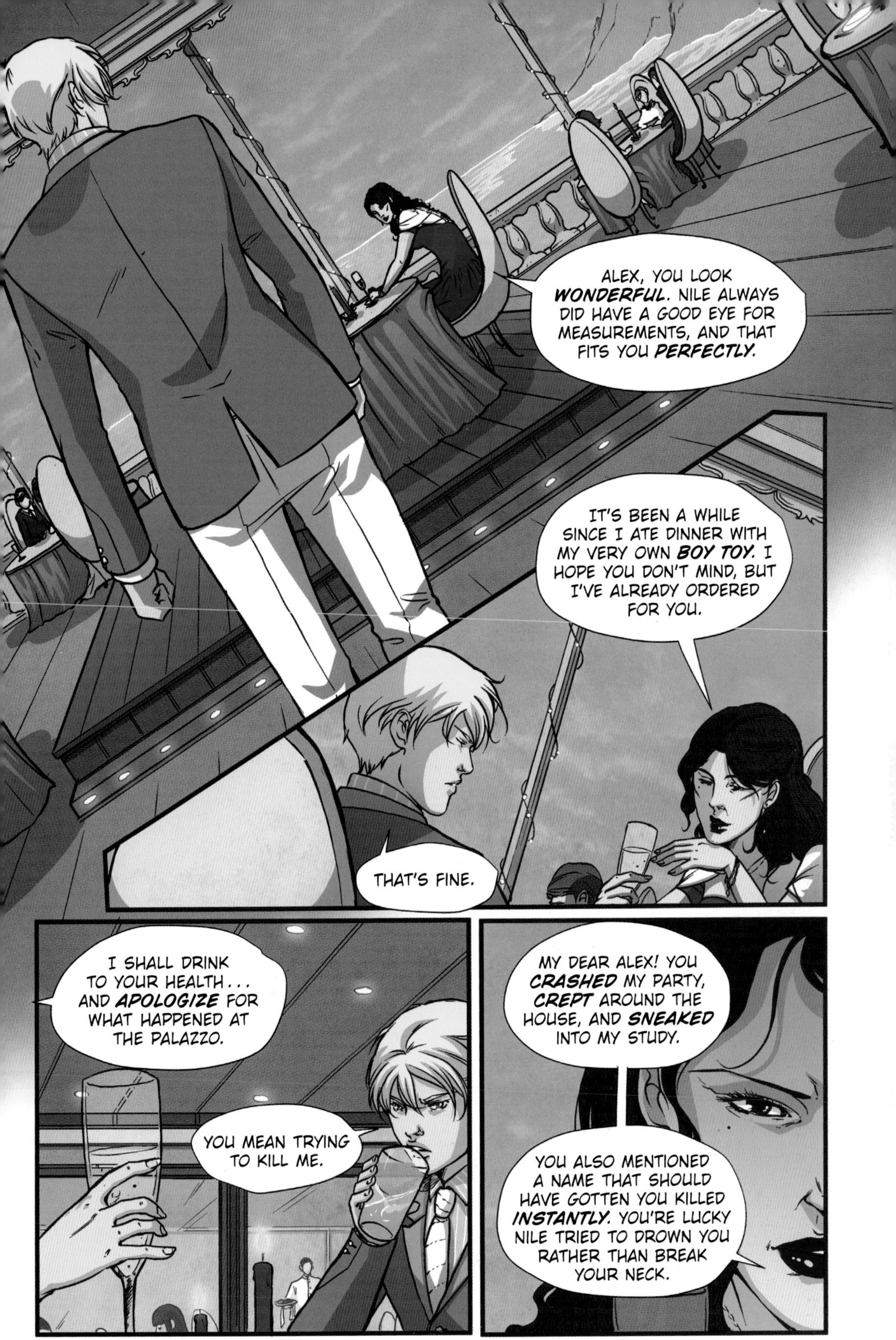
ALEX, YOU LOOK WONDERFUL. NILE ALWAYS DID HAVE A GOOD EYE FOR MEASUREMENTS, AND THAT FITS YOU PERFECTLY.
IT'S BEEN A WHILE SINCE I ATE DINNER WITH MY VERY OWN BOY TOY. I HOPE YOU DON'T MIND, BUT I'VE ALREADY ORDERED FOR YOU.
THAT'S FINE.
I SHALL DRINK TO YOUR HEALTH . . . AND APOLOGIZE FOR WHAT HAPPENED AT THE PALAZZO.
YOU MEAN TRYING TO KILL ME.
MY DEAR ALEX! YOU CRASHED MY PARTY, CREPT AROUND THE HOUSE, AND SNEAKED INTO MY STUDY.
YOU ALSO MENTIONED A NAME THAT SHOULD HAVE GOTTEN YOU KILLED INSTANTLY. YOU'RE LUCKY NILE TRIED TO DROWN YOU RATHER THAN BREAK YOUR NECK.

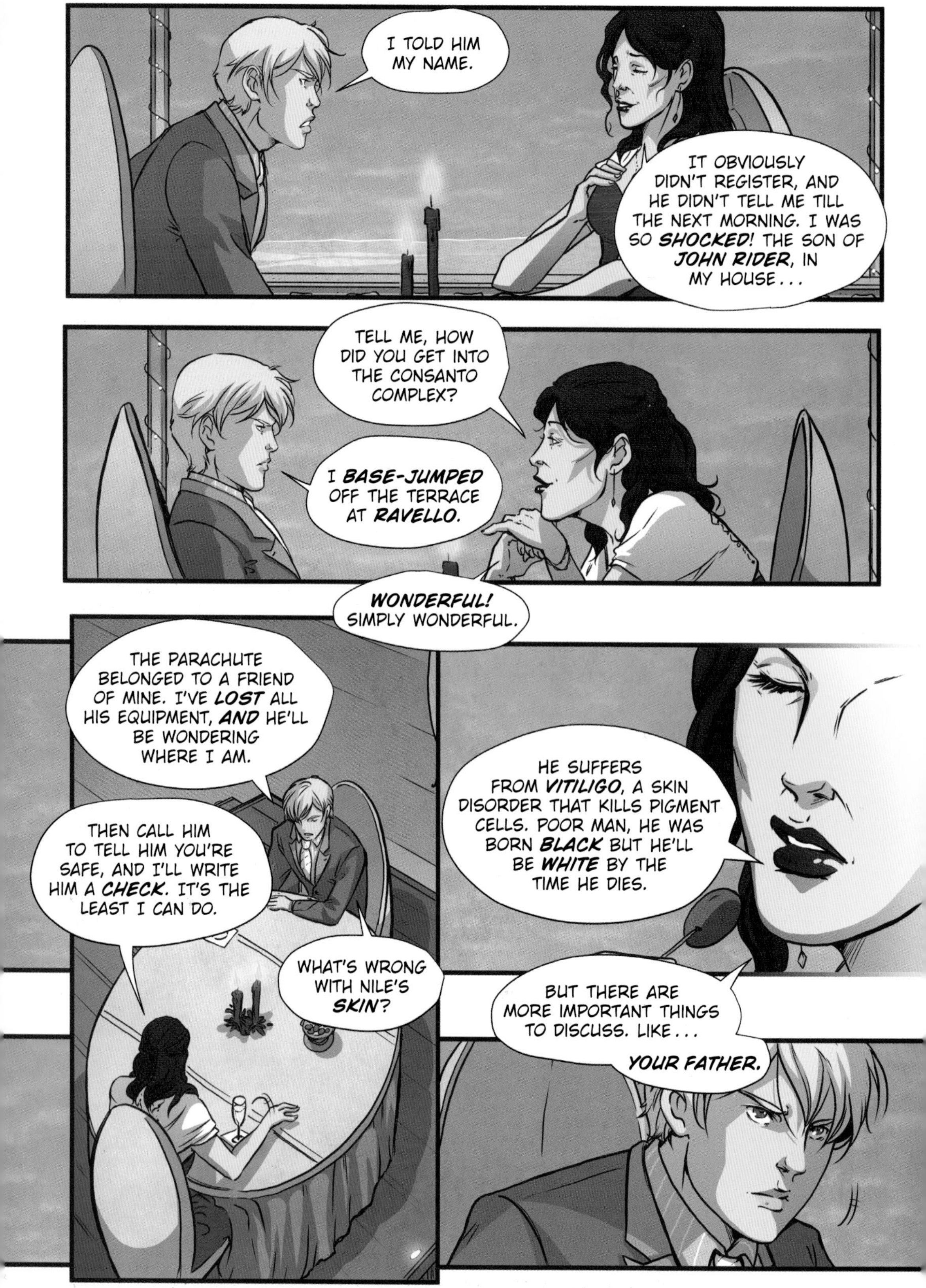
I TOLD HIM MY NAME.
IT OBVIOUSLY DIDN'T REGISTER, AND HE DIDN'T TELL ME TILL THE NEXT MORNING. I WAS SO SHOCKED! THE SON OF JOHN RIDER, IN MY HOUSE . . .
TELL ME, HOW DID YOU GET INTO THE CONSANTO COMPLEX?
I BASE-JUMPED OFF THE TERRACE AT RAVELLO.
WONDERFUL! SIMPLY WONDERFUL.
THE PARACHUTE BELONGED TO A FRIEND OF MINE. I'VE LOST ALL HIS EQUIPMENT, AND HE'LL BE WONDERING WHERE I AM.
THEN CALL HIM TO TELL HIM YOU'RE SAFE, AND I'LL WRITE HIM A CHECK. IT'S THE LEAST I CAN DO.
WHAT'S WRONG WITH NILE'S SKIN?
HE SUFFERS FROM VITILIGO, A SKIN DISORDER THAT KILLS PIGMENT CELLS. POOR MAN, HE WAS BORN BLACK BUT HE'LL BE WHITE BY THE TIME HE DIES.
BUT THERE ARE MORE IMPORTANT THINGS TO DISCUSS. LIKE . . .
YOUR FATHER.

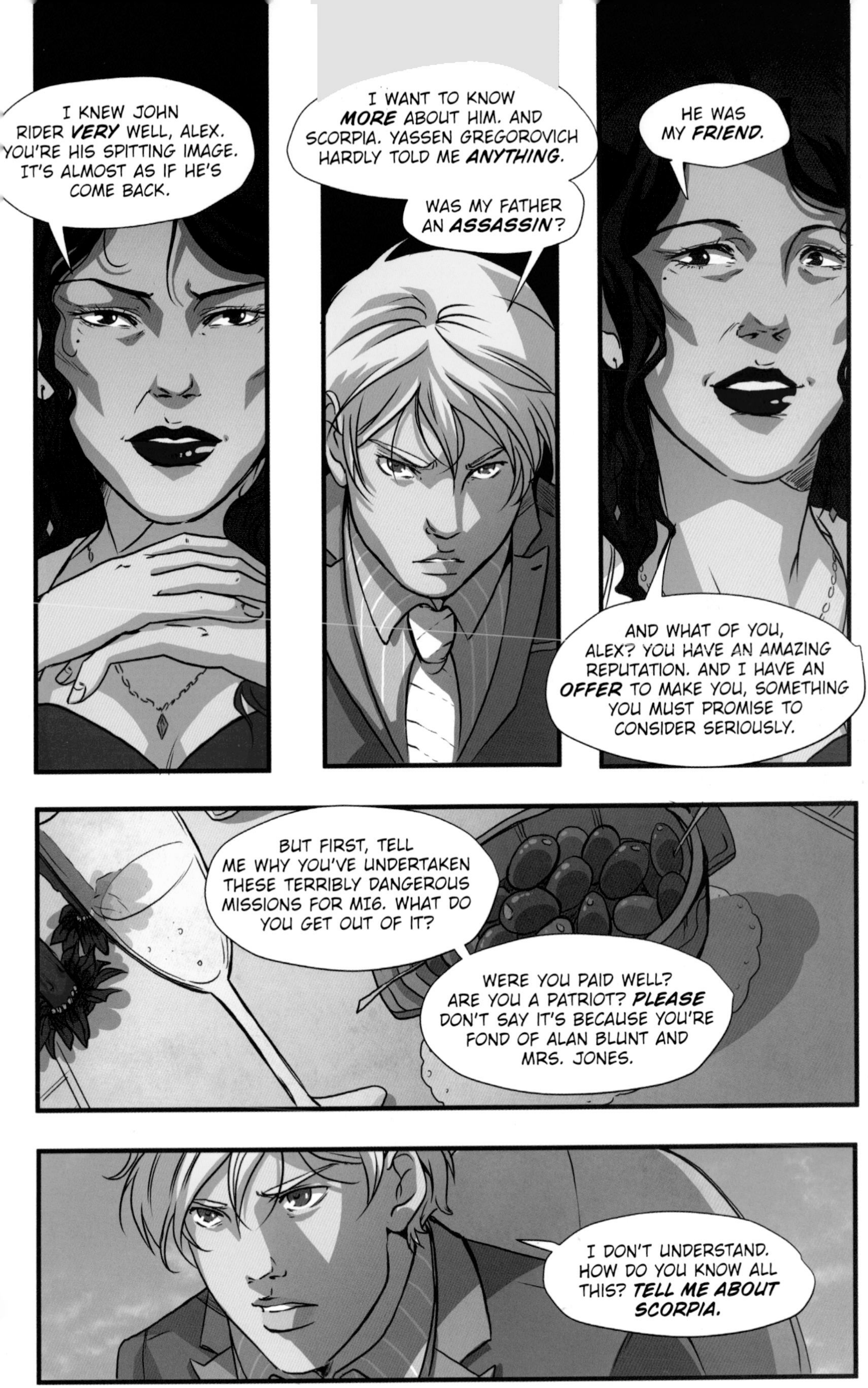
I KNEW JOHN RIDER VERY WELL, ALEX. YOU'RE HIS SPITTING IMAGE. IT'S ALMOST AS IF HE'S COME BACK.
I WANT TO KNOW MORE ABOUT HIM. AND SCORPIA. YASSEN GREGOROVICH HARDLY TOLD ME ANYTHING.
WAS MY FATHER AN ASSASSIN?
HE WAS MY FRIEND.
AND WHAT OF YOU, ALEX? YOU HAVE AN AMAZING REPUTATION. AND I HAVE AN OFFER TO MAKE YOU, SOMETHING YOU MUST PROMISE TO CONSIDER SERIOUSLY.
BUT FIRST, TELL ME WHY YOU'VE UNDERTAKEN THESE TERRIBLY DANGEROUS MISSIONS FOR MI6. WHAT DO YOU GET OUT OF IT?
WERE YOU PAID WELL? ARE YOU A PATRIOT? PLEASE DON'T SAY IT'S BECAUSE YOU'RE FOND OF ALAN BLUNT AND MRS. JONES.
I DON'T UNDERSTAND. HOW DO YOU KNOW ALL THIS? TELL ME ABOUT SCORPIA.

VERY WELL.

IT WAS FORMED DURING THE **COLD WAR**, THE TIME OF HOSTILITY BETWEEN THE SOVIET UNION AND CHINA ON ONE SIDE AND AMERICA AND EUROPE ON THE OTHER.

EVERY GOVERNMENT HAD **SPIES** AND **ASSASSINS** PREPARED TO KILL OR DIE FOR THEIR COUNTRY.

BUT THE COLD WAR **ENDED** IN THE EARLY NINETIES.

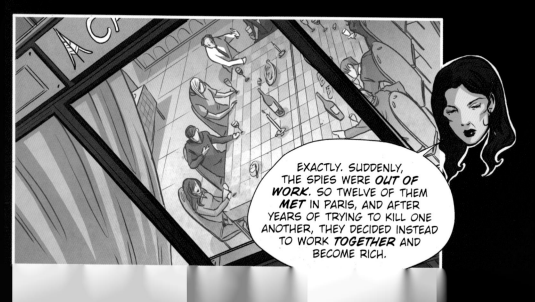

EXACTLY. SUDDENLY, THE SPIES WERE **OUT OF WORK**. SO TWELVE OF THEM **MET** IN PARIS, AND AFTER YEARS OF TRYING TO KILL ONE ANOTHER, THEY DECIDED INSTEAD TO WORK **TOGETHER** AND BECOME RICH.

I HAVE TO GO BACK TO SCHOOL.

I AGREE, AND SCORPIA **HAS** ONE. NILE STUDIED THERE, TOP OF HIS CLASS. HE'D BE PERFECT, IF NOT FOR ONE... **IRRITATING** WEAKNESS.

YOU MEAN HIS **DISEASE?**

NO, IT'S MORE ANNOYING THAN THAT. BUT YOU, ALEX, COULD BE **EVEN BETTER** THAN NILE, IN TIME.

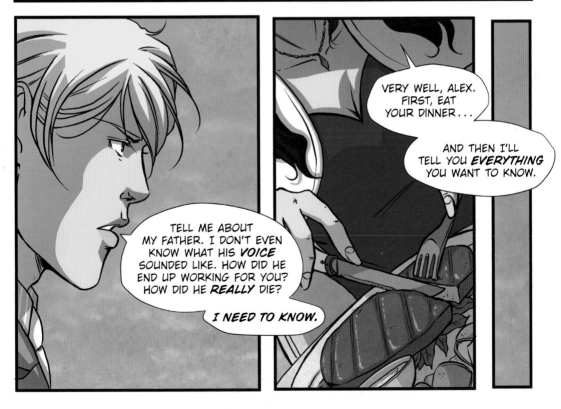

VERY WELL, ALEX. FIRST, EAT YOUR DINNER...

AND THEN I'LL TELL YOU **EVERYTHING** YOU WANT TO KNOW.

TELL ME ABOUT MY FATHER. I DON'T EVEN KNOW WHAT HIS **VOICE** SOUNDED LIKE. HOW DID HE END UP WORKING FOR YOU? HOW DID HE **REALLY** DIE?

I NEED TO KNOW.

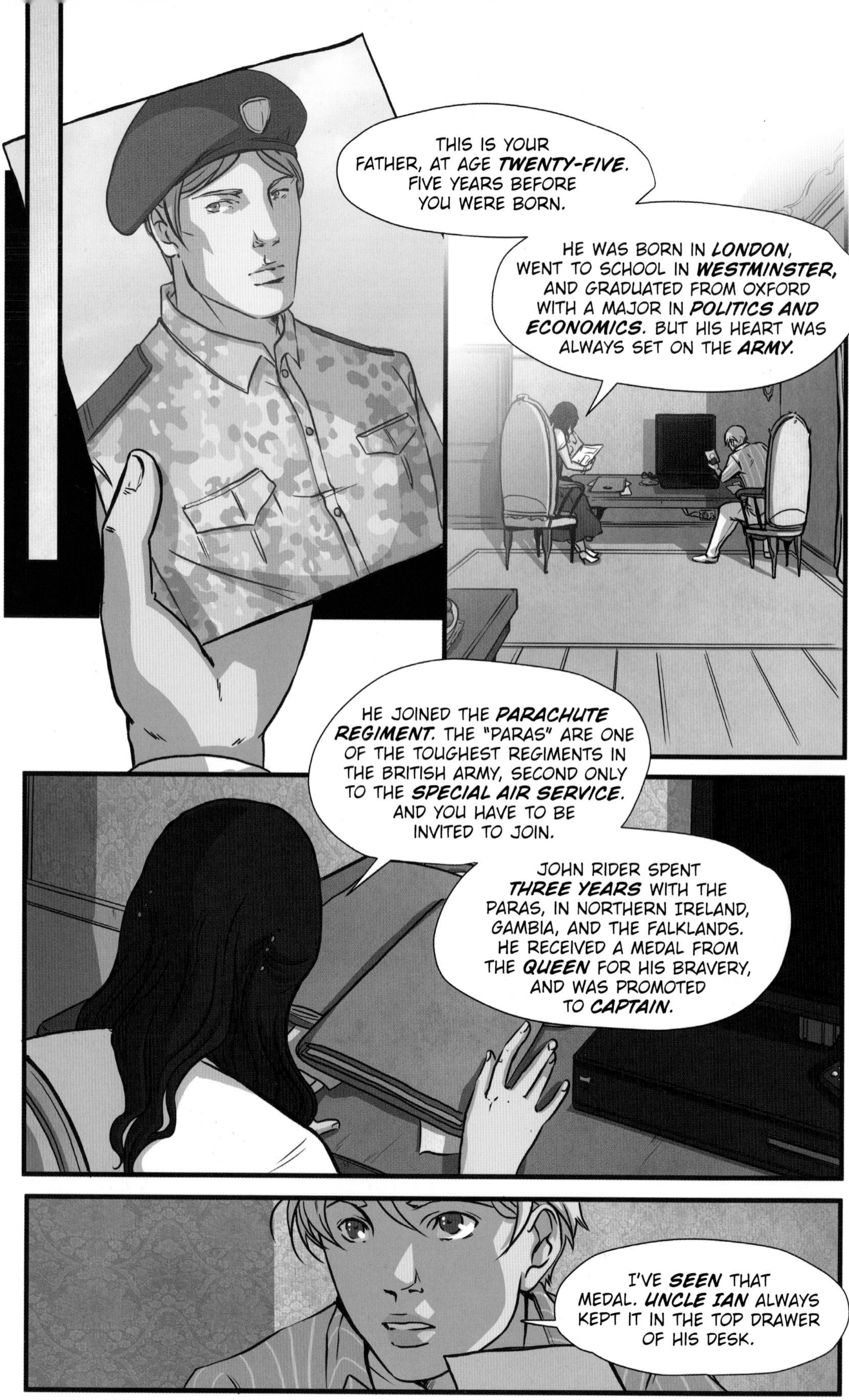

THIS IS YOUR FATHER, AT AGE TWENTY-FIVE. FIVE YEARS BEFORE YOU WERE BORN.
HE WAS BORN IN LONDON, WENT TO SCHOOL IN WESTMINSTER, AND GRADUATED FROM OXFORD WITH A MAJOR IN POLITICS AND ECONOMICS. BUT HIS HEART WAS ALWAYS SET ON THE ARMY.
HE JOINED THE PARACHUTE REGIMENT. THE "PARAS" ARE ONE OF THE TOUGHEST REGIMENTS IN THE BRITISH ARMY, SECOND ONLY TO THE SPECIAL AIR SERVICE. AND YOU HAVE TO BE INVITED TO JOIN.
JOHN RIDER SPENT THREE YEARS WITH THE PARAS, IN NORTHERN IRELAND, GAMBIA, AND THE FALKLANDS. HE RECEIVED A MEDAL FROM THE QUEEN FOR HIS BRAVERY, AND WAS PROMOTED TO CAPTAIN.
I'VE SEEN THAT MEDAL. UNCLE IAN ALWAYS KEPT IT IN THE TOP DRAWER OF HIS DESK.

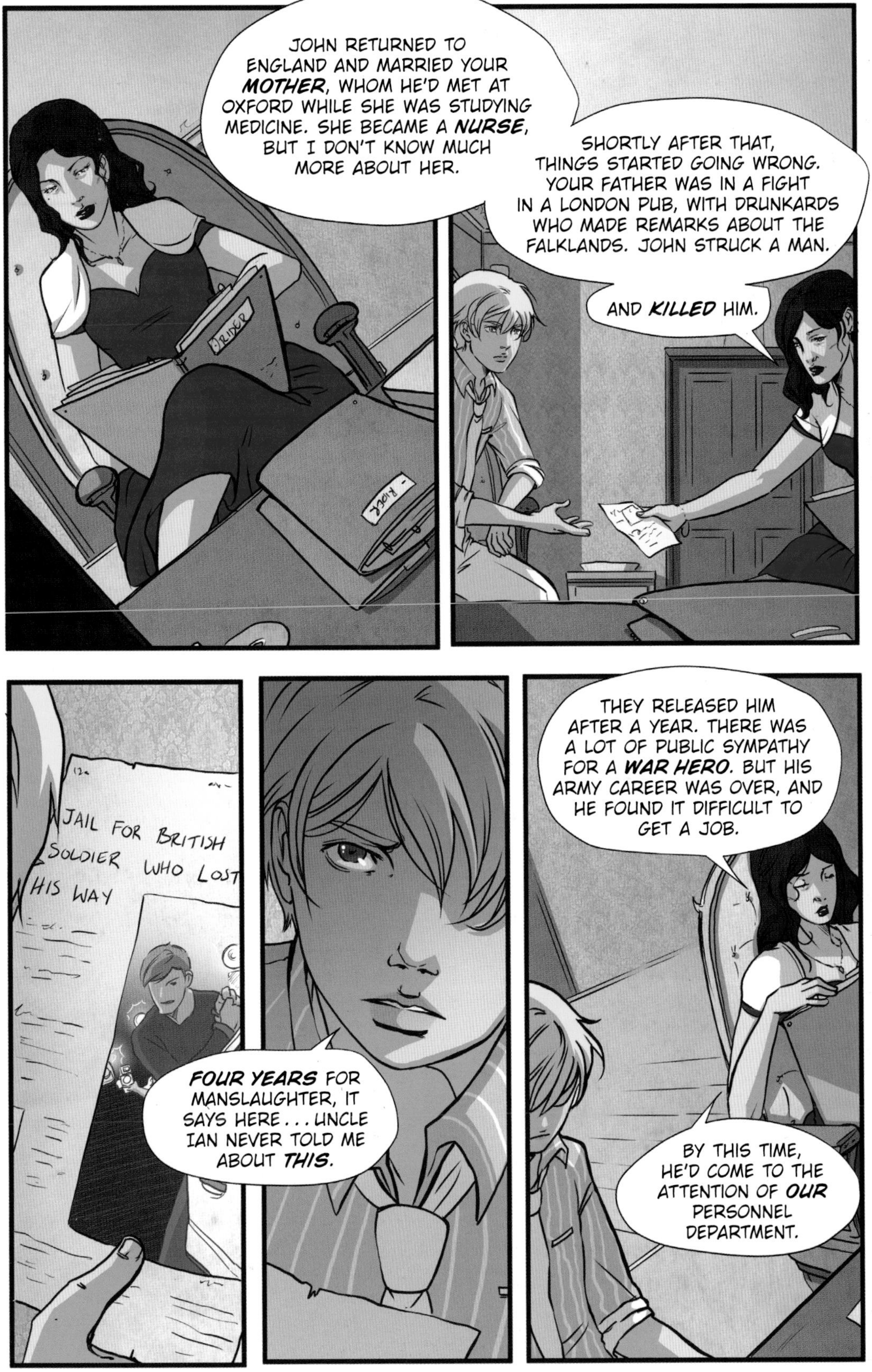
JOHN RETURNED TO ENGLAND AND MARRIED YOUR MOTHER, WHOM HE'D MET AT OXFORD WHILE SHE WAS STUDYING MEDICINE. SHE BECAME A NURSE, BUT I DON'T KNOW MUCH MORE ABOUT HER.
RIDER
SHORTLY AFTER THAT, THINGS STARTED GOING WRONG. YOUR FATHER WAS IN A FIGHT IN A LONDON PUB, WITH DRUNKARDS WHO MADE REMARKS ABOUT THE FALKLANDS. JOHN STRUCK A MAN.
AND KILLED HIM.
JAIL FOR BRITISH SOLDIER WHO LOST HIS WAY
FOUR YEARS FOR MANSLAUGHTER, IT SAYS HERE . . . UNCLE IAN NEVER TOLD ME ABOUT THIS.
THEY RELEASED HIM AFTER A YEAR. THERE WAS A LOT OF PUBLIC SYMPATHY FOR A WAR HERO. BUT HIS ARMY CAREER WAS OVER, AND HE FOUND IT DIFFICULT TO GET A JOB.
BY THIS TIME, HE'D COME TO THE ATTENTION OF OUR PERSONNEL DEPARTMENT.

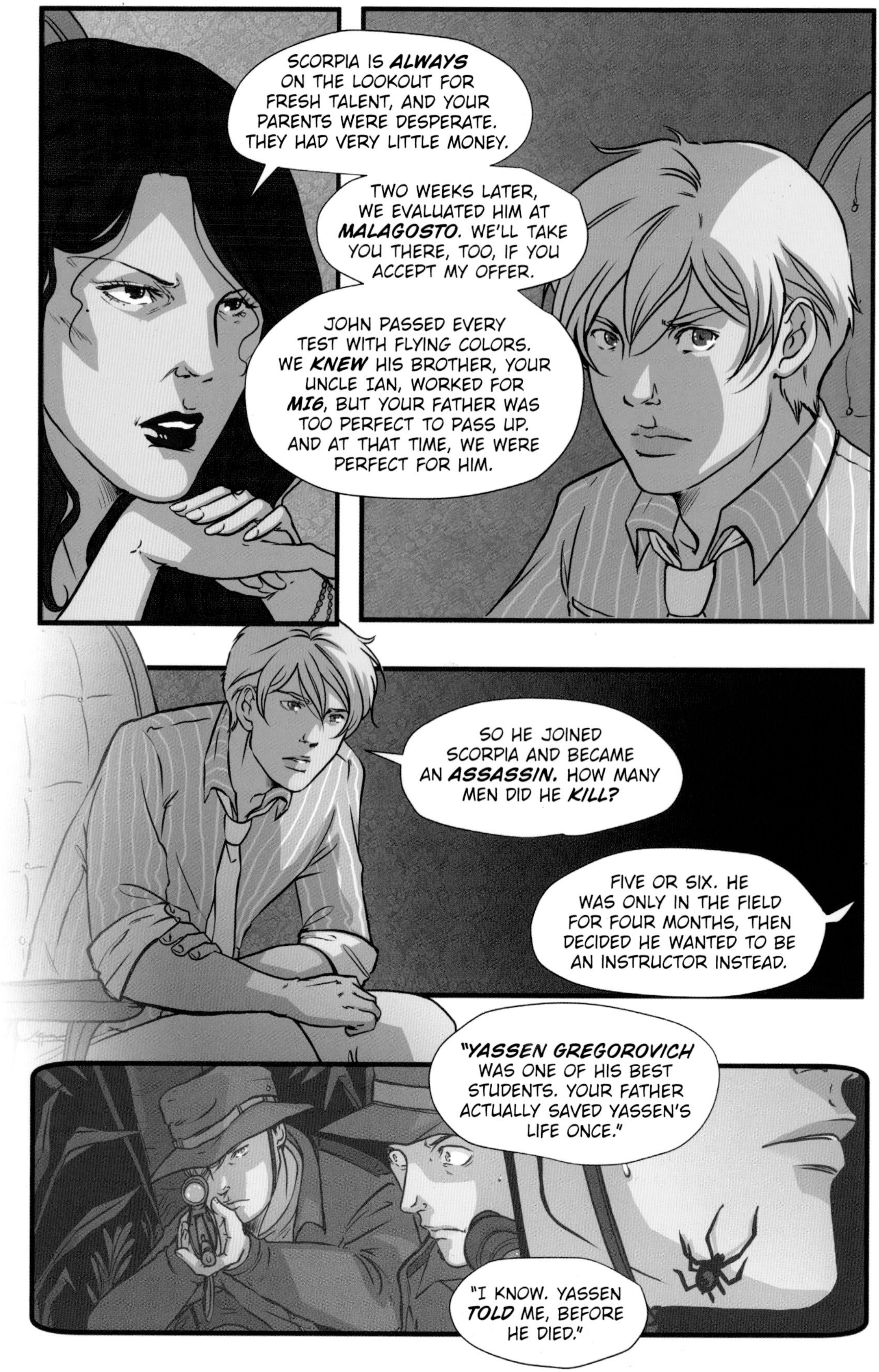

SCORPIA IS ALWAYS ON THE LOOKOUT FOR FRESH TALENT, AND YOUR PARENTS WERE DESPERATE. THEY HAD VERY LITTLE MONEY.
TWO WEEKS LATER, WE EVALUATED HIM AT MALAGOSTO. WE'LL TAKE YOU THERE, TOO, IF YOU ACCEPT MY OFFER.
JOHN PASSED EVERY TEST WITH FLYING COLORS. WE KNEW HIS BROTHER, YOUR UNCLE IAN, WORKED FOR MI6, BUT YOUR FATHER WAS TOO PERFECT TO PASS UP. AND AT THAT TIME, WE WERE PERFECT FOR HIM.
SO HE JOINED SCORPIA AND BECAME AN ASSASSIN. HOW MANY MEN DID HE KILL?
FIVE OR SIX. HE WAS ONLY IN THE FIELD FOR FOUR MONTHS, THEN DECIDED HE WANTED TO BE AN INSTRUCTOR INSTEAD.
"YASSEN GREGOROVICH WAS ONE OF HIS BEST STUDENTS. YOUR FATHER ACTUALLY SAVED YASSEN'S LIFE ONCE."
"I KNOW. YASSEN TOLD ME, BEFORE HE DIED."

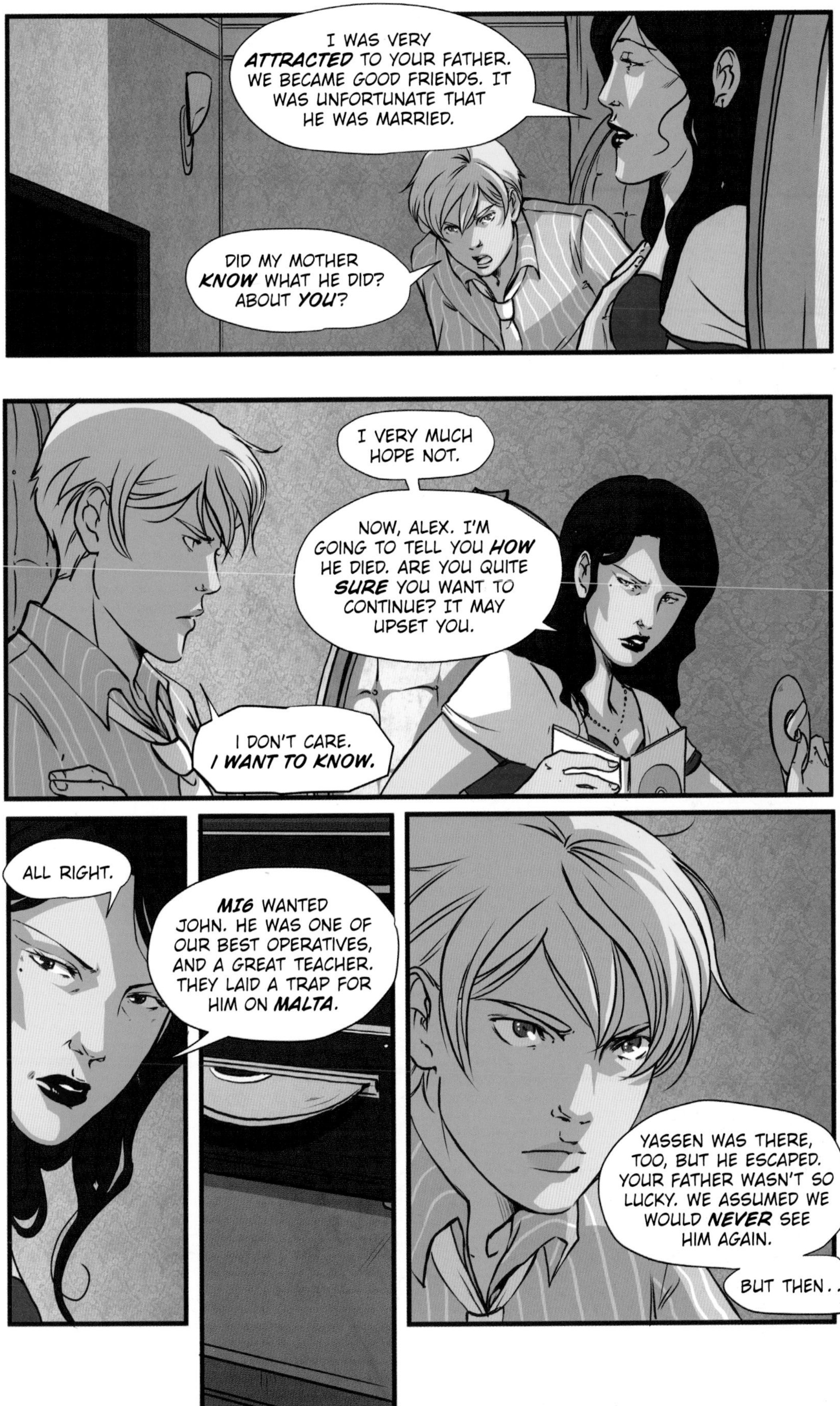
I WAS VERY ATTRACTED TO YOUR FATHER. WE BECAME GOOD FRIENDS. IT WAS UNFORTUNATE THAT HE WAS MARRIED.
DID MY MOTHER KNOW WHAT HE DID? ABOUT YOU?
I VERY MUCH HOPE NOT.
NOW, ALEX. I'M GOING TO TELL YOU HOW HE DIED. ARE YOU QUITE SURE YOU WANT TO CONTINUE? IT MAY UPSET YOU.
I DON'T CARE. I WANT TO KNOW.
ALL RIGHT.
MI6 WANTED JOHN. HE WAS ONE OF OUR BEST OPERATIVES, AND A GREAT TEACHER. THEY LAID A TRAP FOR HIM ON MALTA.
YASSEN WAS THERE, TOO, BUT HE ESCAPED. YOUR FATHER WASN'T SO LUCKY. WE ASSUMED WE WOULD NEVER SEE HIM AGAIN.
BUT THEN . . .

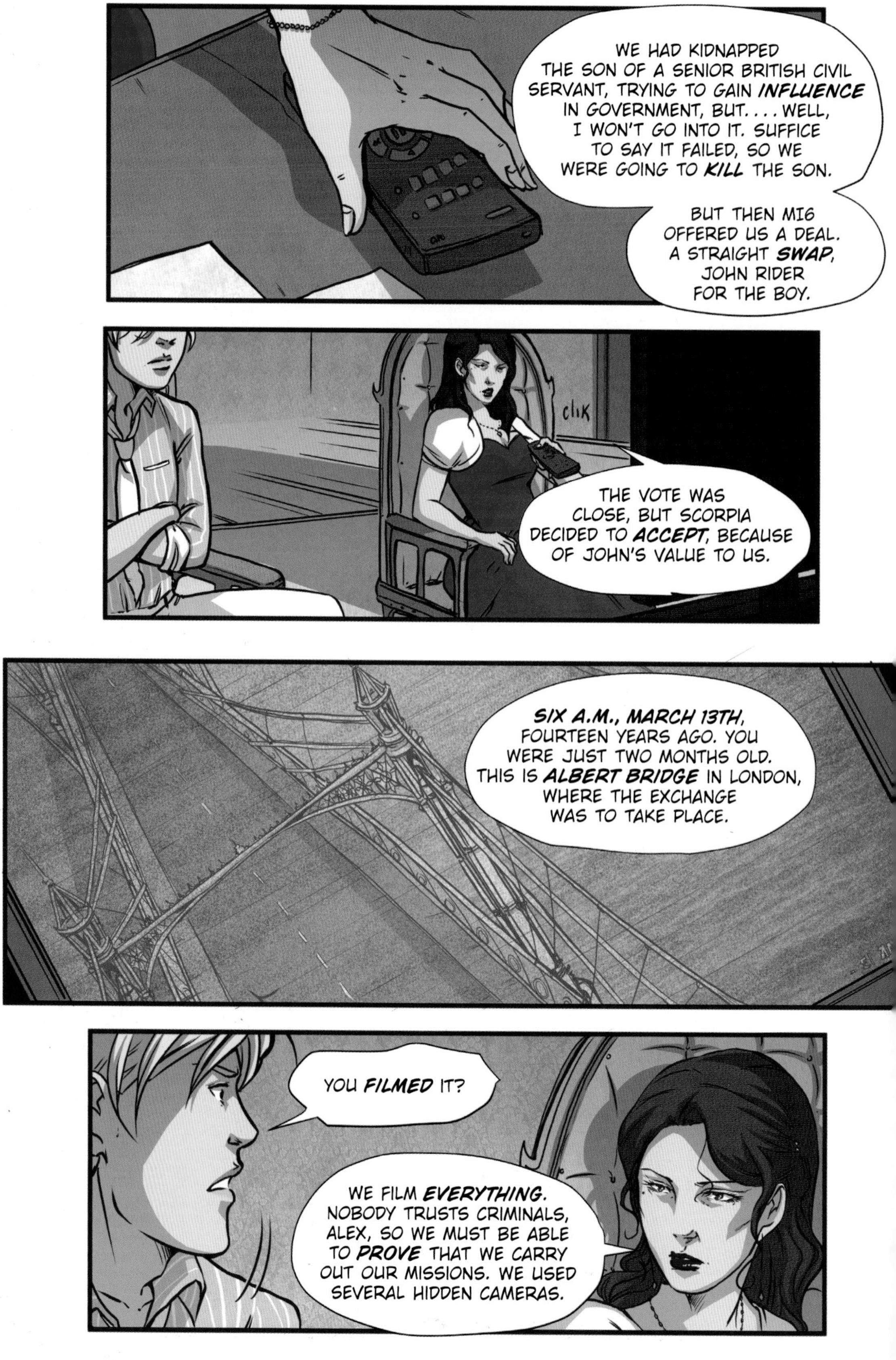
WE HAD KIDNAPPED THE SON OF A SENIOR BRITISH CIVIL SERVANT, TRYING TO GAIN INFLUENCE IN GOVERNMENT, BUT. . . . WELL, I WON'T GO INTO IT. SUFFICE TO SAY IT FAILED, SO WE WERE GOING TO KILL THE SON.
BUT THEN MI6 OFFERED US A DEAL. A STRAIGHT SWAP, JOHN RIDER FOR THE BOY.
CLIK
THE VOTE WAS CLOSE, BUT SCORPIA DECIDED TO ACCEPT, BECAUSE OF JOHN'S VALUE TO US.
SIX A.M., MARCH 13TH, FOURTEEN YEARS AGO. YOU WERE JUST TWO MONTHS OLD. THIS IS ALBERT BRIDGE IN LONDON, WHERE THE EXCHANGE WAS TO TAKE PLACE.
YOU FILMED IT?
WE FILM EVERYTHING. NOBODY TRUSTS CRIMINALS, ALEX, SO WE MUST BE ABLE TO PROVE THAT WE CARRY OUT OUR MISSIONS. WE USED SEVERAL HIDDEN CAMERAS.

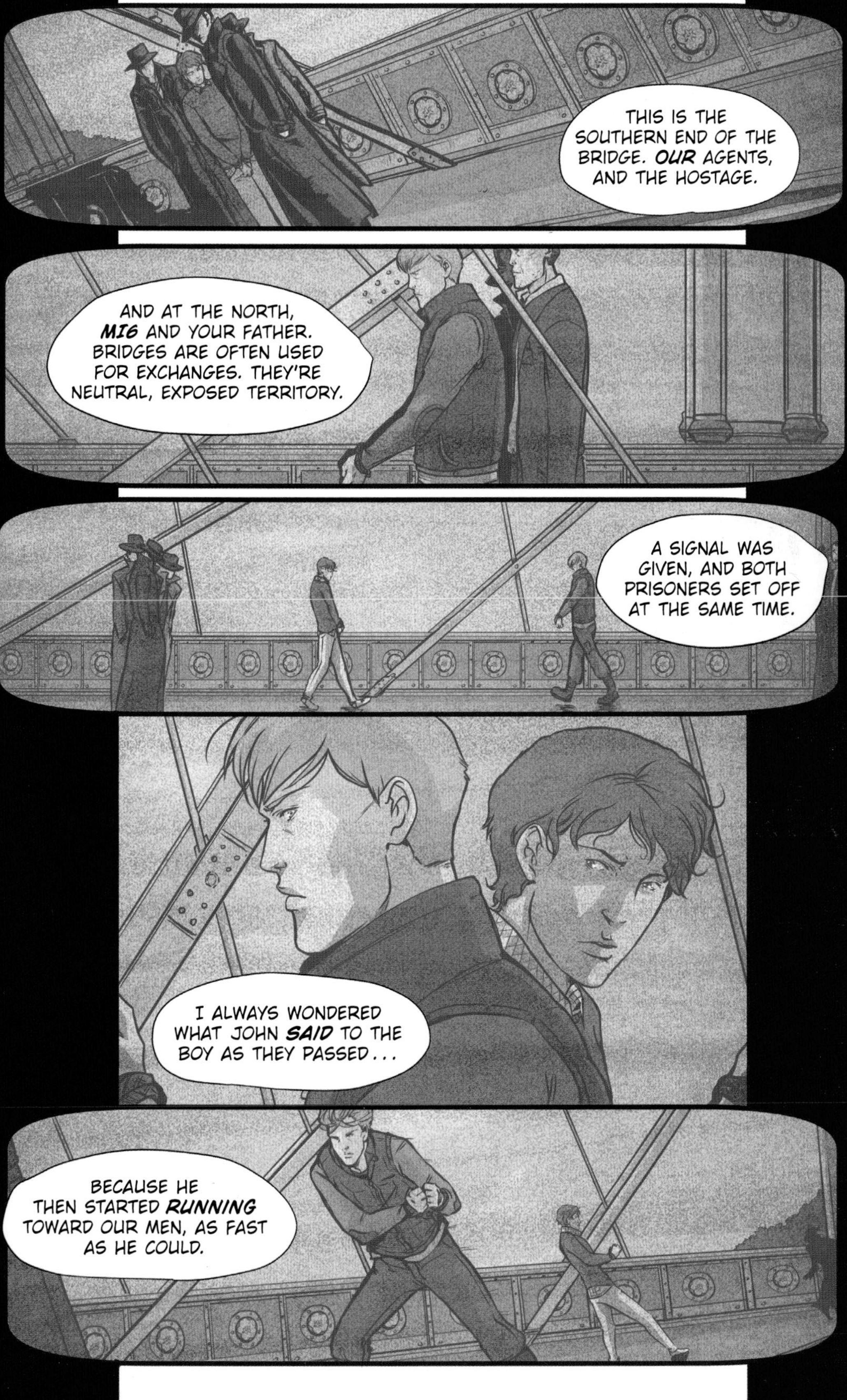
THIS IS THE SOUTHERN END OF THE BRIDGE. OUR AGENTS, AND THE HOSTAGE.
AND AT THE NORTH, MI6 AND YOUR FATHER. BRIDGES ARE OFTEN USED FOR EXCHANGES. THEY'RE NEUTRAL, EXPOSED TERRITORY.
A SIGNAL WAS GIVEN, AND BOTH PRISONERS SET OFF AT THE SAME TIME.
I ALWAYS WONDERED WHAT JOHN SAID TO THE BOY AS THEY PASSED . . .
BECAUSE HE THEN STARTED RUNNING TOWARD OUR MEN, AS FAST AS HE COULD.

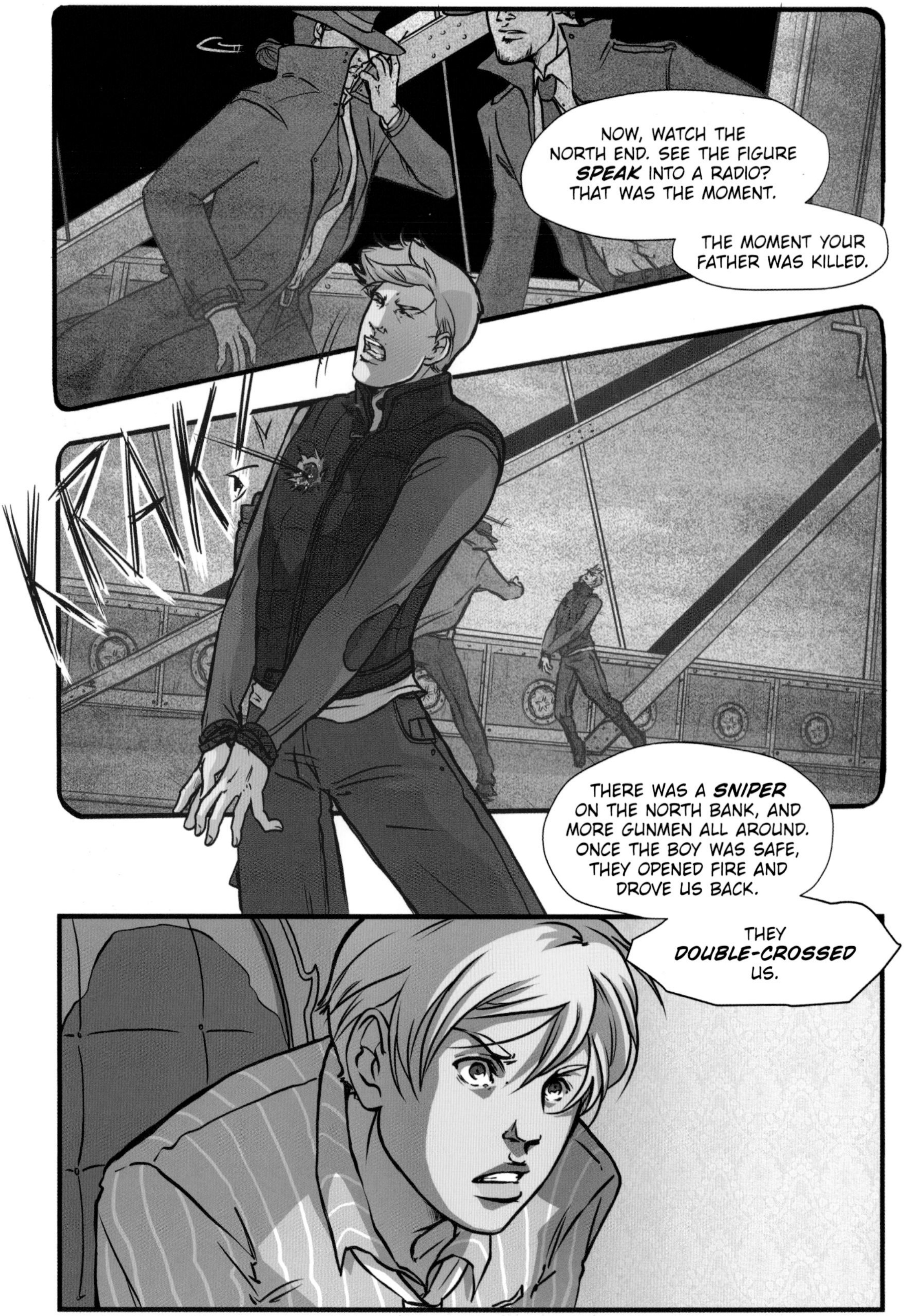
NOW, WATCH THE NORTH END. SEE THE FIGURE SPEAK INTO A RADIO? THAT WAS THE MOMENT.
THE MOMENT YOUR FATHER WAS KILLED.
KRAK!
THERE WAS A SNIPER ON THE NORTH BANK, AND MORE GUNMEN ALL AROUND. ONCE THE BOY WAS SAFE, THEY OPENED FIRE AND DROVE US BACK.
THEY DOUBLE-CROSSED US.

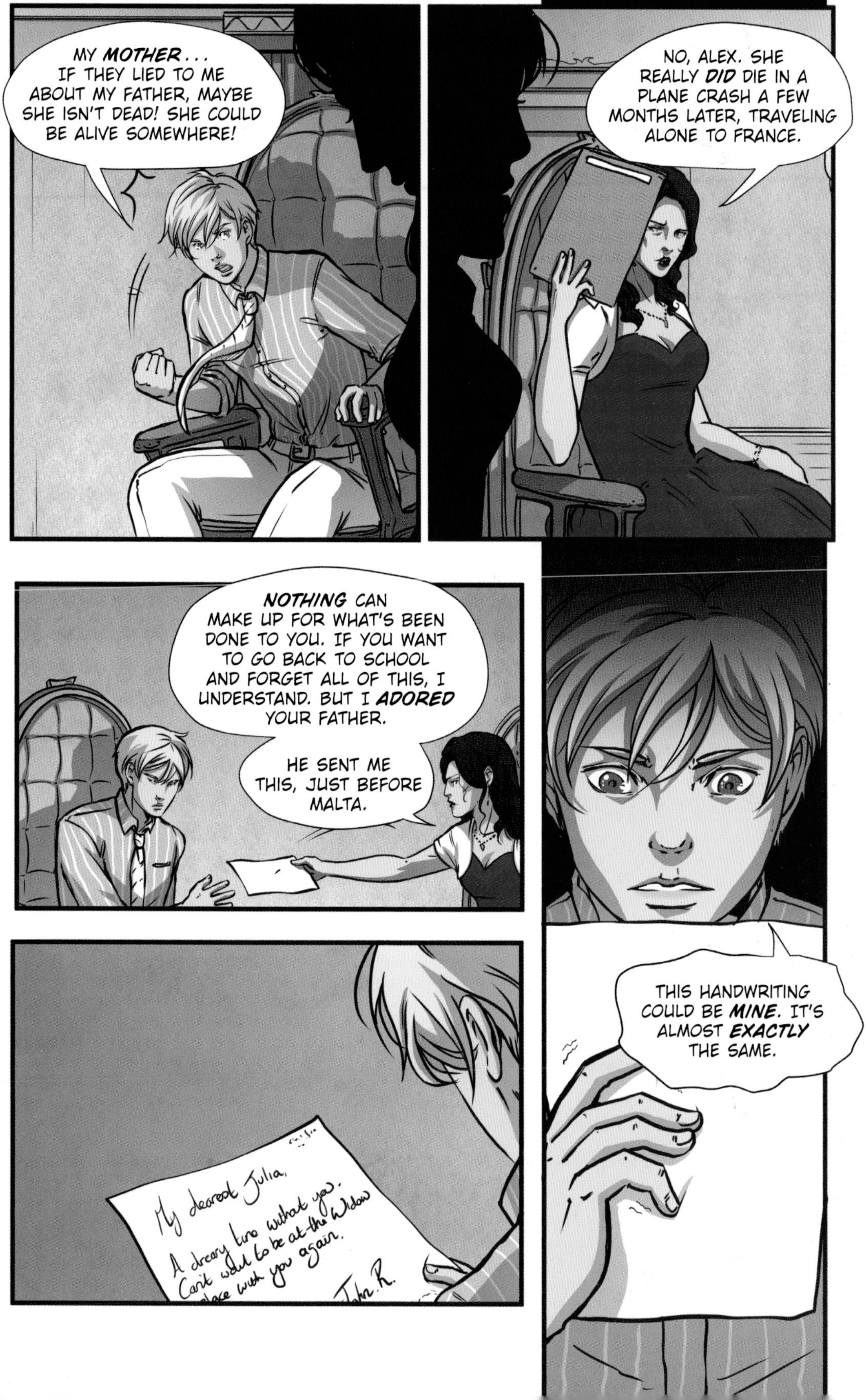
MY MOTHER . . . IF THEY LIED TO ME ABOUT MY FATHER, MAYBE SHE ISN'T DEAD! SHE COULD BE ALIVE SOMEWHERE!
NO, ALEX. SHE REALLY DID DIE IN A PLANE CRASH A FEW MONTHS LATER, TRAVELING ALONE TO FRANCE.
NOTHING CAN MAKE UP FOR WHAT'S BEEN DONE TO YOU. IF YOU WANT TO GO BACK TO SCHOOL AND FORGET ALL OF THIS, I UNDERSTAND. BUT I ADORED YOUR FATHER.
HE SENT ME THIS, JUST BEFORE MALTA.
My dearest Julia,
A dreary time without you.
Can't wait to be at the Widow
John R.
THIS HANDWRITING COULD BE MINE. IT'S ALMOST EXACTLY THE SAME.

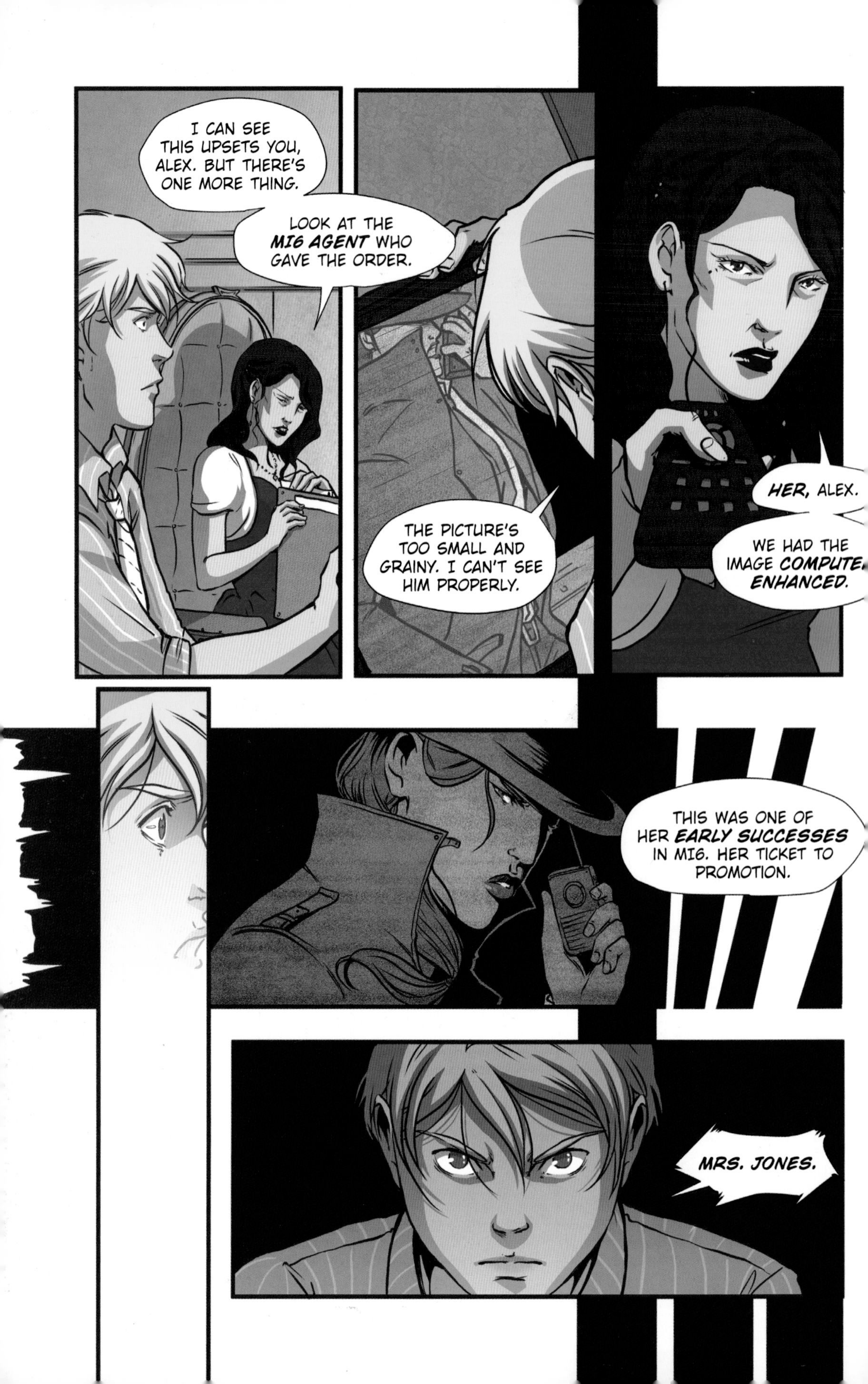
I CAN SEE THIS UPSETS YOU, ALEX. BUT THERE'S ONE MORE THING.
LOOK AT THE MI6 AGENT WHO GAVE THE ORDER.
THE PICTURE'S TOO SMALL AND GRAINY. I CAN'T SEE HIM PROPERLY.
HER, ALEX.
WE HAD THE IMAGE COMPUTE ENHANCED.
THIS WAS ONE OF HER EARLY SUCCESSES IN MI6. HER TICKET TO PROMOTION.
MRS. JONES.

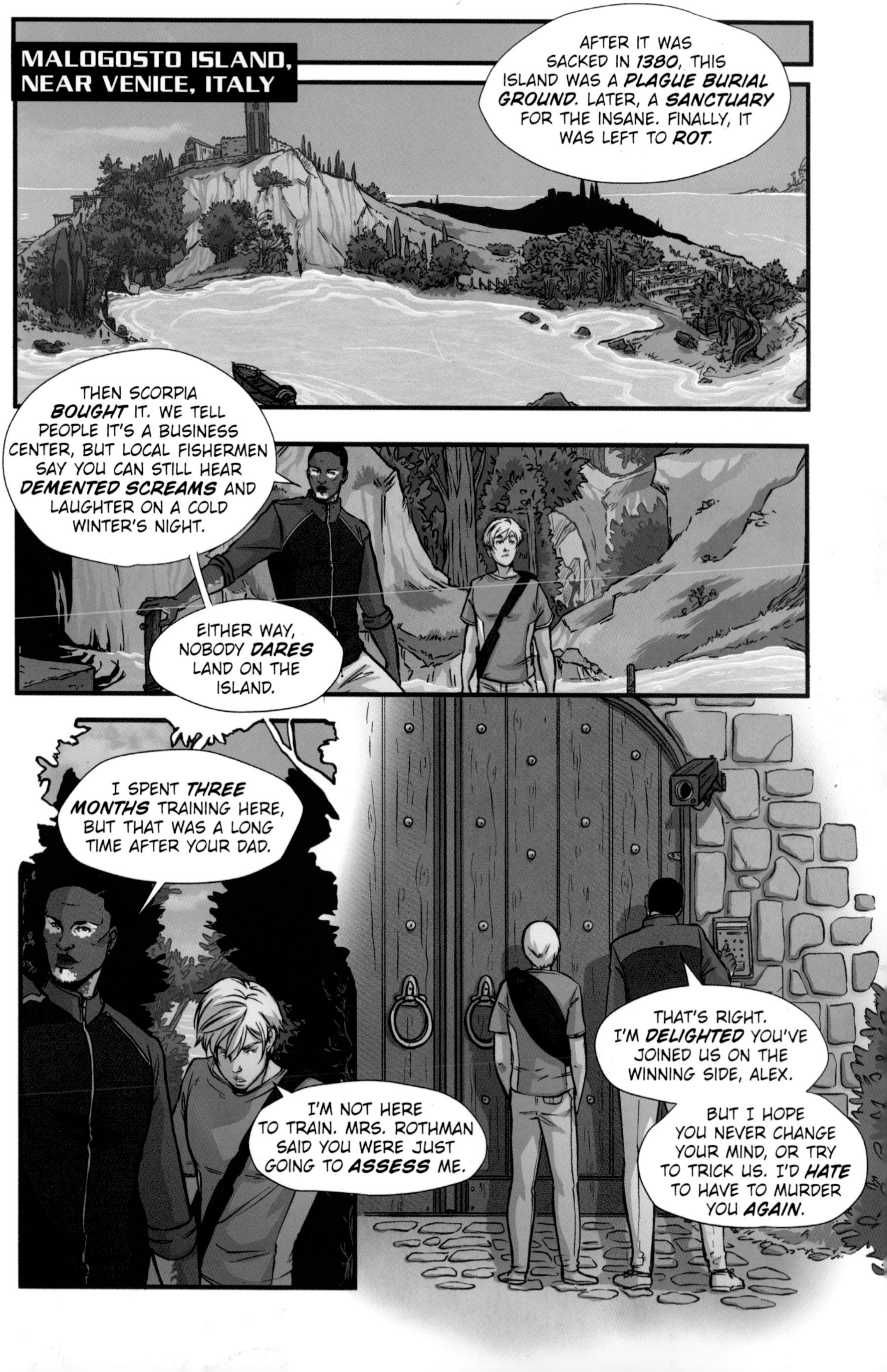
MALOGOSTO ISLAND, NEAR VENICE, ITALY
AFTER IT WAS SACKED IN 1380, THIS ISLAND WAS A PLAGUE BURIAL GROUND. LATER, A SANCTUARY FOR THE INSANE. FINALLY, IT WAS LEFT TO ROT.
THEN SCORPIA BOUGHT IT. WE TELL PEOPLE IT'S A BUSINESS CENTER, BUT LOCAL FISHERMEN SAY YOU CAN STILL HEAR DEMENTED SCREAMS AND LAUGHTER ON A COLD WINTER'S NIGHT.
EITHER WAY, NOBODY DARES LAND ON THE ISLAND.
I SPENT THREE MONTHS TRAINING HERE, BUT THAT WAS A LONG TIME AFTER YOUR DAD.
I'M NOT HERE TO TRAIN. MRS. ROTHMAN SAID YOU WERE JUST GOING TO ASSESS ME.
THAT'S RIGHT. I'M DELIGHTED YOU'VE JOINED US ON THE WINNING SIDE, ALEX.
BUT I HOPE YOU NEVER CHANGE YOUR MIND, OR TRY TO TRICK US. I'D HATE TO HAVE TO MURDER YOU AGAIN.

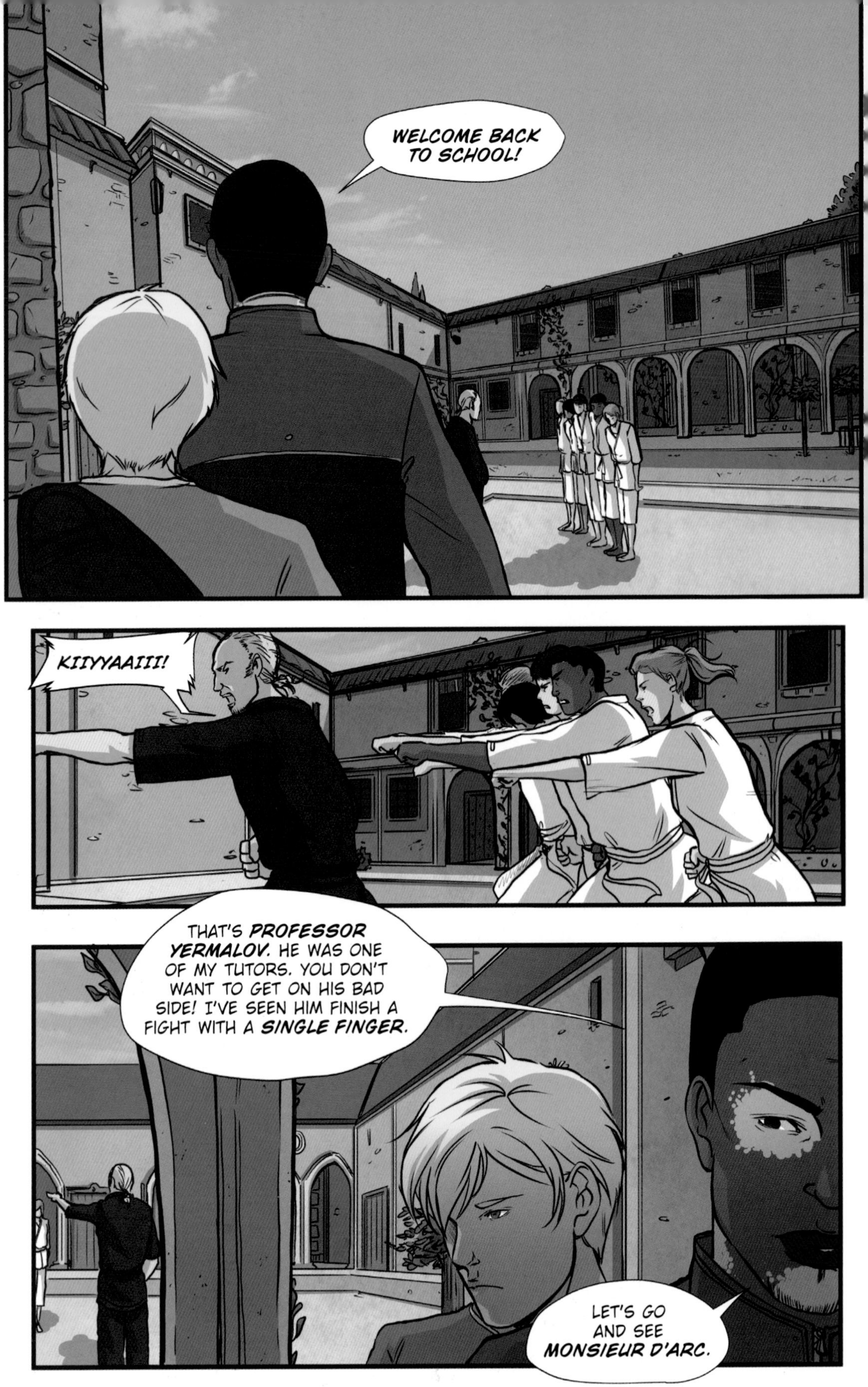
WELCOME BACK TO SCHOOL!
KIIYYAAIII!
THAT'S PROFESSOR YERMALOV. HE WAS ONE OF MY TUTORS. YOU DON'T WANT TO GET ON HIS BAD SIDE! I'VE SEEN HIM FINISH A FIGHT WITH A SINGLE FINGER.
LET'S GO AND SEE MONSIEUR D'ARC.

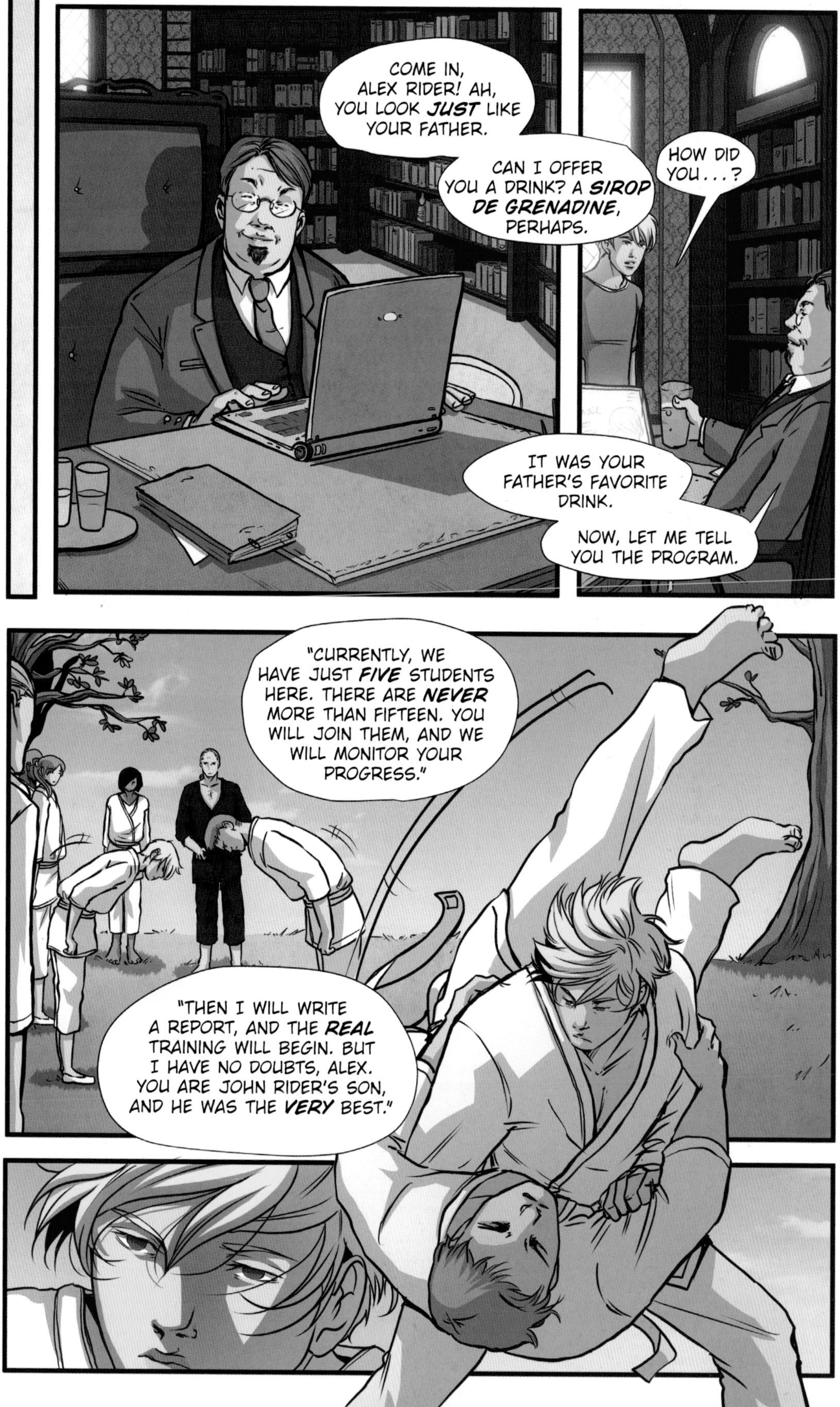
COME IN, ALEX RIDER! AH, YOU LOOK JUST LIKE YOUR FATHER.
CAN I OFFER YOU A DRINK? A SIROP DE GRENADINE, PERHAPS.
HOW DID YOU . . . ?
IT WAS YOUR FATHER'S FAVORITE DRINK.
NOW, LET ME TELL YOU THE PROGRAM.
"CURRENTLY, WE HAVE JUST FIVE STUDENTS HERE. THERE ARE NEVER MORE THAN FIFTEEN. YOU WILL JOIN THEM, AND WE WILL MONITOR YOUR PROGRESS."
"THEN I WILL WRITE A REPORT, AND THE REAL TRAINING WILL BEGIN. BUT I HAVE NO DOUBTS, ALEX. YOU ARE JOHN RIDER'S SON, AND HE WAS THE VERY BEST."

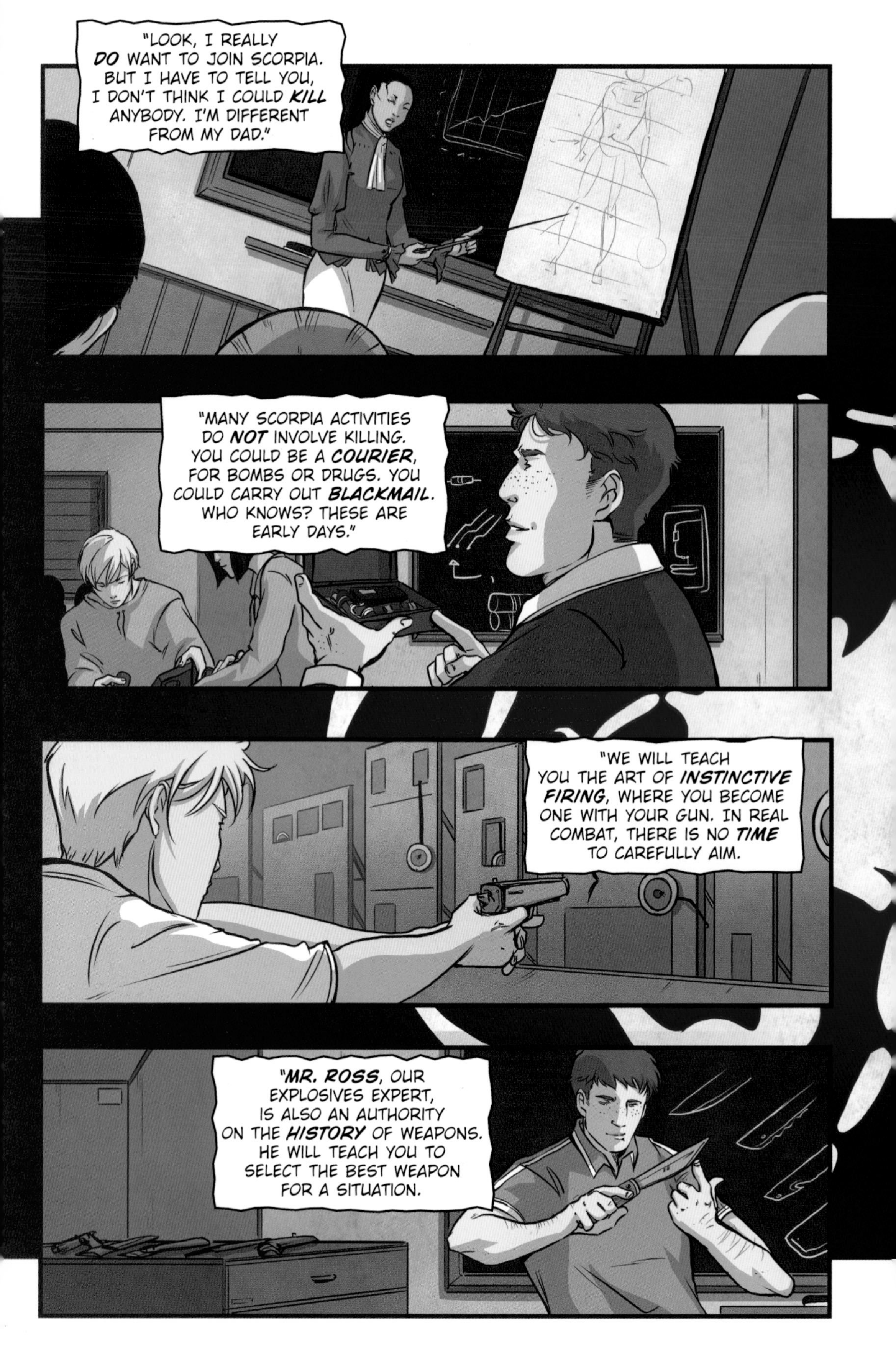
"LOOK, I REALLY DO WANT TO JOIN SCORPIA. BUT I HAVE TO TELL YOU, I DON'T THINK I COULD KILL ANYBODY. I'M DIFFERENT FROM MY DAD."
"MANY SCORPIA ACTIVITIES DO NOT INVOLVE KILLING. YOU COULD BE A COURIER, FOR BOMBS OR DRUGS. YOU COULD CARRY OUT BLACKMAIL. WHO KNOWS? THESE ARE EARLY DAYS."
"WE WILL TEACH YOU THE ART OF INSTINCTIVE FIRING, WHERE YOU BECOME ONE WITH YOUR GUN. IN REAL COMBAT, THERE IS NO TIME TO CAREFULLY AIM.
"MR. ROSS, OUR EXPLOSIVES EXPERT, IS ALSO AN AUTHORITY ON THE HISTORY OF WEAPONS. HE WILL TEACH YOU TO SELECT THE BEST WEAPON FOR A SITUATION.

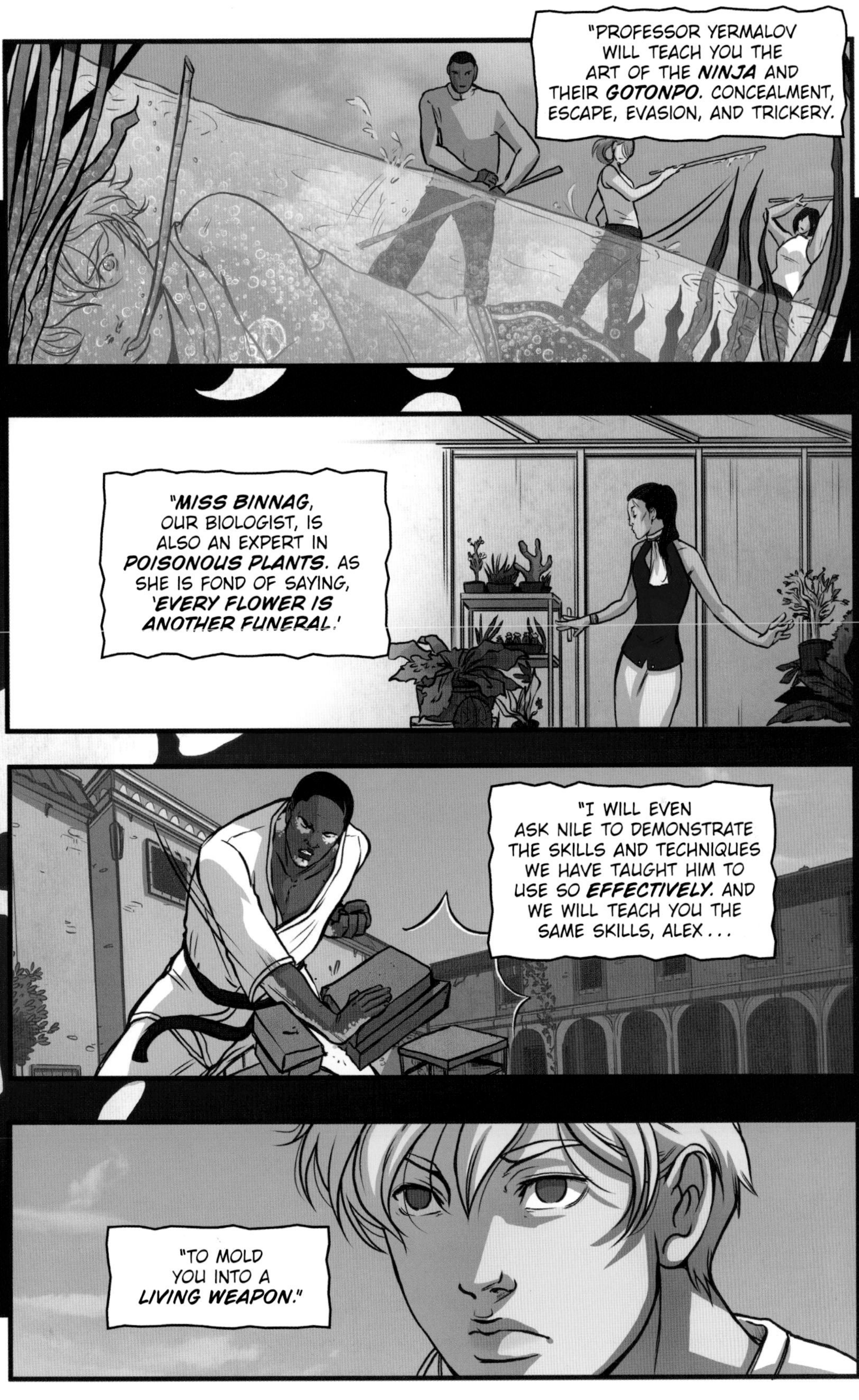
"PROFESSOR YERMALOV WILL TEACH YOU THE ART OF THE NINJA AND THEIR GOTONPO. CONCEALMENT, ESCAPE, EVASION, AND TRICKERY.
"MISS BINNAG, OUR BIOLOGIST, IS ALSO AN EXPERT IN POISONOUS PLANTS. AS SHE IS FOND OF SAYING, 'EVERY FLOWER IS ANOTHER FUNERAL.'
"I WILL EVEN ASK NILE TO DEMONSTRATE THE SKILLS AND TECHNIQUES WE HAVE TAUGHT HIM TO USE SO EFFECTIVELY. AND WE WILL TEACH YOU THE SAME SKILLS, ALEX . . .
"TO MOLD YOU INTO A LIVING WEAPON."

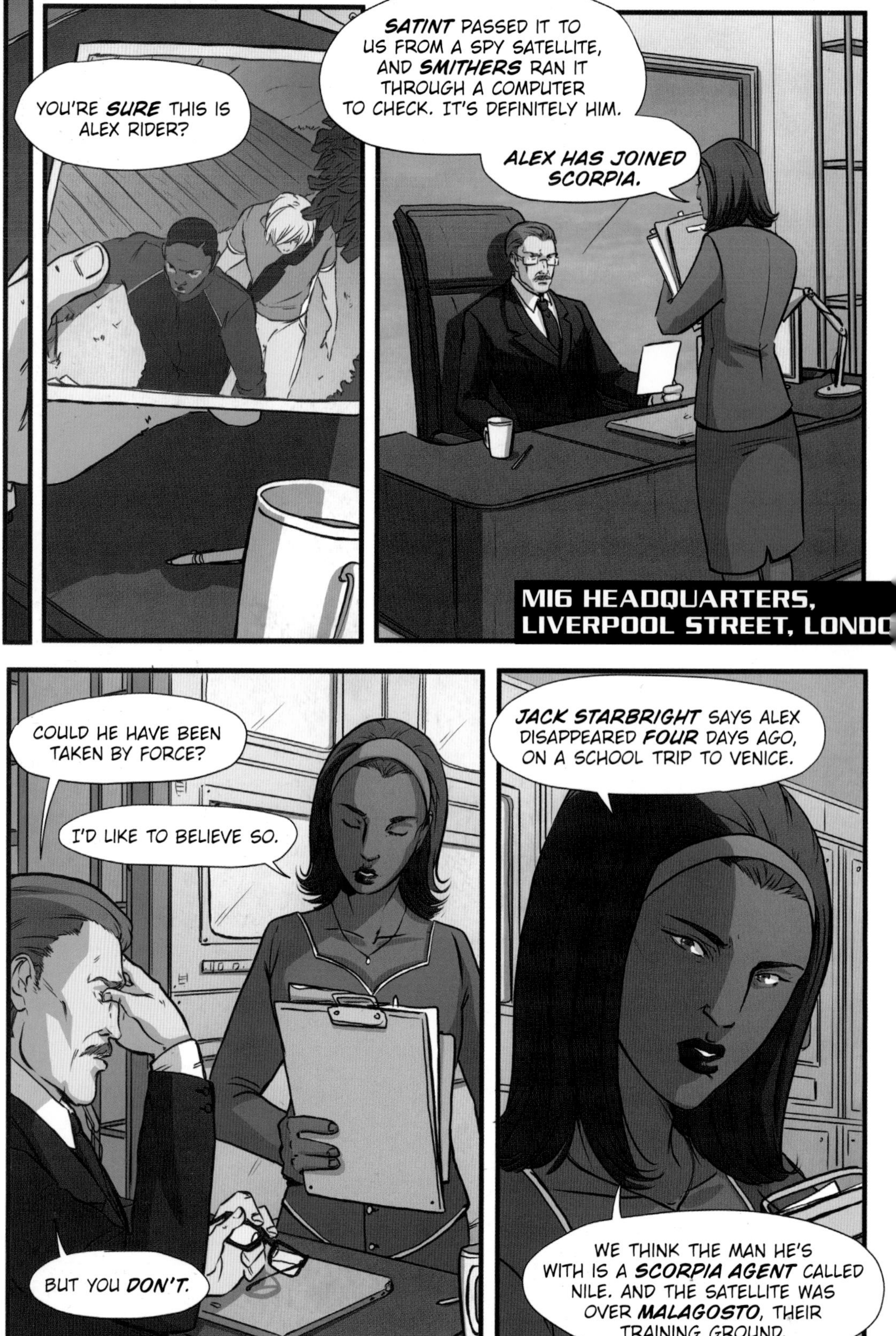
YOU'RE SURE THIS IS ALEX RIDER?
SATINT PASSED IT TO US FROM A SPY SATELLITE, AND SMITHERS RAN IT THROUGH A COMPUTER TO CHECK. IT'S DEFINITELY HIM.
ALEX HAS JOINED SCORPIA.
MI6 HEADQUARTERS, LIVERPOOL STREET, LONDO
COULD HE HAVE BEEN TAKEN BY FORCE?
I'D LIKE TO BELIEVE SO.
BUT YOU DON'T.
JACK STARBRIGHT SAYS ALEX DISAPPEARED FOUR DAYS AGO, ON A SCHOOL TRIP TO VENICE.
WE THINK THE MAN HE'S WITH IS A SCORPIA AGENT CALLED NILE. AND THE SATELLITE WAS OVER MALAGOSTO, THEIR TRAINING GROUND.

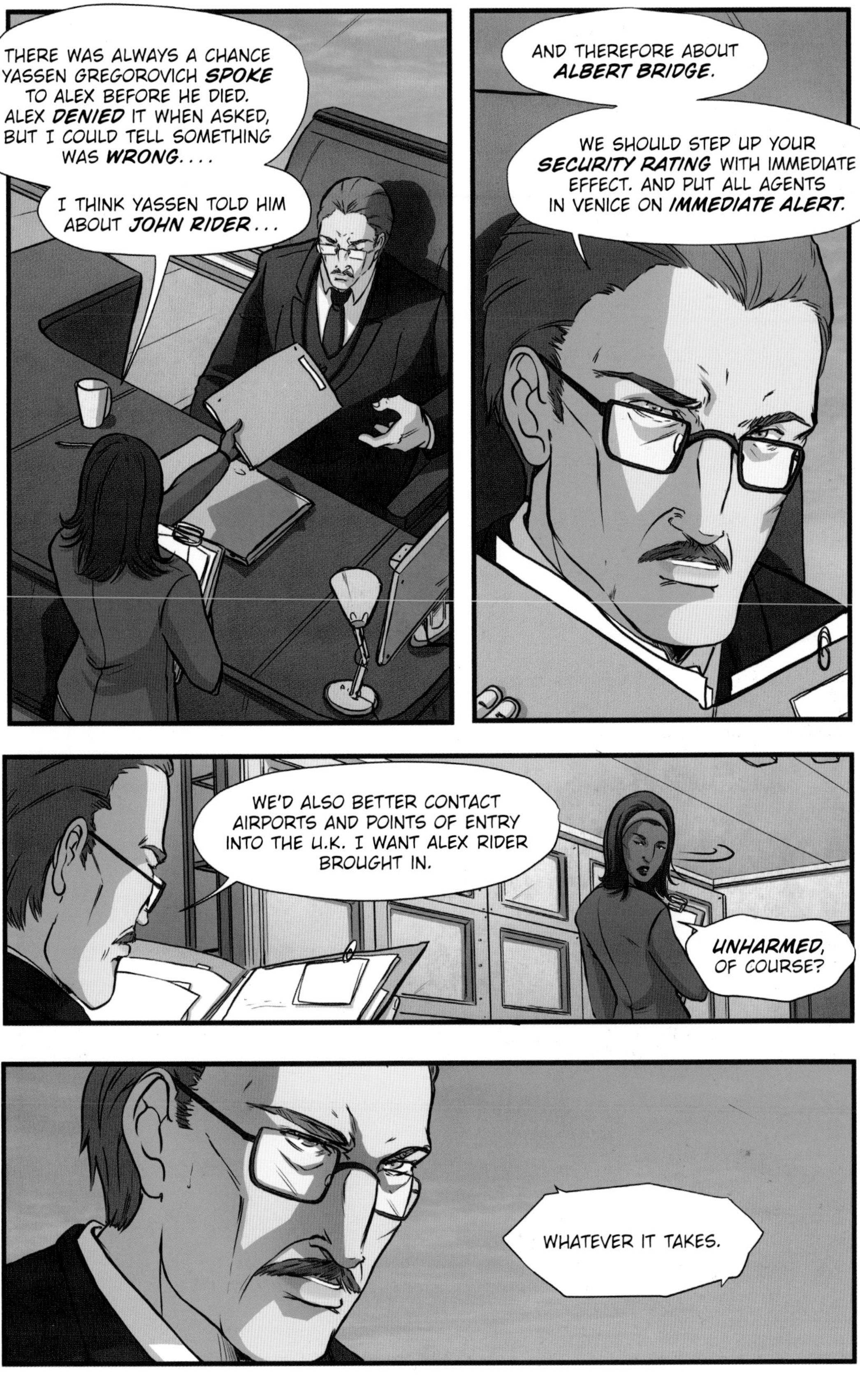
THERE WAS ALWAYS A CHANCE YASSEN GREGOROVICH SPOKE TO ALEX BEFORE HE DIED. ALEX DENIED IT WHEN ASKED, BUT I COULD TELL SOMETHING WAS WRONG. . . .
I THINK YASSEN TOLD HIM ABOUT JOHN RIDER . . .
AND THEREFORE ABOUT ALBERT BRIDGE.
WE SHOULD STEP UP YOUR SECURITY RATING WITH IMMEDIATE EFFECT. AND PUT ALL AGENTS IN VENICE ON IMMEDIATE ALERT.
WE'D ALSO BETTER CONTACT AIRPORTS AND POINTS OF ENTRY INTO THE U.K. I WANT ALEX RIDER BROUGHT IN.
UNHARMED, OF COURSE?
WHATEVER IT TAKES.

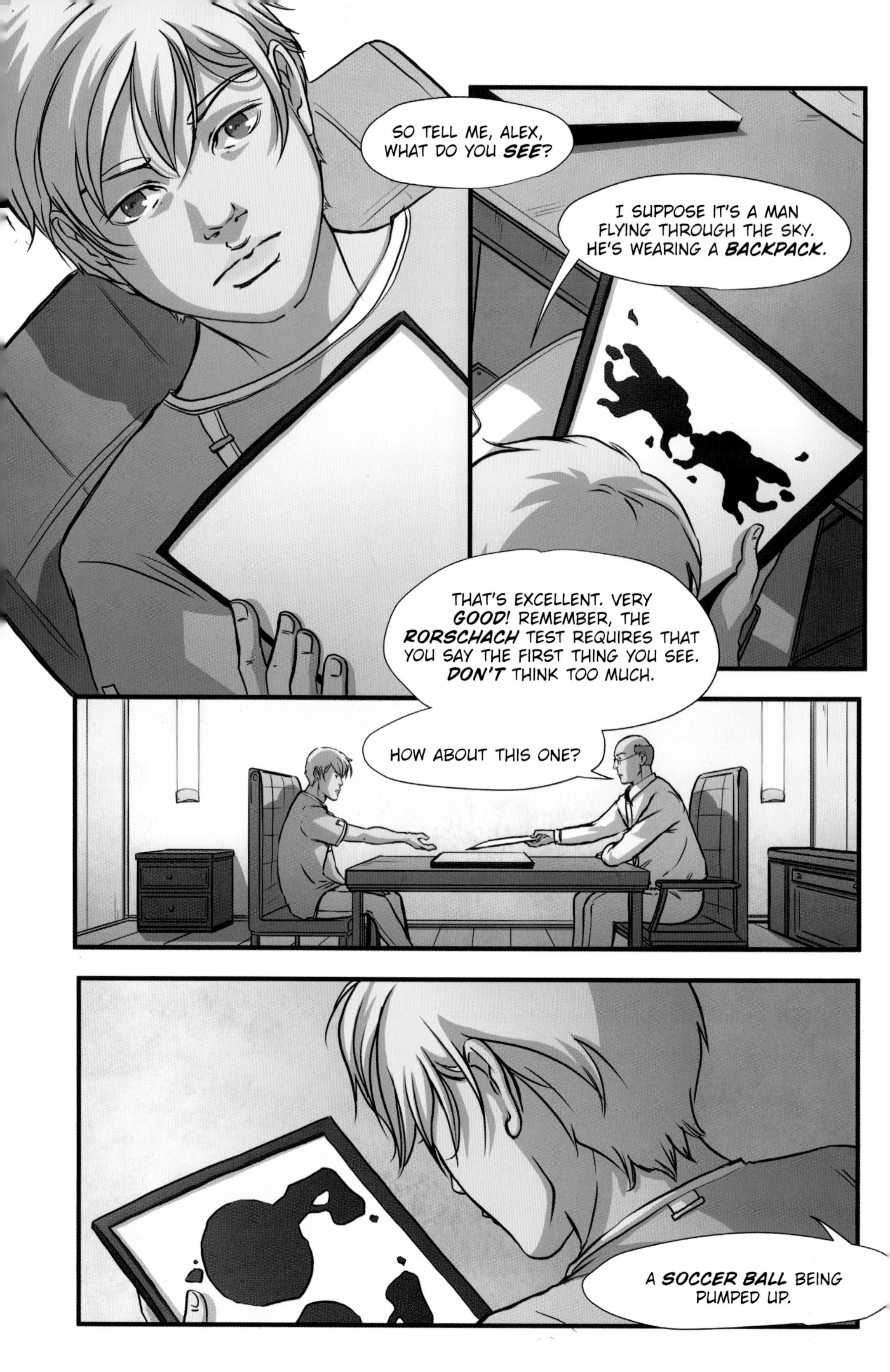
SO TELL ME, ALEX, WHAT DO YOU SEE?
I SUPPOSE IT'S A MAN FLYING THROUGH THE SKY. HE'S WEARING A BACKPACK.
THAT'S EXCELLENT. VERY GOOD! REMEMBER, THE RORSCHACH TEST REQUIRES THAT YOU SAY THE FIRST THING YOU SEE. DON'T THINK TOO MUCH.
HOW ABOUT THIS ONE?
A SOCCER BALL BEING PUMPED UP.

GOOD, THANK YOU.

HOW ARE YOU SETTLING IN?

OK, I GUESS.

YOU HAVE NO *ANXIETIES*? NOTHING YOU WISH TO DISCUSS?

NO. I'M FINE, THANK YOU, DR. STEINER.

YOUR *MEDICAL REPORT* SAYS YOU ARE IN VERY GOOD SHAPE. NOT TOO MUCH FAST FOOD, NO CIGARETTES . . . VERY *SENSIBLE*.

SO, JUST ONE LAST THING.

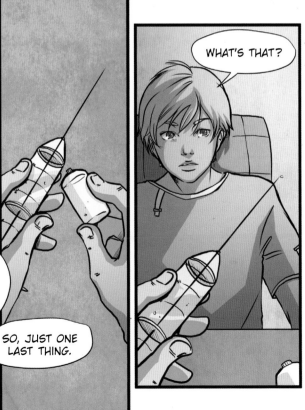

WHAT'S THAT?

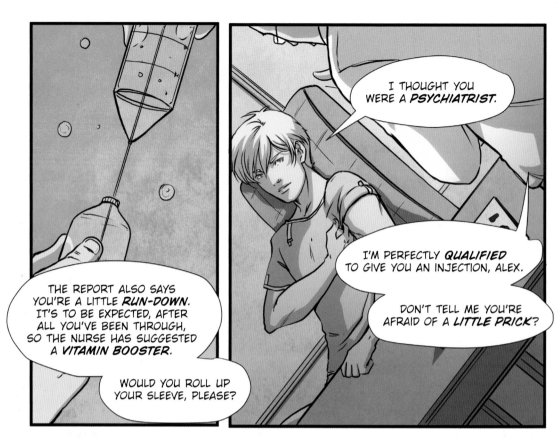

I THOUGHT YOU WERE A *PSYCHIATRIST*.

I'M PERFECTLY *QUALIFIED* TO GIVE YOU AN INJECTION, ALEX.

DON'T TELL ME YOU'RE AFRAID OF A *LITTLE PRICK*?

THE REPORT ALSO SAYS YOU'RE A LITTLE *RUN-DOWN*. IT'S TO BE EXPECTED, AFTER ALL YOU'VE BEEN THROUGH, SO THE NURSE HAS SUGGESTED A *VITAMIN BOOSTER*.

WOULD YOU ROLL UP YOUR SLEEVE, PLEASE?

I WOULDN'T CALL YOU *THAT*. . . .

VERY GOOD. OFF YOU GO! I AM SURE THERE ARE MORE TESTS FOR YOU TO UNDERGO BEFORE YOUR FINAL *REPORT* FROM MONSIEUR D'ARC.

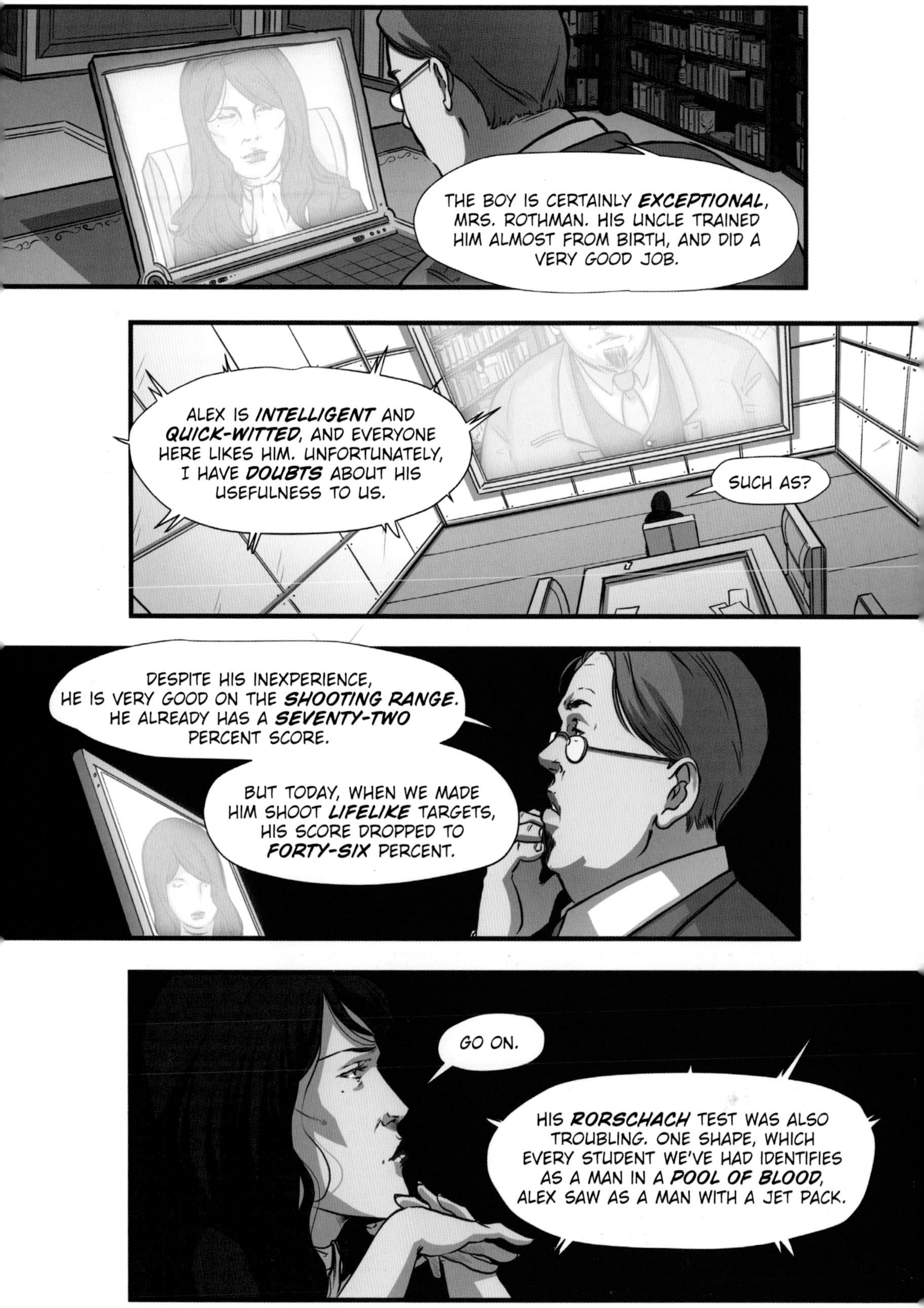
THE BOY IS CERTAINLY EXCEPTIONAL, MRS. ROTHMAN. HIS UNCLE TRAINED HIM ALMOST FROM BIRTH, AND DID A VERY GOOD JOB.
ALEX IS INTELLIGENT AND QUICK-WITTED, AND EVERYONE HERE LIKES HIM. UNFORTUNATELY, I HAVE DOUBTS ABOUT HIS USEFULNESS TO US.
SUCH AS?
DESPITE HIS INEXPERIENCE, HE IS VERY GOOD ON THE SHOOTING RANGE. HE ALREADY HAS A SEVENTY-TWO PERCENT SCORE.
BUT TODAY, WHEN WE MADE HIM SHOOT LIFELIKE TARGETS, HIS SCORE DROPPED TO FORTY-SIX PERCENT.
GO ON.
HIS RORSCHACH TEST WAS ALSO TROUBLING. ONE SHAPE, WHICH EVERY STUDENT WE'VE HAD IDENTIFIES AS A MAN IN A POOL OF BLOOD, ALEX SAW AS A MAN WITH A JET PACK.

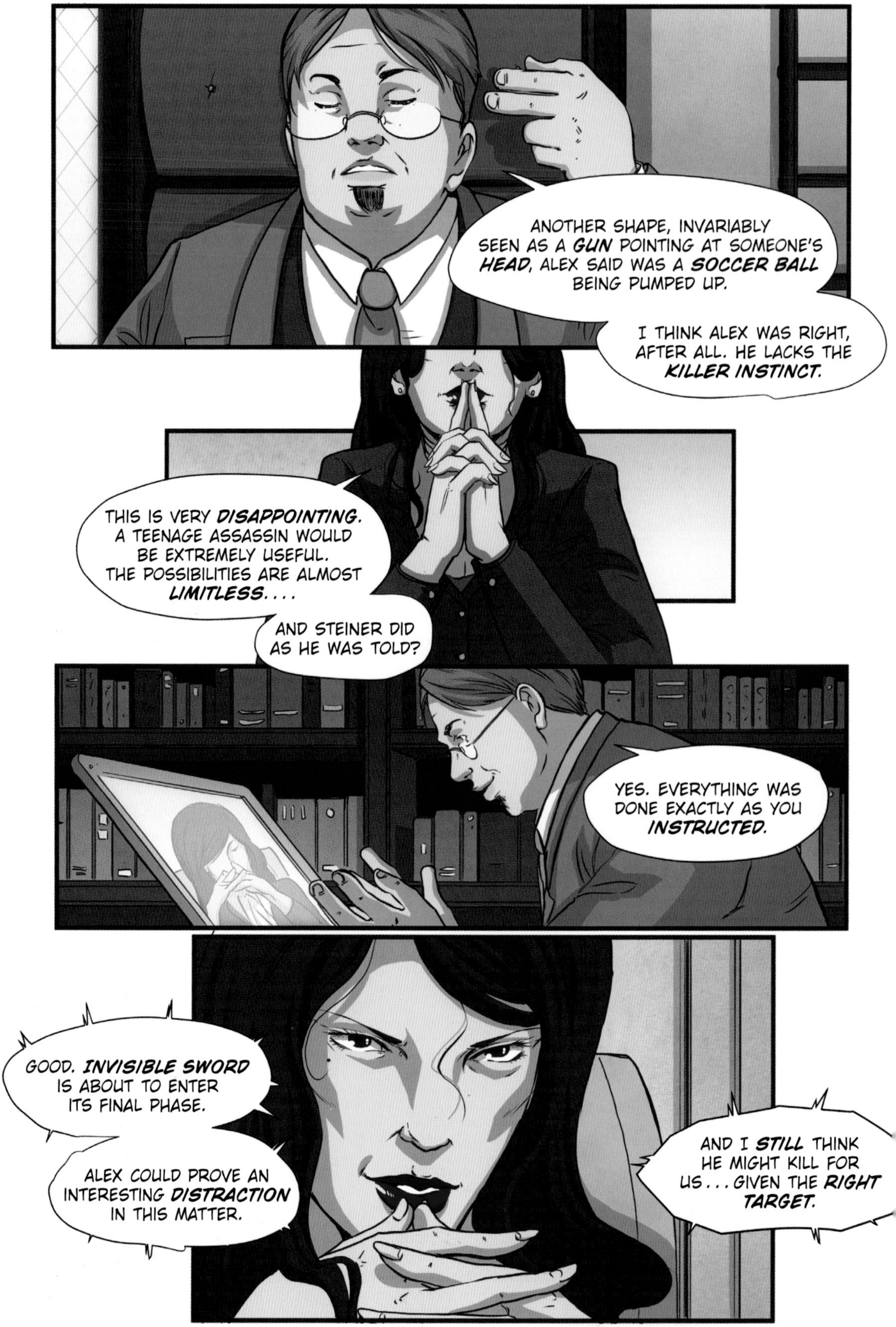
ANOTHER SHAPE, INVARIABLY SEEN AS A GUN POINTING AT SOMEONE'S HEAD, ALEX SAID WAS A SOCCER BALL BEING PUMPED UP.
I THINK ALEX WAS RIGHT, AFTER ALL. HE LACKS THE KILLER INSTINCT.
THIS IS VERY DISAPPOINTING. A TEENAGE ASSASSIN WOULD BE EXTREMELY USEFUL. THE POSSIBILITIES ARE ALMOST LIMITLESS. . . .
AND STEINER DID AS HE WAS TOLD?
YES. EVERYTHING WAS DONE EXACTLY AS YOU INSTRUCTED.
GOOD. INVISIBLE SWORD IS ABOUT TO ENTER ITS FINAL PHASE.
ALEX COULD PROVE AN INTERESTING DISTRACTION IN THIS MATTER.
AND I STILL THINK HE MIGHT KILL FOR US . . . GIVEN THE RIGHT TARGET.

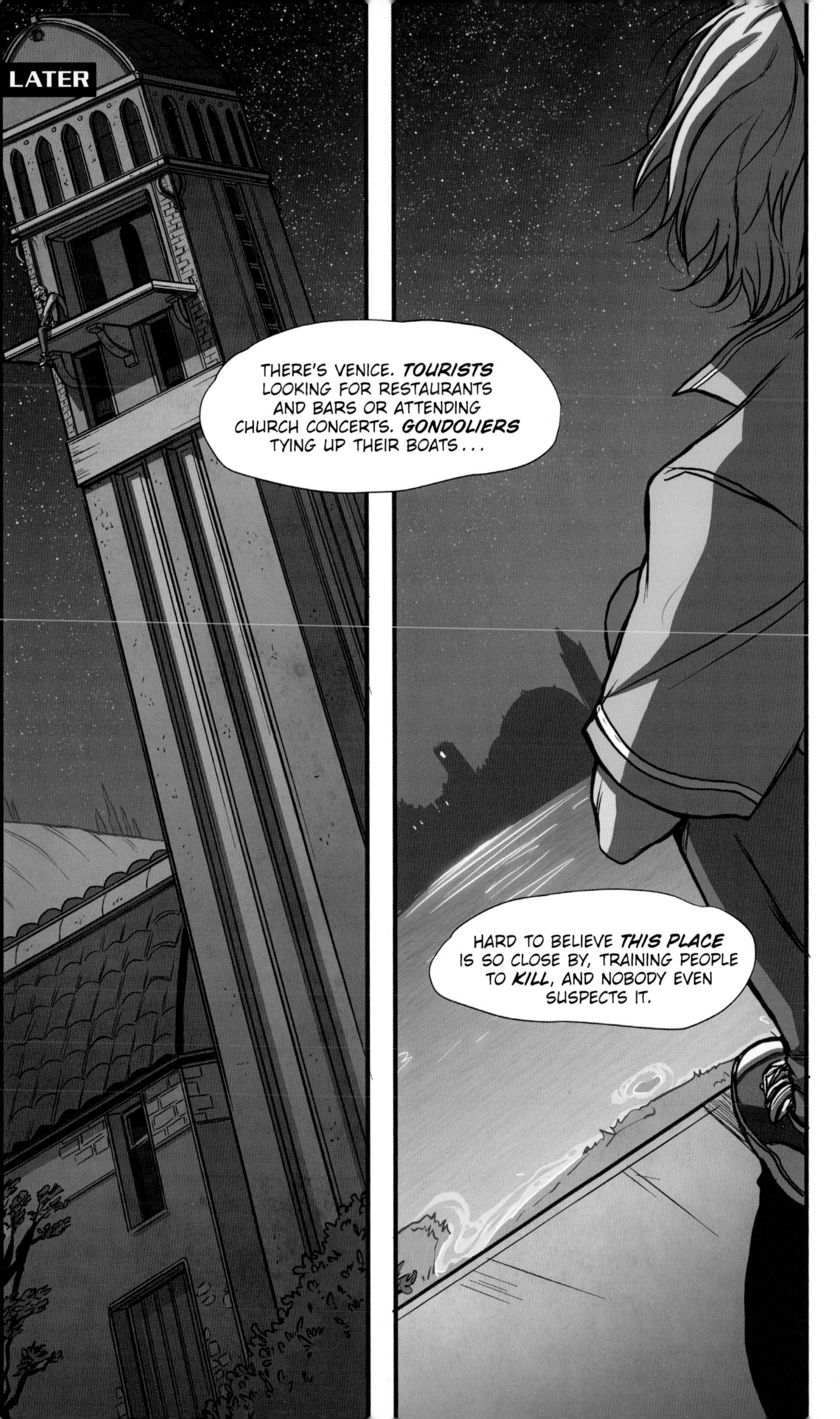
LATER
THERE'S VENICE. TOURISTS LOOKING FOR RESTAURANTS AND BARS OR ATTENDING CHURCH CONCERTS. GONDOLIERS TYING UP THEIR BOATS . . .
HARD TO BELIEVE THIS PLACE IS SO CLOSE BY, TRAINING PEOPLE TO KILL, AND NOBODY EVEN SUSPECTS IT.

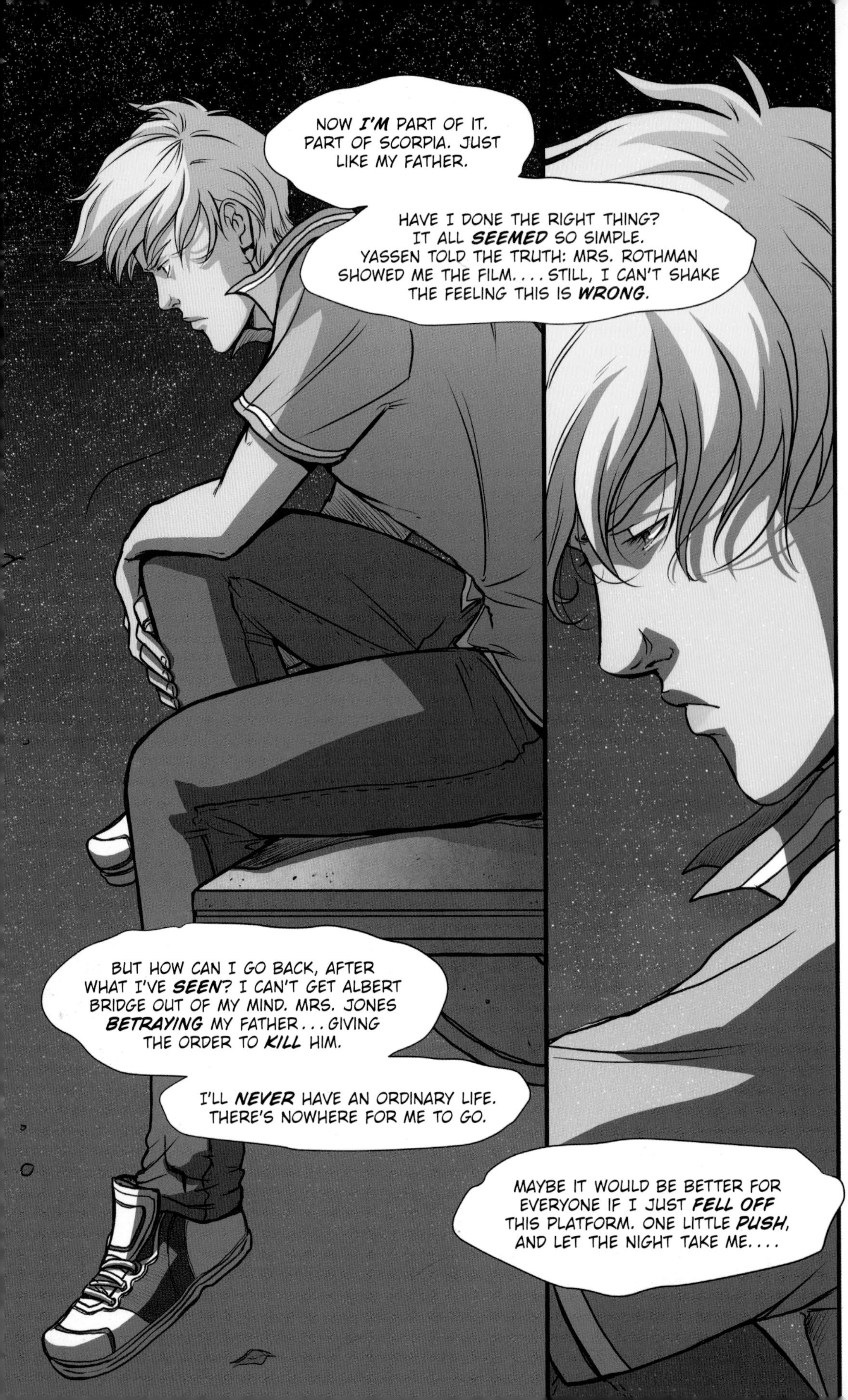
NOW I'M PART OF IT. PART OF SCORPIA. JUST LIKE MY FATHER.
HAVE I DONE THE RIGHT THING? IT ALL SEEMED SO SIMPLE. YASSEN TOLD THE TRUTH: MRS. ROTHMAN SHOWED ME THE FILM. . . . STILL, I CAN'T SHAKE THE FEELING THIS IS WRONG.
BUT HOW CAN I GO BACK, AFTER WHAT I'VE SEEN? I CAN'T GET ALBERT BRIDGE OUT OF MY MIND. MRS. JONES BETRAYING MY FATHER . . . GIVING THE ORDER TO KILL HIM.
I'LL NEVER HAVE AN ORDINARY LIFE. THERE'S NOWHERE FOR ME TO GO.
MAYBE IT WOULD BE BETTER FOR EVERYONE IF I JUST FELL OFF THIS PLATFORM. ONE LITTLE PUSH, AND LET THE NIGHT TAKE ME. . . .

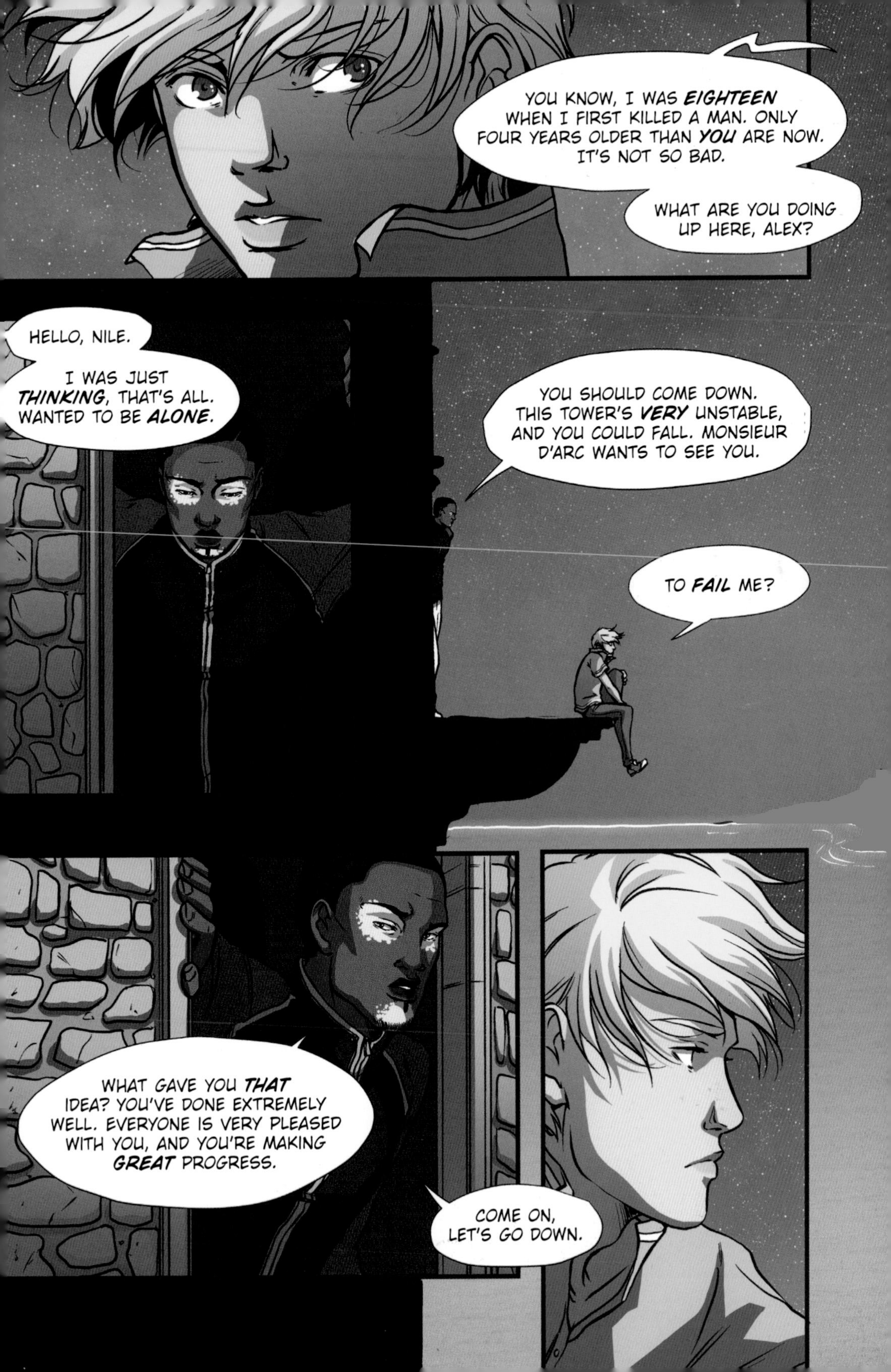
YOU KNOW, I WAS EIGHTEEN WHEN I FIRST KILLED A MAN. ONLY FOUR YEARS OLDER THAN YOU ARE NOW. IT'S NOT SO BAD.
WHAT ARE YOU DOING UP HERE, ALEX?
HELLO, NILE.
I WAS JUST THINKING, THAT'S ALL. WANTED TO BE ALONE.
YOU SHOULD COME DOWN. THIS TOWER'S VERY UNSTABLE, AND YOU COULD FALL. MONSIEUR D'ARC WANTS TO SEE YOU.
TO FAIL ME?
WHAT GAVE YOU THAT IDEA? YOU'VE DONE EXTREMELY WELL. EVERYONE IS VERY PLEASED WITH YOU, AND YOU'RE MAKING GREAT PROGRESS.
COME ON, LET'S GO DOWN.

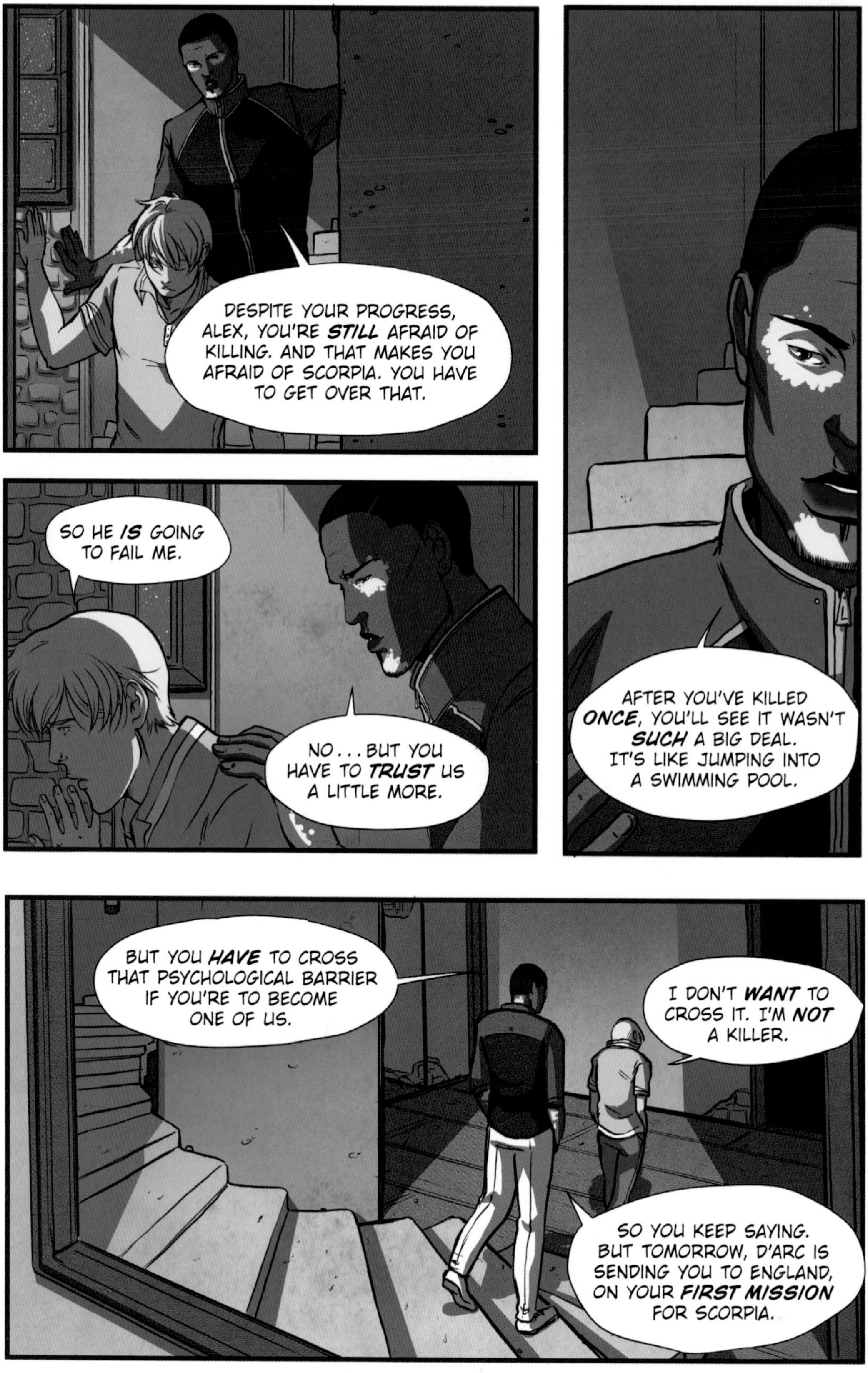
DESPITE YOUR PROGRESS, ALEX, YOU'RE STILL AFRAID OF KILLING. AND THAT MAKES YOU AFRAID OF SCORPIA. YOU HAVE TO GET OVER THAT.
SO HE IS GOING TO FAIL ME.
NO . . . BUT YOU HAVE TO TRUST US A LITTLE MORE.
AFTER YOU'VE KILLED ONCE, YOU'LL SEE IT WASN'T SUCH A BIG DEAL. IT'S LIKE JUMPING INTO A SWIMMING POOL.
BUT YOU HAVE TO CROSS THAT PSYCHOLOGICAL BARRIER IF YOU'RE TO BECOME ONE OF US.
I DON'T WANT TO CROSS IT. I'M NOT A KILLER.
SO YOU KEEP SAYING. BUT TOMORROW, D'ARC IS SENDING YOU TO ENGLAND, ON YOUR FIRST MISSION FOR SCORPIA.

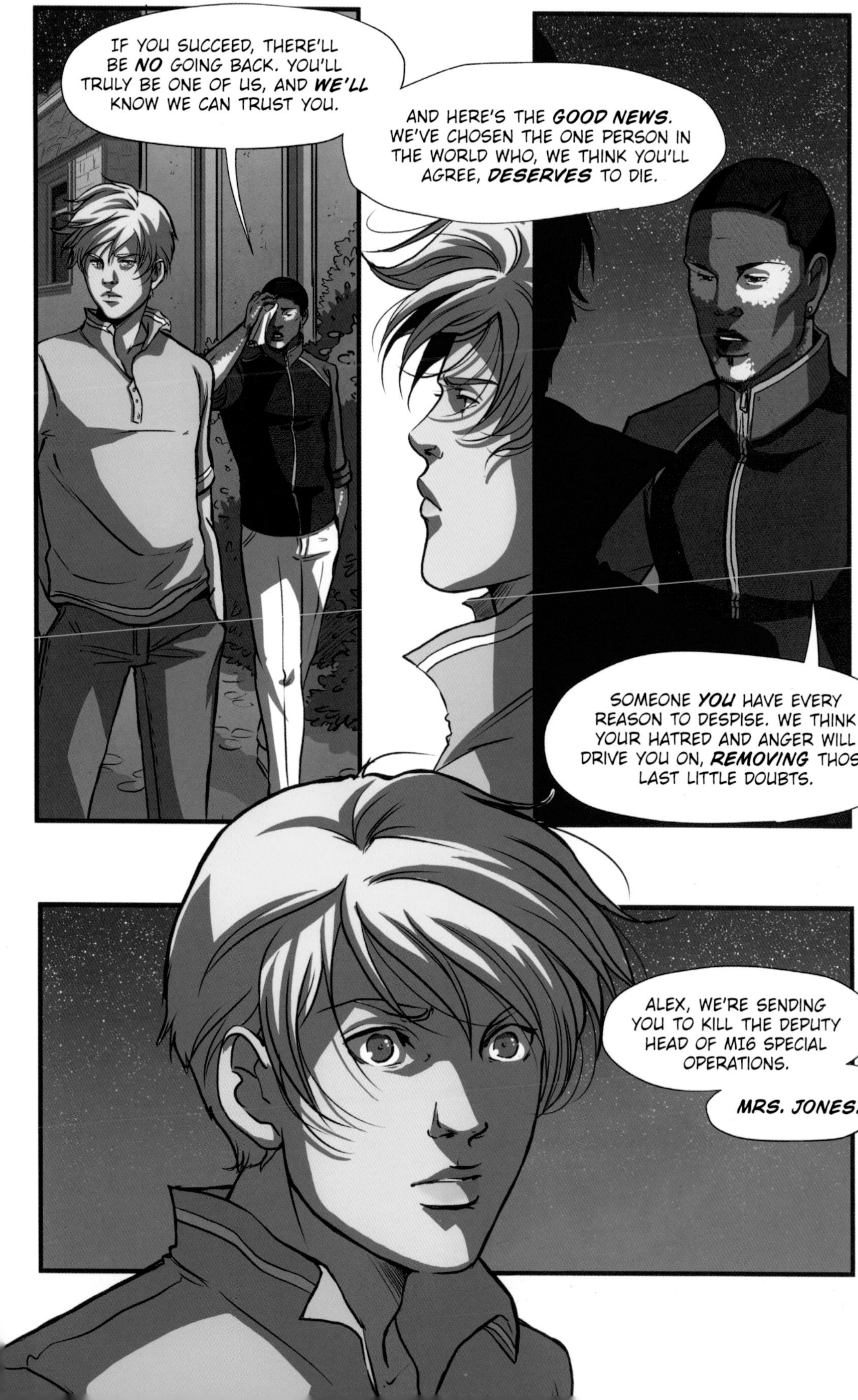
IF YOU SUCCEED, THERE'LL BE NO GOING BACK. YOU'LL TRULY BE ONE OF US, AND WE'LL KNOW WE CAN TRUST YOU.
AND HERE'S THE GOOD NEWS. WE'VE CHOSEN THE ONE PERSON IN THE WORLD WHO, WE THINK YOU'LL AGREE, DESERVES TO DIE.
SOMEONE YOU HAVE EVERY REASON TO DESPISE. WE THINK YOUR HATRED AND ANGER WILL DRIVE YOU ON, REMOVING THOSE LAST LITTLE DOUBTS.
ALEX, WE'RE SENDING YOU TO KILL THE DEPUTY HEAD OF MI6 SPECIAL OPERATIONS.
MRS. JONES.

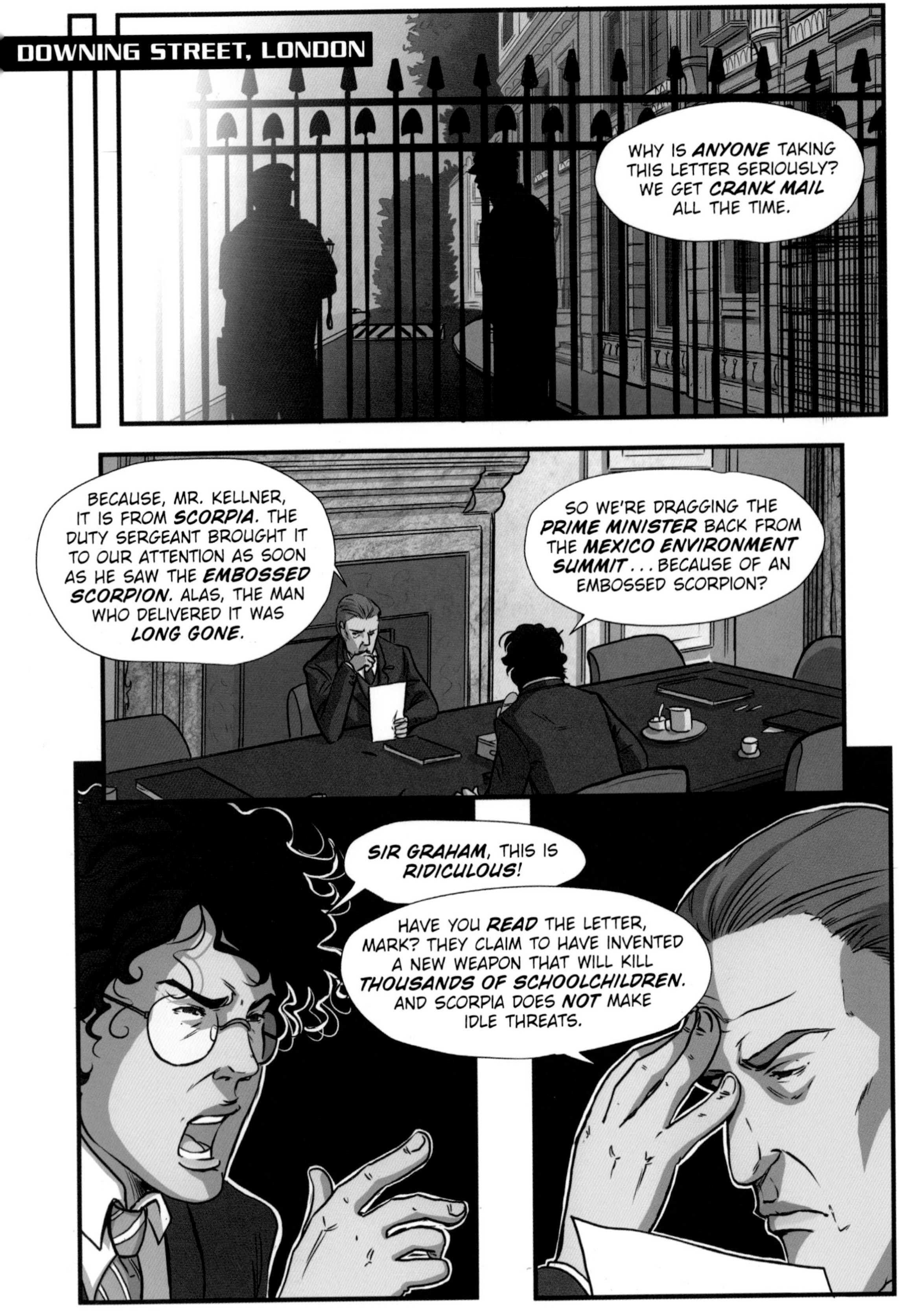
DOWNING STREET, LONDON
WHY IS ANYONE TAKING THIS LETTER SERIOUSLY? WE GET CRANK MAIL ALL THE TIME.
BECAUSE, MR. KELLNER, IT IS FROM SCORPIA. THE DUTY SERGEANT BROUGHT IT TO OUR ATTENTION AS SOON AS HE SAW THE EMBOSSED SCORPION. ALAS, THE MAN WHO DELIVERED IT WAS LONG GONE.
SO WE'RE DRAGGING THE PRIME MINISTER BACK FROM THE MEXICO ENVIRONMENT SUMMIT . . . BECAUSE OF AN EMBOSSED SCORPION?
SIR GRAHAM, THIS IS RIDICULOUS!
HAVE YOU READ THE LETTER, MARK? THEY CLAIM TO HAVE INVENTED A NEW WEAPON THAT WILL KILL THOUSANDS OF SCHOOLCHILDREN. AND SCORPIA DOES NOT MAKE IDLE THREATS.

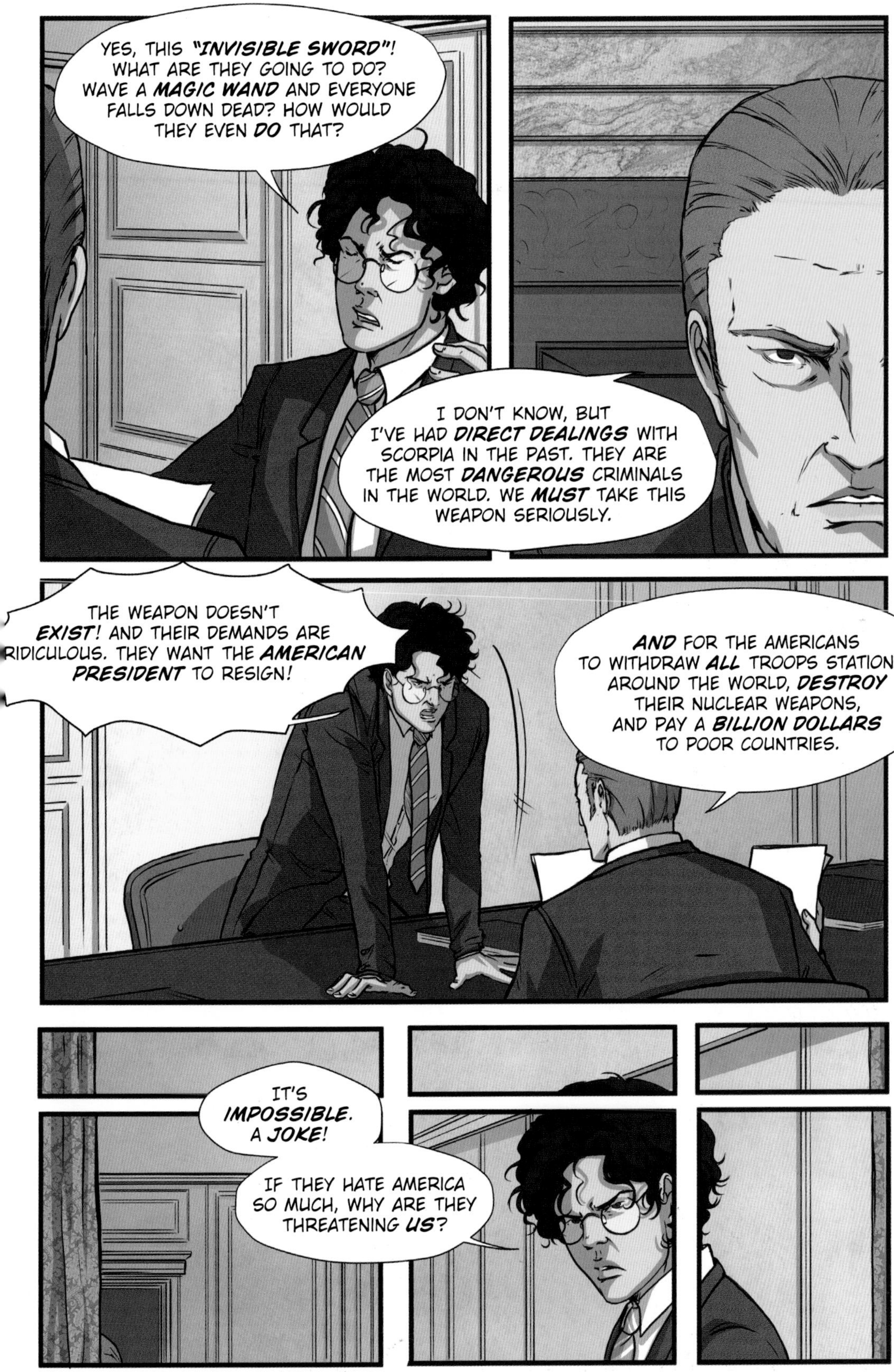
YES, THIS "INVISIBLE SWORD"! WHAT ARE THEY GOING TO DO? WAVE A MAGIC WAND AND EVERYONE FALLS DOWN DEAD? HOW WOULD THEY EVEN DO THAT?
I DON'T KNOW, BUT I'VE HAD DIRECT DEALINGS WITH SCORPIA IN THE PAST. THEY ARE THE MOST DANGEROUS CRIMINALS IN THE WORLD. WE MUST TAKE THIS WEAPON SERIOUSLY.
THE WEAPON DOESN'T EXIST! AND THEIR DEMANDS ARE RIDICULOUS. THEY WANT THE AMERICAN PRESIDENT TO RESIGN!
AND FOR THE AMERICANS TO WITHDRAW ALL TROOPS STATIONED AROUND THE WORLD, DESTROY THEIR NUCLEAR WEAPONS, AND PAY A BILLION DOLLARS TO POOR COUNTRIES.
IT'S IMPOSSIBLE. A JOKE!
IF THEY HATE AMERICA SO MUCH, WHY ARE THEY THREATENING US?

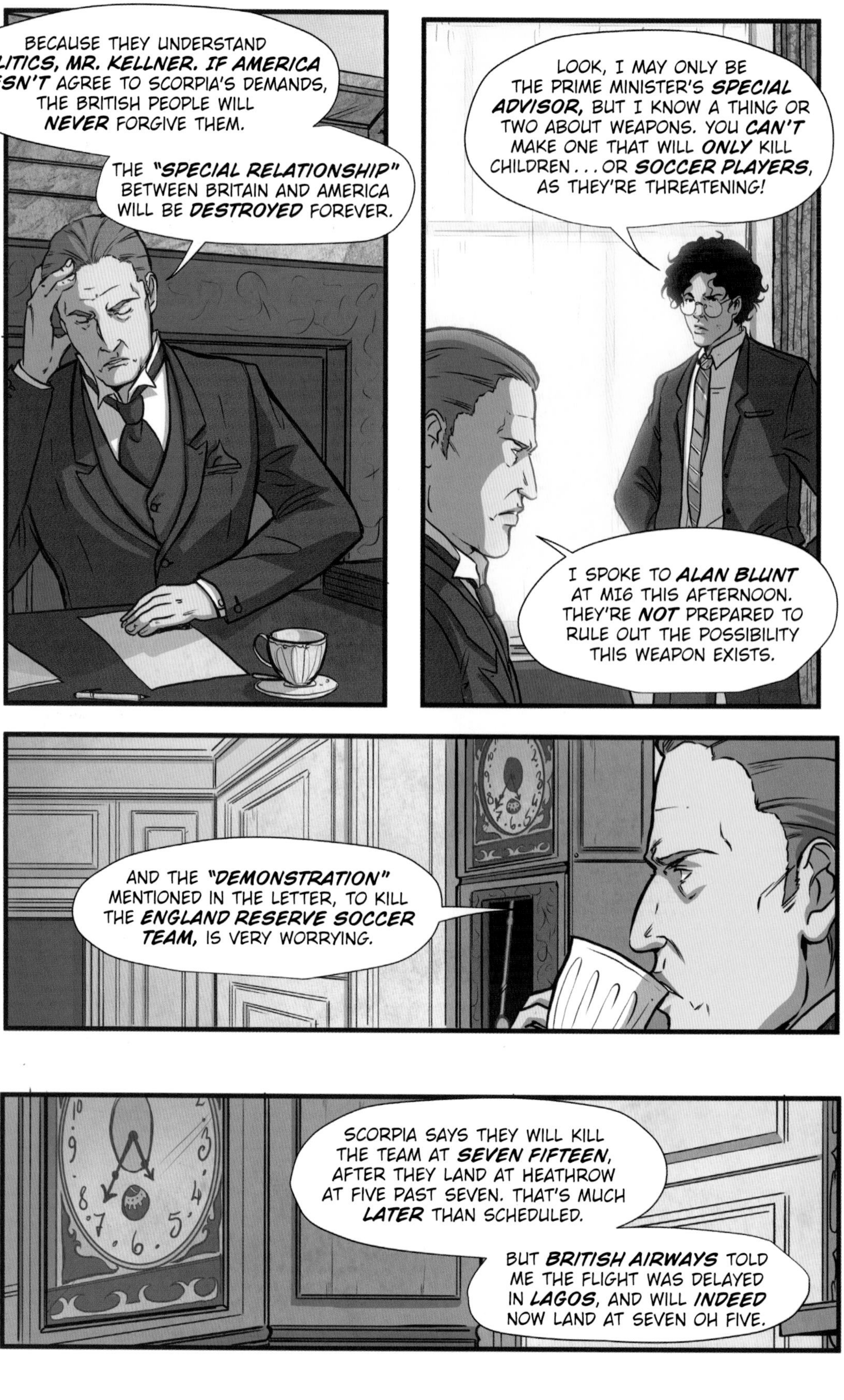
BECAUSE THEY UNDERSTAND POLITICS, MR. KELLNER. IF AMERICA DOESN'T AGREE TO SCORPIA'S DEMANDS, THE BRITISH PEOPLE WILL NEVER FORGIVE THEM.
THE "SPECIAL RELATIONSHIP" BETWEEN BRITAIN AND AMERICA WILL BE DESTROYED FOREVER.
LOOK, I MAY ONLY BE THE PRIME MINISTER'S SPECIAL ADVISOR, BUT I KNOW A THING OR TWO ABOUT WEAPONS. YOU CAN'T MAKE ONE THAT WILL ONLY KILL CHILDREN . . . OR SOCCER PLAYERS, AS THEY'RE THREATENING!
I SPOKE TO ALAN BLUNT AT MI6 THIS AFTERNOON. THEY'RE NOT PREPARED TO RULE OUT THE POSSIBILITY THIS WEAPON EXISTS.
AND THE "DEMONSTRATION" MENTIONED IN THE LETTER, TO KILL THE ENGLAND RESERVE SOCCER TEAM, IS VERY WORRYING.
SCORPIA SAYS THEY WILL KILL THE TEAM AT SEVEN FIFTEEN, AFTER THEY LAND AT HEATHROW AT FIVE PAST SEVEN. THAT'S MUCH LATER THAN SCHEDULED.
BUT BRITISH AIRWAYS TOLD ME THE FLIGHT WAS DELAYED IN LAGOS, AND WILL INDEED NOW LAND AT SEVEN OH FIVE.

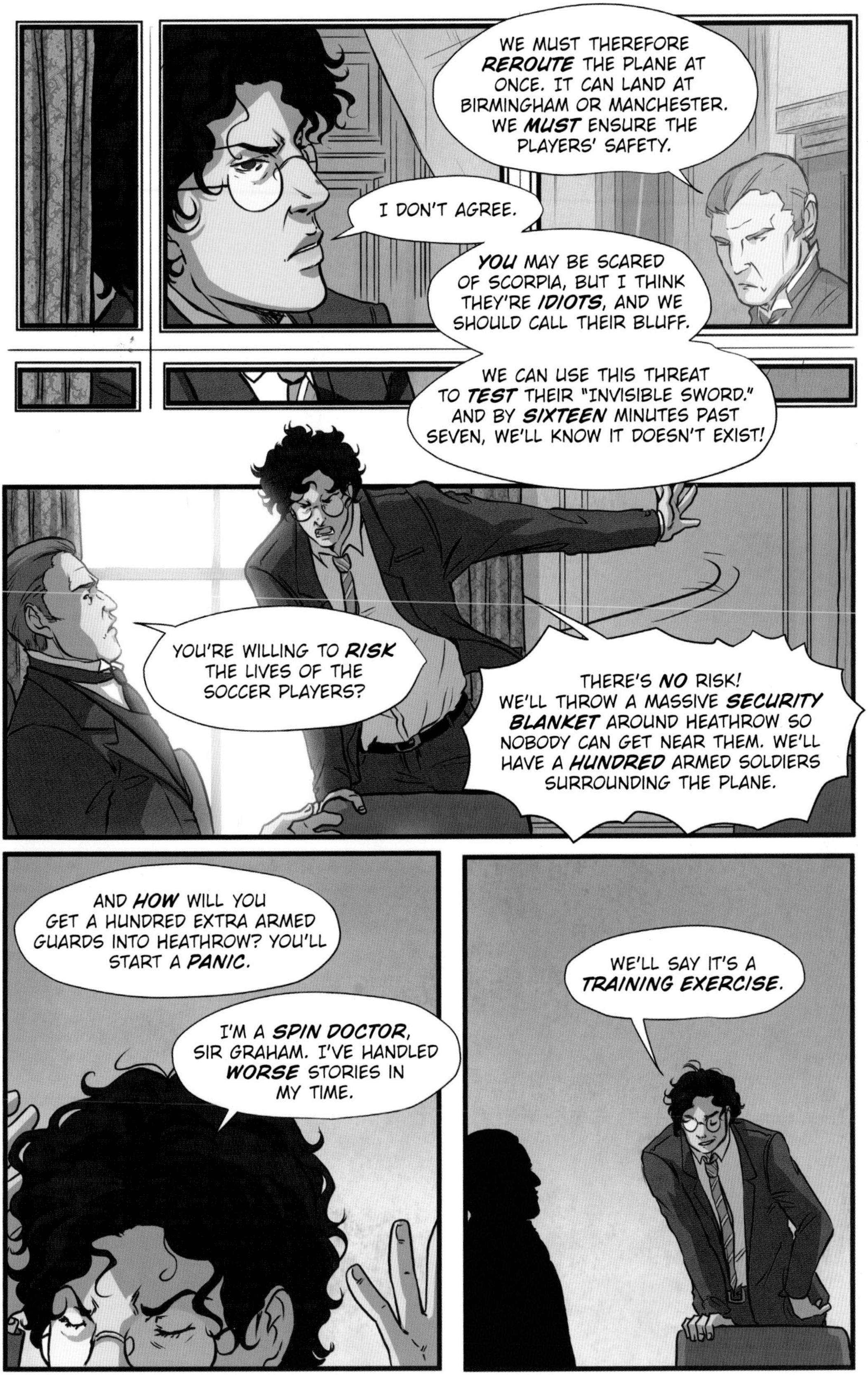
WE MUST THEREFORE REROUTE THE PLANE AT ONCE. IT CAN LAND AT BIRMINGHAM OR MANCHESTER. WE MUST ENSURE THE PLAYERS' SAFETY.
I DON'T AGREE.
YOU MAY BE SCARED OF SCORPIA, BUT I THINK THEY'RE IDIOTS, AND WE SHOULD CALL THEIR BLUFF.
WE CAN USE THIS THREAT TO TEST THEIR "INVISIBLE SWORD." AND BY SIXTEEN MINUTES PAST SEVEN, WE'LL KNOW IT DOESN'T EXIST!
YOU'RE WILLING TO RISK THE LIVES OF THE SOCCER PLAYERS?
THERE'S NO RISK! WE'LL THROW A MASSIVE SECURITY BLANKET AROUND HEATHROW SO NOBODY CAN GET NEAR THEM. WE'LL HAVE A HUNDRED ARMED SOLDIERS SURROUNDING THE PLANE.
AND HOW WILL YOU GET A HUNDRED EXTRA ARMED GUARDS INTO HEATHROW? YOU'LL START A PANIC.
I'M A SPIN DOCTOR, SIR GRAHAM. I'VE HANDLED WORSE STORIES IN MY TIME.
WE'LL SAY IT'S A TRAINING EXERCISE.

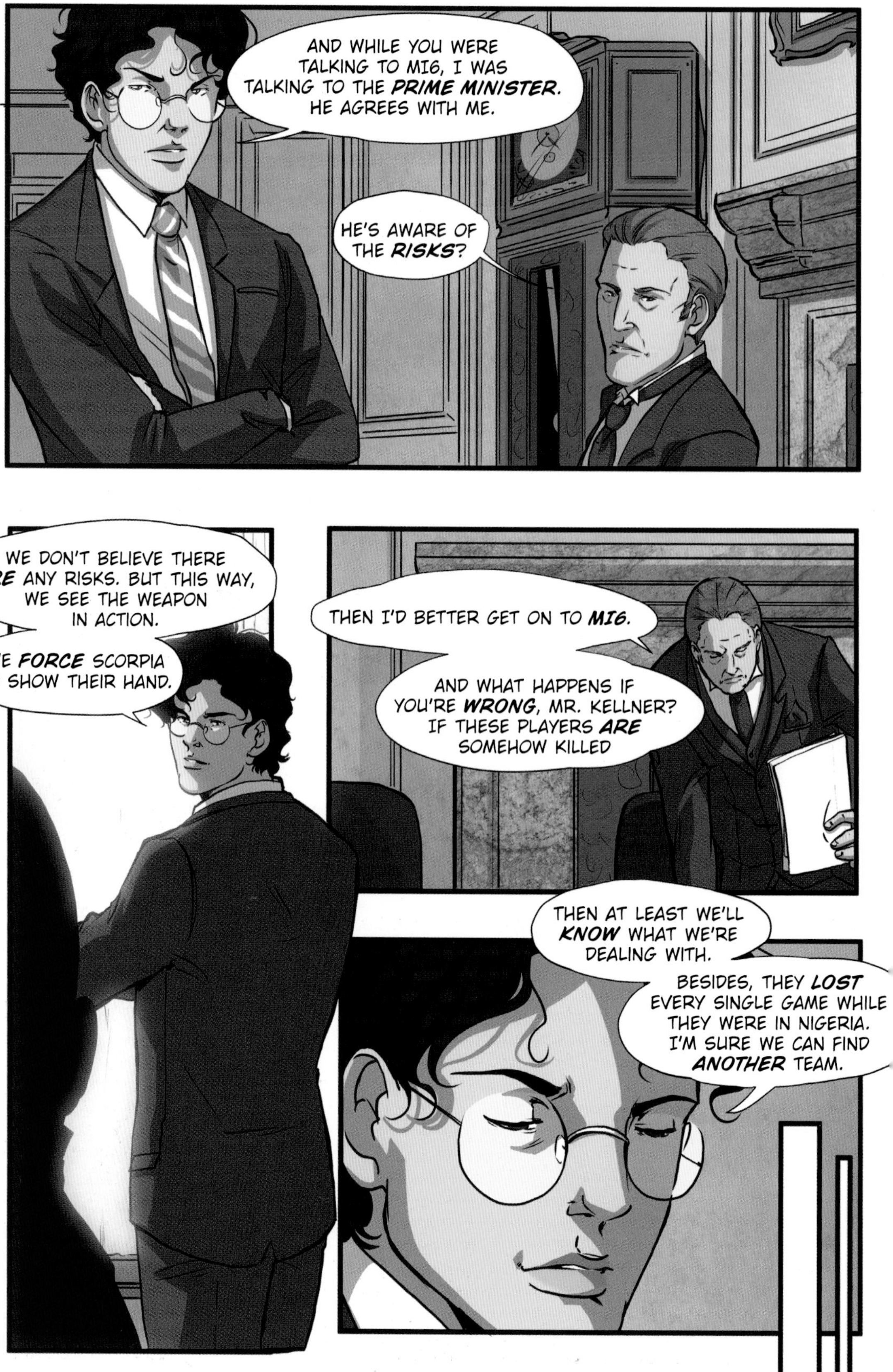
AND WHILE YOU WERE TALKING TO MI6, I WAS TALKING TO THE *PRIME MINISTER*. HE AGREES WITH ME.
HE'S AWARE OF THE *RISKS*?
WE DON'T BELIEVE THERE *ARE* ANY RISKS. BUT THIS WAY, WE SEE THE WEAPON IN ACTION.
WE *FORCE* SCORPIA TO SHOW THEIR HAND.
THEN I'D BETTER GET ON TO *MI6*.
AND WHAT HAPPENS IF YOU'RE *WRONG*, MR. KELLNER? IF THESE PLAYERS *ARE* SOMEHOW KILLED
THEN AT LEAST WE'LL *KNOW* WHAT WE'RE DEALING WITH.
BESIDES, THEY *LOST* EVERY SINGLE GAME WHILE THEY WERE IN NIGERIA. I'M SURE WE CAN FIND *ANOTHER* TEAM.

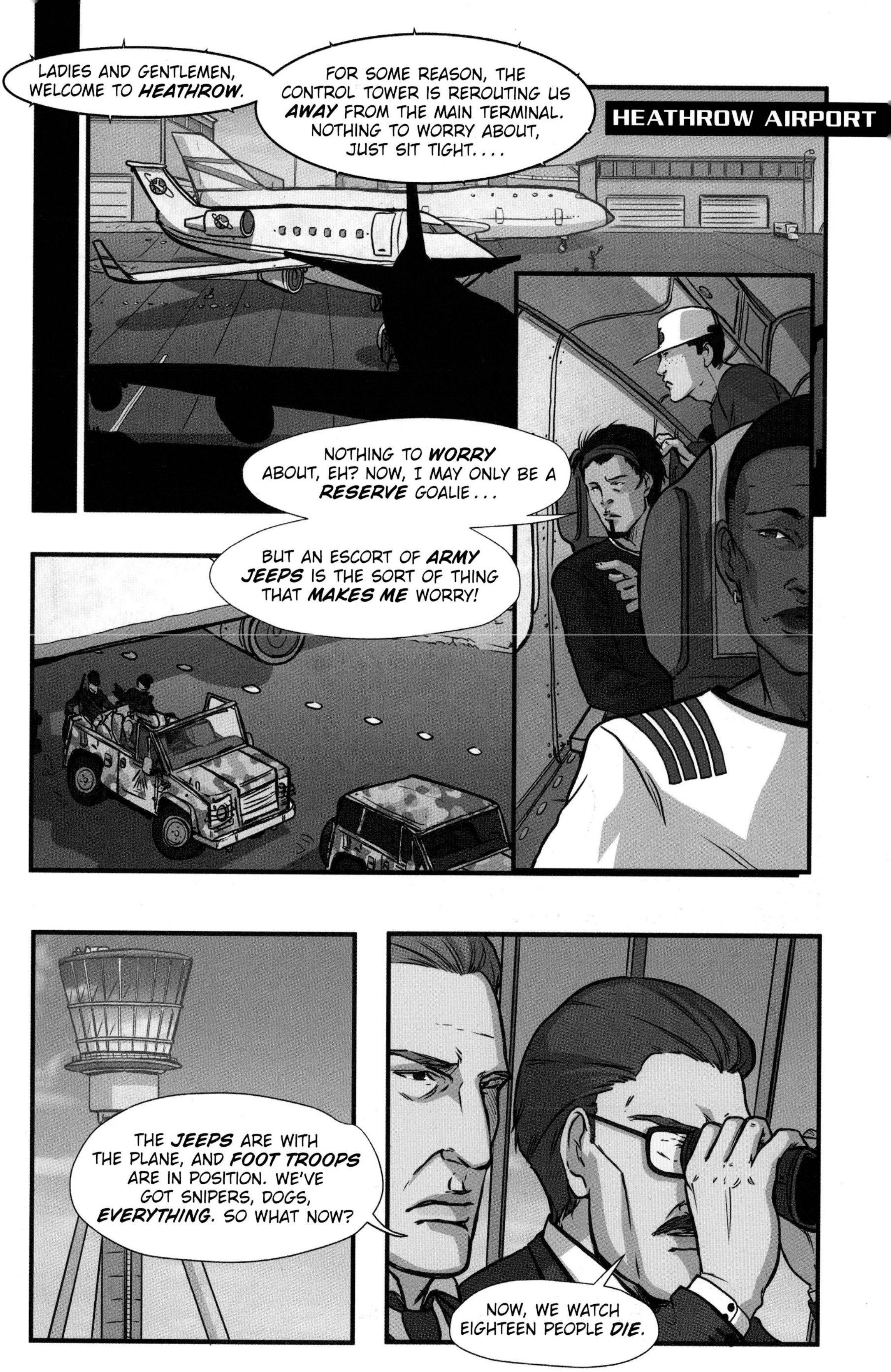
LADIES AND GENTLEMEN, WELCOME TO HEATHROW.
FOR SOME REASON, THE CONTROL TOWER IS REROUTING US AWAY FROM THE MAIN TERMINAL. NOTHING TO WORRY ABOUT, JUST SIT TIGHT. . . .
HEATHROW AIRPORT
NOTHING TO WORRY ABOUT, EH? NOW, I MAY ONLY BE A RESERVE GOALIE . . .
BUT AN ESCORT OF ARMY JEEPS IS THE SORT OF THING THAT MAKES ME WORRY!
THE JEEPS ARE WITH THE PLANE, AND FOOT TROOPS ARE IN POSITION. WE'VE GOT SNIPERS, DOGS, EVERYTHING. SO WHAT NOW?
NOW, WE WATCH EIGHTEEN PEOPLE DIE.

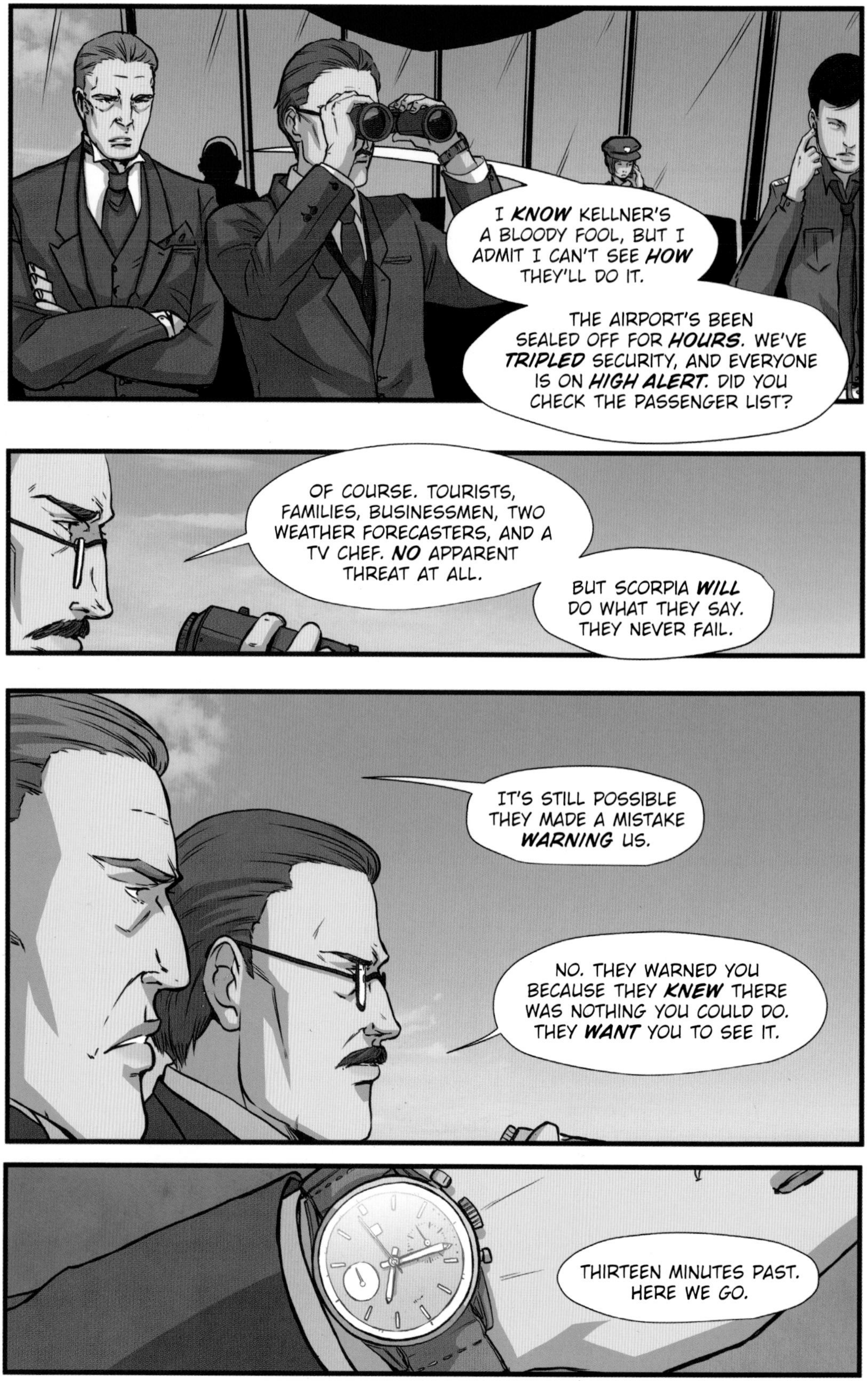
I *KNOW* KELLNER'S A BLOODY FOOL, BUT I ADMIT I CAN'T SEE *HOW* THEY'LL DO IT.
THE AIRPORT'S BEEN SEALED OFF FOR *HOURS*. WE'VE *TRIPLED* SECURITY, AND EVERYONE IS ON *HIGH ALERT*. DID YOU CHECK THE PASSENGER LIST?
OF COURSE. TOURISTS, FAMILIES, BUSINESSMEN, TWO WEATHER FORECASTERS, AND A TV CHEF. *NO* APPARENT THREAT AT ALL.
BUT SCORPIA *WILL* DO WHAT THEY SAY. THEY NEVER FAIL.
IT'S STILL POSSIBLE THEY MADE A MISTAKE *WARNING* US.
NO. THEY WARNED YOU BECAUSE THEY *KNEW* THERE WAS NOTHING YOU COULD DO. THEY *WANT* YOU TO SEE IT.
THIRTEEN MINUTES PAST. HERE WE GO.

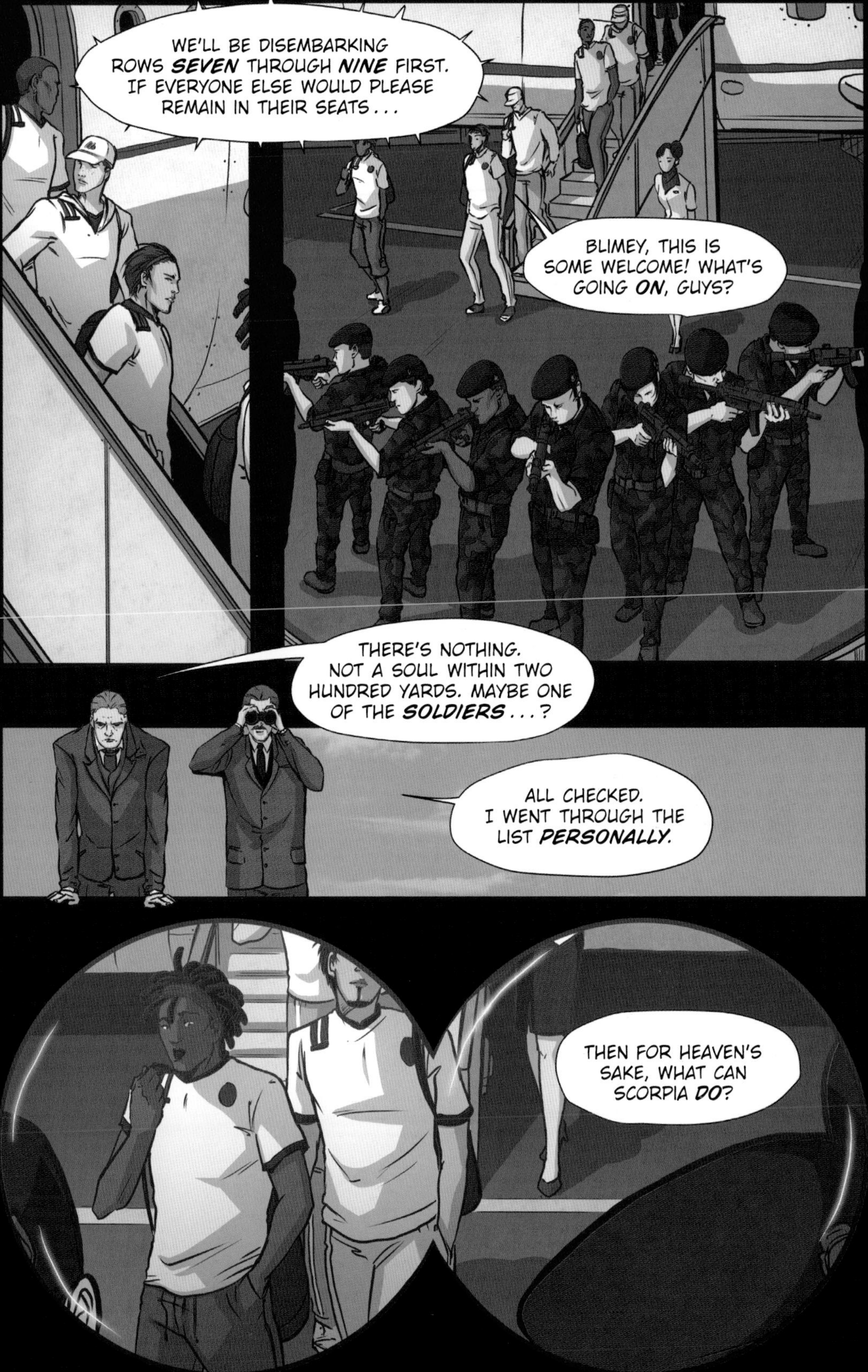
WE'LL BE DISEMBARKING ROWS SEVEN THROUGH NINE FIRST. IF EVERYONE ELSE WOULD PLEASE REMAIN IN THEIR SEATS . . .
BLIMEY, THIS IS SOME WELCOME! WHAT'S GOING ON, GUYS?
THERE'S NOTHING. NOT A SOUL WITHIN TWO HUNDRED YARDS. MAYBE ONE OF THE SOLDIERS . . . ?
ALL CHECKED. I WENT THROUGH THE LIST PERSONALLY.
THEN FOR HEAVEN'S SAKE, WHAT CAN SCORPIA DO?

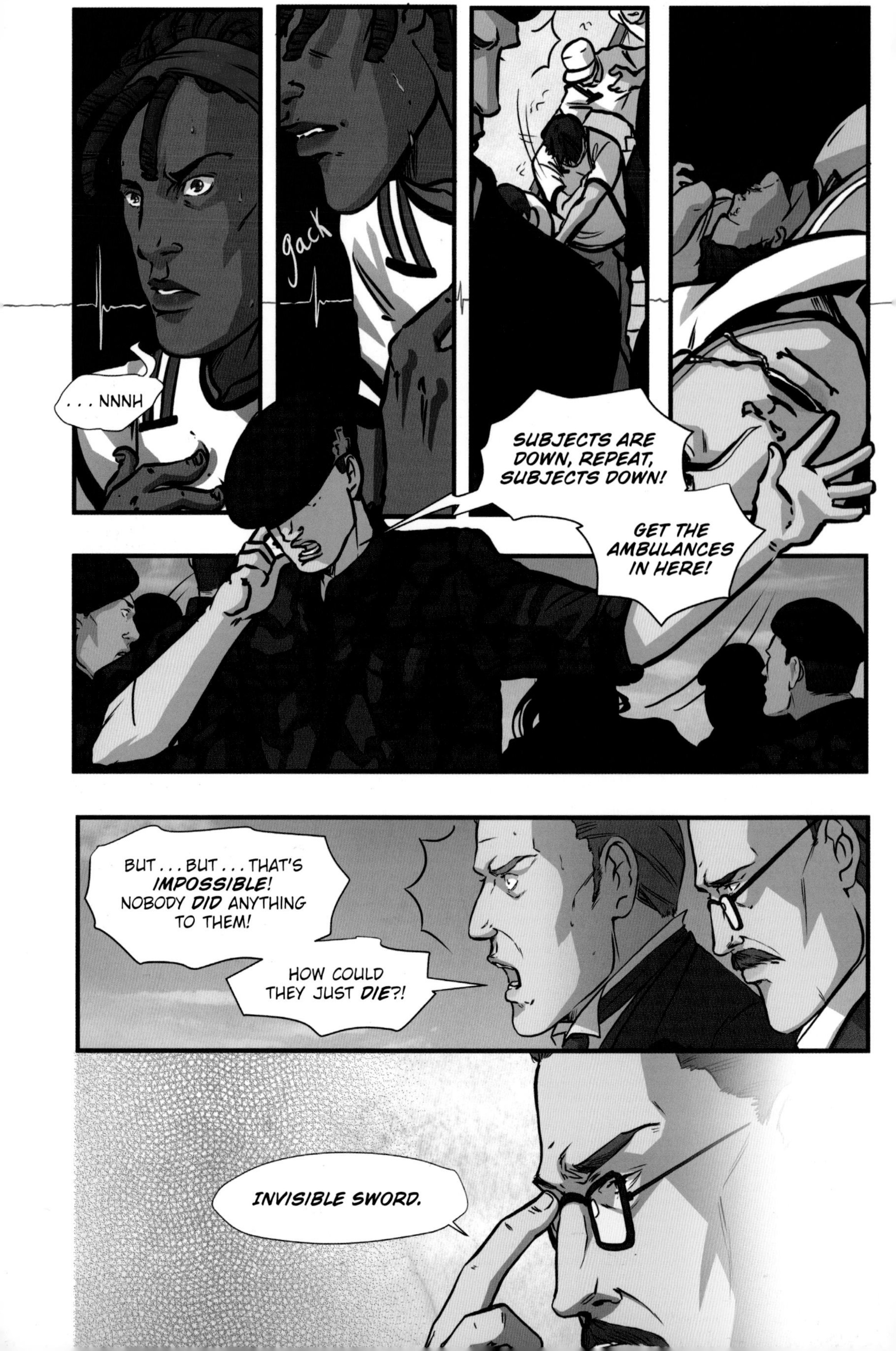
. . . NNNH
gack
SUBJECTS ARE DOWN, REPEAT, SUBJECTS DOWN!
GET THE AMBULANCES IN HERE!
BUT . . . BUT . . . THAT'S *IMPOSSIBLE*! NOBODY *DID* ANYTHING TO THEM!
HOW COULD THEY JUST *DIE*?!
INVISIBLE SWORD.

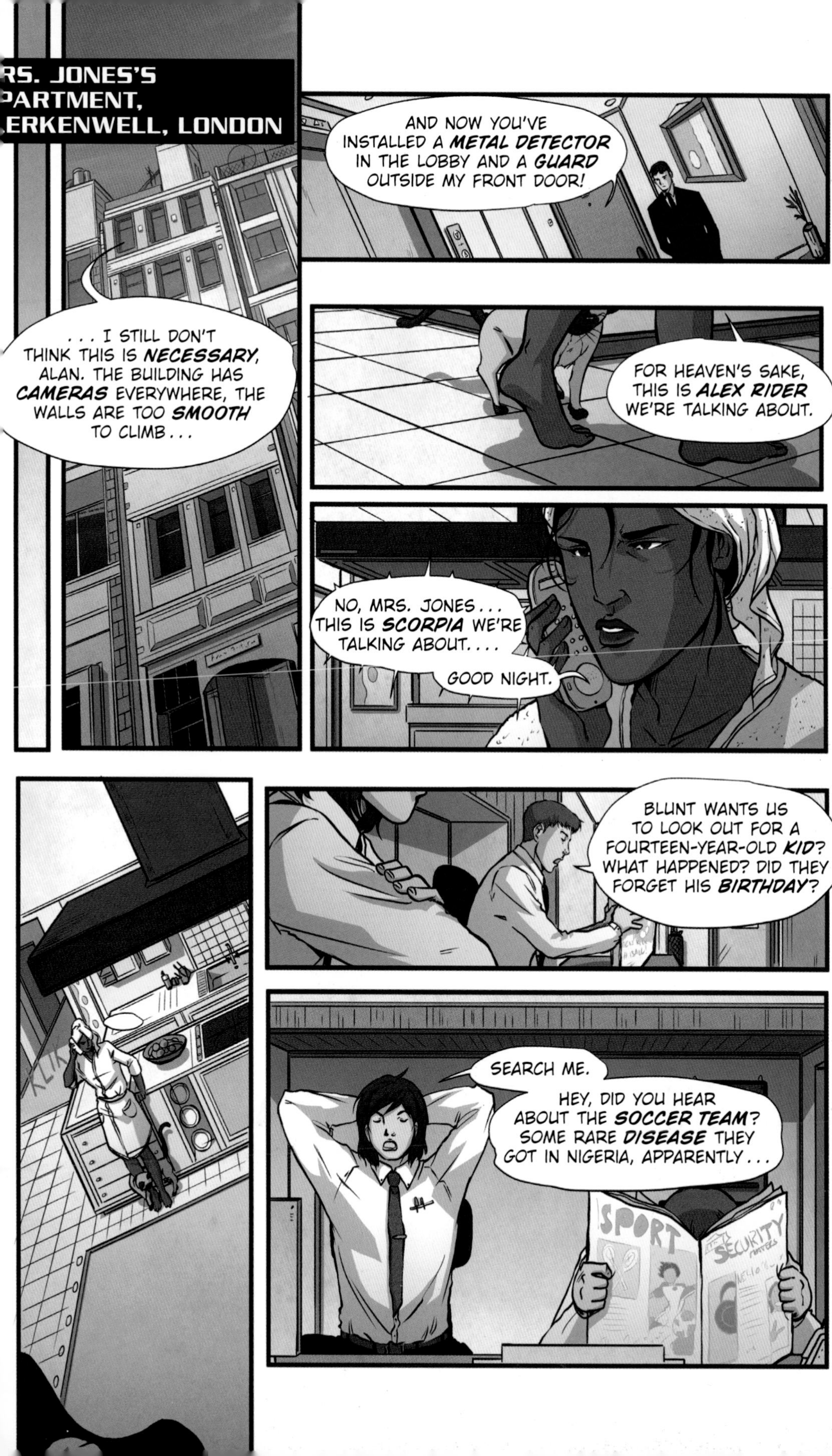

RS. JONES'S
PARTMENT,
ERKENWELL, LONDON
. . . I STILL DON'T THINK THIS IS NECESSARY, ALAN. THE BUILDING HAS CAMERAS EVERYWHERE, THE WALLS ARE TOO SMOOTH TO CLIMB . . .
AND NOW YOU'VE INSTALLED A METAL DETECTOR IN THE LOBBY AND A GUARD OUTSIDE MY FRONT DOOR!
FOR HEAVEN'S SAKE, THIS IS ALEX RIDER WE'RE TALKING ABOUT.
NO, MRS. JONES . . . THIS IS SCORPIA WE'RE TALKING ABOUT. . . .
GOOD NIGHT.
KLIK
BLUNT WANTS US TO LOOK OUT FOR A FOURTEEN-YEAR-OLD KID? WHAT HAPPENED? DID THEY FORGET HIS BIRTHDAY?
SEARCH ME.
HEY, DID YOU HEAR ABOUT THE SOCCER TEAM? SOME RARE DISEASE THEY GOT IN NIGERIA, APPARENTLY . . .
SPORT
SECURITY

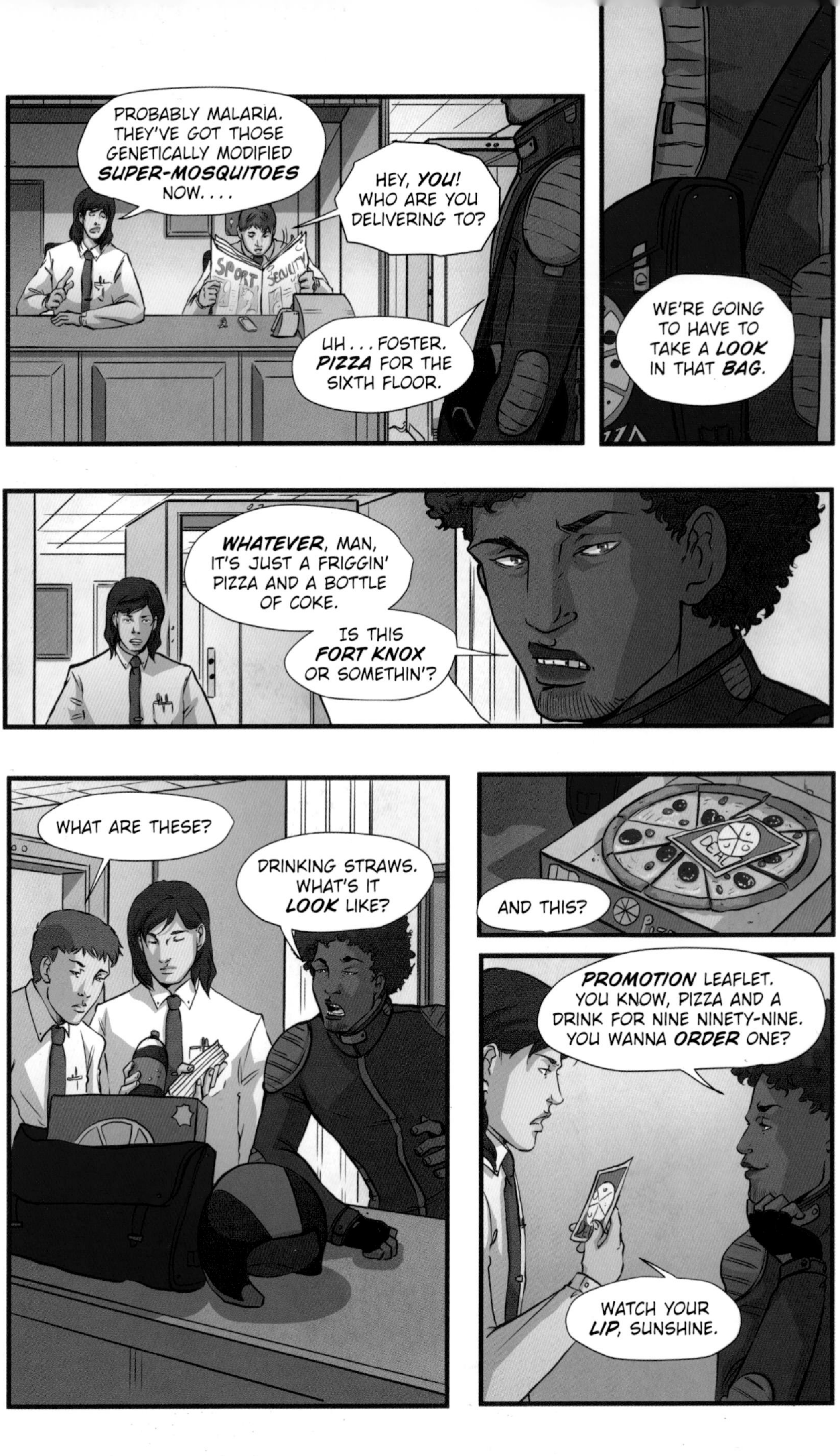
PROBABLY MALARIA. THEY'VE GOT THOSE GENETICALLY MODIFIED SUPER-MOSQUITOES NOW. . . .
HEY, YOU! WHO ARE YOU DELIVERING TO?
UH . . . FOSTER. PIZZA FOR THE SIXTH FLOOR.
WE'RE GOING TO HAVE TO TAKE A LOOK IN THAT BAG.
WHATEVER, MAN, IT'S JUST A FRIGGIN' PIZZA AND A BOTTLE OF COKE.
IS THIS FORT KNOX OR SOMETHIN'?
WHAT ARE THESE?
DRINKING STRAWS. WHAT'S IT LOOK LIKE?
AND THIS?
PROMOTION LEAFLET. YOU KNOW, PIZZA AND A DRINK FOR NINE NINETY-NINE. YOU WANNA ORDER ONE?
WATCH YOUR LIP, SUNSHINE.

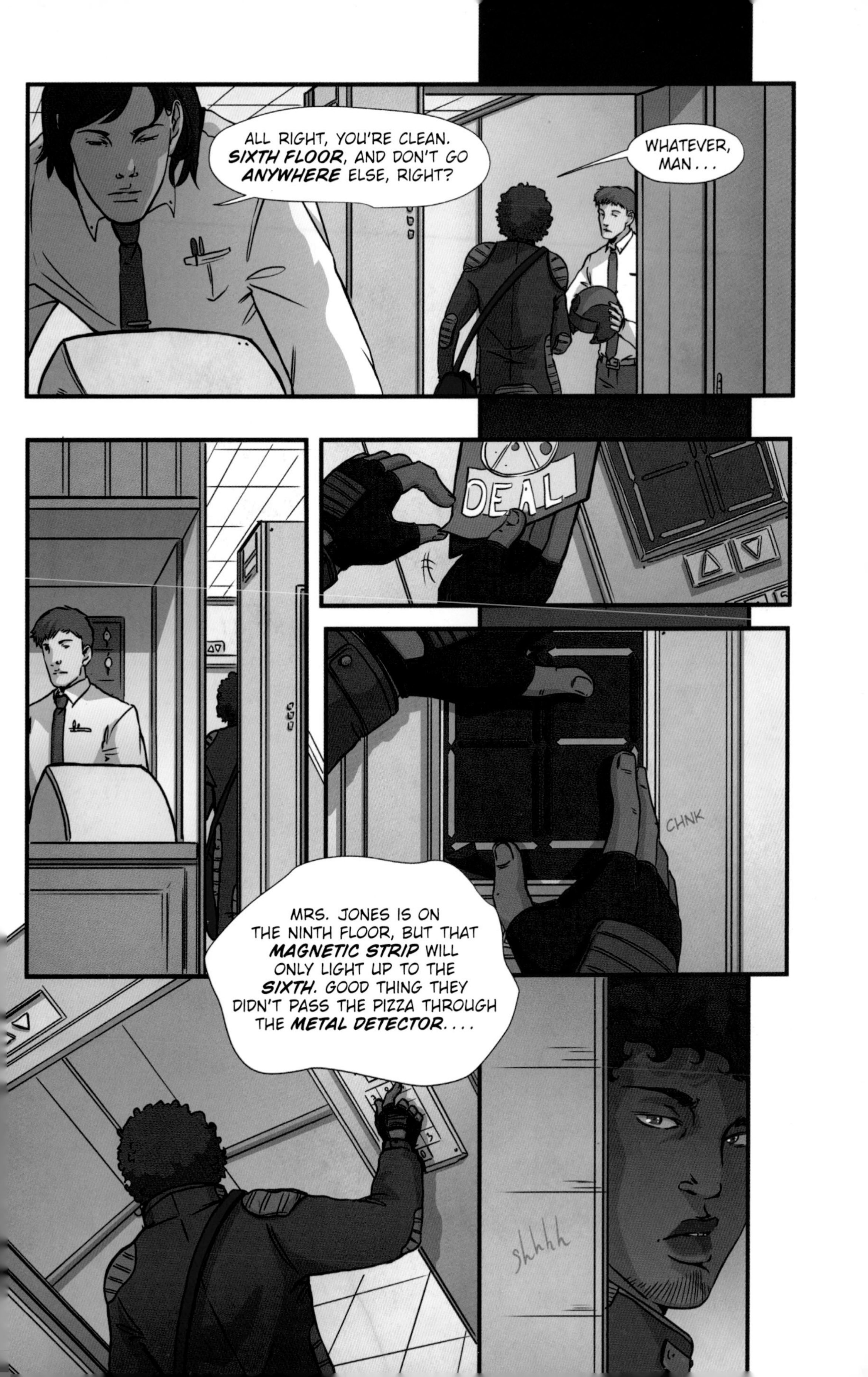
ALL RIGHT, YOU'RE CLEAN. SIXTH FLOOR, AND DON'T GO ANYWHERE ELSE, RIGHT?
WHATEVER, MAN . . .
DEAL
CHNK
MRS. JONES IS ON THE NINTH FLOOR, BUT THAT MAGNETIC STRIP WILL ONLY LIGHT UP TO THE SIXTH. GOOD THING THEY DIDN'T PASS THE PIZZA THROUGH THE METAL DETECTOR. . . .
shhhh

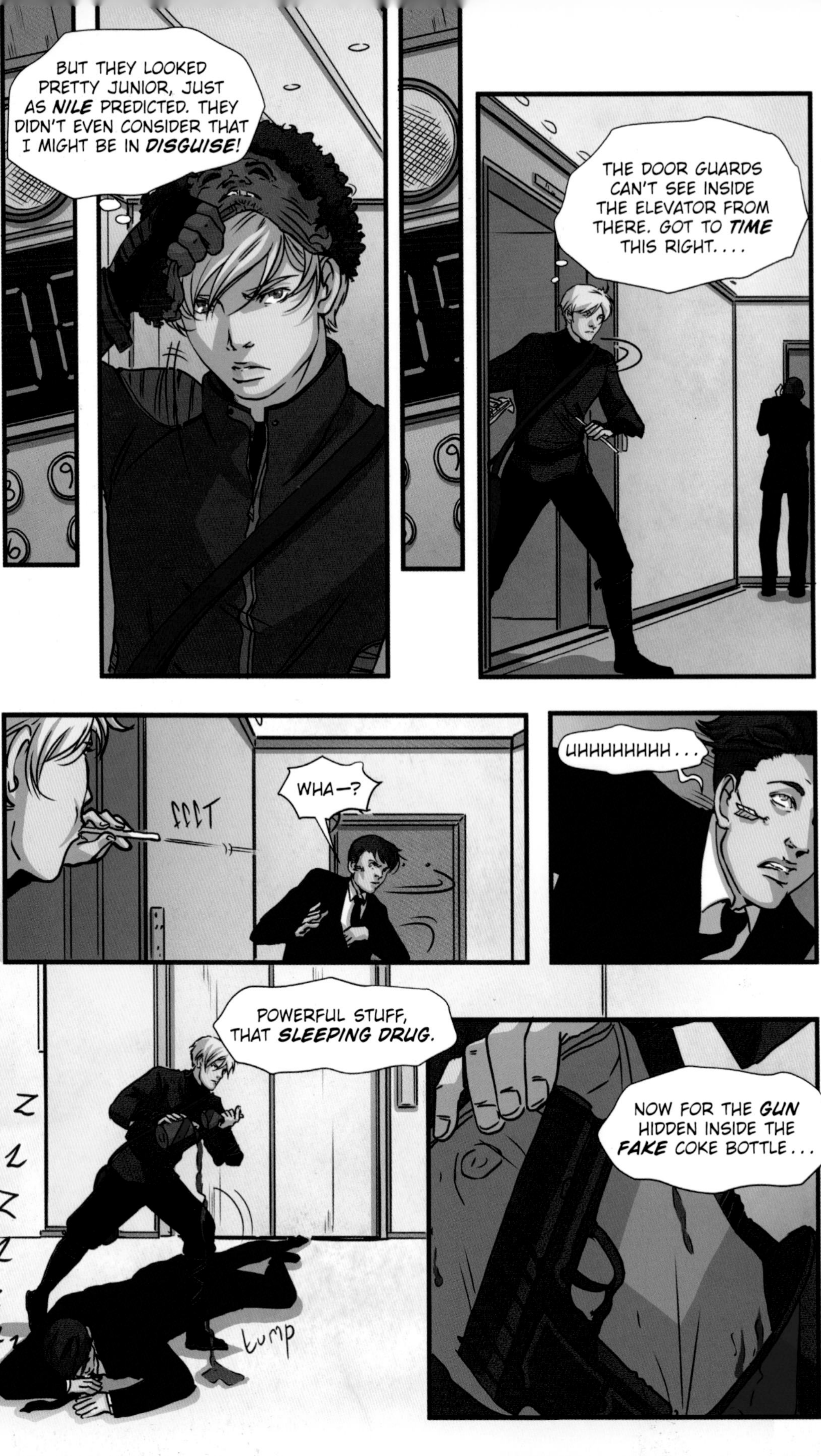
BUT THEY LOOKED PRETTY JUNIOR, JUST AS NILE PREDICTED. THEY DIDN'T EVEN CONSIDER THAT I MIGHT BE IN DISGUISE!
THE DOOR GUARDS CAN'T SEE INSIDE THE ELEVATOR FROM THERE. GOT TO TIME THIS RIGHT. . . .
FFFT
WHA—?
UHHHHHHHH. . .
POWERFUL STUFF, THAT SLEEPING DRUG.
Z Z Z Z Z Z
LUMP
NOW FOR THE GUN HIDDEN INSIDE THE FAKE COKE BOTTLE. . .

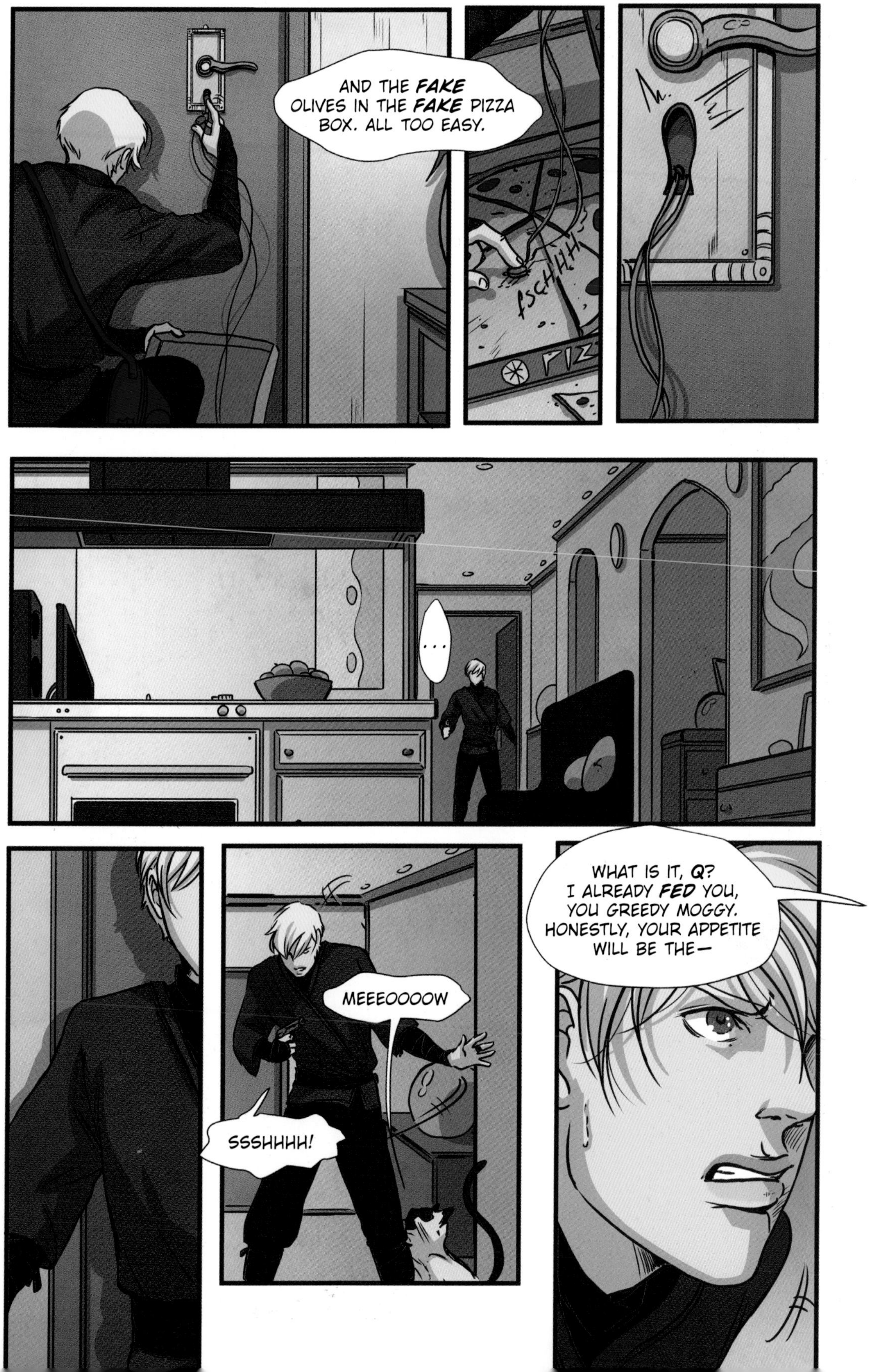
AND THE FAKE OLIVES IN THE FAKE PIZZA BOX. ALL TOO EASY.
FSCHHH
PIZ
...
MEEEOOOOW
SSSHHHH!
WHAT IS IT, Q? I ALREADY FED YOU, YOU GREEDY MOGGY. HONESTLY, YOUR APPETITE WILL BE THE—

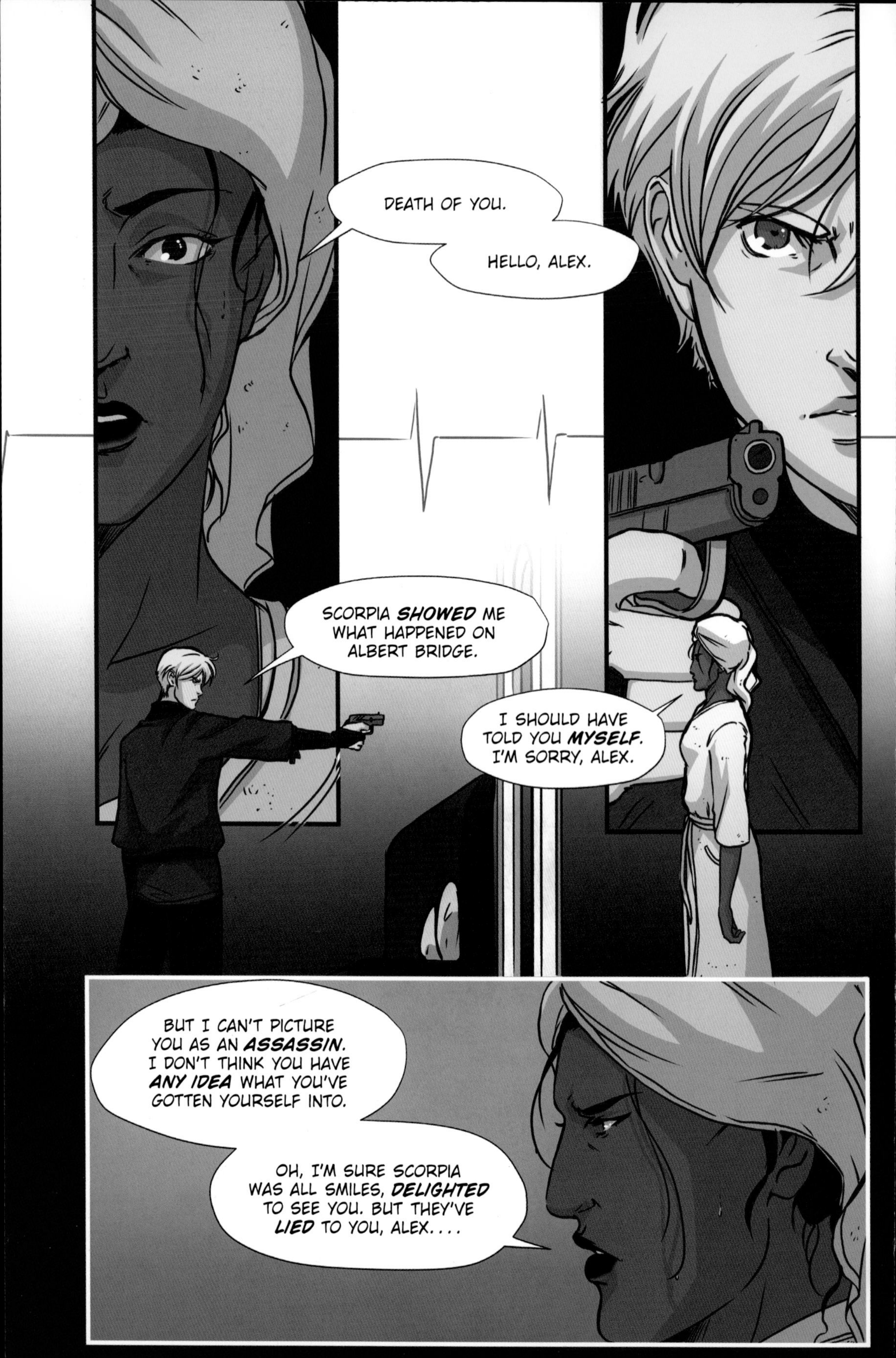
DEATH OF YOU.
HELLO, ALEX.
SCORPIA SHOWED ME WHAT HAPPENED ON ALBERT BRIDGE.
I SHOULD HAVE TOLD YOU MYSELF. I'M SORRY, ALEX.
BUT I CAN'T PICTURE YOU AS AN ASSASSIN. I DON'T THINK YOU HAVE ANY IDEA WHAT YOU'VE GOTTEN YOURSELF INTO.
OH, I'M SURE SCORPIA WAS ALL SMILES, DELIGHTED TO SEE YOU. BUT THEY'VE LIED TO YOU, ALEX. . . .

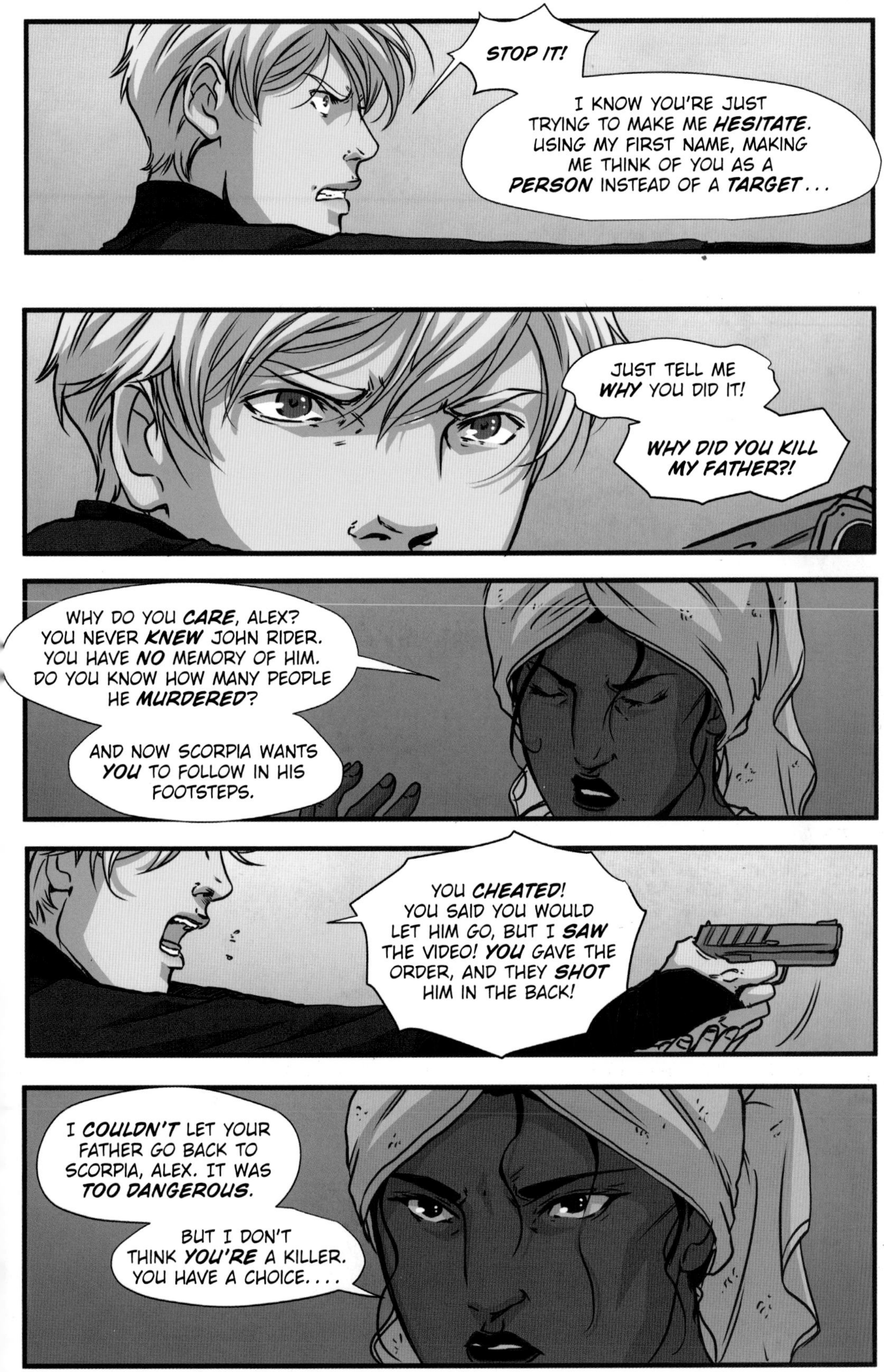
STOP IT!
I KNOW YOU'RE JUST TRYING TO MAKE ME HESITATE. USING MY FIRST NAME, MAKING ME THINK OF YOU AS A PERSON INSTEAD OF A TARGET . . .
JUST TELL ME WHY YOU DID IT!
WHY DID YOU KILL MY FATHER?!
WHY DO YOU CARE, ALEX? YOU NEVER KNEW JOHN RIDER. YOU HAVE NO MEMORY OF HIM. DO YOU KNOW HOW MANY PEOPLE HE MURDERED?
AND NOW SCORPIA WANTS YOU TO FOLLOW IN HIS FOOTSTEPS.
YOU CHEATED! YOU SAID YOU WOULD LET HIM GO, BUT I SAW THE VIDEO! YOU GAVE THE ORDER, AND THEY SHOT HIM IN THE BACK!
I COULDN'T LET YOUR FATHER GO BACK TO SCORPIA, ALEX. IT WAS TOO DANGEROUS.
BUT I DON'T THINK YOU'RE A KILLER. YOU HAVE A CHOICE. . . .

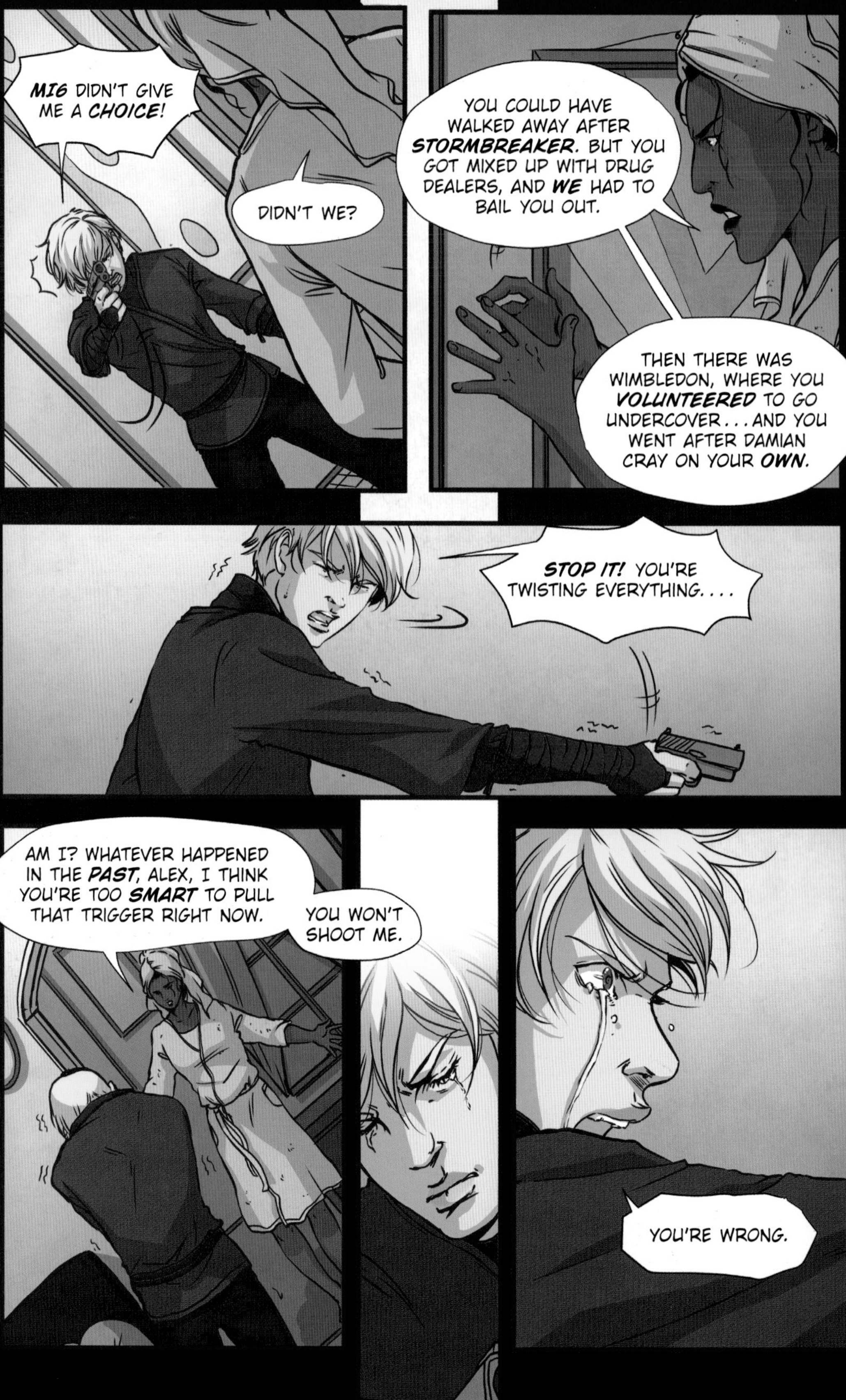
MI6 DIDN'T GIVE ME A CHOICE!
DIDN'T WE?
YOU COULD HAVE WALKED AWAY AFTER STORMBREAKER. BUT YOU GOT MIXED UP WITH DRUG DEALERS, AND WE HAD TO BAIL YOU OUT.
THEN THERE WAS WIMBLEDON, WHERE YOU VOLUNTEERED TO GO UNDERCOVER . . . AND YOU WENT AFTER DAMIAN CRAY ON YOUR OWN.
STOP IT! YOU'RE TWISTING EVERYTHING. . . .
AM I? WHATEVER HAPPENED IN THE PAST, ALEX, I THINK YOU'RE TOO SMART TO PULL THAT TRIGGER RIGHT NOW.
YOU WON'T SHOOT ME.
YOU'RE WRONG.

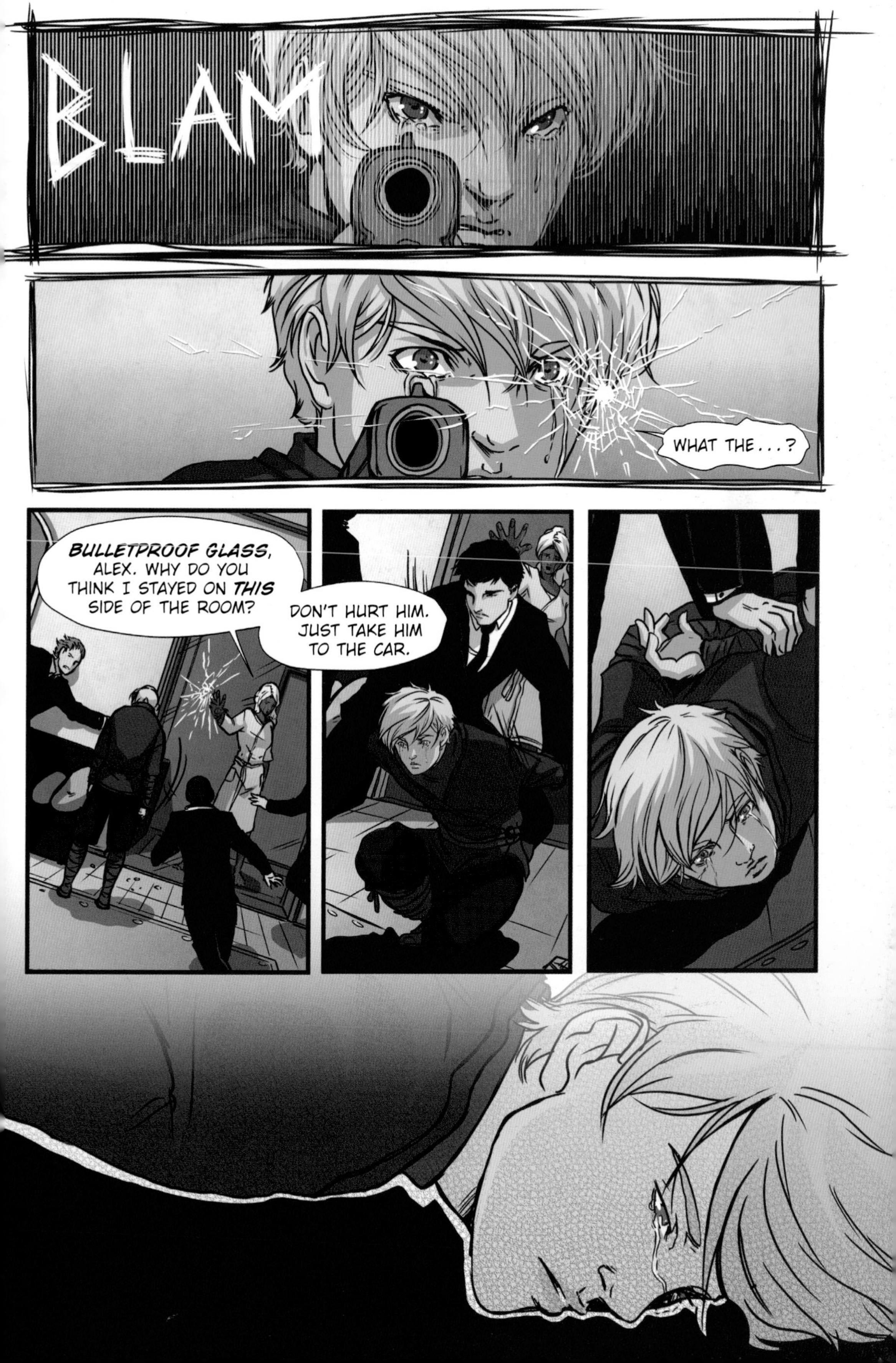
BLAM
WHAT THE . . . ?
BULLETPROOF GLASS, ALEX. WHY DO YOU THINK I STAYED ON THIS SIDE OF THE ROOM?
DON'T HURT HIM. JUST TAKE HIM TO THE CAR.

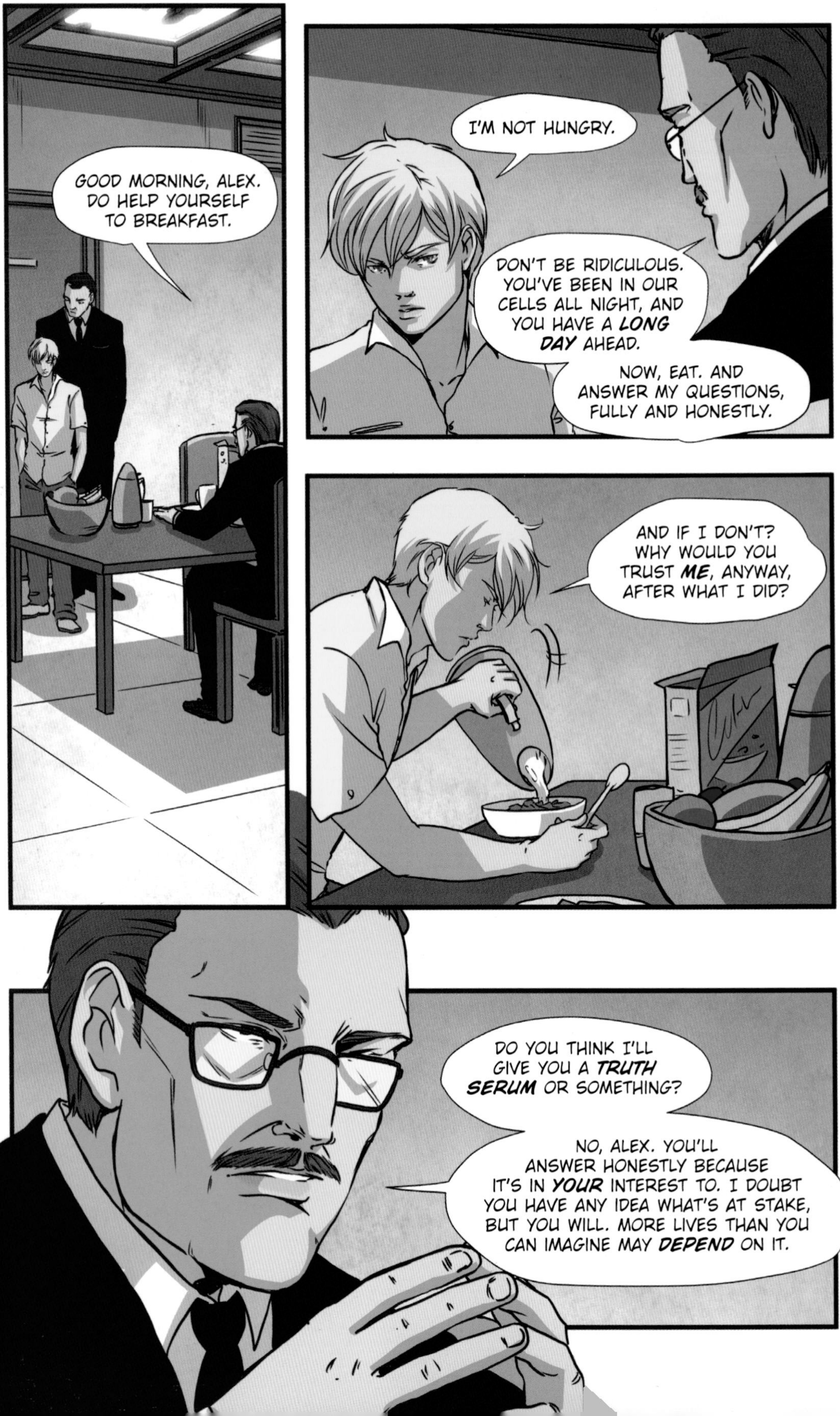

GOOD MORNING, ALEX. DO HELP YOURSELF TO BREAKFAST.
I'M NOT HUNGRY.
DON'T BE RIDICULOUS. YOU'VE BEEN IN OUR CELLS ALL NIGHT, AND YOU HAVE A LONG DAY AHEAD.
NOW, EAT. AND ANSWER MY QUESTIONS, FULLY AND HONESTLY.
AND IF I DON'T? WHY WOULD YOU TRUST ME, ANYWAY, AFTER WHAT I DID?
DO YOU THINK I'LL GIVE YOU A TRUTH SERUM OR SOMETHING?
NO, ALEX. YOU'LL ANSWER HONESTLY BECAUSE IT'S IN YOUR INTEREST TO. I DOUBT YOU HAVE ANY IDEA WHAT'S AT STAKE, BUT YOU WILL. MORE LIVES THAN YOU CAN IMAGINE MAY DEPEND ON IT.

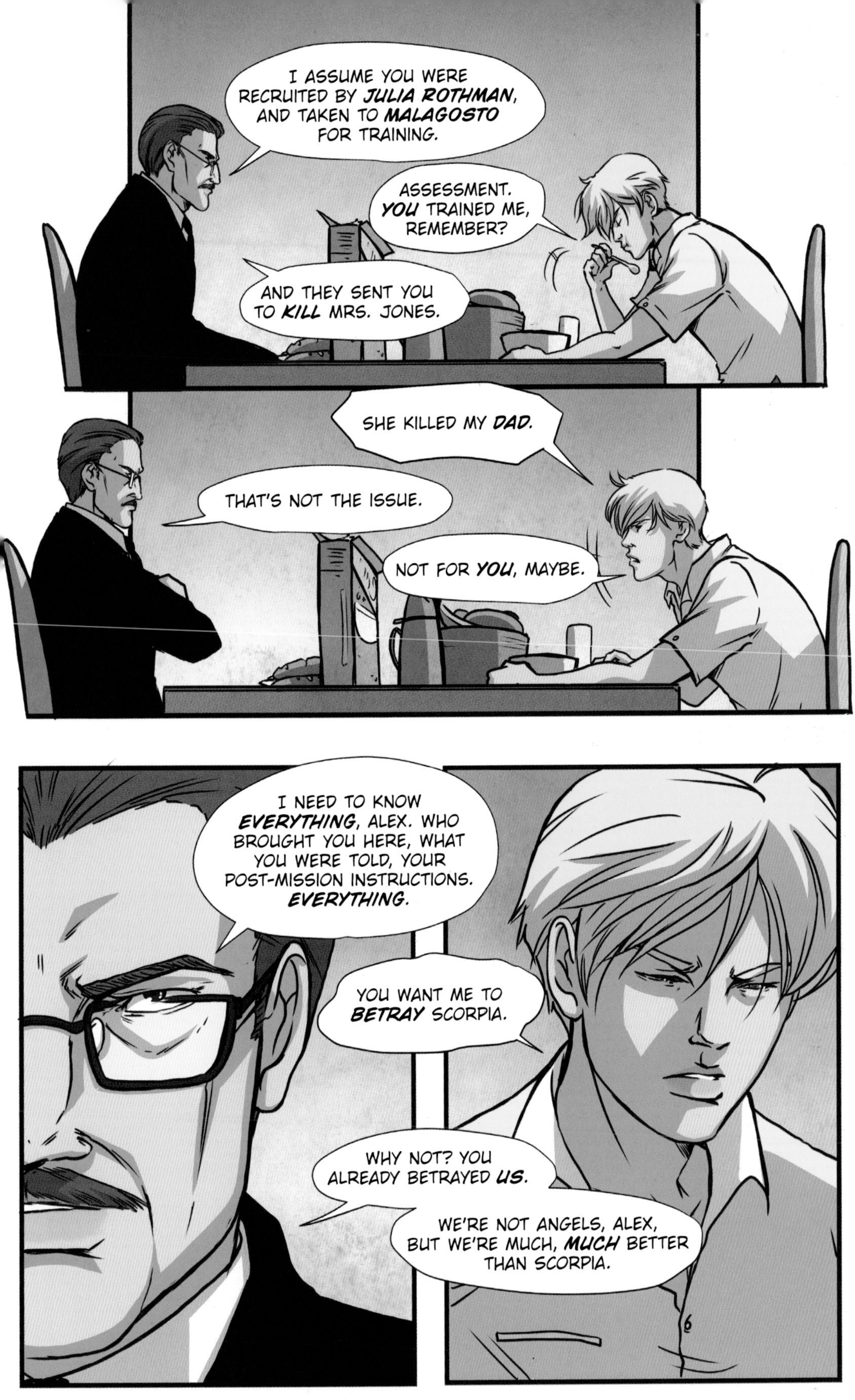
I ASSUME YOU WERE RECRUITED BY JULIA ROTHMAN, AND TAKEN TO MALAGOSTO FOR TRAINING.
ASSESSMENT. YOU TRAINED ME, REMEMBER?
AND THEY SENT YOU TO KILL MRS. JONES.
SHE KILLED MY DAD.
THAT'S NOT THE ISSUE.
NOT FOR YOU, MAYBE.
I NEED TO KNOW EVERYTHING, ALEX. WHO BROUGHT YOU HERE, WHAT YOU WERE TOLD, YOUR POST-MISSION INSTRUCTIONS. EVERYTHING.
YOU WANT ME TO BETRAY SCORPIA.
WHY NOT? YOU ALREADY BETRAYED US.
WE'RE NOT ANGELS, ALEX, BUT WE'RE MUCH, MUCH BETTER THAN SCORPIA.

TWO AGENTS BROUGHT ME IN THROUGH **HEATHROW**, DISGUISED AS AN **ITALIAN** FAMILY. I DON'T KNOW THEIR NAMES.

THEY HAD A **LAYOUT** OF MRS. JONES'S APARTMENT. EVERYTHING EXCEPT FOR THAT **GLASS PANEL**. ALL I HAD TO DO WAS WAIT FOR HER.

THEY GAVE ME A **NUMBER** TO CALL WHEN I'D KILLED HER. BUT THEY'LL KNOW **YOU'VE** GOT ME NOW.

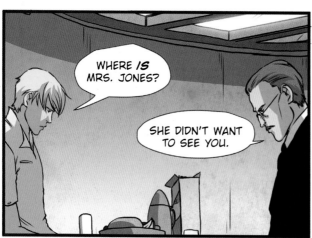

WHERE **IS** MRS. JONES?

SHE DIDN'T WANT TO SEE YOU.

I JUST WANT TO GO BACK TO SCHOOL. I DON'T WANT TO SEE **ANY** OF YOU, **EVER** AGAIN. NOT YOU, NOT SCORPIA—YOU CAN **ALL** GO TO **HELL**!

ALEX . . . YOU'VE BEEN **MORE** USEFUL TO US THAN I COULD POSSIBLY HAVE CALCULATED.

BUT IN TRUTH, I WISH WE HAD NEVER MET, BECAUSE YOU DON'T BELONG IN MY WORLD ANY MORE THAN I BELONG IN YOURS.

UNFORTUNATELY, I **CAN'T** LET YOU GO BACK TO SCHOOL. . . .

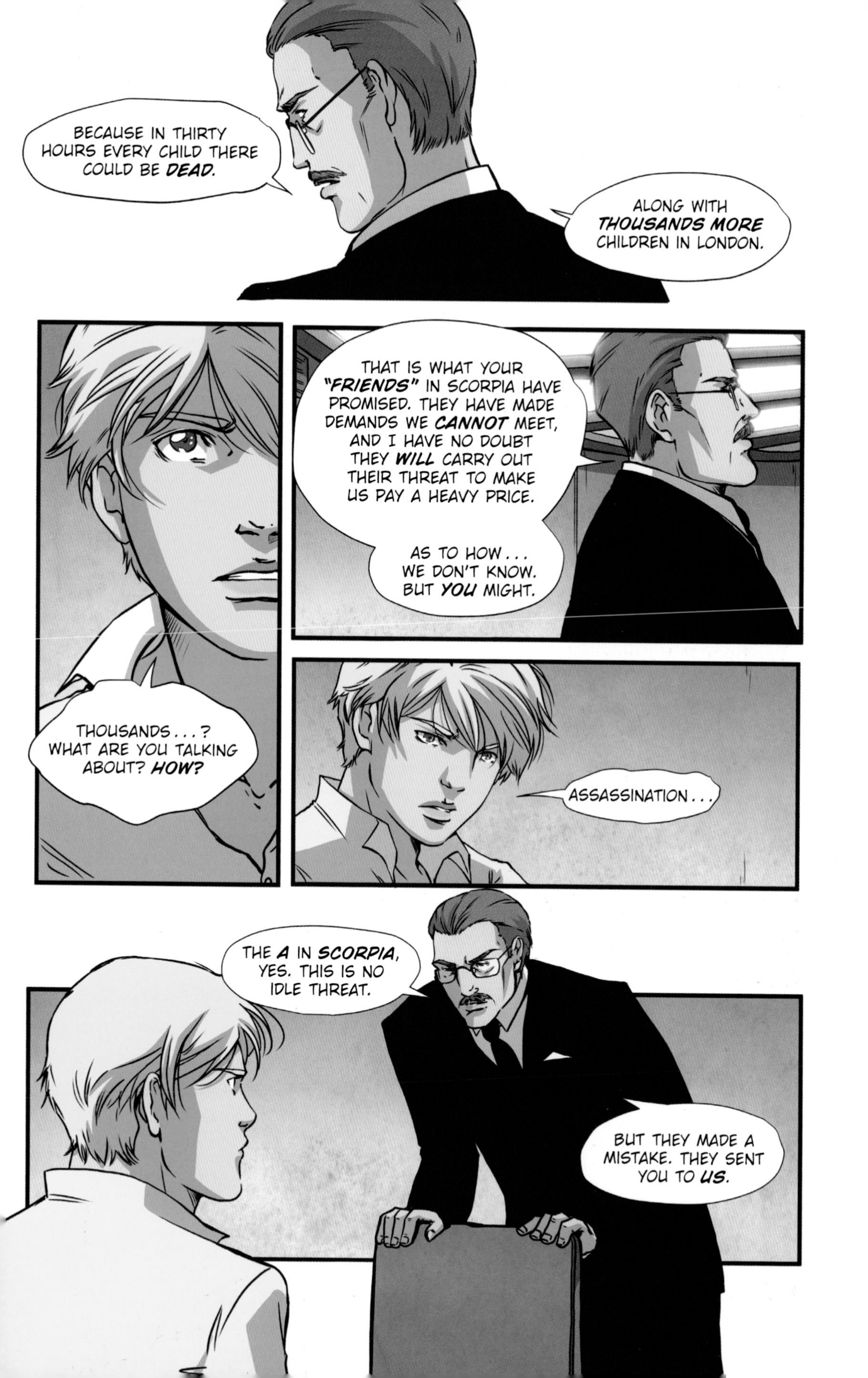
BECAUSE IN THIRTY HOURS EVERY CHILD THERE COULD BE **DEAD.**
ALONG WITH **THOUSANDS MORE** CHILDREN IN LONDON.
THOUSANDS . . . ? WHAT ARE YOU TALKING ABOUT? **HOW?**
THAT IS WHAT YOUR **"FRIENDS"** IN SCORPIA HAVE PROMISED. THEY HAVE MADE DEMANDS WE **CANNOT** MEET, AND I HAVE NO DOUBT THEY **WILL** CARRY OUT THEIR THREAT TO MAKE US PAY A HEAVY PRICE.
AS TO HOW . . . WE DON'T KNOW. BUT **YOU** MIGHT.
ASSASSINATION . . .
THE **A** IN **SCORPIA**, YES. THIS IS NO IDLE THREAT.
BUT THEY MADE A MISTAKE. THEY SENT YOU TO **US**.

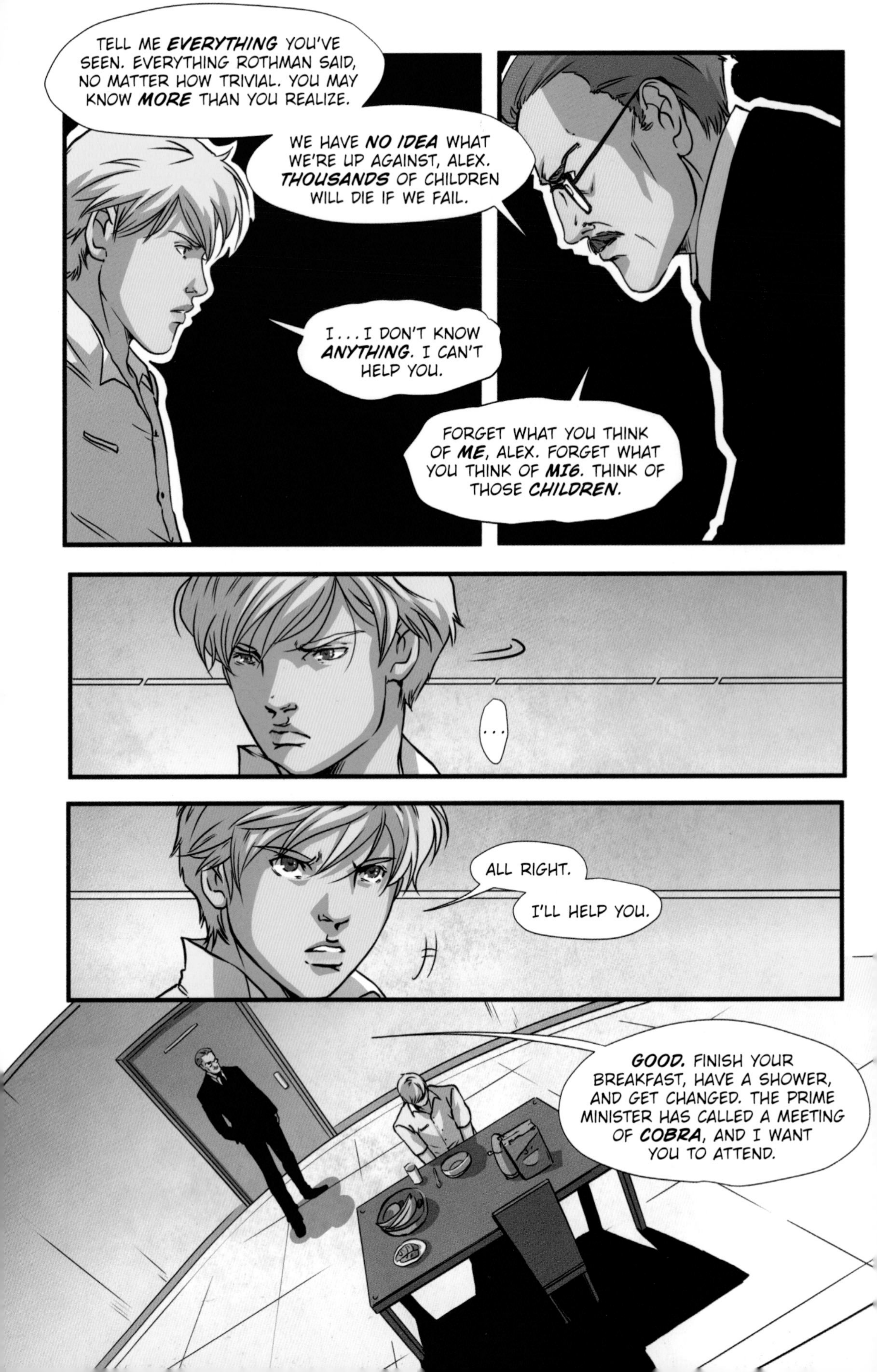
TELL ME EVERYTHING YOU'VE SEEN. EVERYTHING ROTHMAN SAID, NO MATTER HOW TRIVIAL. YOU MAY KNOW MORE THAN YOU REALIZE.
WE HAVE NO IDEA WHAT WE'RE UP AGAINST, ALEX. THOUSANDS OF CHILDREN WILL DIE IF WE FAIL.
I . . . I DON'T KNOW ANYTHING. I CAN'T HELP YOU.
FORGET WHAT YOU THINK OF ME, ALEX. FORGET WHAT YOU THINK OF MI6. THINK OF THOSE CHILDREN.
. . .
ALL RIGHT.
I'LL HELP YOU.
GOOD. FINISH YOUR BREAKFAST, HAVE A SHOWER, AND GET CHANGED. THE PRIME MINISTER HAS CALLED A MEETING OF COBRA, AND I WANT YOU TO ATTEND.

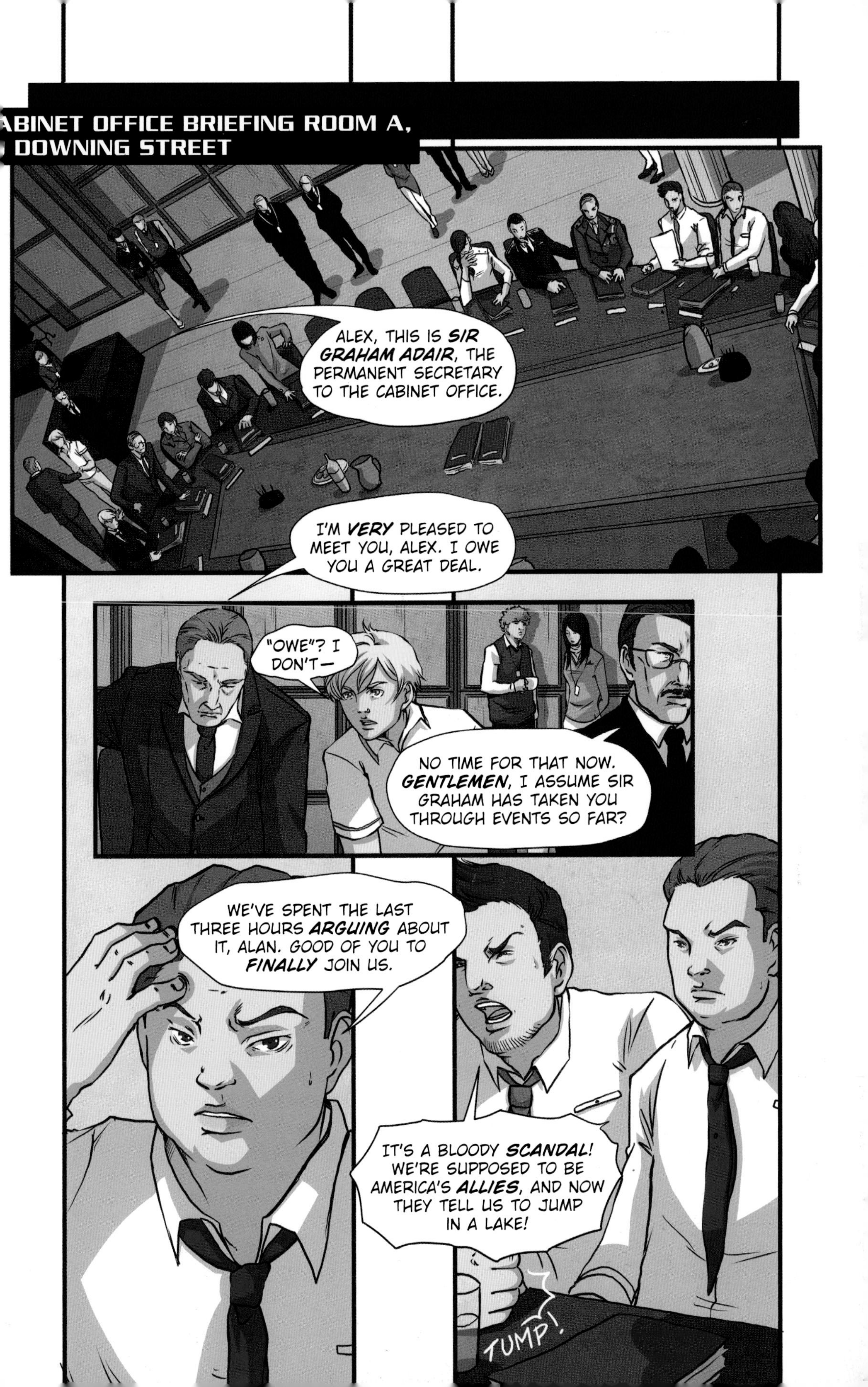
ABINET OFFICE BRIEFING ROOM A,
DOWNING STREET
ALEX, THIS IS SIR GRAHAM ADAIR, THE PERMANENT SECRETARY TO THE CABINET OFFICE.
I'M VERY PLEASED TO MEET YOU, ALEX. I OWE YOU A GREAT DEAL.
"OWE"? I DON'T—
NO TIME FOR THAT NOW. GENTLEMEN, I ASSUME SIR GRAHAM HAS TAKEN YOU THROUGH EVENTS SO FAR?
WE'VE SPENT THE LAST THREE HOURS ARGUING ABOUT IT, ALAN. GOOD OF YOU TO FINALLY JOIN US.
IT'S A BLOODY SCANDAL! WE'RE SUPPOSED TO BE AMERICA'S ALLIES, AND NOW THEY TELL US TO JUMP IN A LAKE!
TUMP!

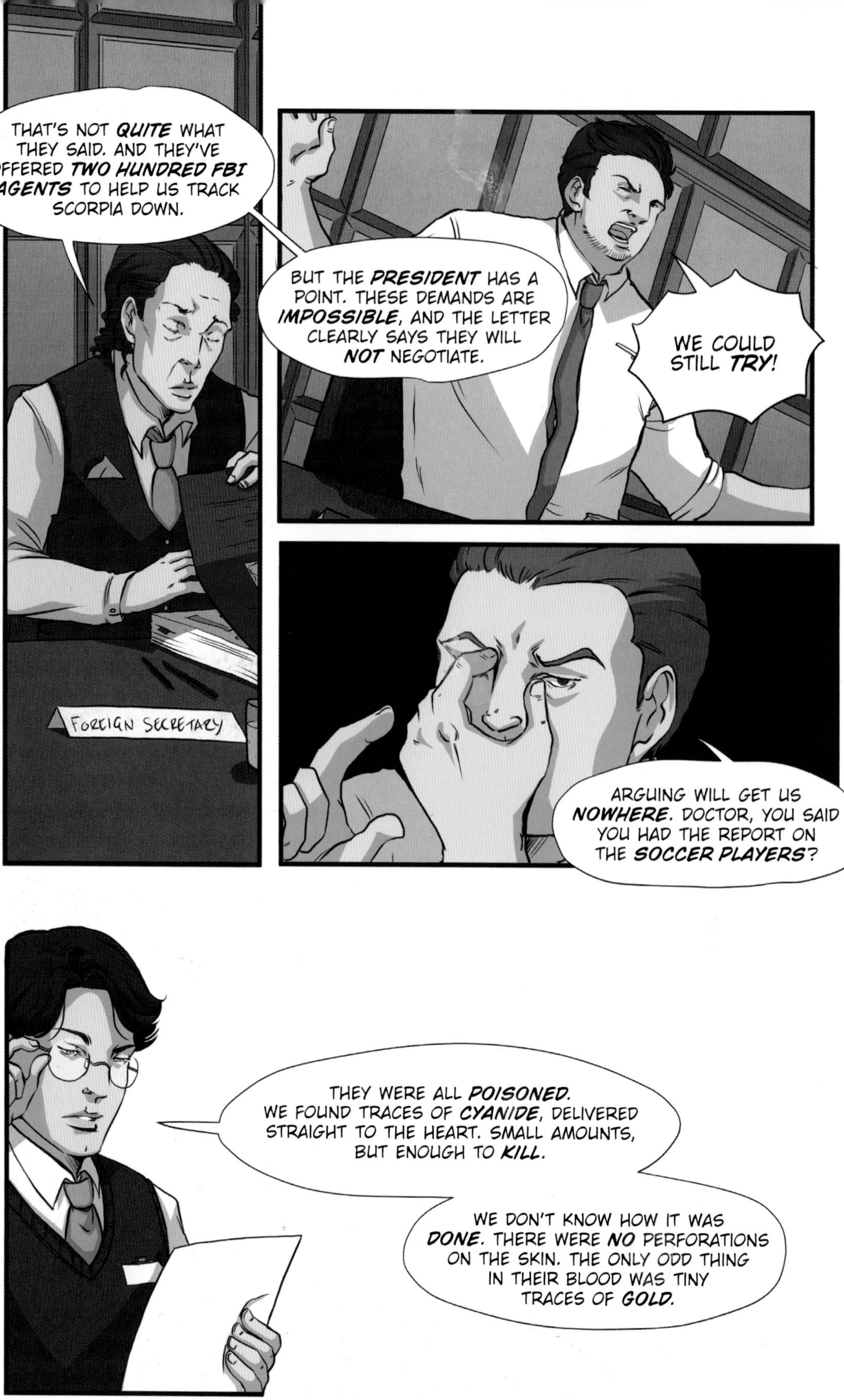
THAT'S NOT QUITE WHAT THEY SAID. AND THEY'VE OFFERED TWO HUNDRED FBI AGENTS TO HELP US TRACK SCORPIA DOWN.
FOREIGN SECRETARY
BUT THE PRESIDENT HAS A POINT. THESE DEMANDS ARE IMPOSSIBLE, AND THE LETTER CLEARLY SAYS THEY WILL NOT NEGOTIATE.
WE COULD STILL TRY!
ARGUING WILL GET US NOWHERE. DOCTOR, YOU SAID YOU HAD THE REPORT ON THE SOCCER PLAYERS?
THEY WERE ALL POISONED. WE FOUND TRACES OF CYANIDE, DELIVERED STRAIGHT TO THE HEART. SMALL AMOUNTS, BUT ENOUGH TO KILL.
WE DON'T KNOW HOW IT WAS DONE. THERE WERE NO PERFORATIONS ON THE SKIN. THE ONLY ODD THING IN THEIR BLOOD WAS TINY TRACES OF GOLD.

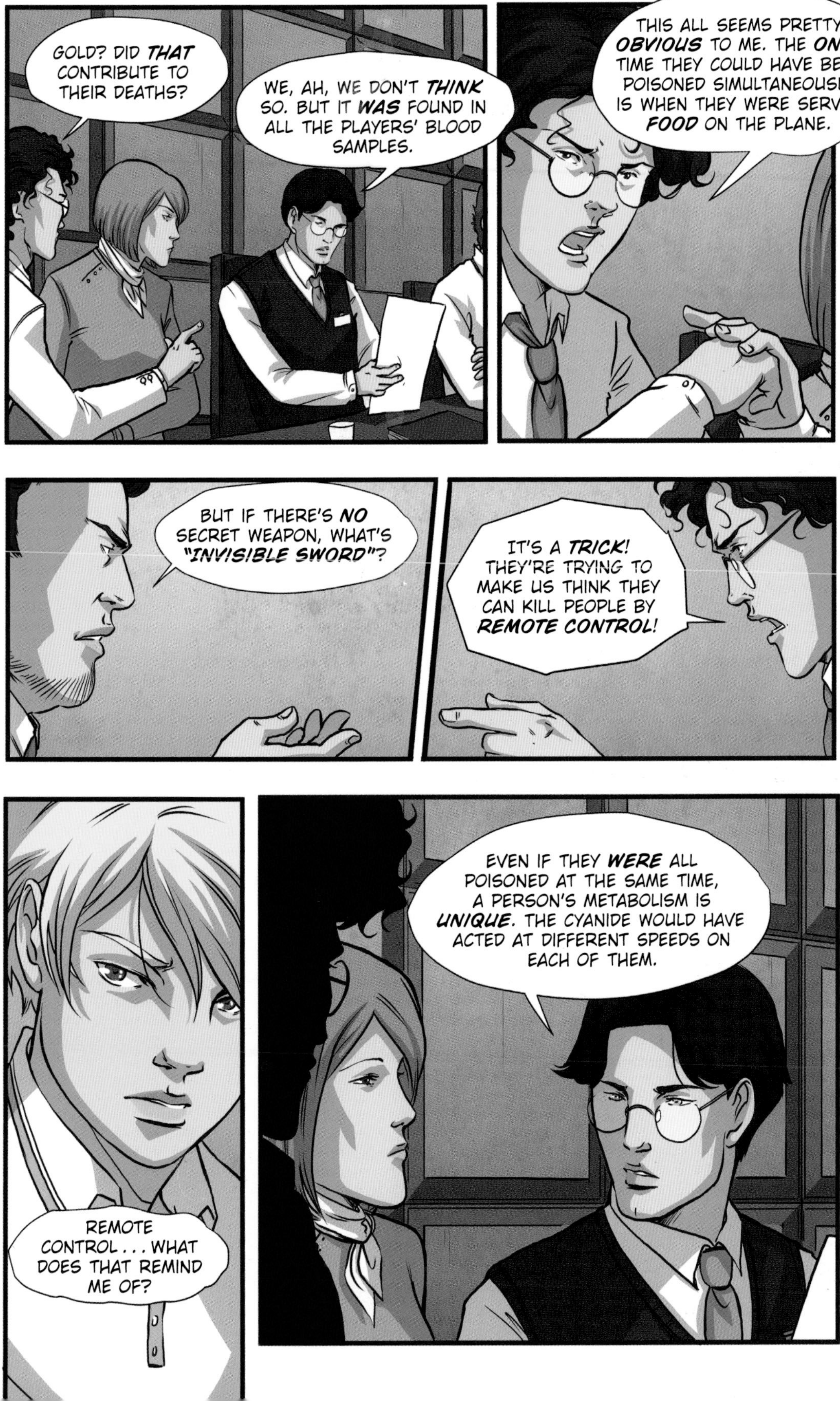
GOLD? DID THAT CONTRIBUTE TO THEIR DEATHS?
WE, AH, WE DON'T THINK SO. BUT IT WAS FOUND IN ALL THE PLAYERS' BLOOD SAMPLES.
THIS ALL SEEMS PRETTY OBVIOUS TO ME. THE ONLY TIME THEY COULD HAVE BEEN POISONED SIMULTANEOUSLY IS WHEN THEY WERE SERVED FOOD ON THE PLANE.
BUT IF THERE'S NO SECRET WEAPON, WHAT'S "INVISIBLE SWORD"?
IT'S A TRICK! THEY'RE TRYING TO MAKE US THINK THEY CAN KILL PEOPLE BY REMOTE CONTROL!
REMOTE CONTROL . . . WHAT DOES THAT REMIND ME OF?
EVEN IF THEY WERE ALL POISONED AT THE SAME TIME, A PERSON'S METABOLISM IS UNIQUE. THE CYANIDE WOULD HAVE ACTED AT DIFFERENT SPEEDS ON EACH OF THEM.

THEY WERE ALL *ATHLETES*! NOT VERY GOOD ATHLETES, BUT STILL. . . . THEIR METABOLISMS WOULD BE SIMILAR ENOUGH. THE WHOLE THING IS A *BLUFF*!

THAT ISN'T *NORMALLY* SCORPIA'S WAY.

WE'VE DEALT WITH THEM BEFORE, AND THEY'VE *NEVER* YET MADE A HOLLOW THREAT.

YOU WERE *AT* HEATHROW, ALAN. WHAT DO *YOU* THINK HAPPENED?

I DON'T KNOW.

WELL, THAT'S *VERY* HELPFUL, ISN'T IT? SO MUCH FOR THE *"INTELLIGENCE"* SERVICES!

COULD YOU AT LEAST TELL US WHY YOU'VE BROUGHT YOUR *SON* ALONG?

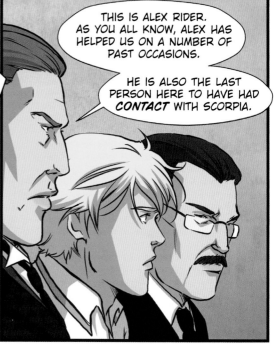

THIS IS ALEX RIDER. AS YOU ALL KNOW, ALEX HAS HELPED US ON A NUMBER OF PAST OCCASIONS.

HE IS ALSO THE LAST PERSON HERE TO HAVE HAD *CONTACT* WITH SCORPIA.

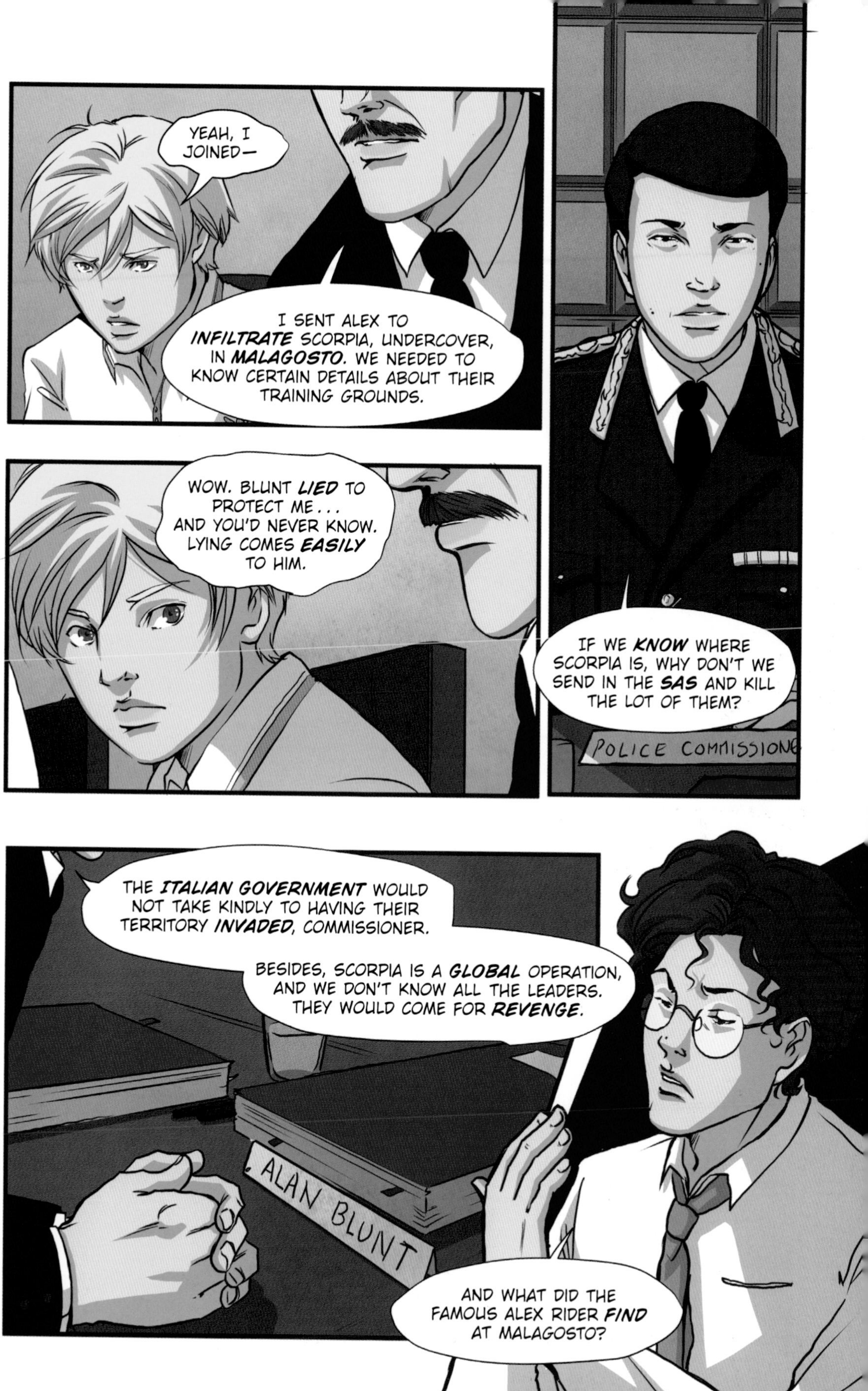
YEAH, I JOINED—
I SENT ALEX TO INFILTRATE SCORPIA, UNDERCOVER, IN MALAGOSTO. WE NEEDED TO KNOW CERTAIN DETAILS ABOUT THEIR TRAINING GROUNDS.
WOW. BLUNT LIED TO PROTECT ME . . . AND YOU'D NEVER KNOW. LYING COMES EASILY TO HIM.
IF WE KNOW WHERE SCORPIA IS, WHY DON'T WE SEND IN THE SAS AND KILL THE LOT OF THEM?
POLICE COMMISSIONE
THE ITALIAN GOVERNMENT WOULD NOT TAKE KINDLY TO HAVING THEIR TERRITORY INVADED, COMMISSIONER.
BESIDES, SCORPIA IS A GLOBAL OPERATION, AND WE DON'T KNOW ALL THE LEADERS. THEY WOULD COME FOR REVENGE.
ALAN BLUNT
AND WHAT DID THE FAMOUS ALEX RIDER FIND AT MALAGOSTO?

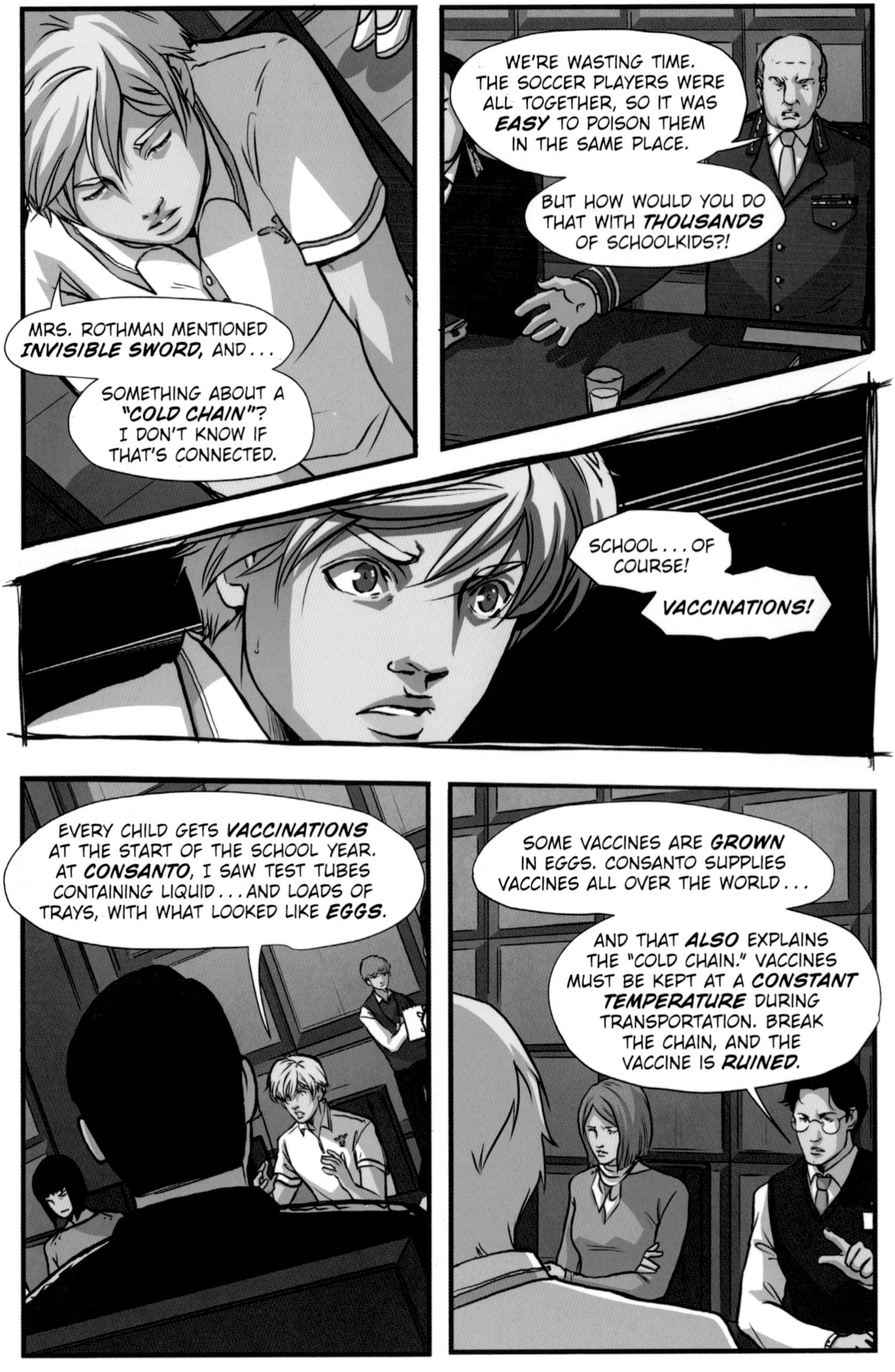
MRS. ROTHMAN MENTIONED INVISIBLE SWORD, AND . . .
SOMETHING ABOUT A "COLD CHAIN"? I DON'T KNOW IF THAT'S CONNECTED.
WE'RE WASTING TIME. THE SOCCER PLAYERS WERE ALL TOGETHER, SO IT WAS EASY TO POISON THEM IN THE SAME PLACE.
BUT HOW WOULD YOU DO THAT WITH THOUSANDS OF SCHOOLKIDS?!
SCHOOL . . . OF COURSE!
VACCINATIONS!
EVERY CHILD GETS VACCINATIONS AT THE START OF THE SCHOOL YEAR. AT CONSANTO, I SAW TEST TUBES CONTAINING LIQUID . . . AND LOADS OF TRAYS, WITH WHAT LOOKED LIKE EGGS.
SOME VACCINES ARE GROWN IN EGGS. CONSANTO SUPPLIES VACCINES ALL OVER THE WORLD . . .
AND THAT ALSO EXPLAINS THE "COLD CHAIN." VACCINES MUST BE KEPT AT A CONSTANT TEMPERATURE DURING TRANSPORTATION. BREAK THE CHAIN, AND THE VACCINE IS RUINED.

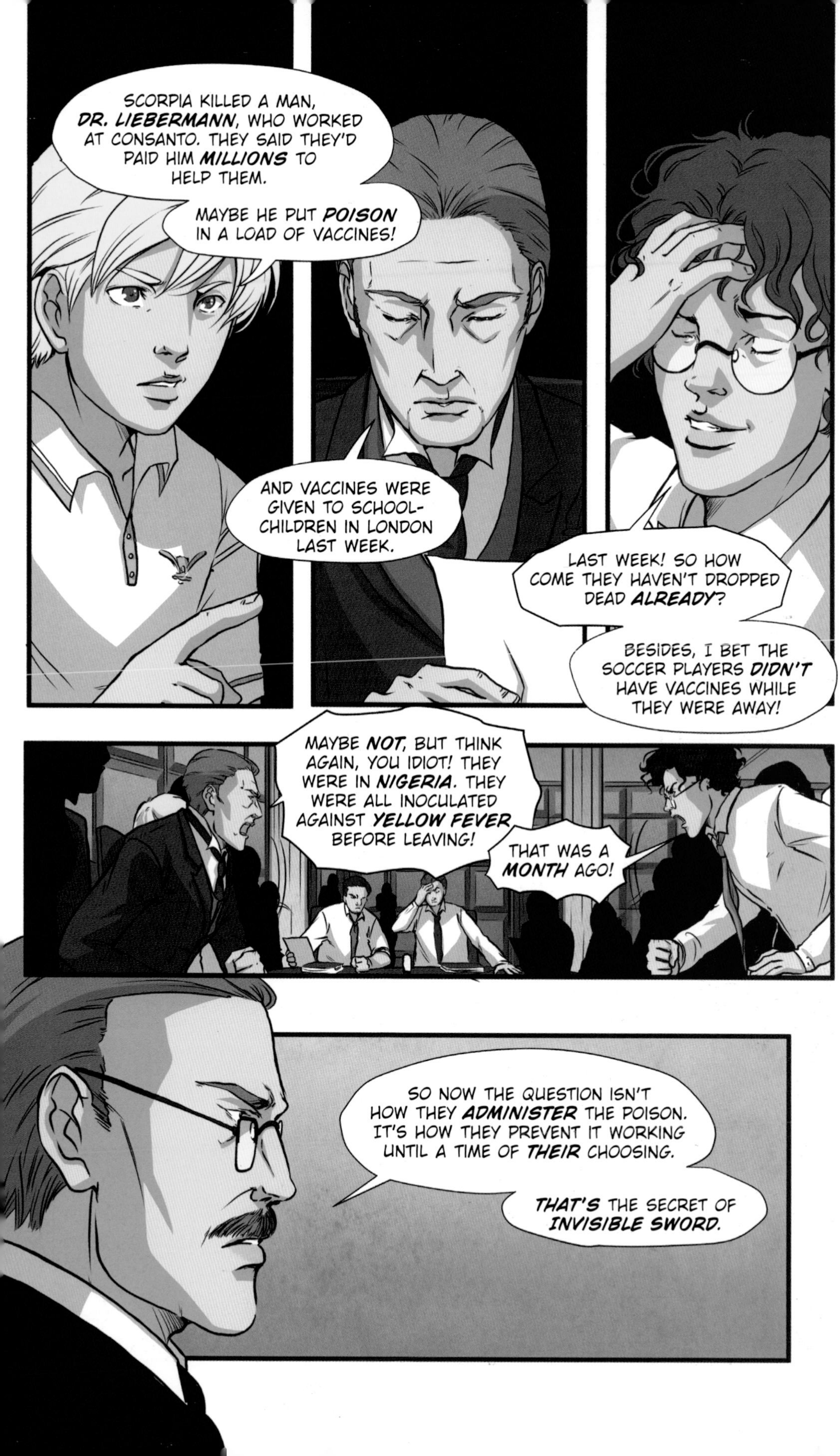
SCORPIA KILLED A MAN, DR. LIEBERMANN, WHO WORKED AT CONSANTO. THEY SAID THEY'D PAID HIM MILLIONS TO HELP THEM.
MAYBE HE PUT POISON IN A LOAD OF VACCINES!
AND VACCINES WERE GIVEN TO SCHOOL-CHILDREN IN LONDON LAST WEEK.
LAST WEEK! SO HOW COME THEY HAVEN'T DROPPED DEAD ALREADY?
BESIDES, I BET THE SOCCER PLAYERS DIDN'T HAVE VACCINES WHILE THEY WERE AWAY!
MAYBE NOT, BUT THINK AGAIN, YOU IDIOT! THEY WERE IN NIGERIA. THEY WERE ALL INOCULATED AGAINST YELLOW FEVER BEFORE LEAVING!
THAT WAS A MONTH AGO!
SO NOW THE QUESTION ISN'T HOW THEY ADMINISTER THE POISON. IT'S HOW THEY PREVENT IT WORKING UNTIL A TIME OF THEIR CHOOSING.
THAT'S THE SECRET OF INVISIBLE SWORD.

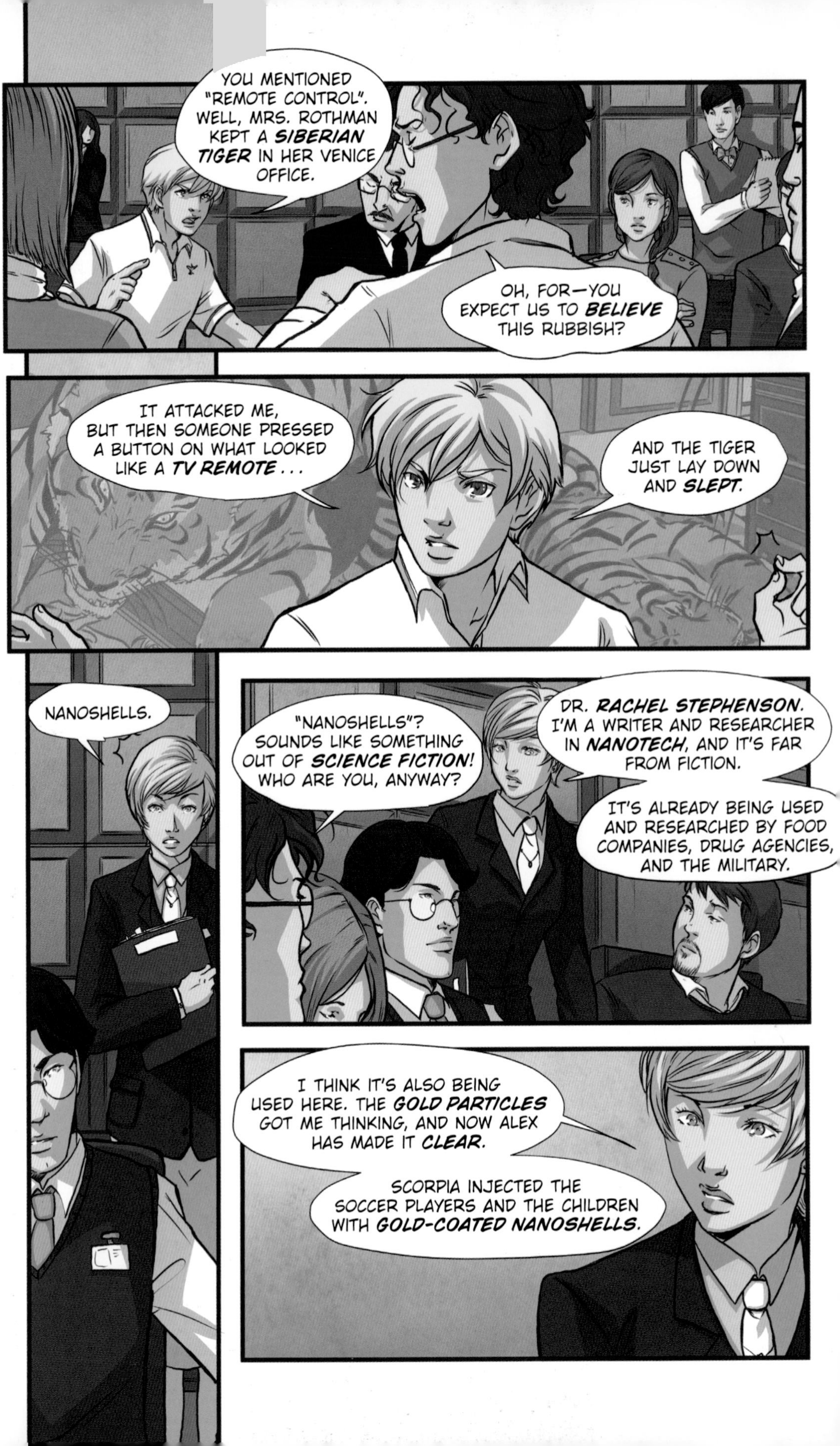
YOU MENTIONED "REMOTE CONTROL". WELL, MRS. ROTHMAN KEPT A SIBERIAN TIGER IN HER VENICE OFFICE.
OH, FOR—YOU EXPECT US TO BELIEVE THIS RUBBISH?
IT ATTACKED ME, BUT THEN SOMEONE PRESSED A BUTTON ON WHAT LOOKED LIKE A TV REMOTE . . .
AND THE TIGER JUST LAY DOWN AND SLEPT.
NANOSHELLS.
"NANOSHELLS"? SOUNDS LIKE SOMETHING OUT OF SCIENCE FICTION! WHO ARE YOU, ANYWAY?
DR. RACHEL STEPHENSON. I'M A WRITER AND RESEARCHER IN NANOTECH, AND IT'S FAR FROM FICTION.
IT'S ALREADY BEING USED AND RESEARCHED BY FOOD COMPANIES, DRUG AGENCIES, AND THE MILITARY.
I THINK IT'S ALSO BEING USED HERE. THE GOLD PARTICLES GOT ME THINKING, AND NOW ALEX HAS MADE IT CLEAR.
SCORPIA INJECTED THE SOCCER PLAYERS AND THE CHILDREN WITH GOLD-COATED NANOSHELLS.

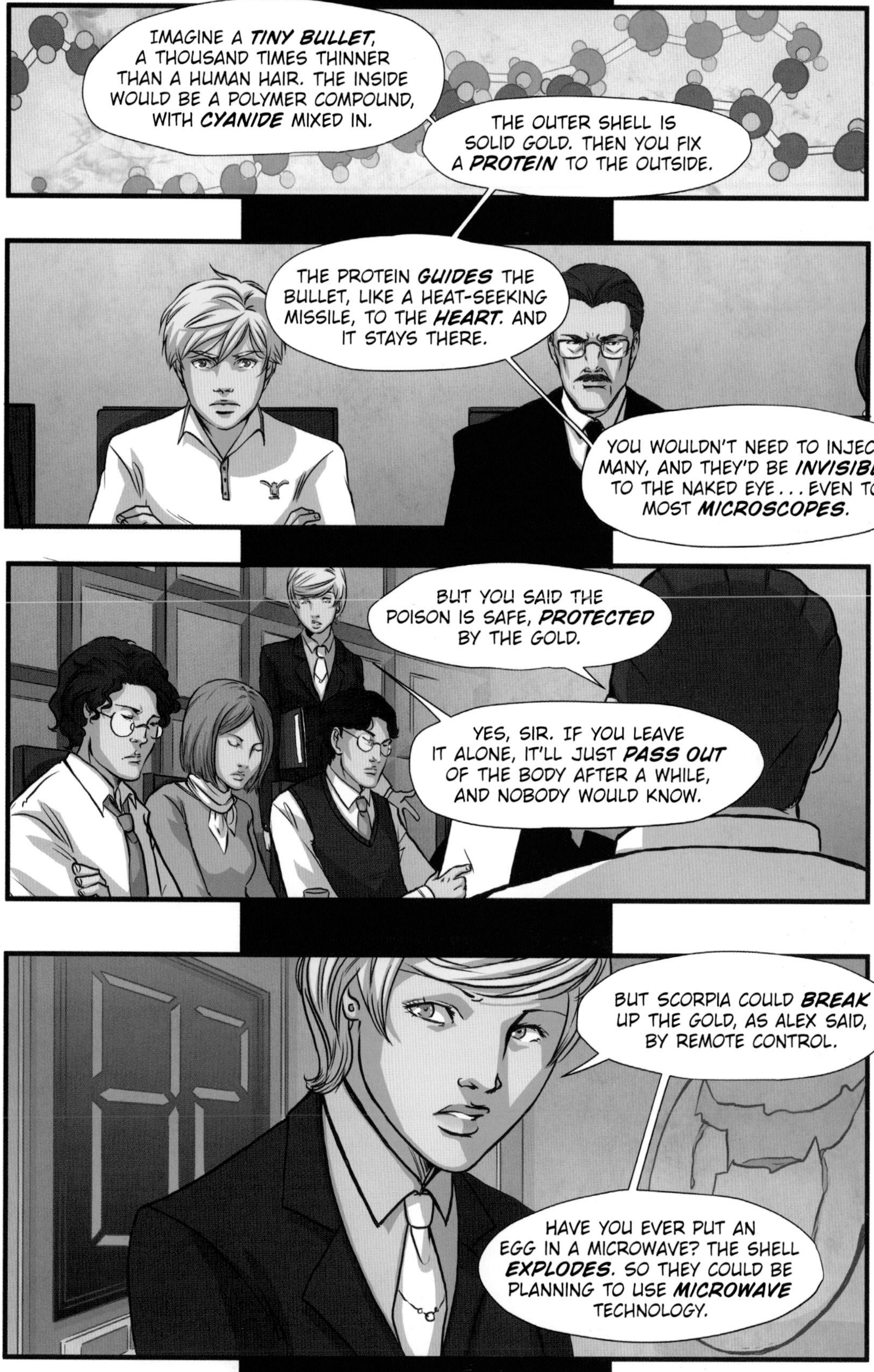
IMAGINE A TINY BULLET, A THOUSAND TIMES THINNER THAN A HUMAN HAIR. THE INSIDE WOULD BE A POLYMER COMPOUND, WITH CYANIDE MIXED IN.
THE OUTER SHELL IS SOLID GOLD. THEN YOU FIX A PROTEIN TO THE OUTSIDE.
THE PROTEIN GUIDES THE BULLET, LIKE A HEAT-SEEKING MISSILE, TO THE HEART. AND IT STAYS THERE.
YOU WOULDN'T NEED TO INJECT MANY, AND THEY'D BE INVISIBLE TO THE NAKED EYE . . . EVEN TO MOST MICROSCOPES.
BUT YOU SAID THE POISON IS SAFE, PROTECTED BY THE GOLD.
YES, SIR. IF YOU LEAVE IT ALONE, IT'LL JUST PASS OUT OF THE BODY AFTER A WHILE, AND NOBODY WOULD KNOW.
BUT SCORPIA COULD BREAK UP THE GOLD, AS ALEX SAID, BY REMOTE CONTROL.
HAVE YOU EVER PUT AN EGG IN A MICROWAVE? THE SHELL EXPLODES. SO THEY COULD BE PLANNING TO USE MICROWAVE TECHNOLOGY.

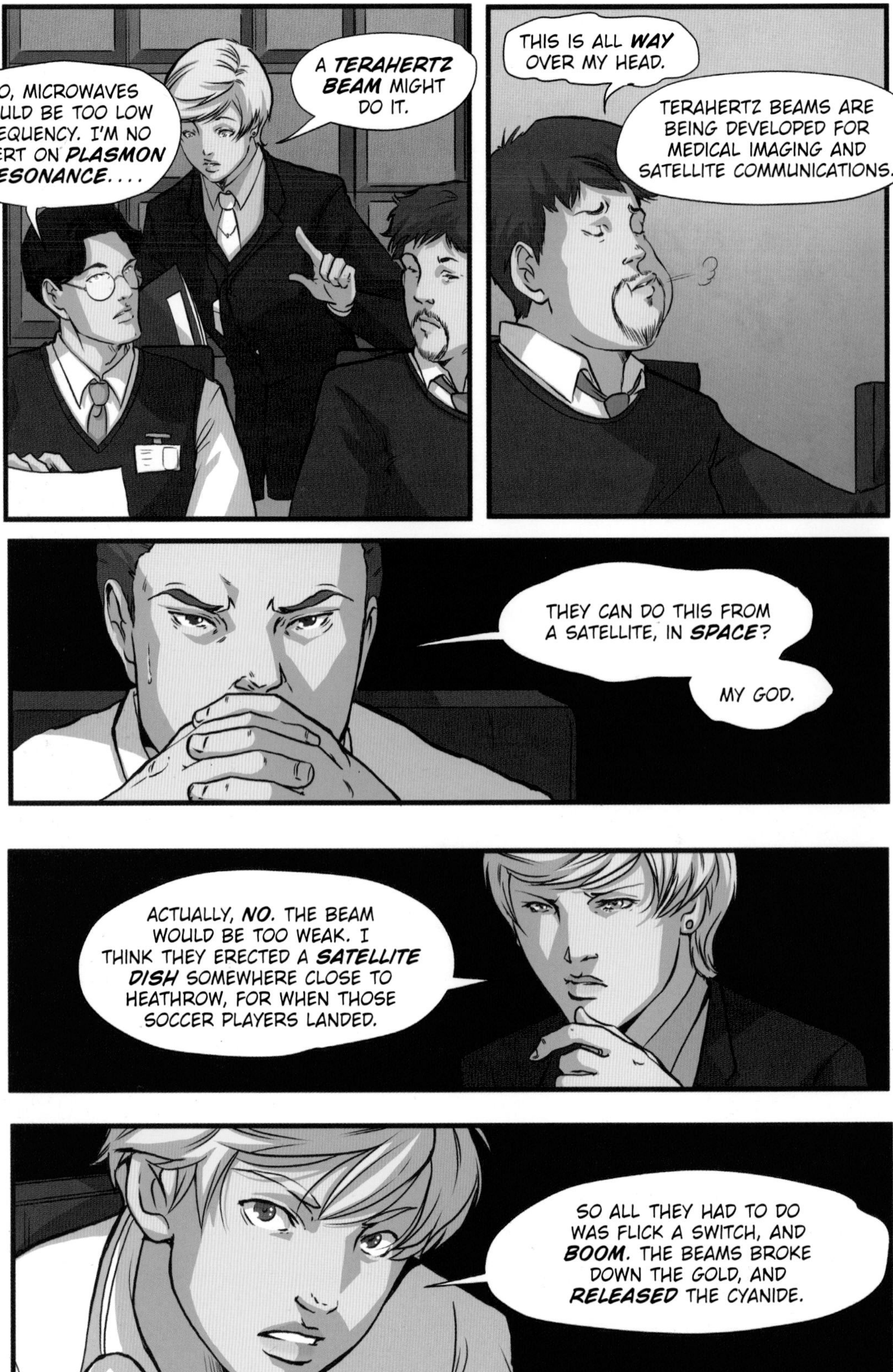
NO, MICROWAVES WOULD BE TOO LOW FREQUENCY. I'M NO EXPERT ON PLASMON RESONANCE....
A TERAHERTZ BEAM MIGHT DO IT.
THIS IS ALL WAY OVER MY HEAD.
TERAHERTZ BEAMS ARE BEING DEVELOPED FOR MEDICAL IMAGING AND SATELLITE COMMUNICATIONS.
THEY CAN DO THIS FROM A SATELLITE, IN SPACE?
MY GOD.
ACTUALLY, NO. THE BEAM WOULD BE TOO WEAK. I THINK THEY ERECTED A SATELLITE DISH SOMEWHERE CLOSE TO HEATHROW, FOR WHEN THOSE SOCCER PLAYERS LANDED.
SO ALL THEY HAD TO DO WAS FLICK A SWITCH, AND BOOM. THE BEAMS BROKE DOWN THE GOLD, AND RELEASED THE CYANIDE.

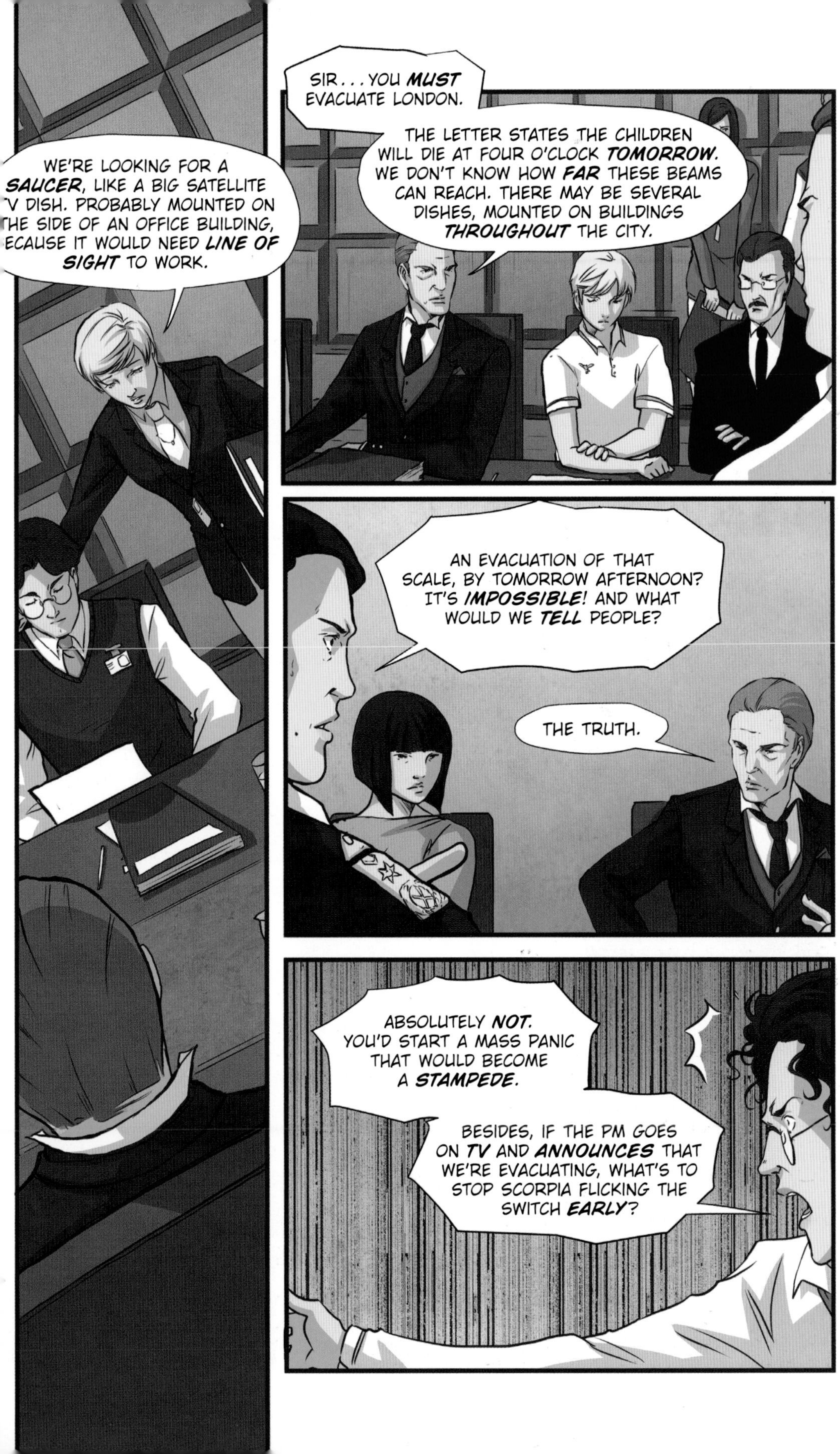
WE'RE LOOKING FOR A SAUCER, LIKE A BIG SATELLITE 'V DISH. PROBABLY MOUNTED ON HE SIDE OF AN OFFICE BUILDING, ECAUSE IT WOULD NEED LINE OF SIGHT TO WORK.
SIR . . . YOU MUST EVACUATE LONDON.
THE LETTER STATES THE CHILDREN WILL DIE AT FOUR O'CLOCK TOMORROW. WE DON'T KNOW HOW FAR THESE BEAMS CAN REACH. THERE MAY BE SEVERAL DISHES, MOUNTED ON BUILDINGS THROUGHOUT THE CITY.
AN EVACUATION OF THAT SCALE, BY TOMORROW AFTERNOON? IT'S IMPOSSIBLE! AND WHAT WOULD WE TELL PEOPLE?
THE TRUTH.
ABSOLUTELY NOT. YOU'D START A MASS PANIC THAT WOULD BECOME A STAMPEDE.
BESIDES, IF THE PM GOES ON TV AND ANNOUNCES THAT WE'RE EVACUATING, WHAT'S TO STOP SCORPIA FLICKING THE SWITCH EARLY?

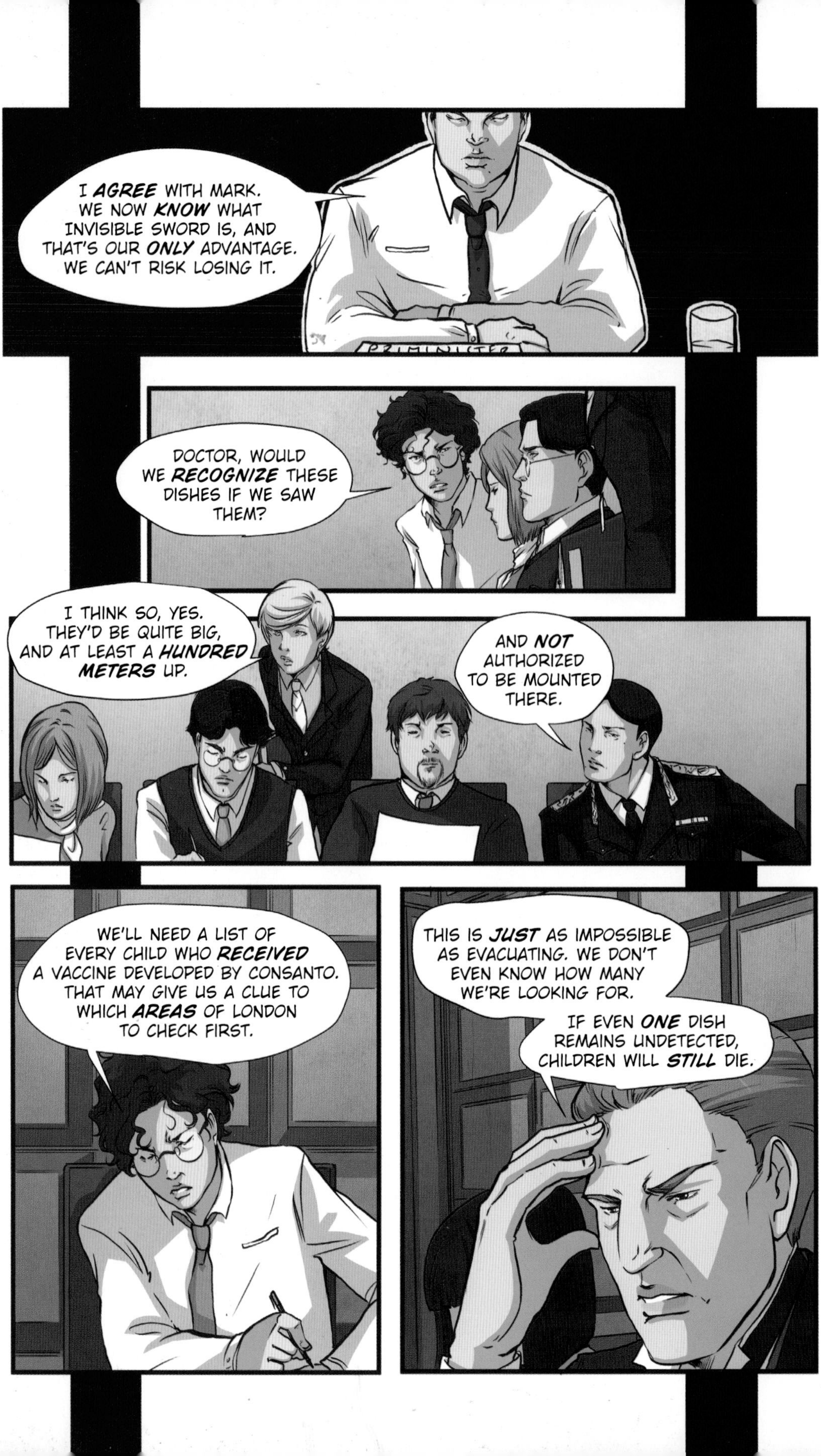
I AGREE WITH MARK. WE NOW KNOW WHAT INVISIBLE SWORD IS, AND THAT'S OUR ONLY ADVANTAGE. WE CAN'T RISK LOSING IT.
DOCTOR, WOULD WE RECOGNIZE THESE DISHES IF WE SAW THEM?
I THINK SO, YES. THEY'D BE QUITE BIG, AND AT LEAST A HUNDRED METERS UP.
AND NOT AUTHORIZED TO BE MOUNTED THERE.
WE'LL NEED A LIST OF EVERY CHILD WHO RECEIVED A VACCINE DEVELOPED BY CONSANTO. THAT MAY GIVE US A CLUE TO WHICH AREAS OF LONDON TO CHECK FIRST.
THIS IS JUST AS IMPOSSIBLE AS EVACUATING. WE DON'T EVEN KNOW HOW MANY WE'RE LOOKING FOR.
IF EVEN ONE DISH REMAINS UNDETECTED, CHILDREN WILL STILL DIE.

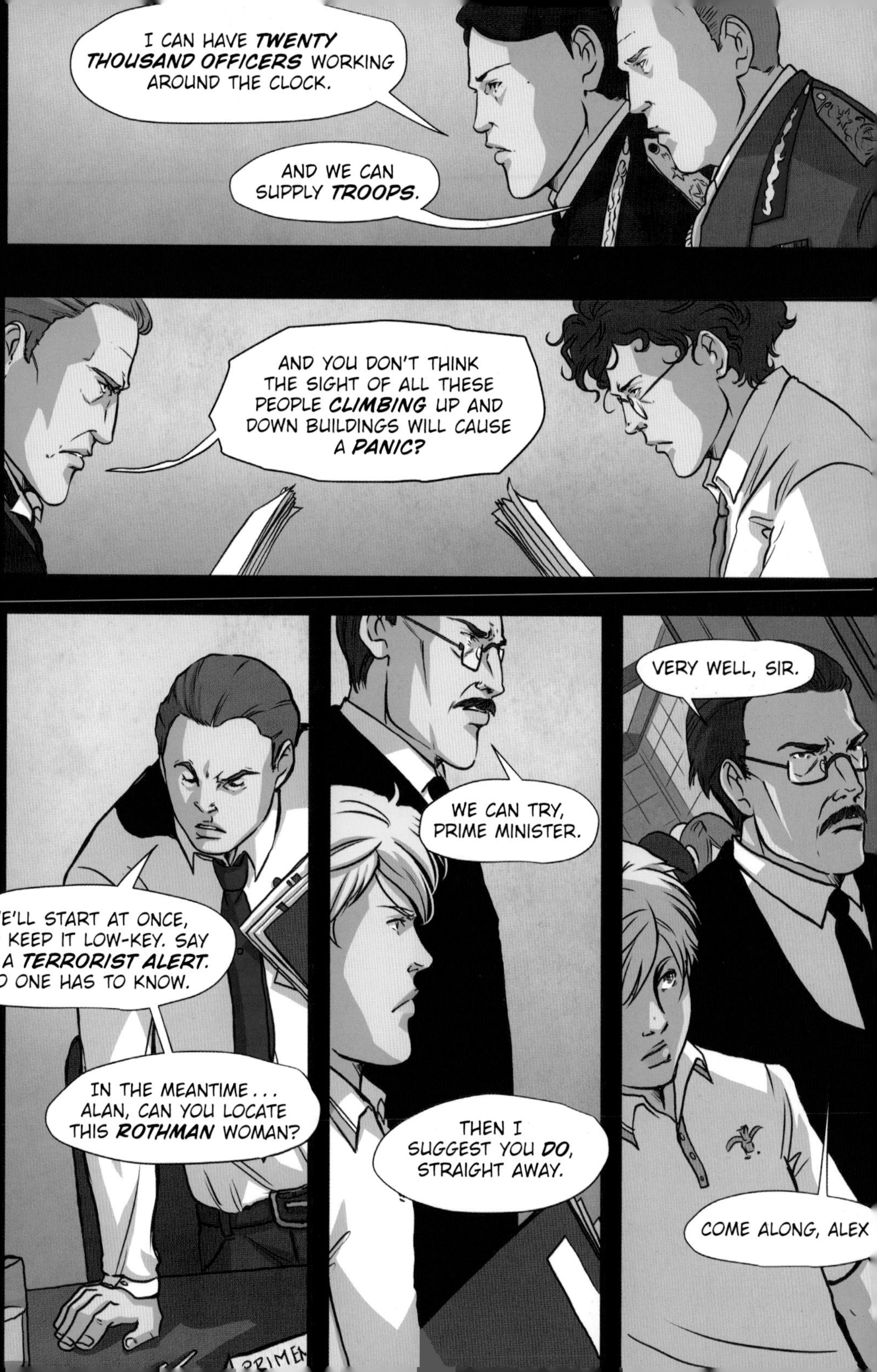

I CAN HAVE **TWENTY THOUSAND OFFICERS** WORKING AROUND THE CLOCK.
AND WE CAN SUPPLY **TROOPS**.
AND YOU DON'T THINK THE SIGHT OF ALL THESE PEOPLE **CLIMBING** UP AND DOWN BUILDINGS WILL CAUSE A **PANIC?**
E'LL START AT ONCE, KEEP IT LOW-KEY. SAY A **TERRORIST ALERT**. O ONE HAS TO KNOW.
IN THE MEANTIME . . . ALAN, CAN YOU LOCATE THIS **ROTHMAN** WOMAN?
WE CAN TRY, PRIME MINISTER.
THEN I SUGGEST YOU **DO**, STRAIGHT AWAY.
VERY WELL, SIR.
COME ALONG, ALEX

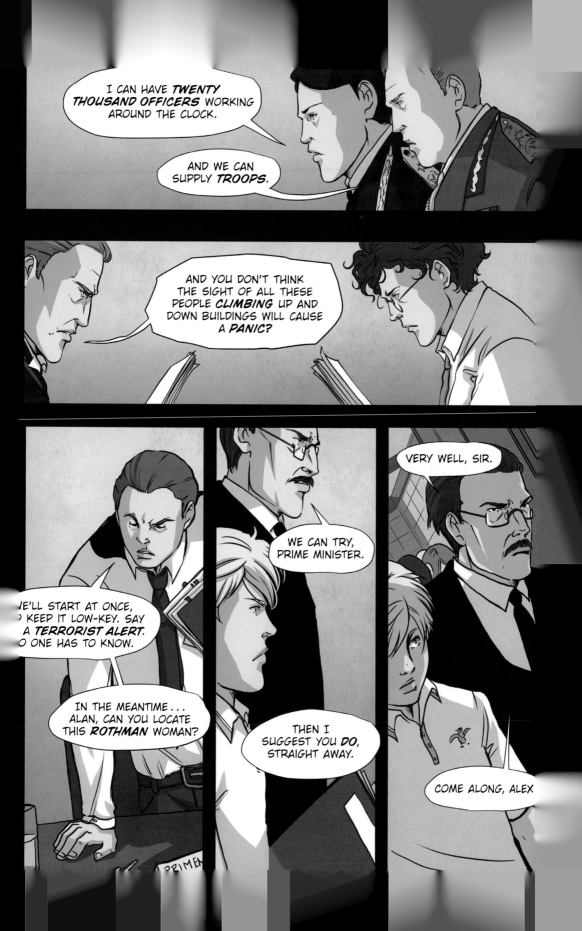

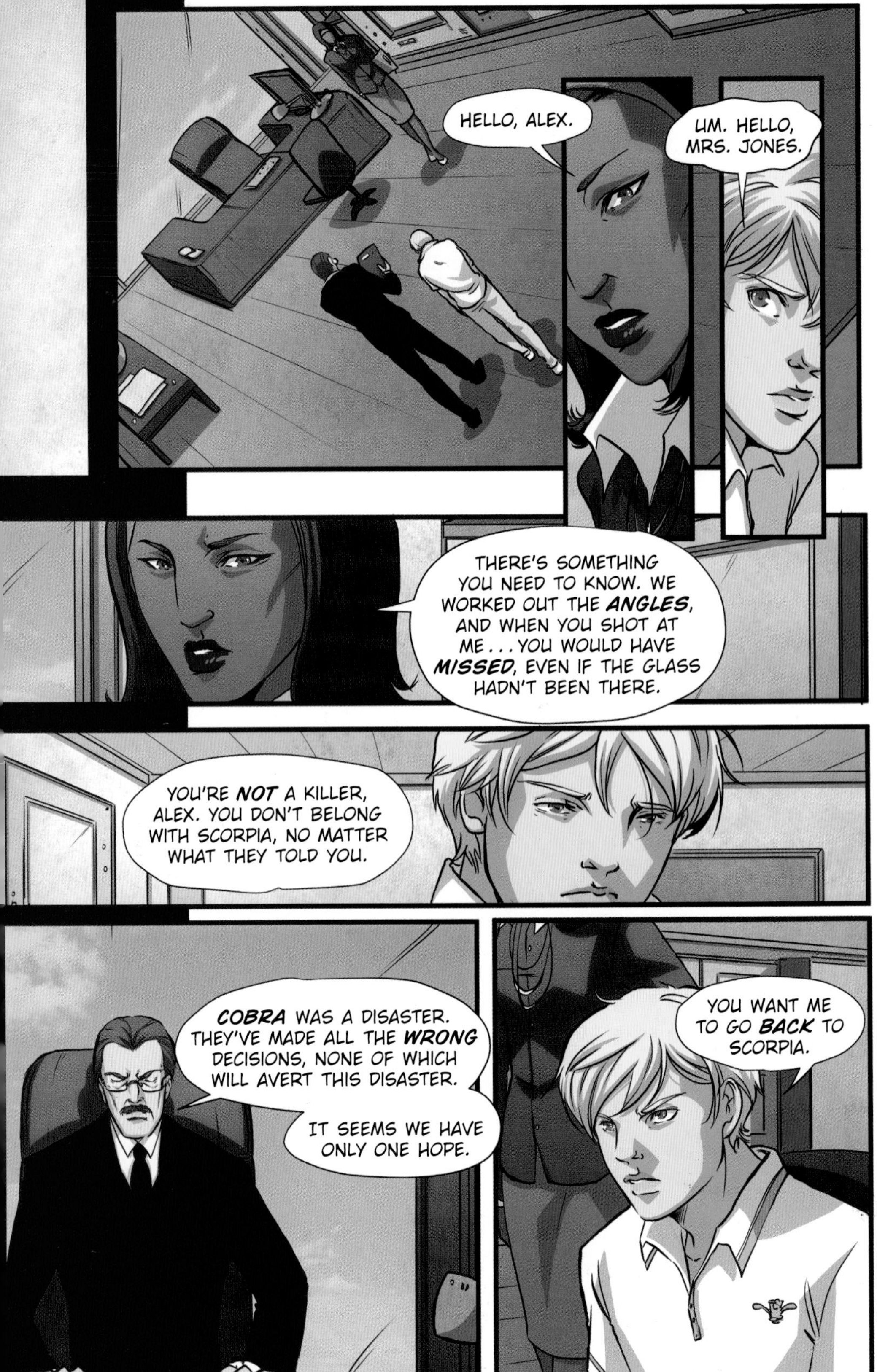
HELLO, ALEX.
UM. HELLO, MRS. JONES.
THERE'S SOMETHING YOU NEED TO KNOW. WE WORKED OUT THE ANGLES, AND WHEN YOU SHOT AT ME . . . YOU WOULD HAVE MISSED, EVEN IF THE GLASS HADN'T BEEN THERE.
YOU'RE NOT A KILLER, ALEX. YOU DON'T BELONG WITH SCORPIA, NO MATTER WHAT THEY TOLD YOU.
COBRA WAS A DISASTER. THEY'VE MADE ALL THE WRONG DECISIONS, NONE OF WHICH WILL AVERT THIS DISASTER.
IT SEEMS WE HAVE ONLY ONE HOPE.
YOU WANT ME TO GO BACK TO SCORPIA.

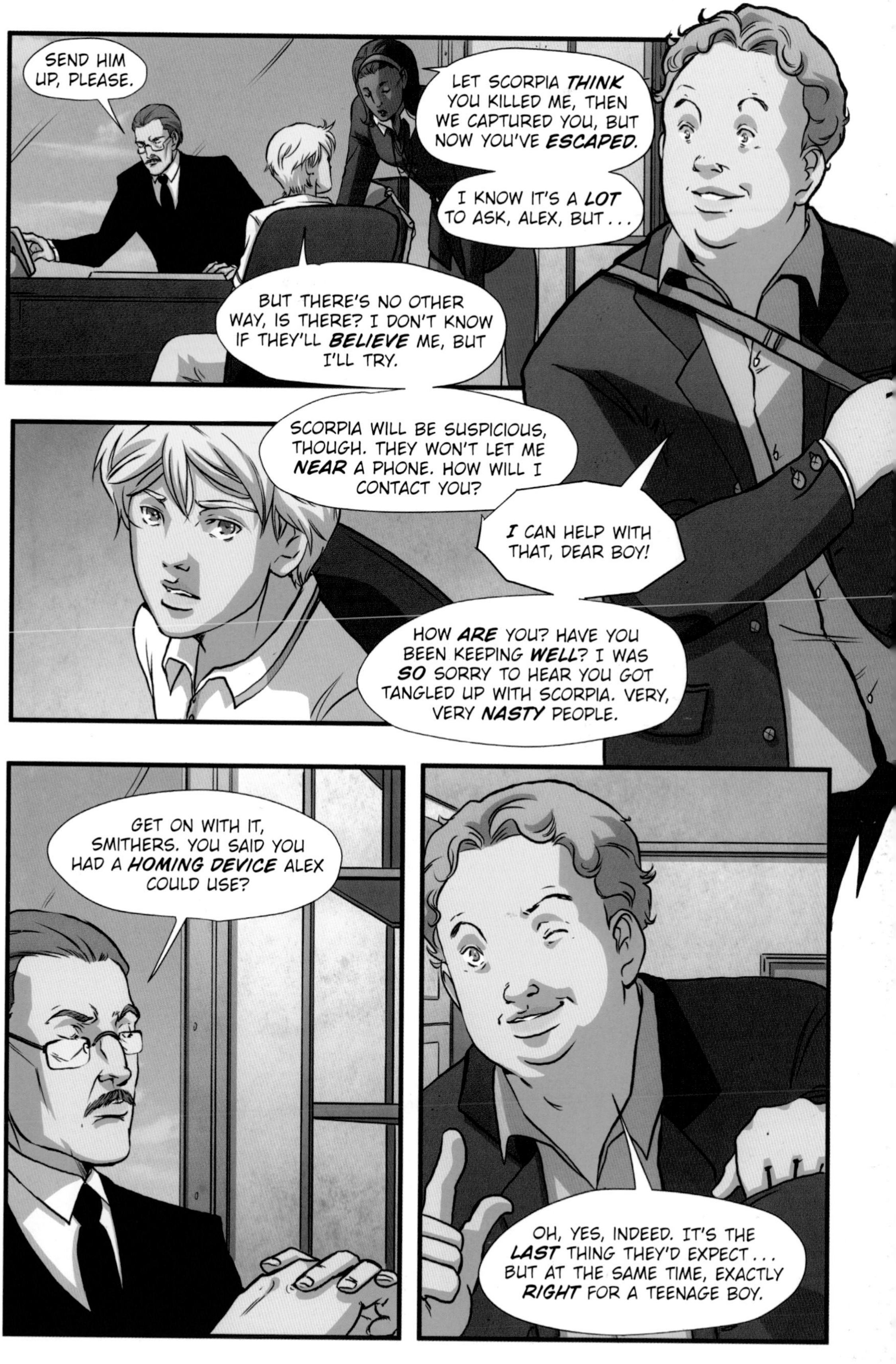
SEND HIM UP, PLEASE.
LET SCORPIA THINK YOU KILLED ME, THEN WE CAPTURED YOU, BUT NOW YOU'VE ESCAPED.
I KNOW IT'S A LOT TO ASK, ALEX, BUT . . .
BUT THERE'S NO OTHER WAY, IS THERE? I DON'T KNOW IF THEY'LL BELIEVE ME, BUT I'LL TRY.
SCORPIA WILL BE SUSPICIOUS, THOUGH. THEY WON'T LET ME NEAR A PHONE. HOW WILL I CONTACT YOU?
I CAN HELP WITH THAT, DEAR BOY!
HOW ARE YOU? HAVE YOU BEEN KEEPING WELL? I WAS SO SORRY TO HEAR YOU GOT TANGLED UP WITH SCORPIA. VERY, VERY NASTY PEOPLE.
GET ON WITH IT, SMITHERS. YOU SAID YOU HAD A HOMING DEVICE ALEX COULD USE?
OH, YES, INDEED. IT'S THE LAST THING THEY'D EXPECT . . . BUT AT THE SAME TIME, EXACTLY RIGHT FOR A TEENAGE BOY.

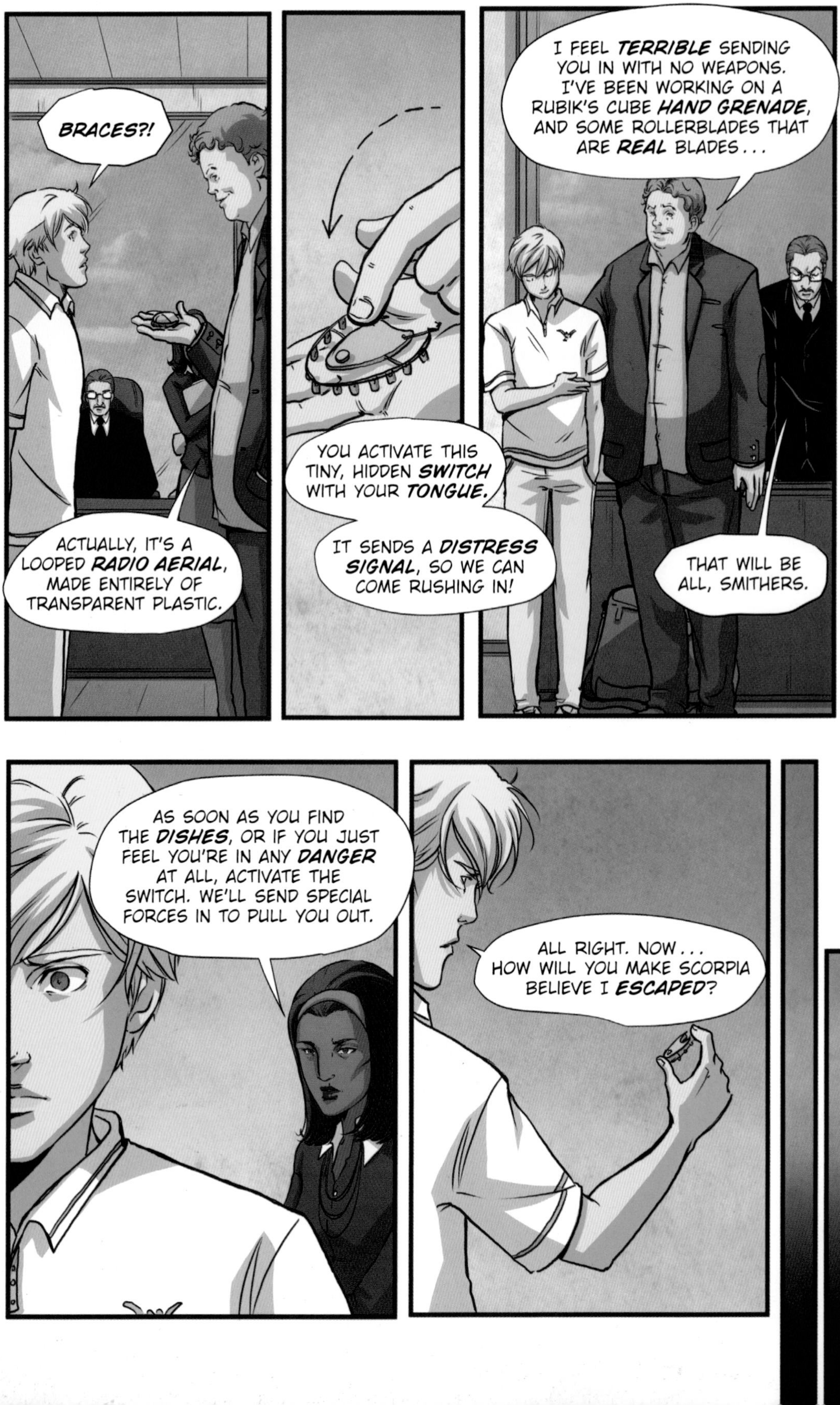
BRACES?!
ACTUALLY, IT'S A LOOPED RADIO AERIAL, MADE ENTIRELY OF TRANSPARENT PLASTIC.
YOU ACTIVATE THIS TINY, HIDDEN SWITCH WITH YOUR TONGUE.
IT SENDS A DISTRESS SIGNAL, SO WE CAN COME RUSHING IN!
I FEEL TERRIBLE SENDING YOU IN WITH NO WEAPONS. I'VE BEEN WORKING ON A RUBIK'S CUBE HAND GRENADE, AND SOME ROLLERBLADES THAT ARE REAL BLADES . . .
THAT WILL BE ALL, SMITHERS.
AS SOON AS YOU FIND THE DISHES, OR IF YOU JUST FEEL YOU'RE IN ANY DANGER AT ALL, ACTIVATE THE SWITCH. WE'LL SEND SPECIAL FORCES IN TO PULL YOU OUT.
ALL RIGHT. NOW . . . HOW WILL YOU MAKE SCORPIA BELIEVE I ESCAPED?

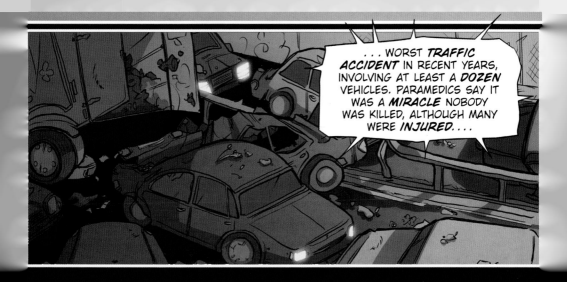

. . . WORST TRAFFIC ACCIDENT IN RECENT YEARS, INVOLVING AT LEAST A DOZEN VEHICLES. PARAMEDICS SAY IT WAS A MIRACLE NOBODY WAS KILLED, ALTHOUGH MANY WERE INJURED. . . .
WITNESSES SAY A TEENAGE BOY TRAVELING IN THE FIRST CAR FLED THE SCENE, PURSUED BY A MAN IN A DARK SUIT AND SUNGLASSES. NEITHER HAS YET BEEN LOCATED. . . .
BREAKING NEWS
THIS IS ALEX RIDER. I NEED TO TALK TO NILE.
FIRST TELL US WHAT HAPPENED. IS THE WOMAN DEAD?
BREAKING NEWS
YES, BUT THEY CAUGHT ME ON THE WAY OUT. THEY WERE TAKING ME SOMEWHERE THIS AFTERNOON, AND I MANAGED TO ESCAPE.
LOOK, YOU SAID YOU'D BRING ME IN WHEN I'D DONE IT. I'M IN A PHONE BOX, EVERYONE'S LOOKING FOR ME. . . .

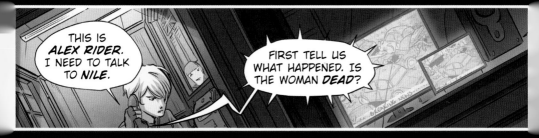

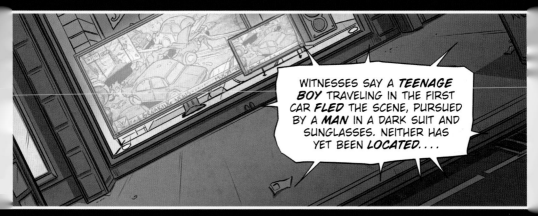

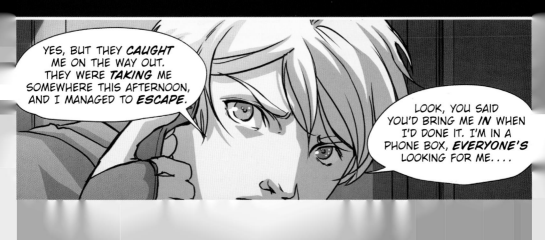

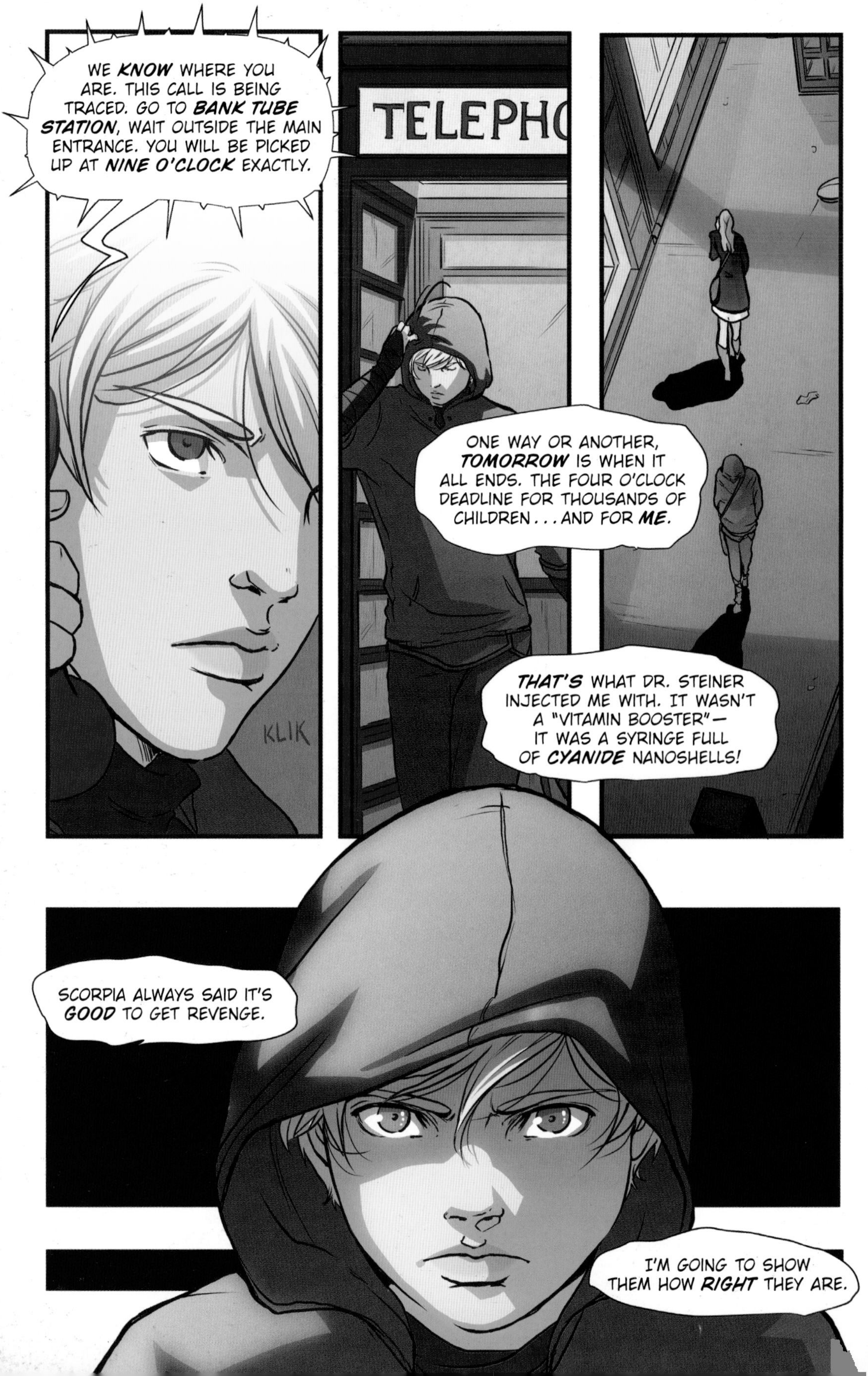
WE KNOW WHERE YOU ARE. THIS CALL IS BEING TRACED. GO TO BANK TUBE STATION, WAIT OUTSIDE THE MAIN ENTRANCE. YOU WILL BE PICKED UP AT NINE O'CLOCK EXACTLY.
KLIK
TELEPHO
ONE WAY OR ANOTHER, TOMORROW IS WHEN IT ALL ENDS. THE FOUR O'CLOCK DEADLINE FOR THOUSANDS OF CHILDREN . . . AND FOR ME.
THAT'S WHAT DR. STEINER INJECTED ME WITH. IT WASN'T A "VITAMIN BOOSTER"— IT WAS A SYRINGE FULL OF CYANIDE NANOSHELLS!
SCORPIA ALWAYS SAID IT'S GOOD TO GET REVENGE.
I'M GOING TO SHOW THEM HOW RIGHT THEY ARE.

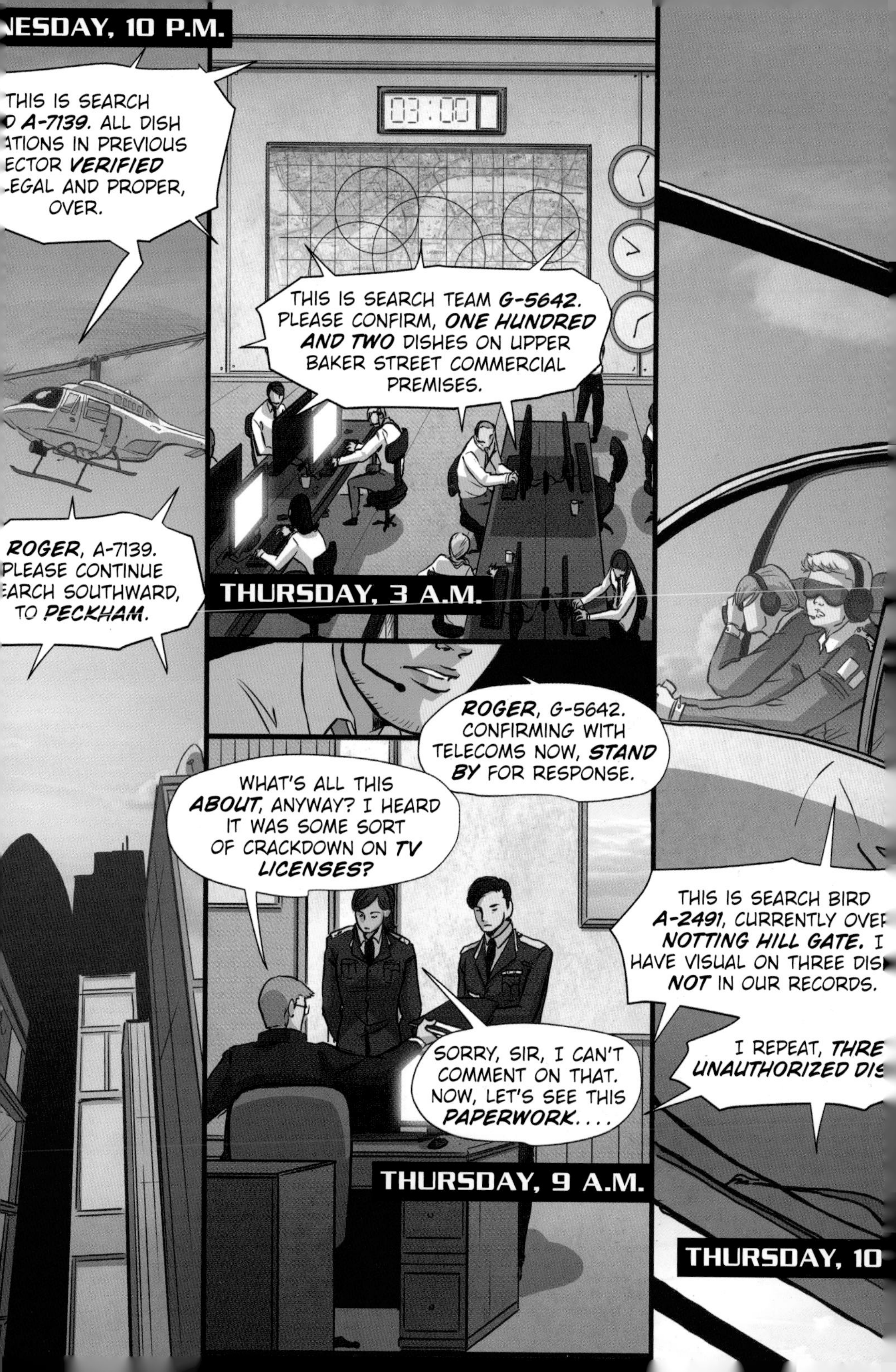

NESDAY, 10 P.M.
THIS IS SEARCH D A-7139. ALL DISH ATIONS IN PREVIOUS ECTOR VERIFIED EGAL AND PROPER, OVER.
ROGER, A-7139. PLEASE CONTINUE EARCH SOUTHWARD, TO PECKHAM.
03:00
THIS IS SEARCH TEAM G-5642. PLEASE CONFIRM, ONE HUNDRED AND TWO DISHES ON UPPER BAKER STREET COMMERCIAL PREMISES.
THURSDAY, 3 A.M.
ROGER, G-5642. CONFIRMING WITH TELECOMS NOW, STAND BY FOR RESPONSE.
WHAT'S ALL THIS ABOUT, ANYWAY? I HEARD IT WAS SOME SORT OF CRACKDOWN ON TV LICENSES?
SORRY, SIR, I CAN'T COMMENT ON THAT. NOW, LET'S SEE THIS PAPERWORK. . . .
THURSDAY, 9 A.M.
THIS IS SEARCH BIRD A-2491, CURRENTLY OVE NOTTING HILL GATE. I HAVE VISUAL ON THREE DIS NOT IN OUR RECORDS.
I REPEAT, THRE UNAUTHORIZED DIS
THURSDAY, 10

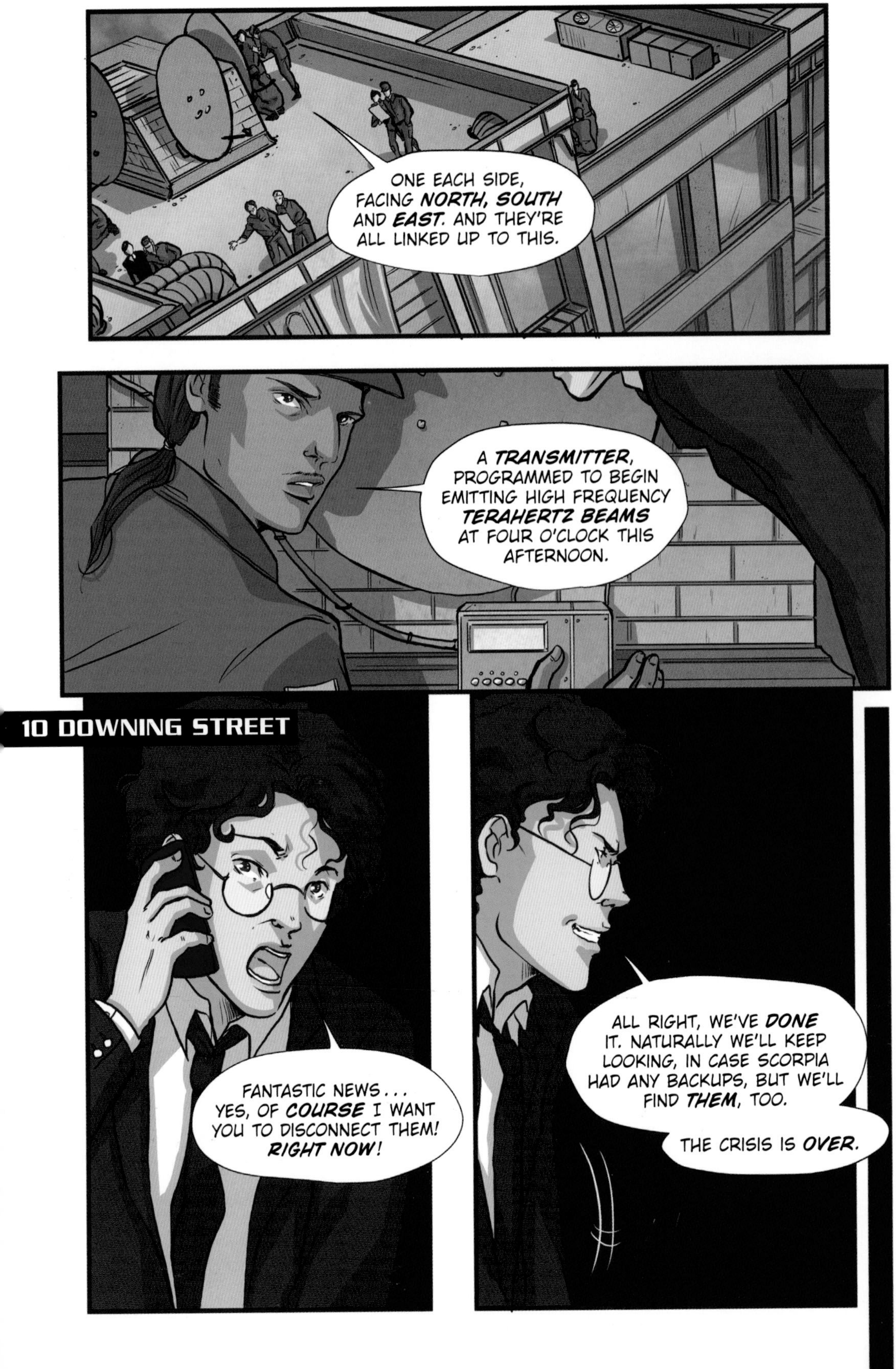
ONE EACH SIDE, FACING NORTH, SOUTH AND EAST. AND THEY'RE ALL LINKED UP TO THIS.
A TRANSMITTER, PROGRAMMED TO BEGIN EMITTING HIGH FREQUENCY TERAHERTZ BEAMS AT FOUR O'CLOCK THIS AFTERNOON.
10 DOWNING STREET
FANTASTIC NEWS . . . YES, OF COURSE I WANT YOU TO DISCONNECT THEM! RIGHT NOW!
ALL RIGHT, WE'VE DONE IT. NATURALLY WE'LL KEEP LOOKING, IN CASE SCORPIA HAD ANY BACKUPS, BUT WE'LL FIND THEM, TOO.
THE CRISIS IS OVER.

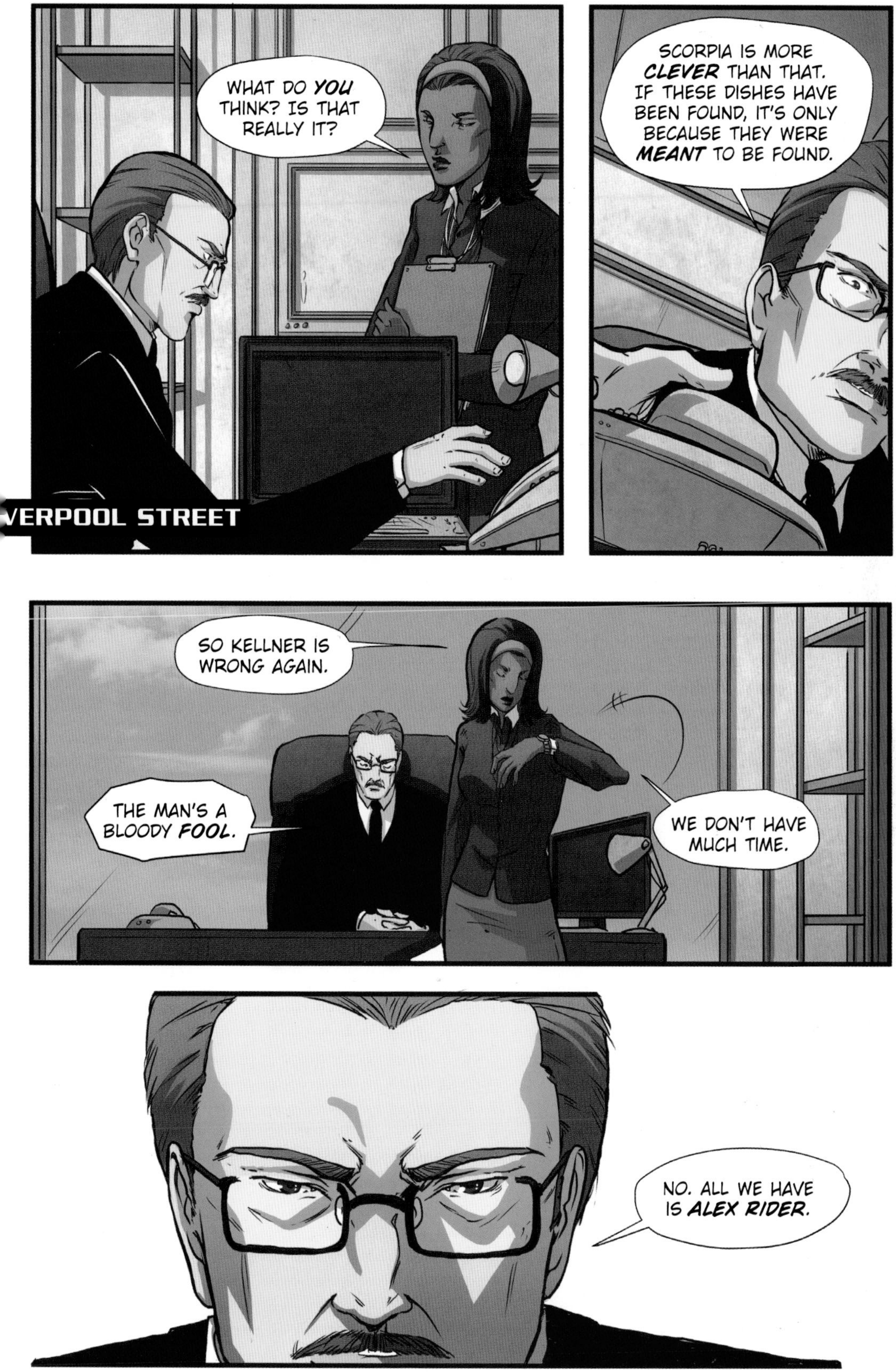

VERPOOL STREET
WHAT DO YOU THINK? IS THAT REALLY IT?
SCORPIA IS MORE CLEVER THAN THAT. IF THESE DISHES HAVE BEEN FOUND, IT'S ONLY BECAUSE THEY WERE MEANT TO BE FOUND.
SO KELLNER IS WRONG AGAIN.
THE MAN'S A BLOODY FOOL.
WE DON'T HAVE MUCH TIME.
NO. ALL WE HAVE IS ALEX RIDER.

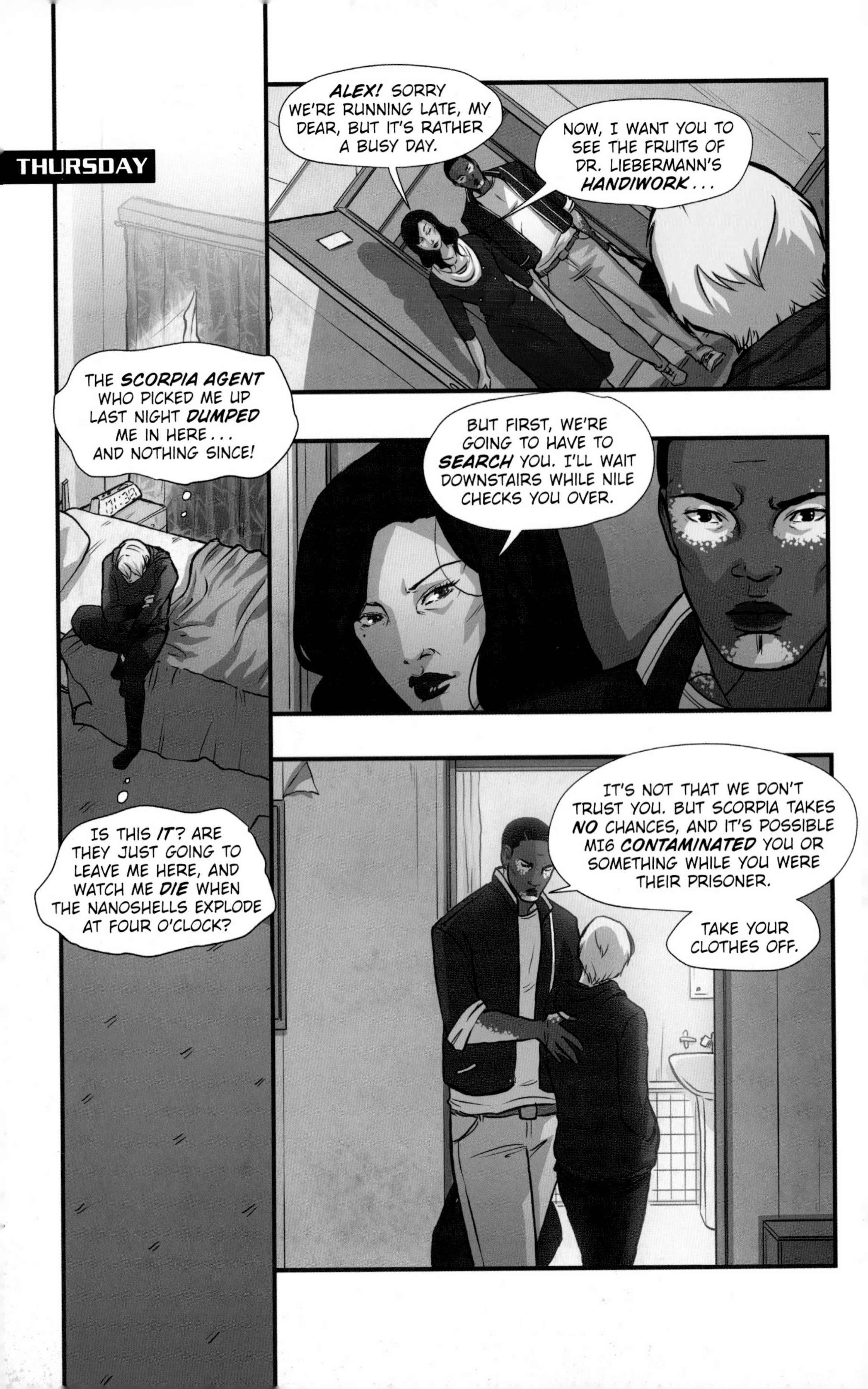
THURSDAY
ALEX! SORRY WE'RE RUNNING LATE, MY DEAR, BUT IT'S RATHER A BUSY DAY.
NOW, I WANT YOU TO SEE THE FRUITS OF DR. LIEBERMANN'S HANDIWORK . . .
THE SCORPIA AGENT WHO PICKED ME UP LAST NIGHT DUMPED ME IN HERE . . . AND NOTHING SINCE!
BUT FIRST, WE'RE GOING TO HAVE TO SEARCH YOU. I'LL WAIT DOWNSTAIRS WHILE NILE CHECKS YOU OVER.
IS THIS IT? ARE THEY JUST GOING TO LEAVE ME HERE, AND WATCH ME DIE WHEN THE NANOSHELLS EXPLODE AT FOUR O'CLOCK?
IT'S NOT THAT WE DON'T TRUST YOU. BUT SCORPIA TAKES NO CHANCES, AND IT'S POSSIBLE MI6 CONTAMINATED YOU OR SOMETHING WHILE YOU WERE THEIR PRISONER.
TAKE YOUR CLOTHES OFF.

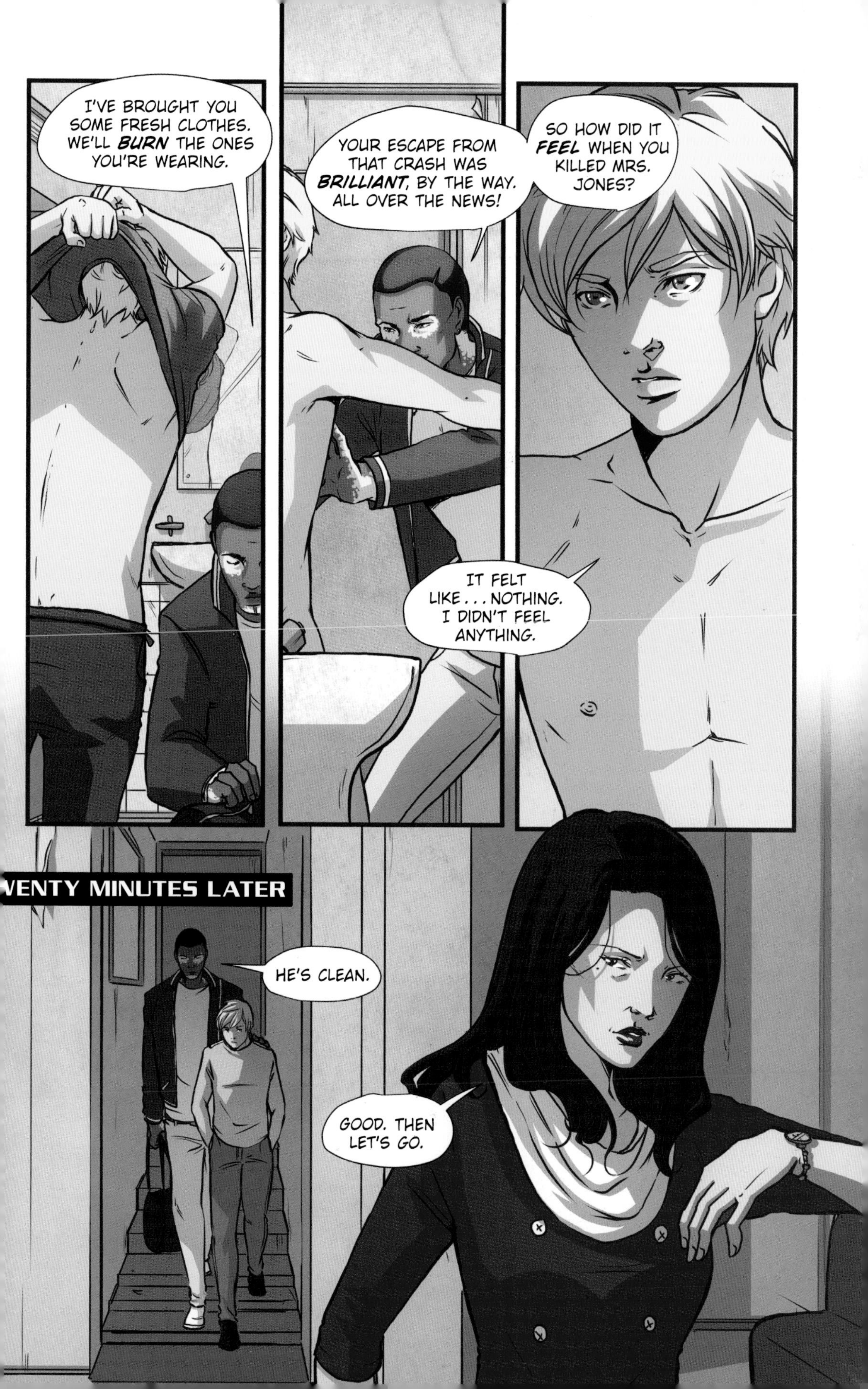
I'VE BROUGHT YOU SOME FRESH CLOTHES. WE'LL **BURN** THE ONES YOU'RE WEARING.
YOUR ESCAPE FROM THAT CRASH WAS **BRILLIANT**, BY THE WAY. ALL OVER THE NEWS!
SO HOW DID IT **FEEL** WHEN YOU KILLED MRS. JONES?
IT FELT LIKE . . . NOTHING. I DIDN'T FEEL ANYTHING.
VENTY MINUTES LATER
HE'S CLEAN.
GOOD. THEN LET'S GO.

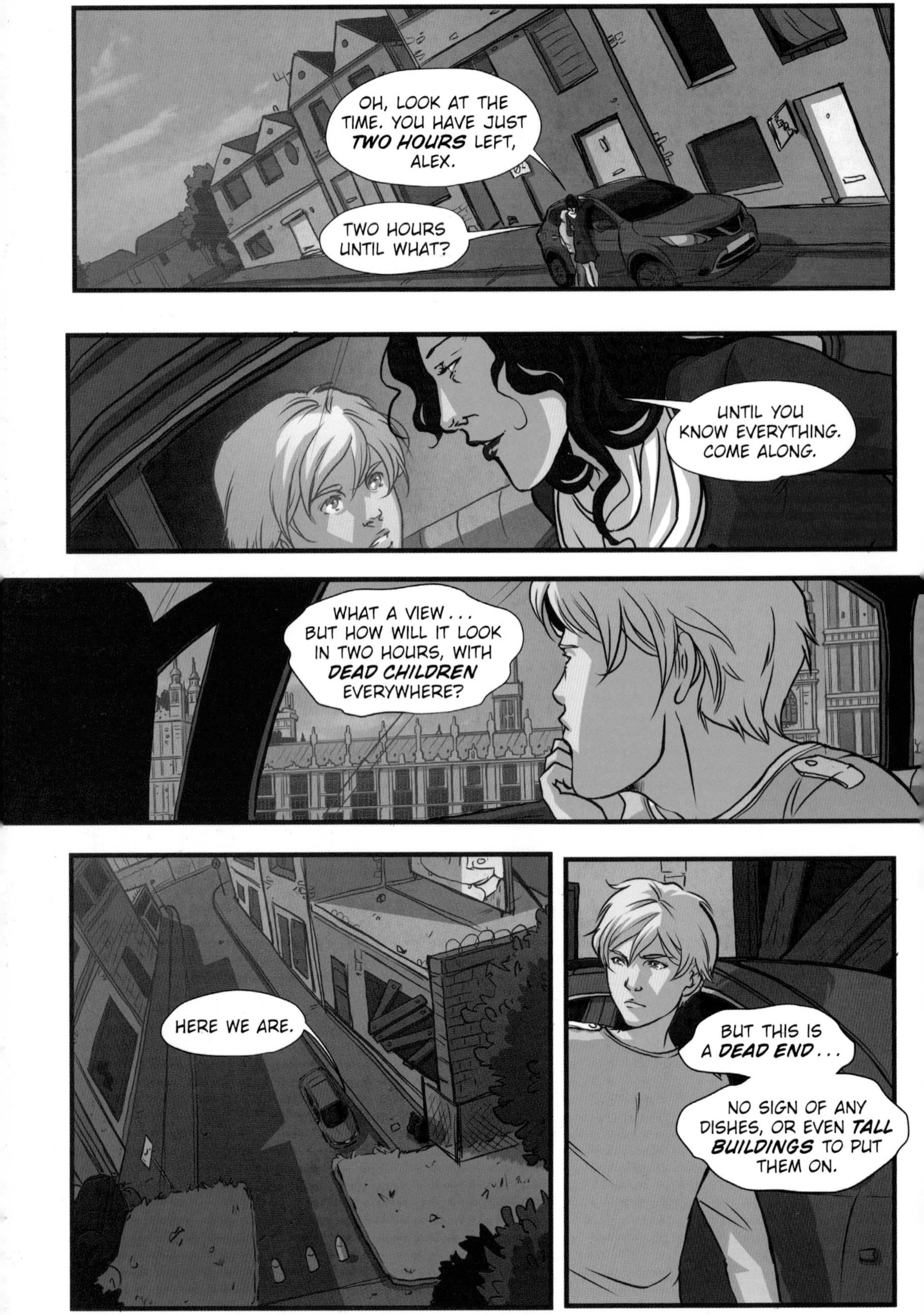
OH, LOOK AT THE TIME. YOU HAVE JUST **TWO HOURS** LEFT, ALEX.
TWO HOURS UNTIL WHAT?
UNTIL YOU KNOW EVERYTHING. COME ALONG.
WHAT A VIEW . . . BUT HOW WILL IT LOOK IN TWO HOURS, WITH **DEAD CHILDREN** EVERYWHERE?
HERE WE ARE.
BUT THIS IS A **DEAD END** . . .
NO SIGN OF ANY DISHES, OR EVEN **TALL BUILDINGS** TO PUT THEM ON.

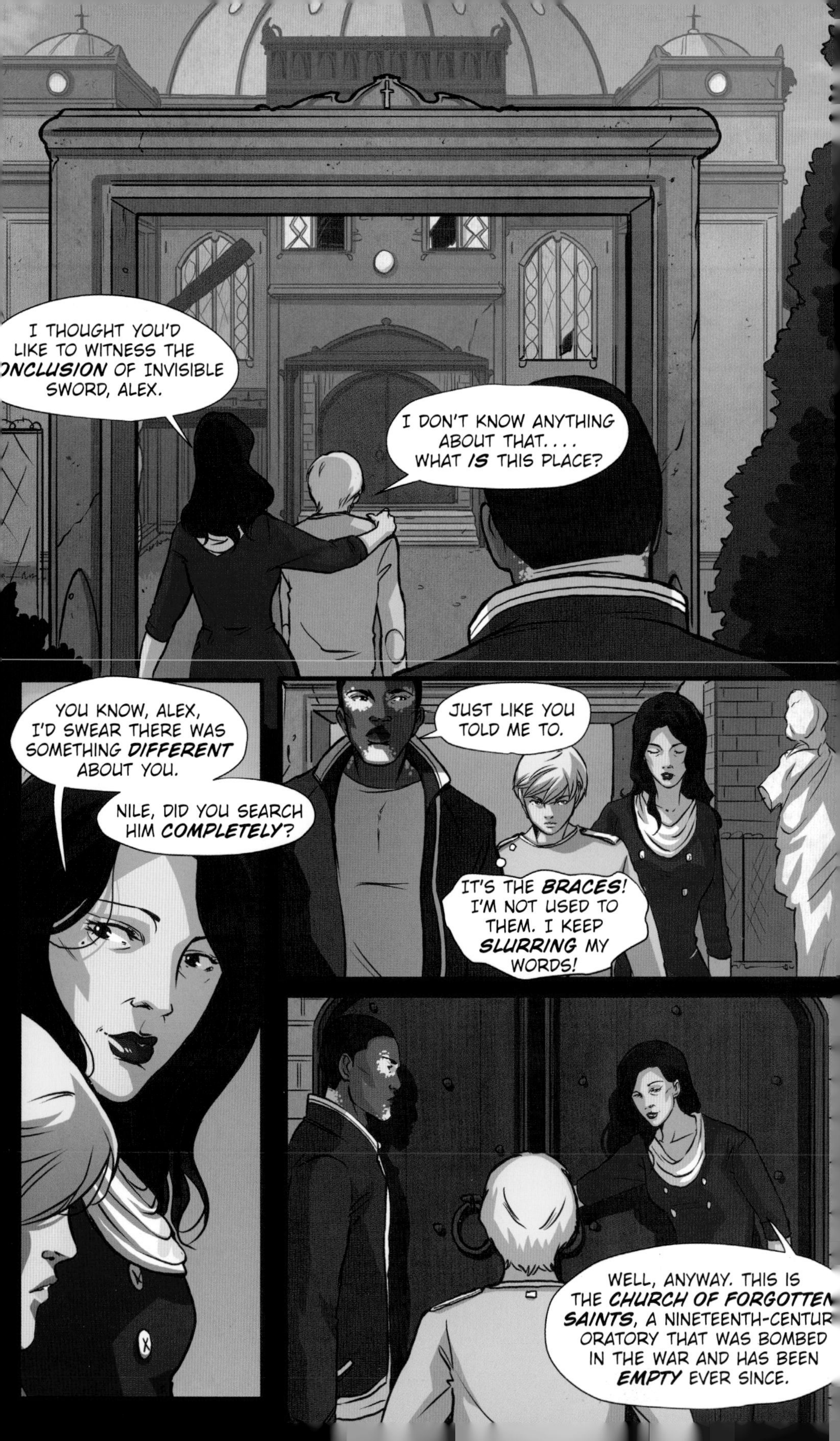

I THOUGHT YOU'D LIKE TO WITNESS THE ONCLUSION OF INVISIBLE SWORD, ALEX.
I DON'T KNOW ANYTHING ABOUT THAT. . . . WHAT IS THIS PLACE?
YOU KNOW, ALEX, I'D SWEAR THERE WAS SOMETHING DIFFERENT ABOUT YOU.
NILE, DID YOU SEARCH HIM COMPLETELY?
JUST LIKE YOU TOLD ME TO.
IT'S THE BRACES! I'M NOT USED TO THEM. I KEEP SLURRING MY WORDS!
WELL, ANYWAY. THIS IS THE CHURCH OF FORGOTTEN SAINTS, A NINETEENTH-CENTUR ORATORY THAT WAS BOMBED IN THE WAR AND HAS BEEN EMPTY EVER SINCE.

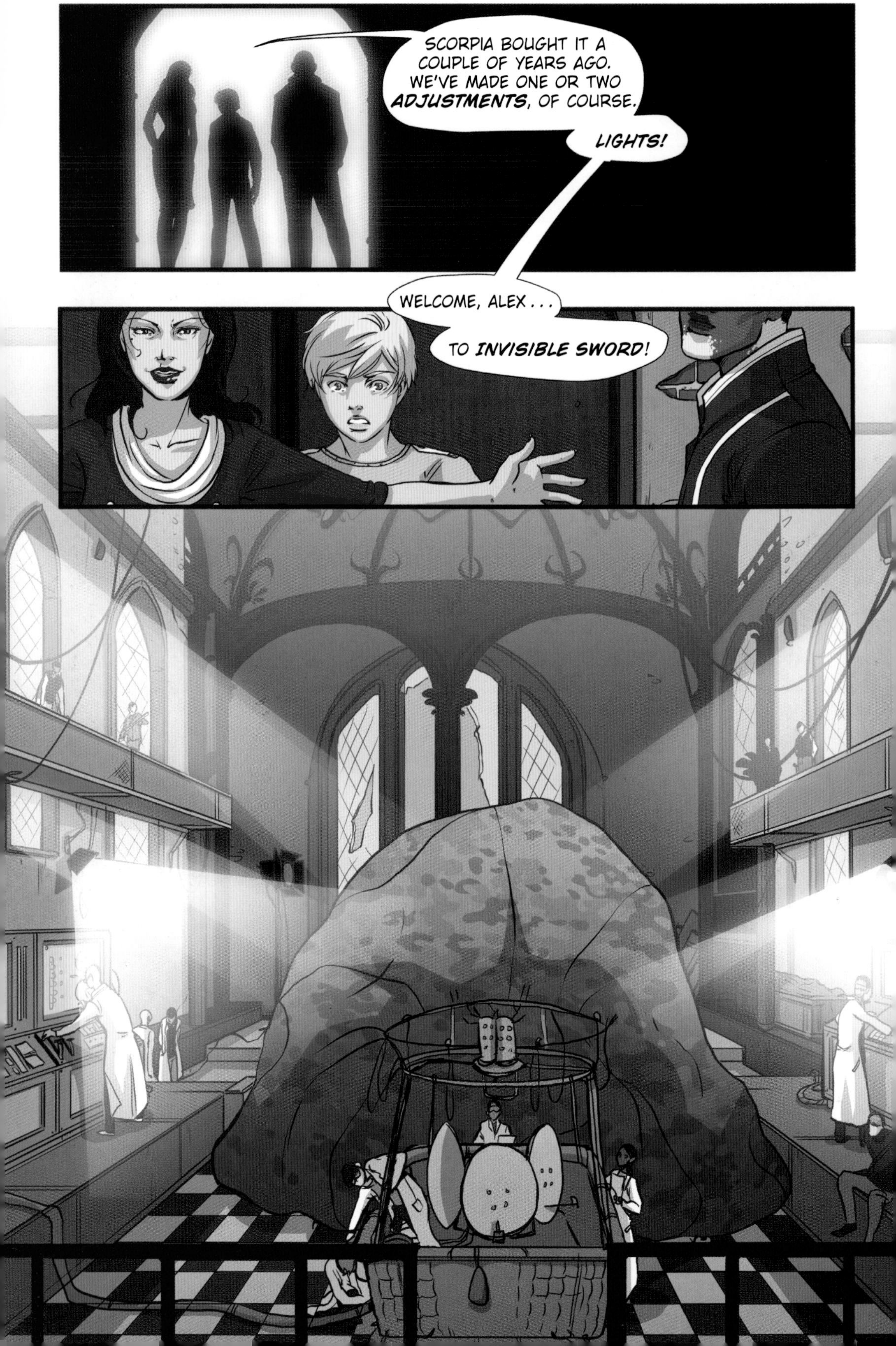
SCORPIA BOUGHT IT A COUPLE OF YEARS AGO. WE'VE MADE ONE OR TWO ADJUSTMENTS, OF COURSE.
LIGHTS!
WELCOME, ALEX . . .
TO INVISIBLE SWORD!

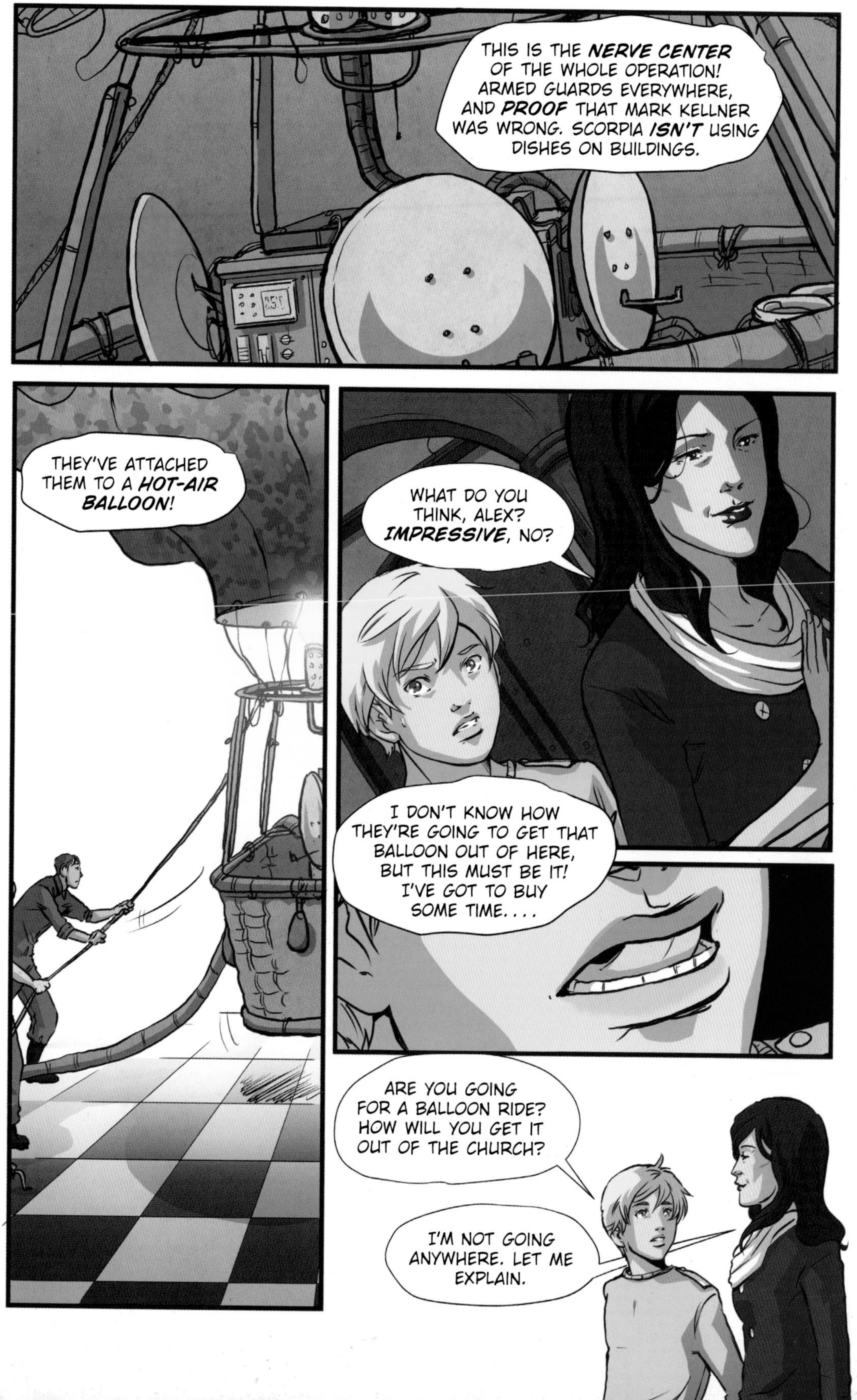
THIS IS THE NERVE CENTER OF THE WHOLE OPERATION! ARMED GUARDS EVERYWHERE, AND PROOF THAT MARK KELLNER WAS WRONG. SCORPIA ISN'T USING DISHES ON BUILDINGS.
THEY'VE ATTACHED THEM TO A HOT-AIR BALLOON!
WHAT DO YOU THINK, ALEX? IMPRESSIVE, NO?
I DON'T KNOW HOW THEY'RE GOING TO GET THAT BALLOON OUT OF HERE, BUT THIS MUST BE IT! I'VE GOT TO BUY SOME TIME. . . .
ARE YOU GOING FOR A BALLOON RIDE? HOW WILL YOU GET IT OUT OF THE CHURCH?
I'M NOT GOING ANYWHERE. LET ME EXPLAIN.

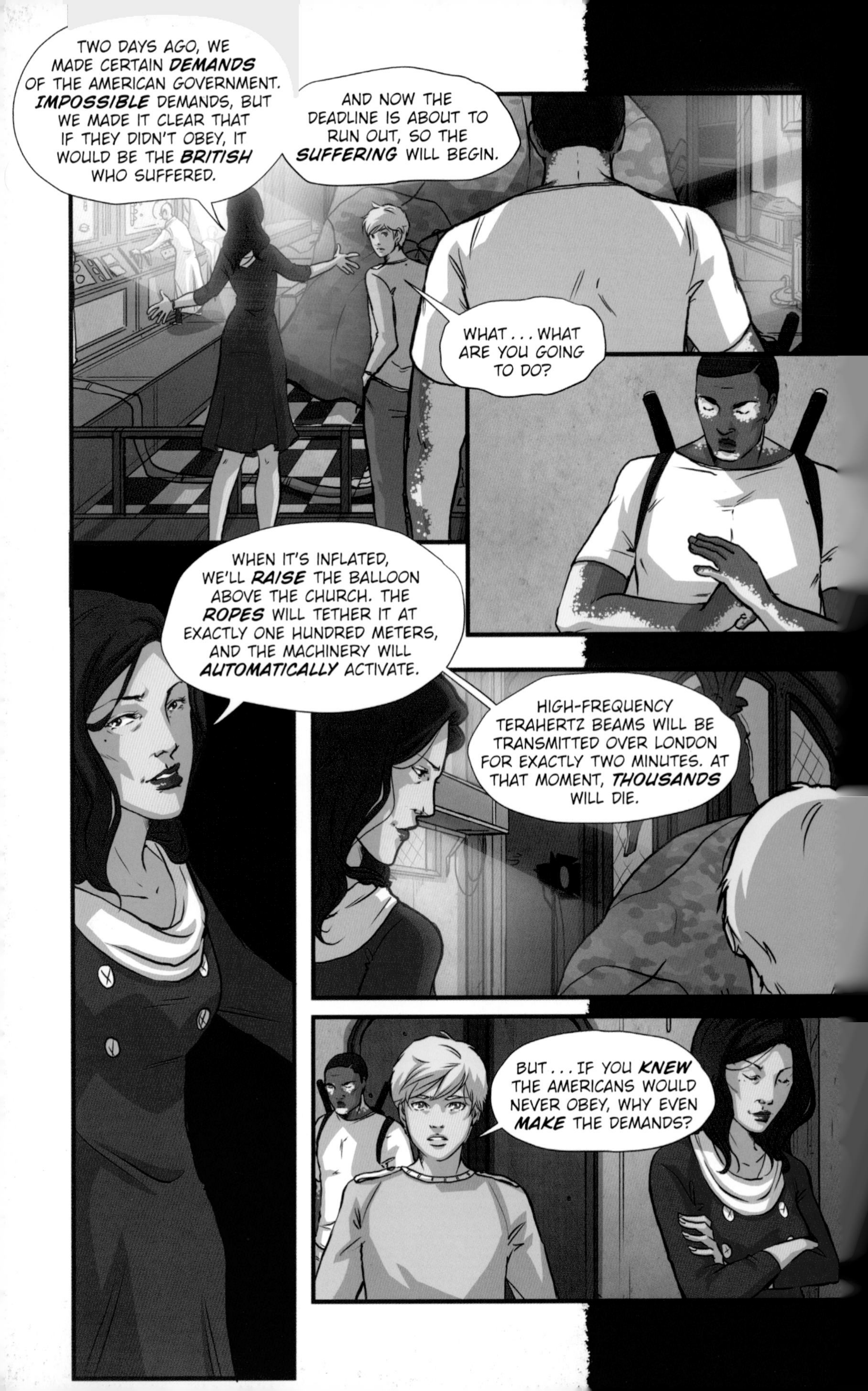
TWO DAYS AGO, WE MADE CERTAIN DEMANDS OF THE AMERICAN GOVERNMENT. IMPOSSIBLE DEMANDS, BUT WE MADE IT CLEAR THAT IF THEY DIDN'T OBEY, IT WOULD BE THE BRITISH WHO SUFFERED.
AND NOW THE DEADLINE IS ABOUT TO RUN OUT, SO THE SUFFERING WILL BEGIN.
WHAT . . . WHAT ARE YOU GOING TO DO?
WHEN IT'S INFLATED, WE'LL RAISE THE BALLOON ABOVE THE CHURCH. THE ROPES WILL TETHER IT AT EXACTLY ONE HUNDRED METERS, AND THE MACHINERY WILL AUTOMATICALLY ACTIVATE.
HIGH-FREQUENCY TERAHERTZ BEAMS WILL BE TRANSMITTED OVER LONDON FOR EXACTLY TWO MINUTES. AT THAT MOMENT, THOUSANDS WILL DIE.
BUT . . . IF YOU KNEW THE AMERICANS WOULD NEVER OBEY, WHY EVEN MAKE THE DEMANDS?

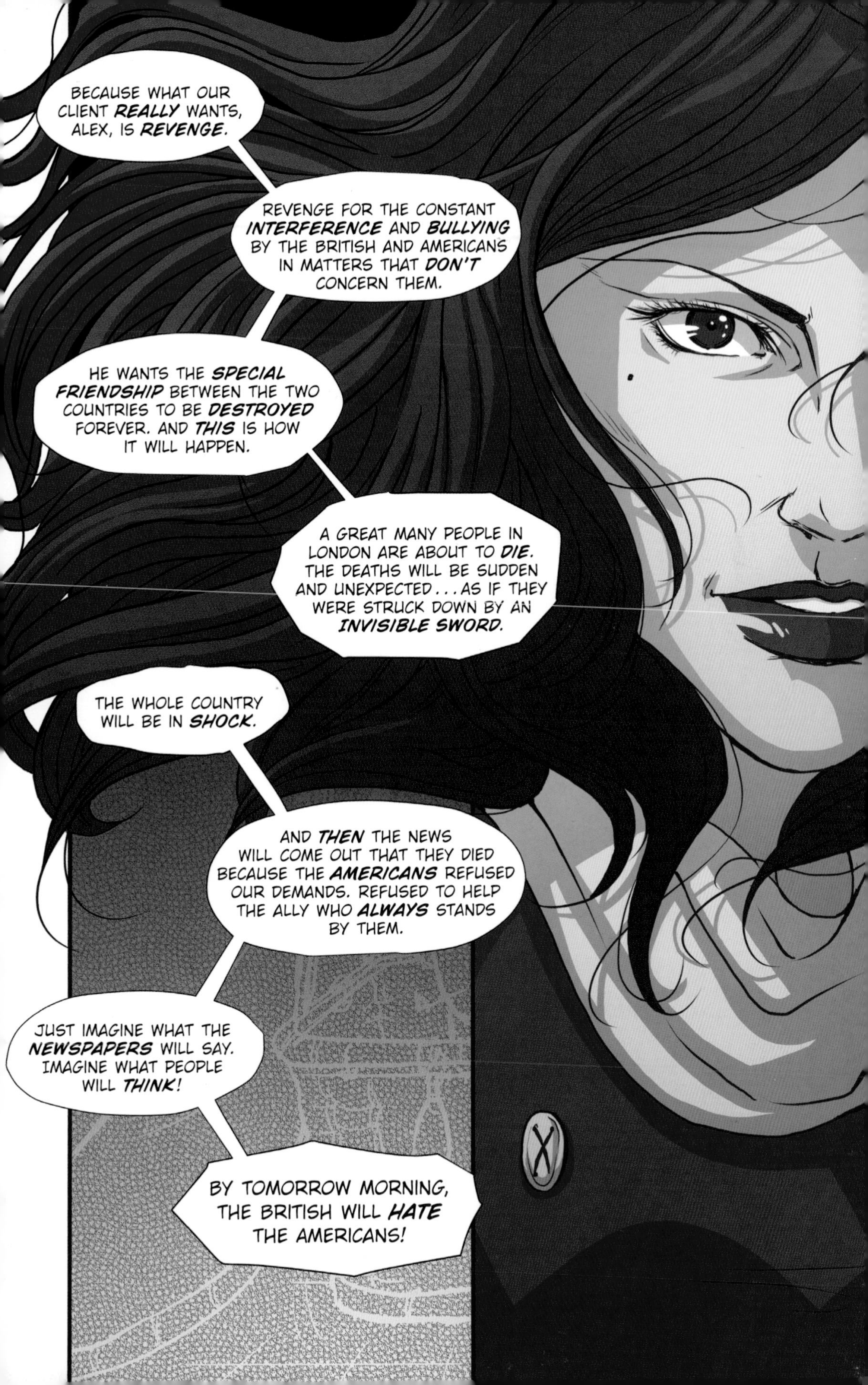
BECAUSE WHAT OUR CLIENT *REALLY* WANTS, ALEX, IS *REVENGE.*
REVENGE FOR THE CONSTANT *INTERFERENCE* AND *BULLYING* BY THE BRITISH AND AMERICANS IN MATTERS THAT *DON'T* CONCERN THEM.
HE WANTS THE *SPECIAL FRIENDSHIP* BETWEEN THE TWO COUNTRIES TO BE *DESTROYED* FOREVER. AND *THIS* IS HOW IT WILL HAPPEN.
A GREAT MANY PEOPLE IN LONDON ARE ABOUT TO *DIE.* THE DEATHS WILL BE SUDDEN AND UNEXPECTED . . . AS IF THEY WERE STRUCK DOWN BY AN *INVISIBLE SWORD.*
THE WHOLE COUNTRY WILL BE IN *SHOCK.*
AND *THEN* THE NEWS WILL COME OUT THAT THEY DIED BECAUSE THE *AMERICANS* REFUSED OUR DEMANDS. REFUSED TO HELP THE ALLY WHO *ALWAYS* STANDS BY THEM.
JUST IMAGINE WHAT THE *NEWSPAPERS* WILL SAY. IMAGINE WHAT PEOPLE WILL *THINK!*
BY TOMORROW MORNING, THE BRITISH WILL *HATE* THE AMERICANS!

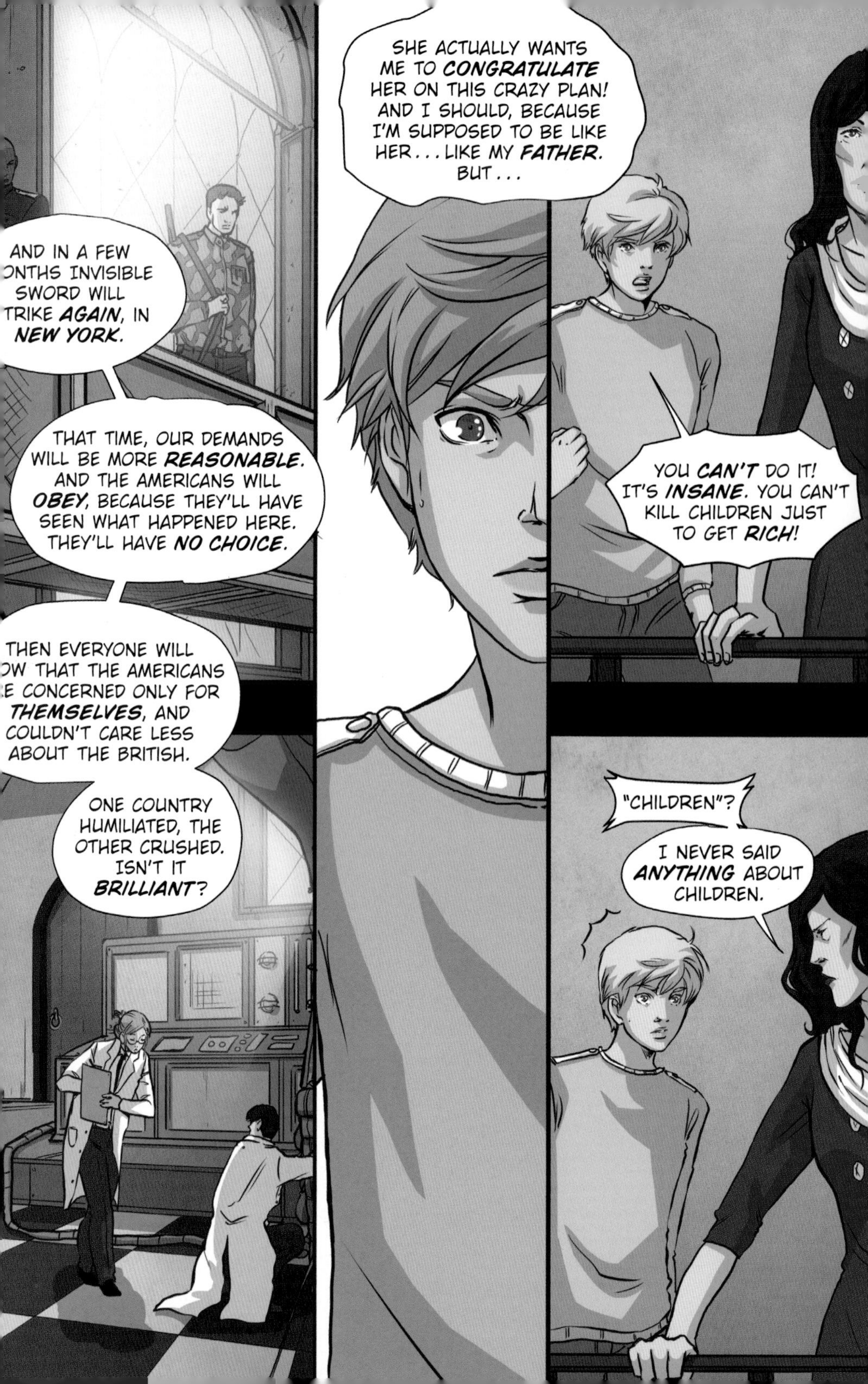

AND IN A FEW
ONTHS INVISIBLE
SWORD WILL
TRIKE AGAIN, IN
NEW YORK.
THAT TIME, OUR DEMANDS WILL BE MORE REASONABLE. AND THE AMERICANS WILL OBEY, BECAUSE THEY'LL HAVE SEEN WHAT HAPPENED HERE. THEY'LL HAVE NO CHOICE.
THEN EVERYONE WILL OW THAT THE AMERICANS E CONCERNED ONLY FOR THEMSELVES, AND COULDN'T CARE LESS ABOUT THE BRITISH.
ONE COUNTRY HUMILIATED, THE OTHER CRUSHED. ISN'T IT BRILLIANT?
SHE ACTUALLY WANTS ME TO CONGRATULATE HER ON THIS CRAZY PLAN! AND I SHOULD, BECAUSE I'M SUPPOSED TO BE LIKE HER . . . LIKE MY FATHER. BUT . . .
YOU CAN'T DO IT! IT'S INSANE. YOU CAN'T KILL CHILDREN JUST TO GET RICH!
"CHILDREN"?
I NEVER SAID ANYTHING ABOUT CHILDREN.

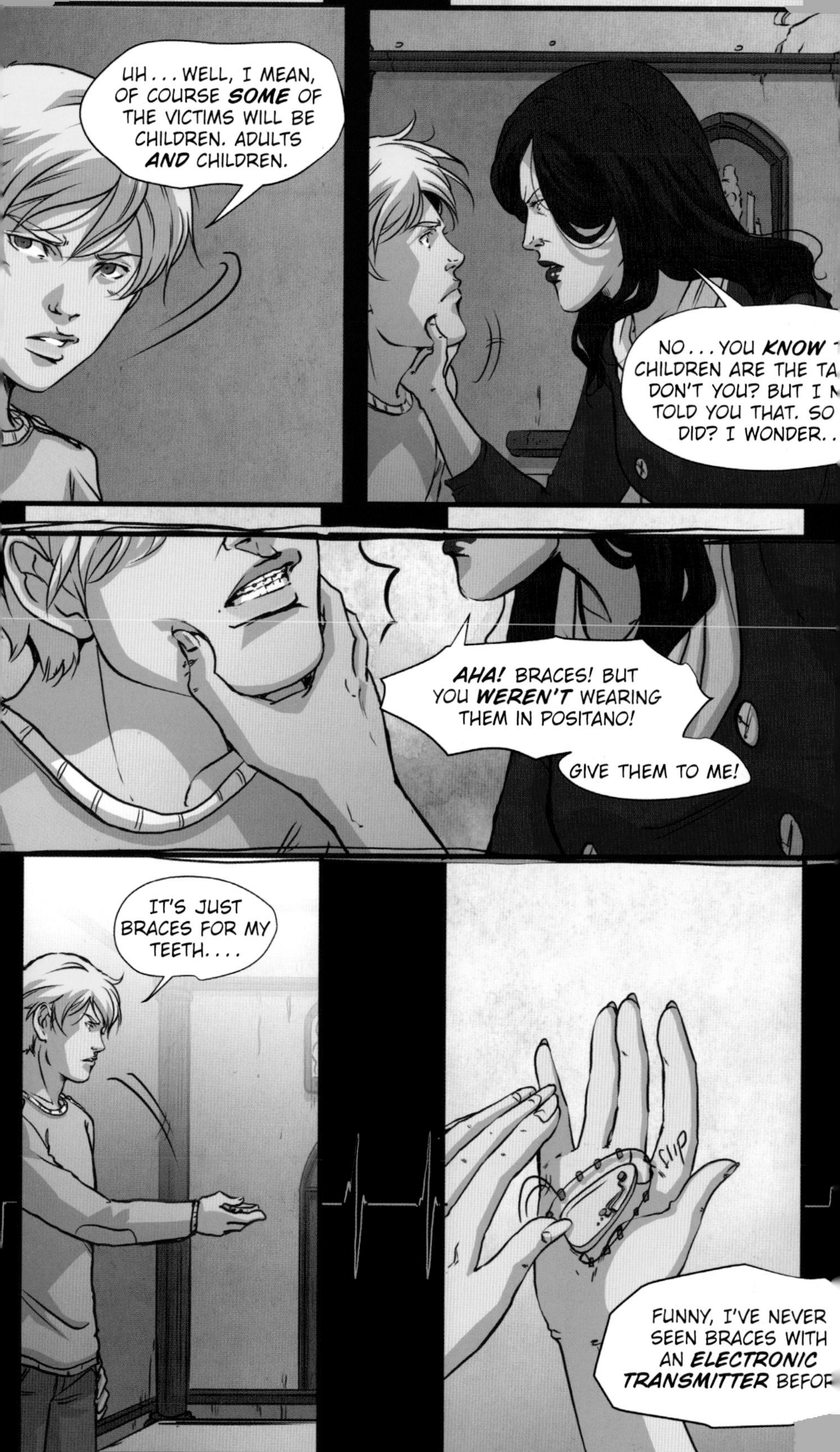
UH . . . WELL, I MEAN, OF COURSE SOME OF THE VICTIMS WILL BE CHILDREN. ADULTS AND CHILDREN.
NO . . . YOU KNOW CHILDREN ARE THE TA DON'T YOU? BUT I TOLD YOU THAT. SO DID? I WONDER. .
AHA! BRACES! BUT YOU WEREN'T WEARING THEM IN POSITANO!
GIVE THEM TO ME!
IT'S JUST BRACES FOR MY TEETH. . . .
SLIP
FUNNY, I'VE NEVER SEEN BRACES WITH AN ELECTRONIC TRANSMITTER BEFOR

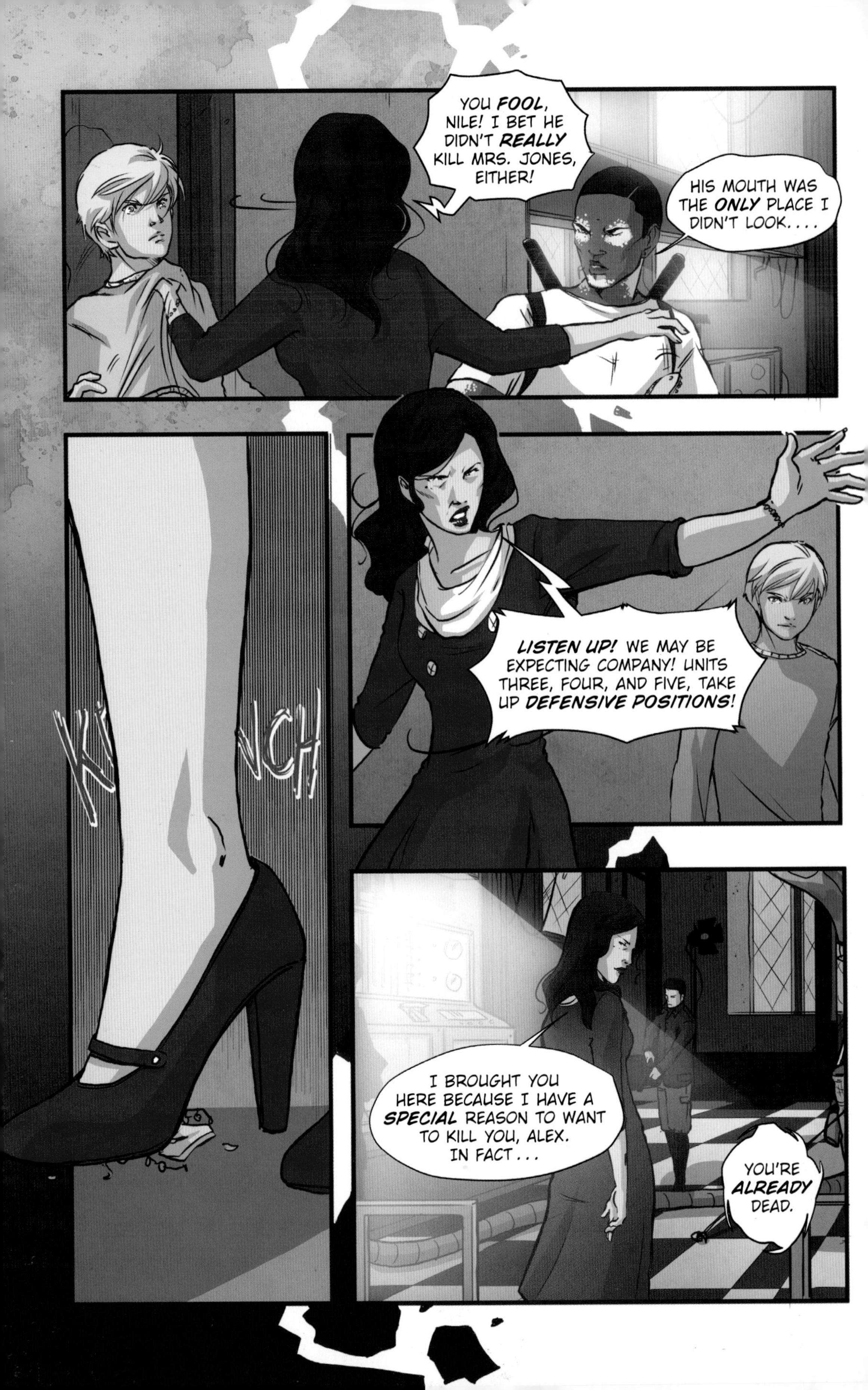
YOU FOOL, NILE! I BET HE DIDN'T REALLY KILL MRS. JONES, EITHER!
HIS MOUTH WAS THE ONLY PLACE I DIDN'T LOOK. . . .
LISTEN UP! WE MAY BE EXPECTING COMPANY! UNITS THREE, FOUR, AND FIVE, TAKE UP DEFENSIVE POSITIONS!
I BROUGHT YOU HERE BECAUSE I HAVE A SPECIAL REASON TO WANT TO KILL YOU, ALEX. IN FACT . . .
YOU'RE ALREADY DEAD.

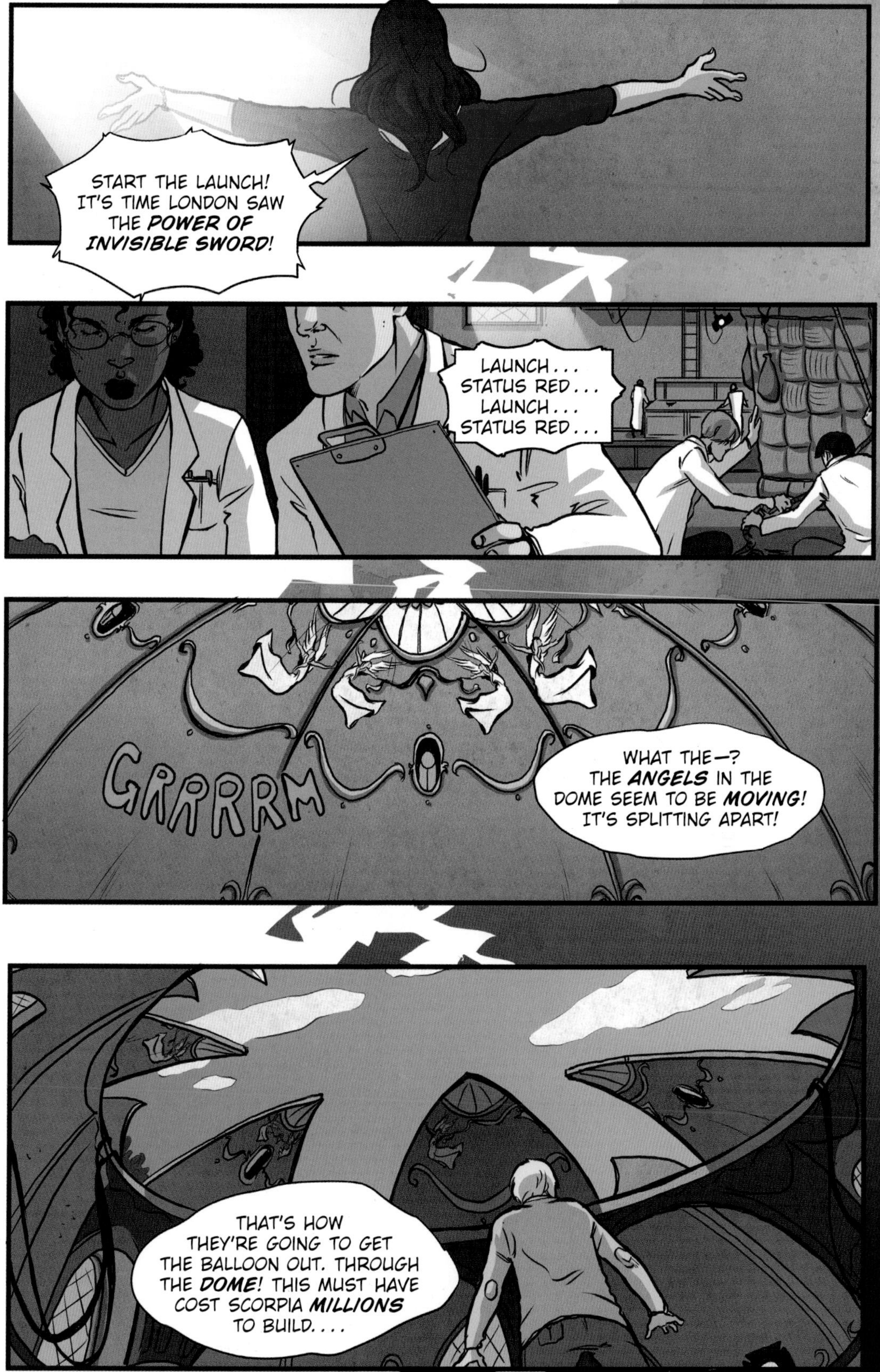
START THE LAUNCH! IT'S TIME LONDON SAW THE **POWER OF INVISIBLE SWORD**!
LAUNCH . . . STATUS RED . . . LAUNCH . . . STATUS RED . . .
GRRRRM
WHAT THE—? THE **ANGELS** IN THE DOME SEEM TO BE **MOVING**! IT'S SPLITTING APART!
THAT'S HOW THEY'RE GOING TO GET THE BALLOON OUT. THROUGH THE **DOME**! THIS MUST HAVE COST SCORPIA **MILLIONS** TO BUILD. . . .

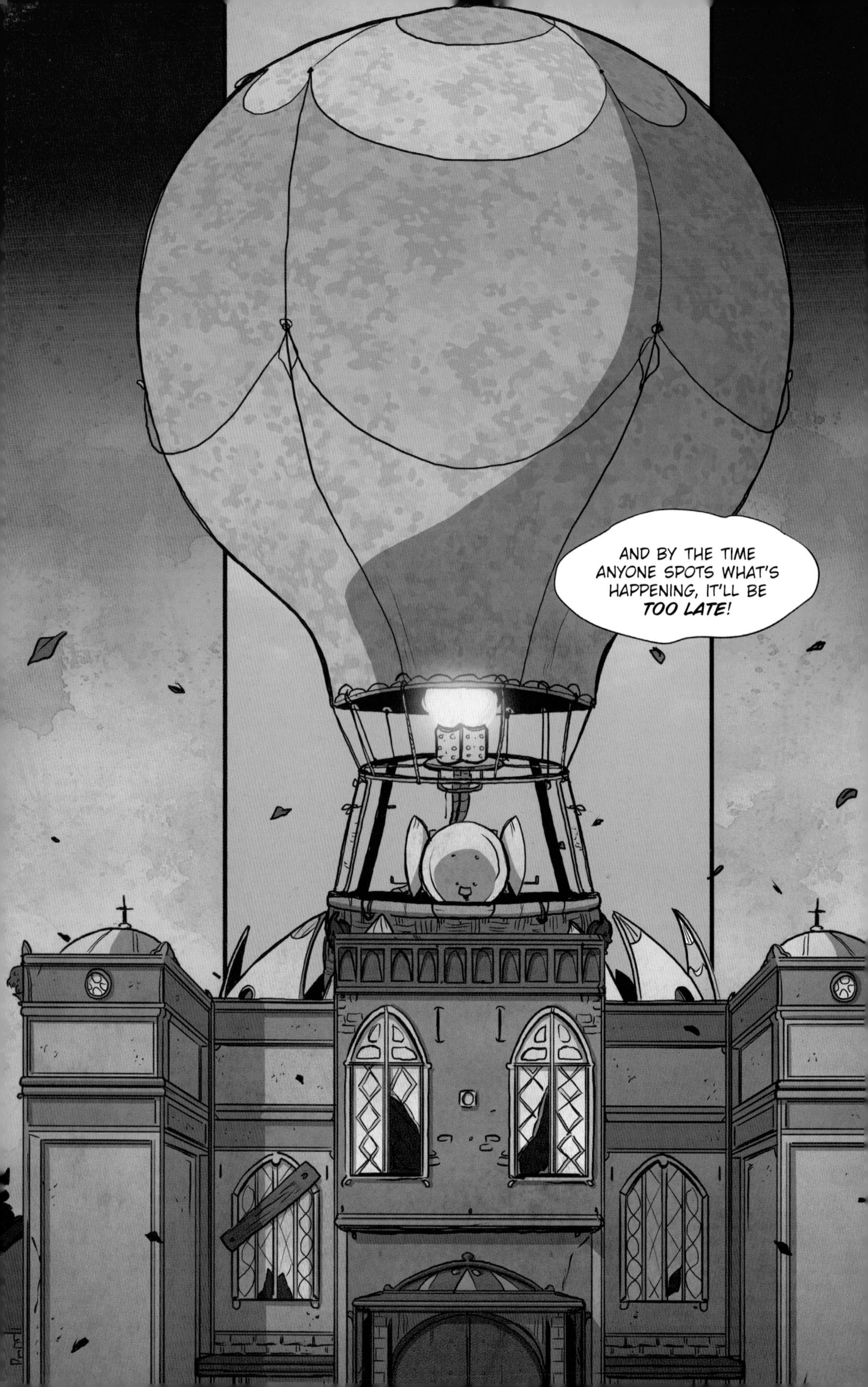
AND BY THE TIME ANYONE SPOTS WHAT'S HAPPENING, IT'LL BE *TOO LATE!*

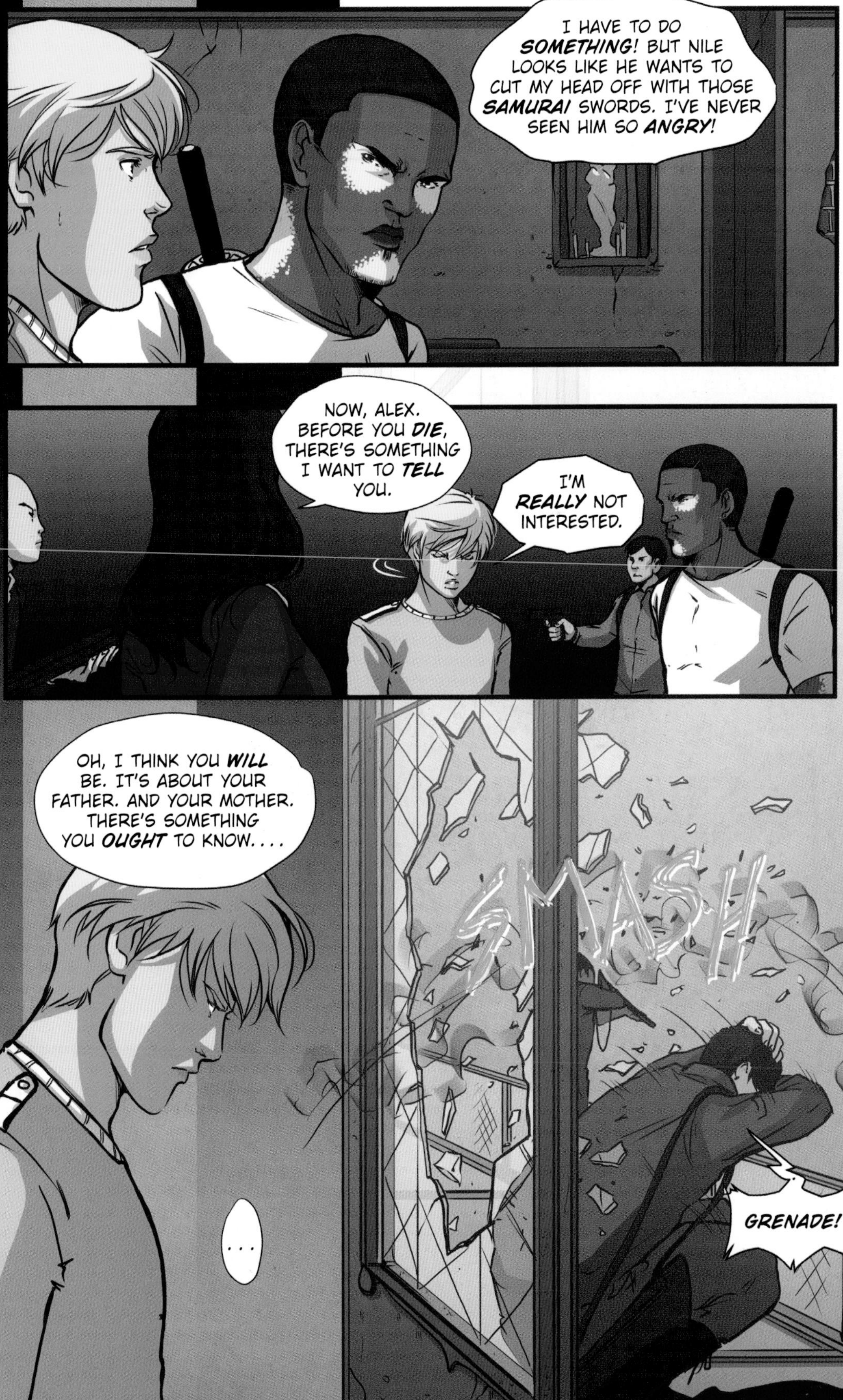
I HAVE TO DO SOMETHING! BUT NILE LOOKS LIKE HE WANTS TO CUT MY HEAD OFF WITH THOSE SAMURAI SWORDS. I'VE NEVER SEEN HIM SO ANGRY!
NOW, ALEX. BEFORE YOU DIE, THERE'S SOMETHING I WANT TO TELL YOU.
I'M REALLY NOT INTERESTED.
OH, I THINK YOU WILL BE. IT'S ABOUT YOUR FATHER. AND YOUR MOTHER. THERE'S SOMETHING YOU OUGHT TO KNOW. . . .
. . .
SMASH
GRENADE!

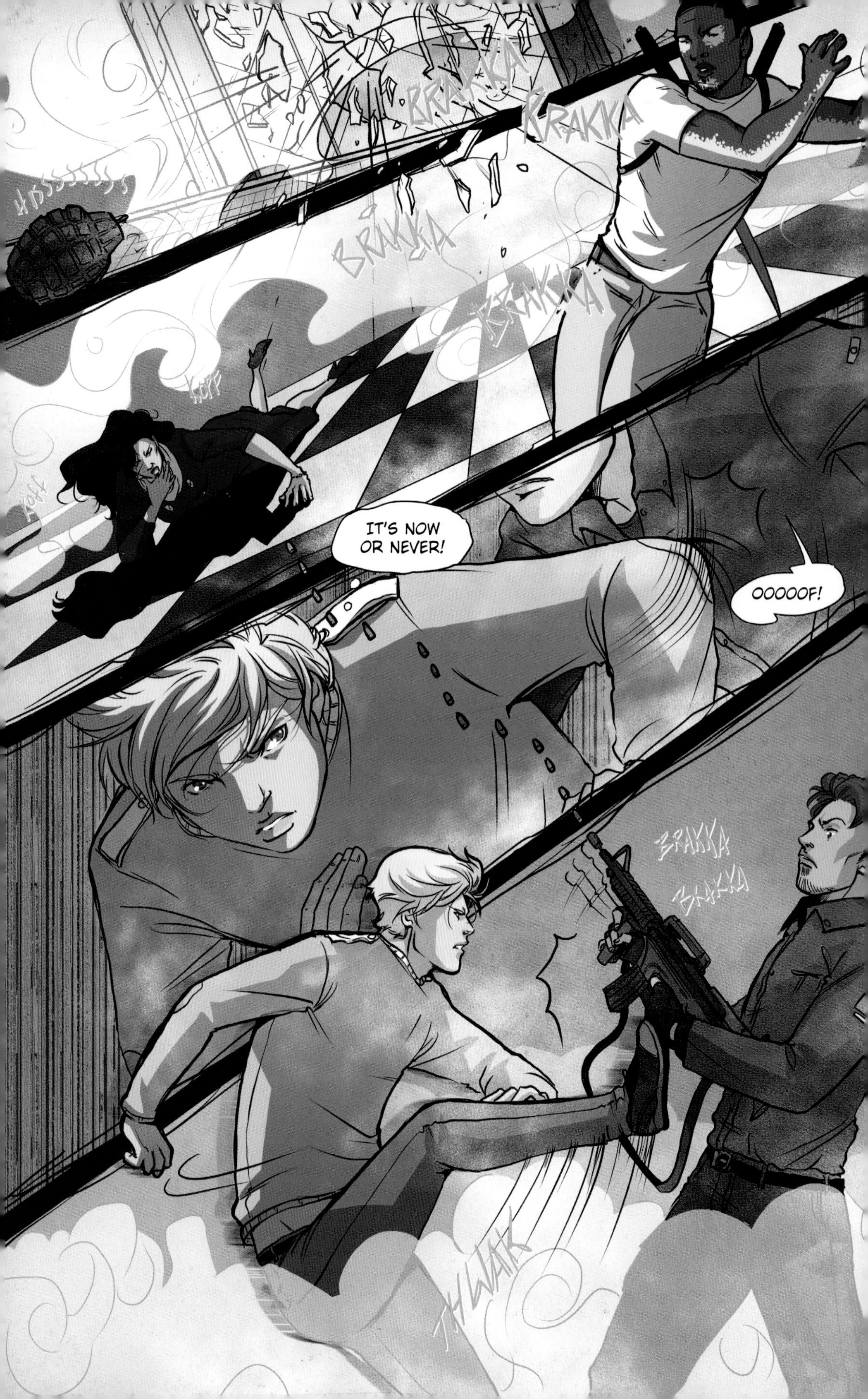

HISSSSSSSS
BRAKKA
BRAKKA
BRAKKA
BRAKKA
KOFF
KOFF
IT'S NOW OR NEVER!
OOOOOF!
BRAKKA
BRAKKA
THWAK

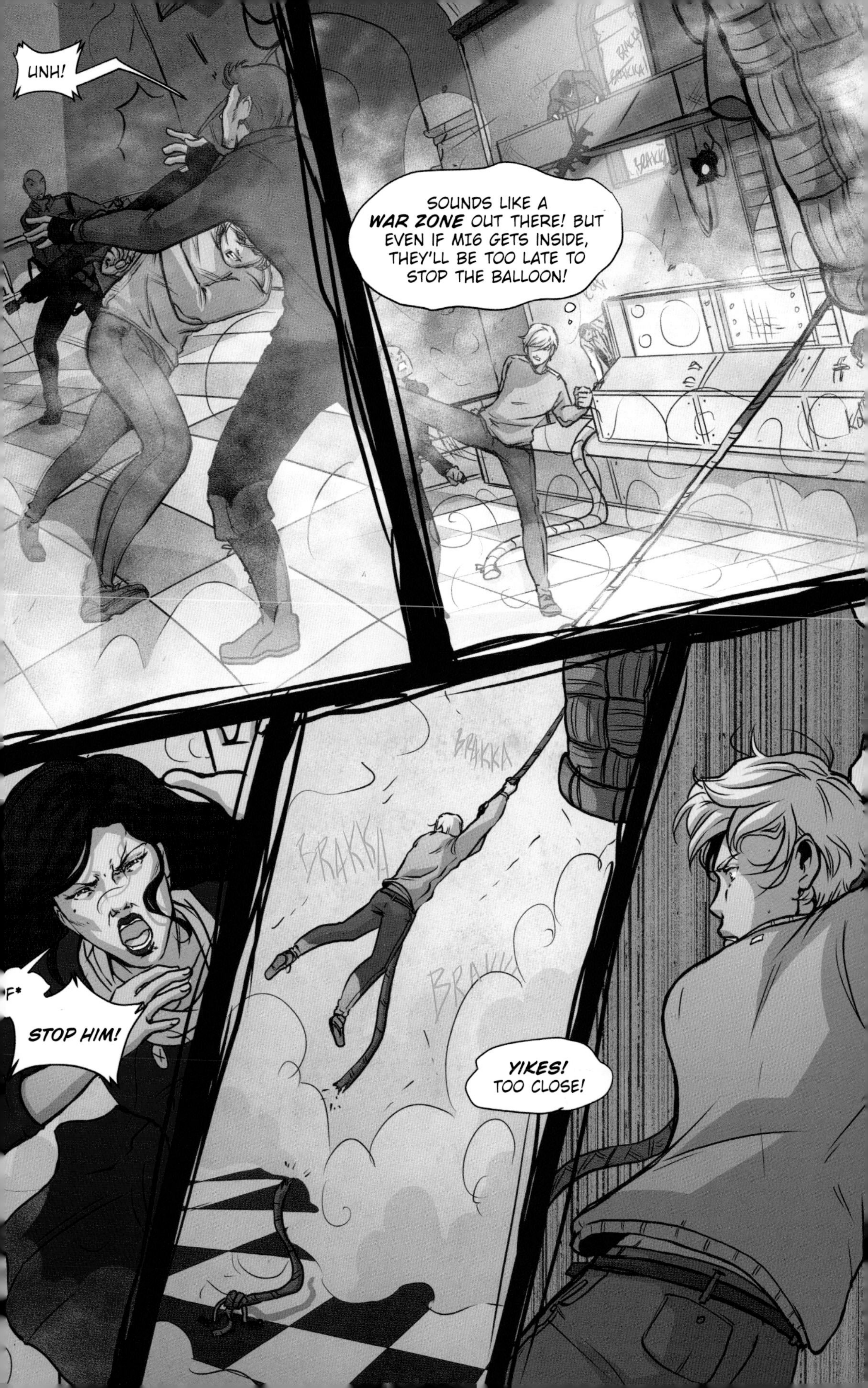
UNH!
SOUNDS LIKE A WAR ZONE OUT THERE! BUT EVEN IF MI6 GETS INSIDE, THEY'LL BE TOO LATE TO STOP THE BALLOON!
F*
STOP HIM!
BRAKKA
BRAKKA
YIKES! TOO CLOSE!

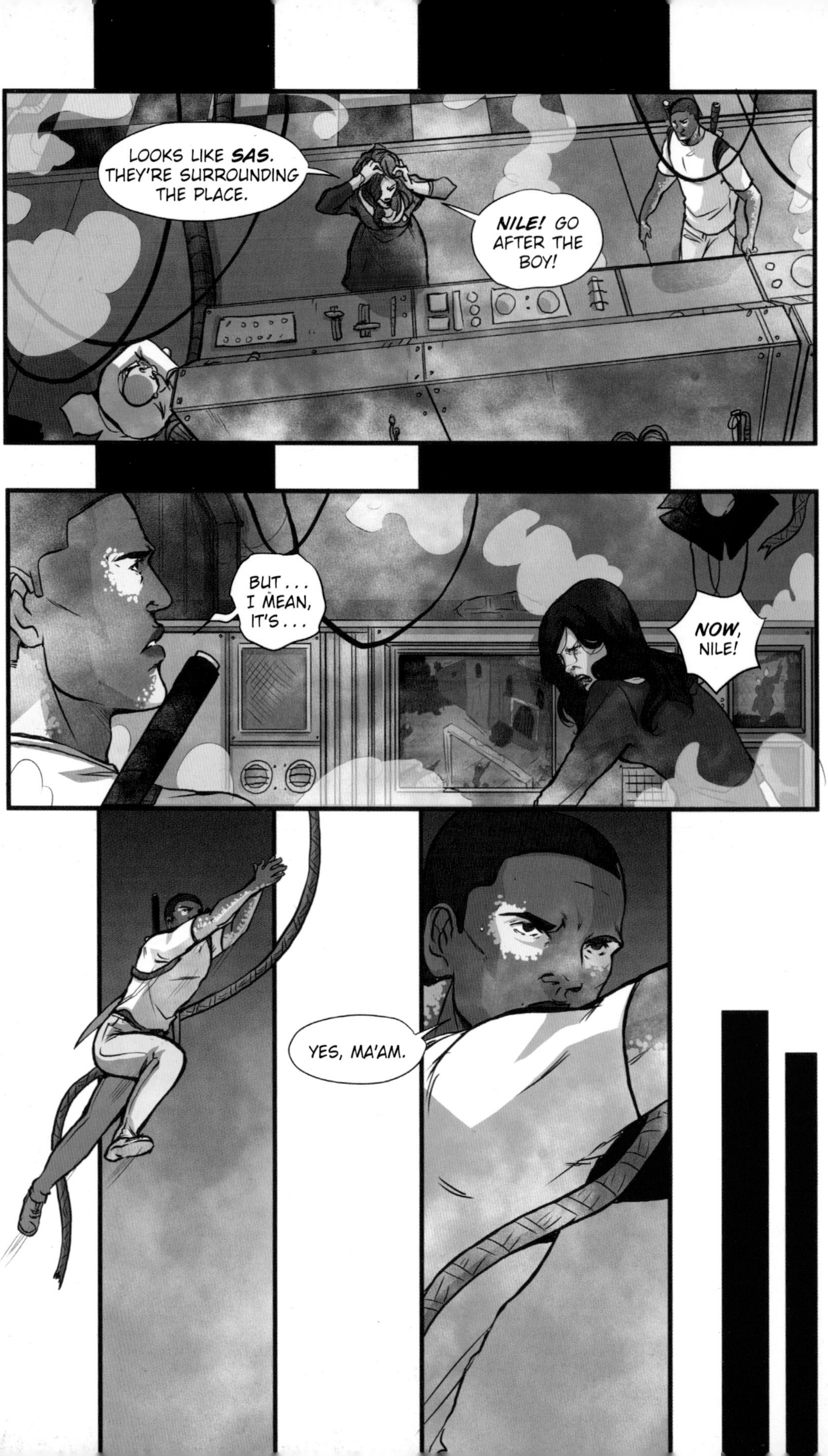
LOOKS LIKE **SAS**. THEY'RE SURROUNDING THE PLACE.
NILE! GO AFTER THE BOY!
BUT . . . I MEAN, IT'S . . .
NOW, NILE!
YES, MA'AM.

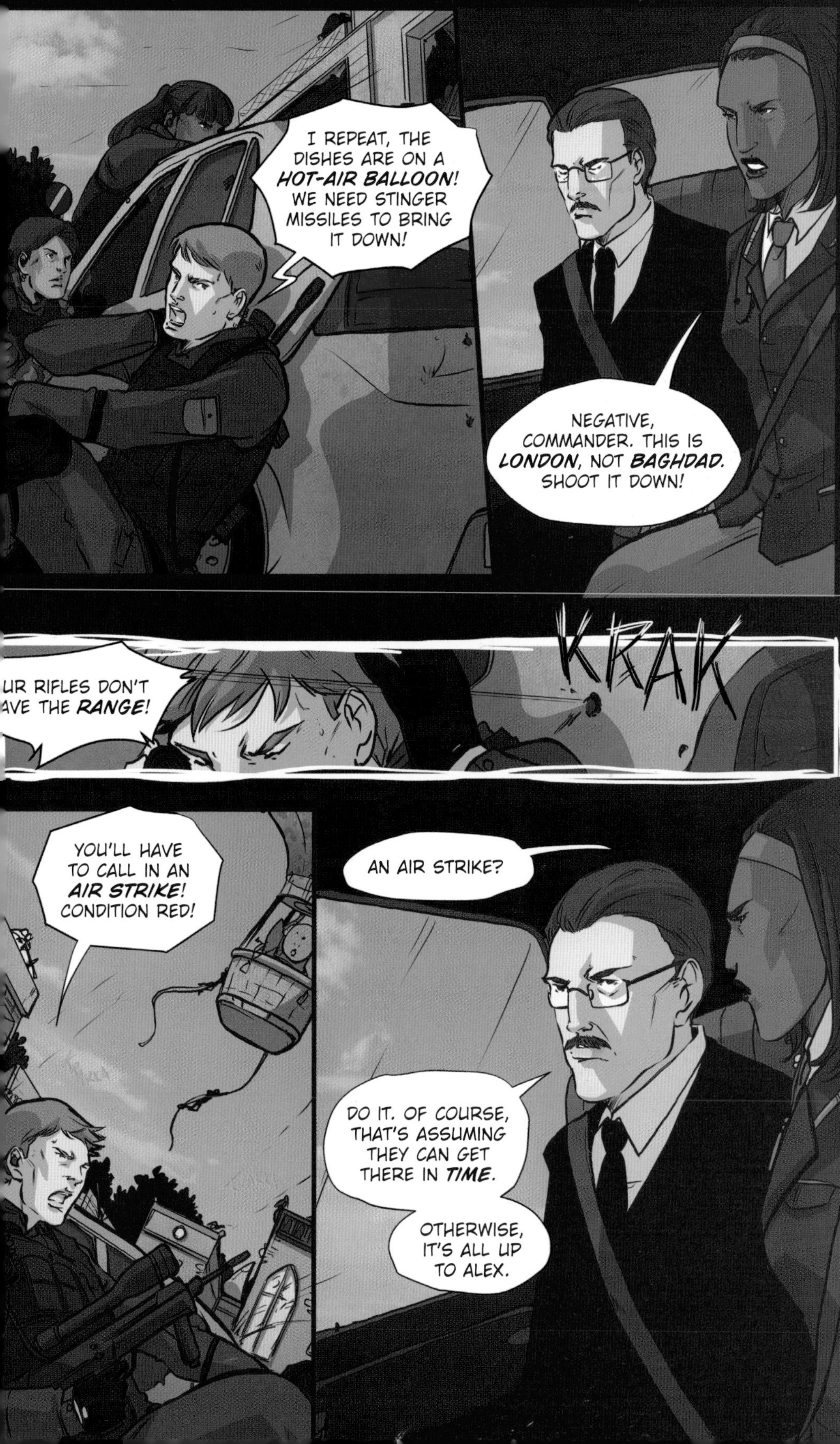
I REPEAT, THE DISHES ARE ON A ***HOT-AIR BALLOON***! WE NEED STINGER MISSILES TO BRING IT DOWN!
NEGATIVE, COMMANDER. THIS IS ***LONDON***, NOT ***BAGHDAD***. SHOOT IT DOWN!
UR RIFLES DON'T AVE THE ***RANGE***!
KRAK
YOU'LL HAVE TO CALL IN AN ***AIR STRIKE***! CONDITION RED!
AN AIR STRIKE?
DO IT. OF COURSE, THAT'S ASSUMING THEY CAN GET THERE IN ***TIME***.
OTHERWISE, IT'S ALL UP TO ALEX.

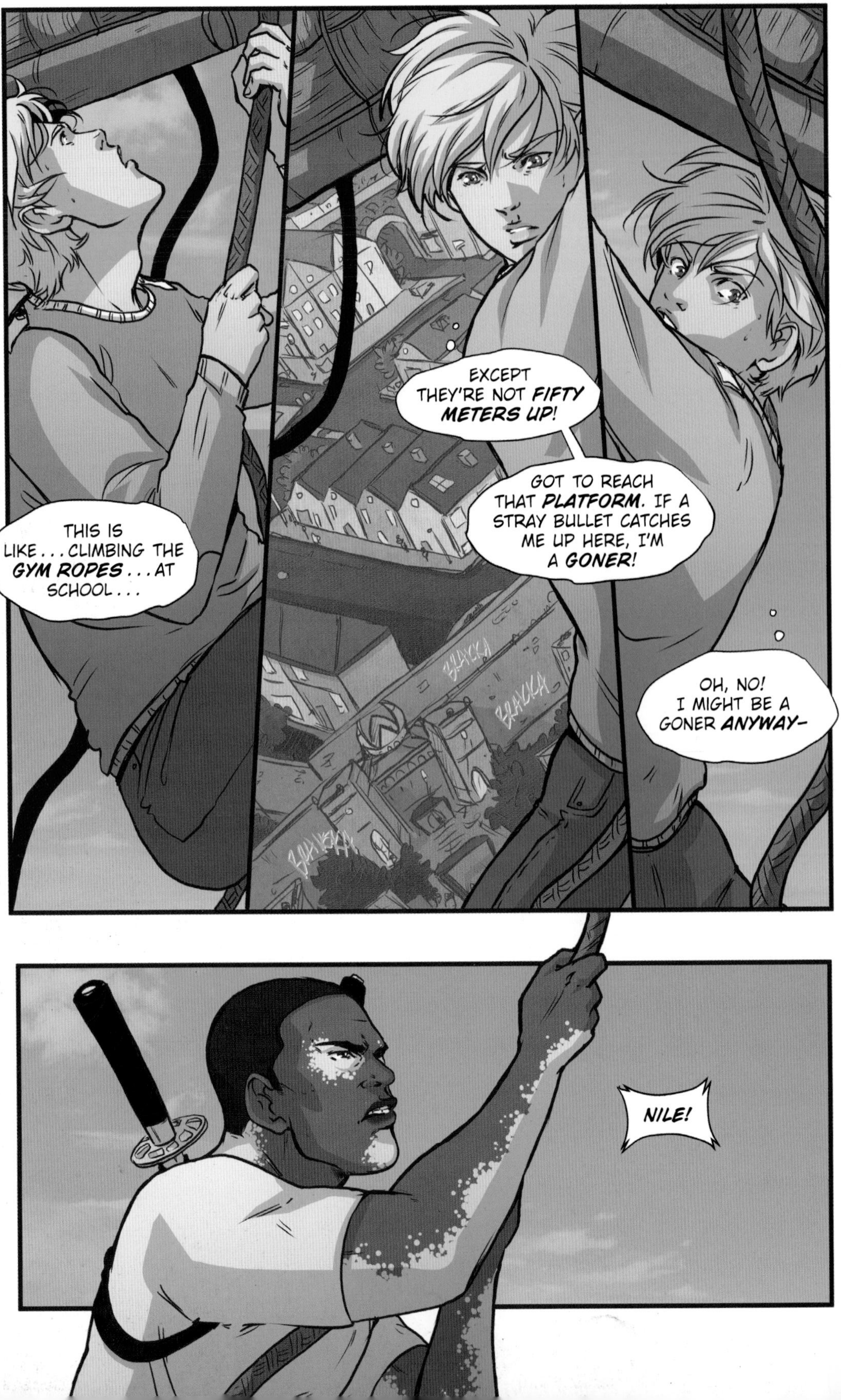
THIS IS LIKE . . . CLIMBING THE **GYM ROPES** . . . AT SCHOOL . . .
EXCEPT THEY'RE NOT ***FIFTY METERS UP***!
GOT TO REACH THAT ***PLATFORM.*** IF A STRAY BULLET CATCHES ME UP HERE, I'M A ***GONER***!
OH, NO! I MIGHT BE A GONER ***ANYWAY***-
NILE!

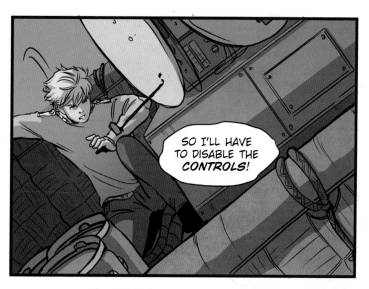

SO I'LL HAVE TO DISABLE THE *CONTROLS!*

DISHES... ARE SECURED *TIGHT*...CAN'T PULL THEM OFF...

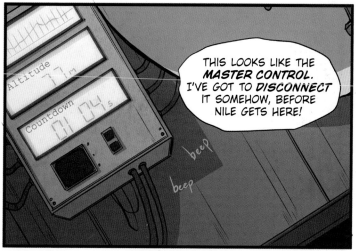

Altitude

Countdown

THIS LOOKS LIKE THE *MASTER CONTROL.* I'VE GOT TO *DISCONNECT* IT SOMEHOW, BEFORE NILE GETS HERE!

beep

beep

NNNGH! STUCK... TIGHT!

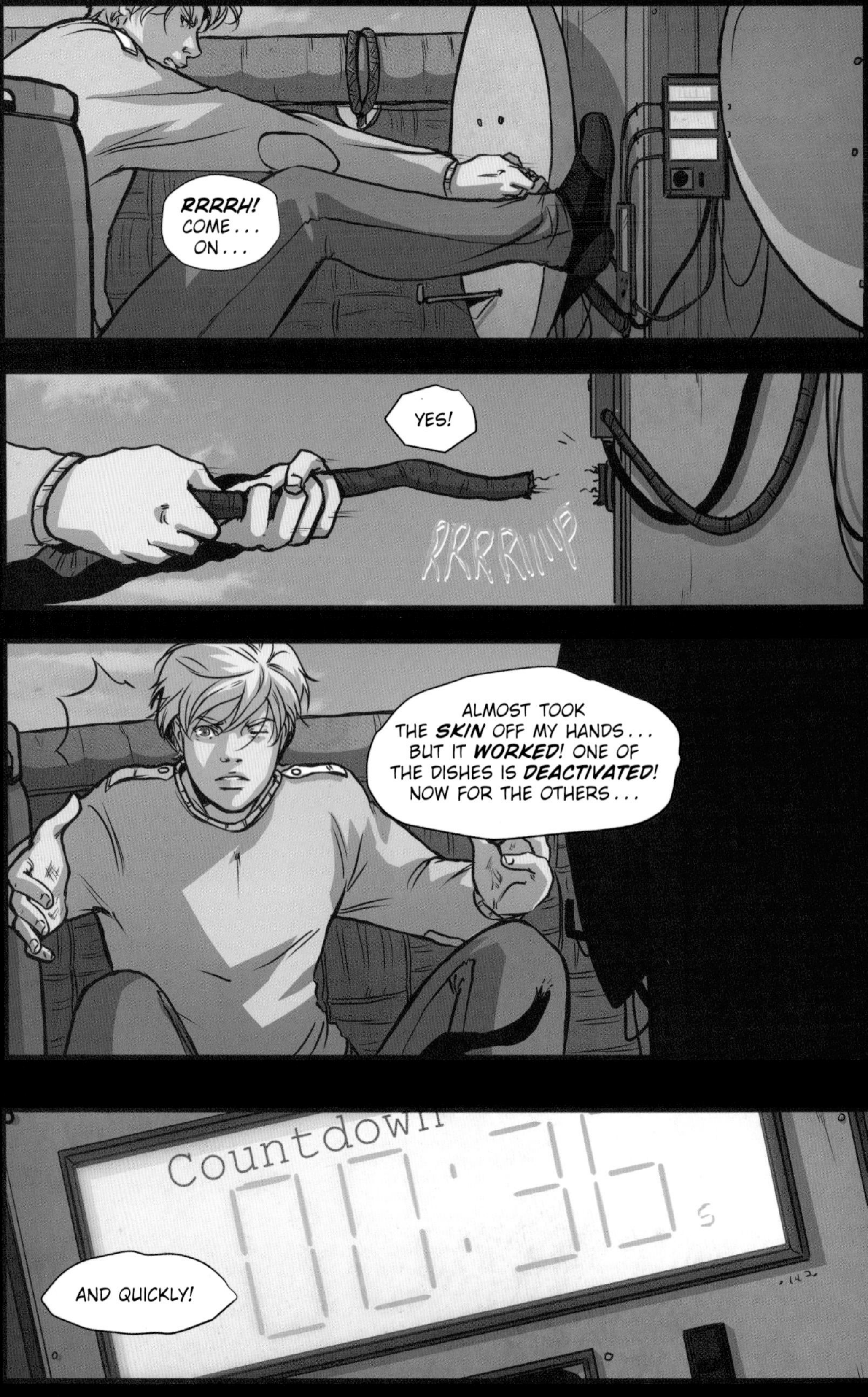

RRRRH! COME . . . ON . . .
YES!
RRRRIIIP
ALMOST TOOK THE SKIN OFF MY HANDS . . . BUT IT WORKED! ONE OF THE DISHES IS DEACTIVATED! NOW FOR THE OTHERS . . .
Countdown
00:35 s
AND QUICKLY!

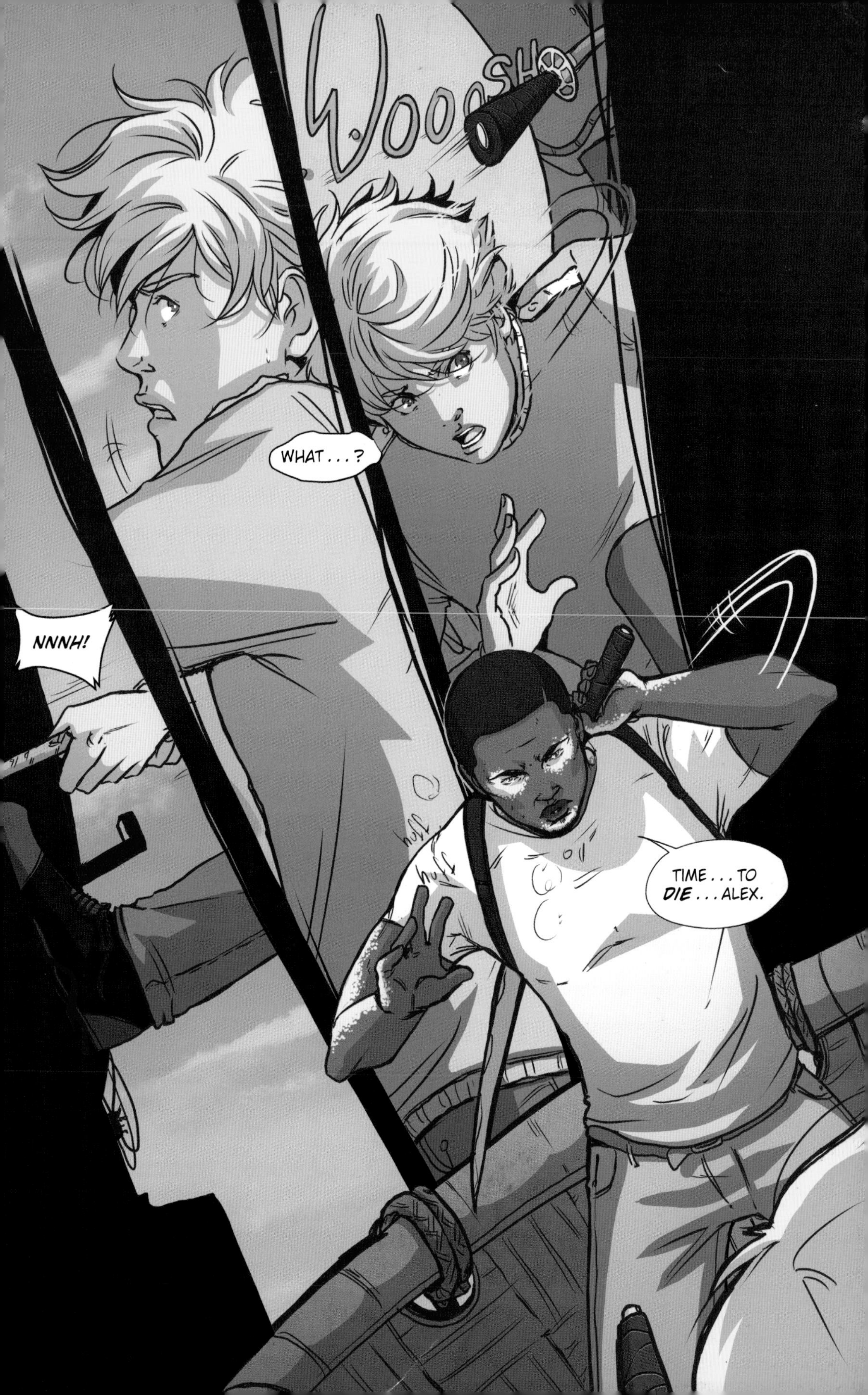
WOOOSH
WHAT . . . ?
NNNH!
huff
huff
TIME . . . TO DIE . . . ALEX.

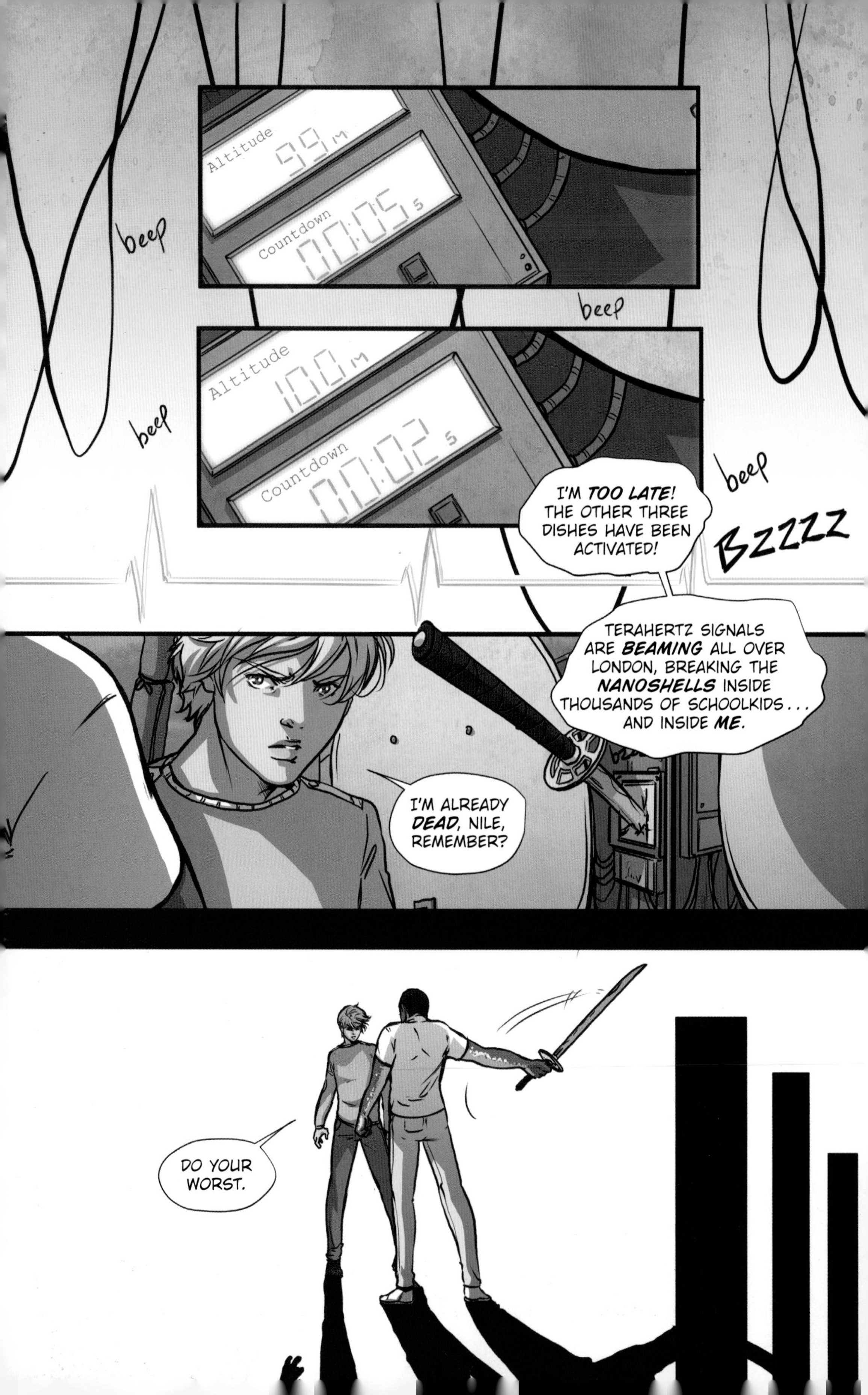
Altitude 99 M
Countdown 00:05 s
beep
beep
Altitude 100 M
Countdown 00:02 s
beep
beep
I'M TOO LATE! THE OTHER THREE DISHES HAVE BEEN ACTIVATED!
BZZZZ
TERAHERTZ SIGNALS ARE BEAMING ALL OVER LONDON, BREAKING THE NANOSHELLS INSIDE THOUSANDS OF SCHOOLKIDS . . . AND INSIDE ME.
I'M ALREADY DEAD, NILE, REMEMBER?
DO YOUR WORST.

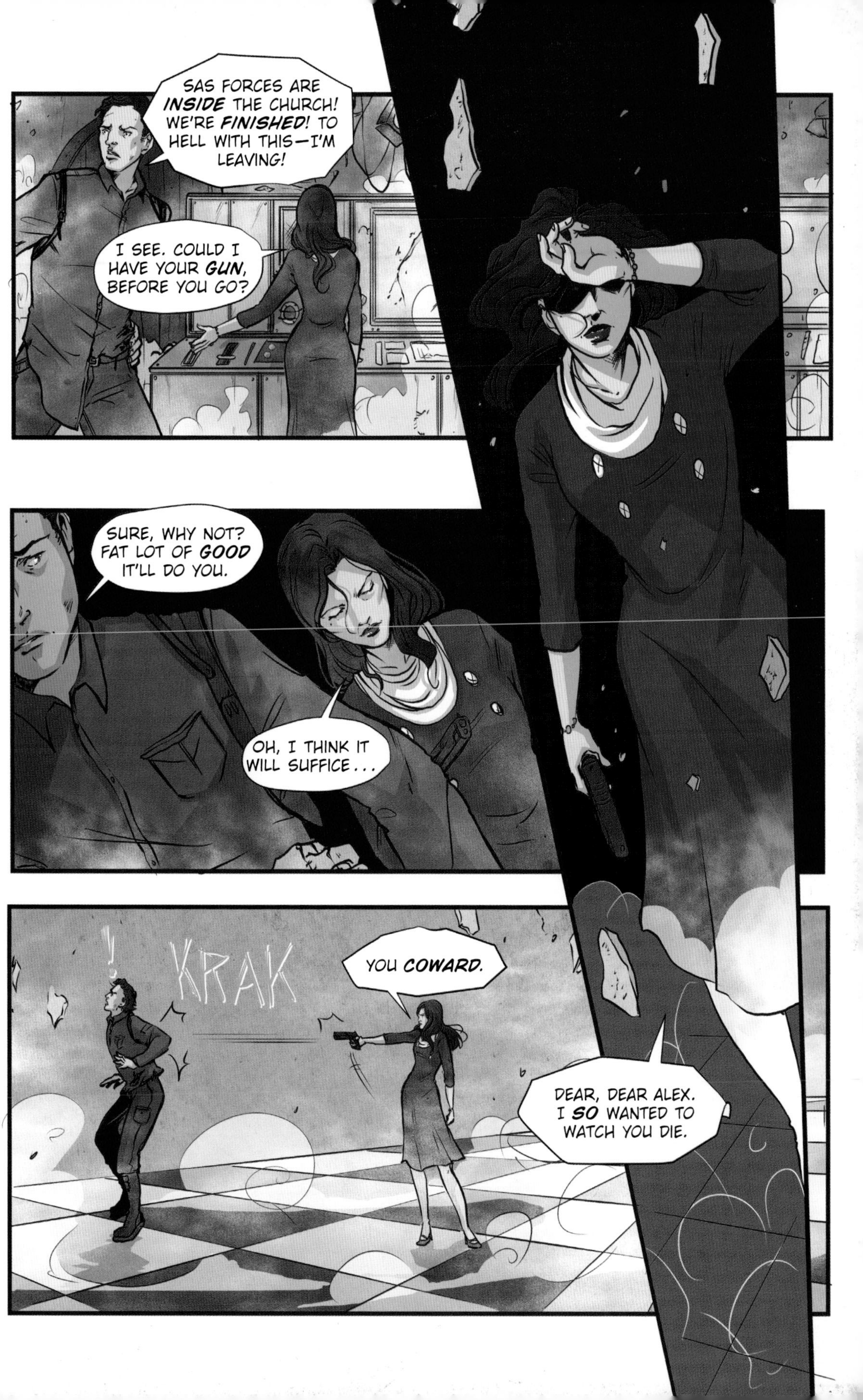
SAS FORCES ARE INSIDE THE CHURCH! WE'RE FINISHED! TO HELL WITH THIS—I'M LEAVING!
I SEE. COULD I HAVE YOUR GUN, BEFORE YOU GO?
SURE, WHY NOT? FAT LOT OF GOOD IT'LL DO YOU.
OH, I THINK IT WILL SUFFICE . . .
!
KRAK
YOU COWARD.
DEAR, DEAR ALEX. I SO WANTED TO WATCH YOU DIE.

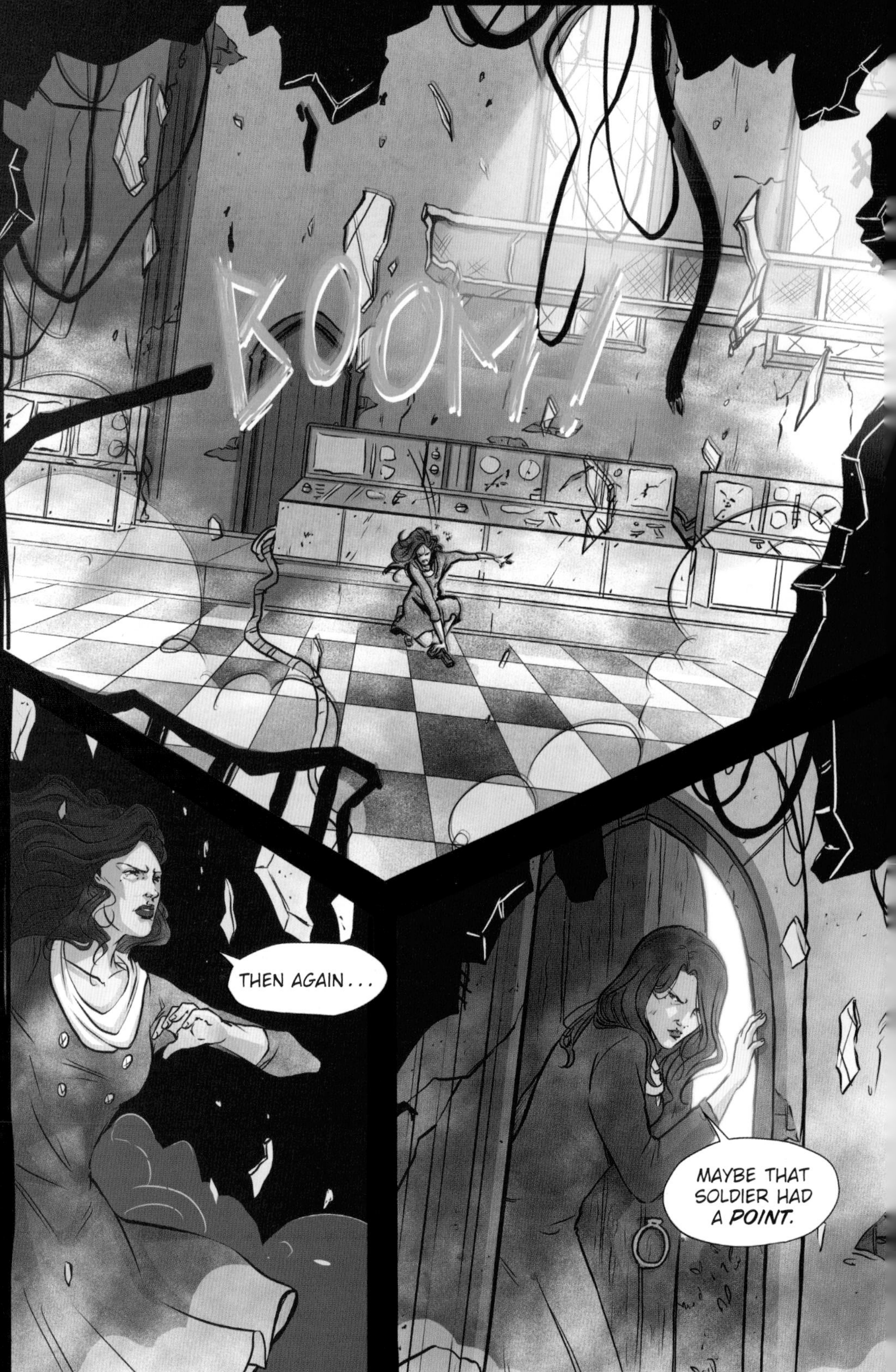
BOOM!!
THEN AGAIN . . .
MAYBE THAT SOLDIER HAD A *POINT.*

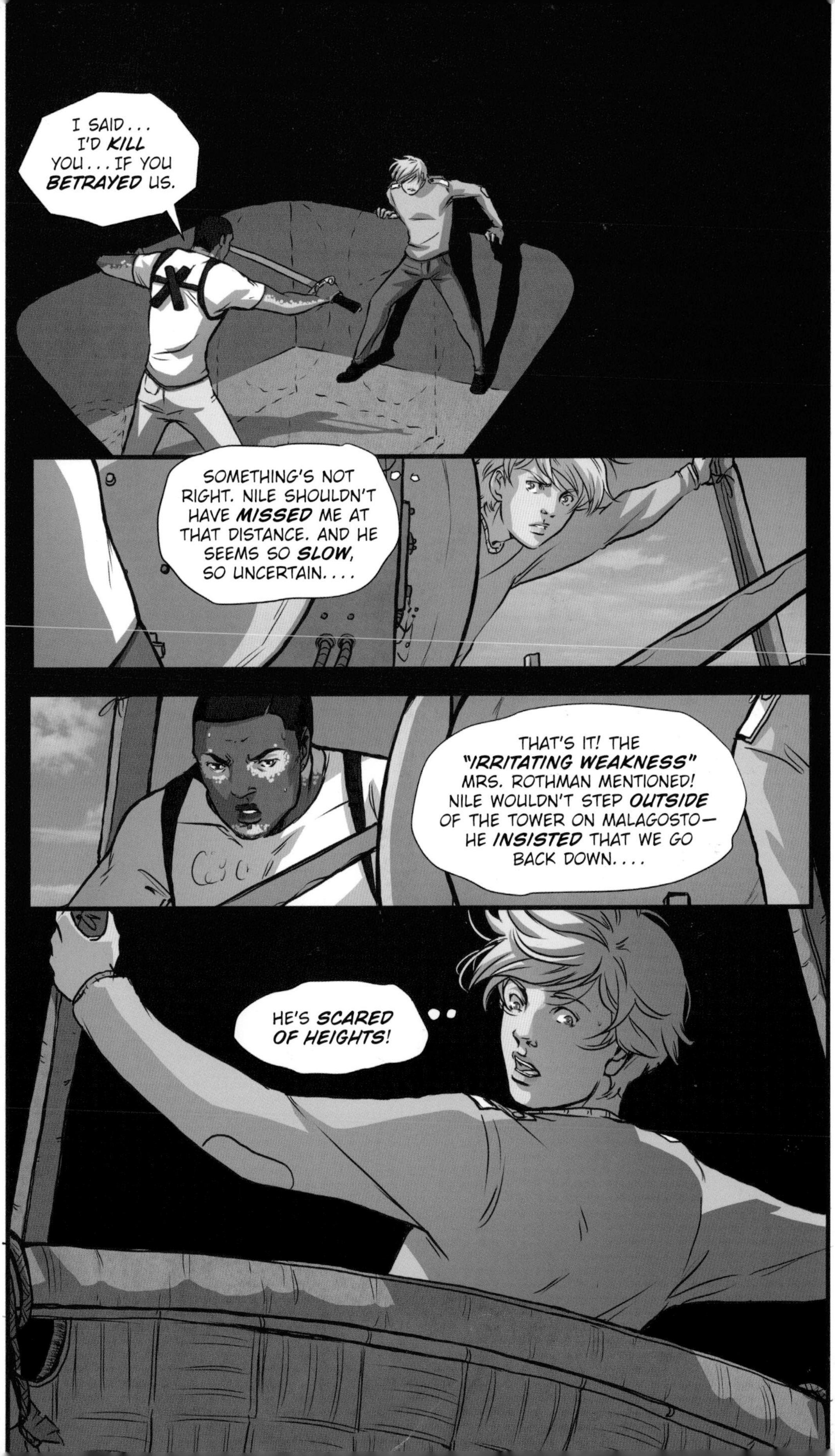
I SAID... I'D KILL YOU... IF YOU BETRAYED US.
SOMETHING'S NOT RIGHT. NILE SHOULDN'T HAVE MISSED ME AT THAT DISTANCE. AND HE SEEMS SO SLOW, SO UNCERTAIN....
THAT'S IT! THE "IRRITATING WEAKNESS" MRS. ROTHMAN MENTIONED! NILE WOULDN'T STEP OUTSIDE OF THE TOWER ON MALAGOSTO— HE INSISTED THAT WE GO BACK DOWN....
HE'S SCARED OF HEIGHTS!

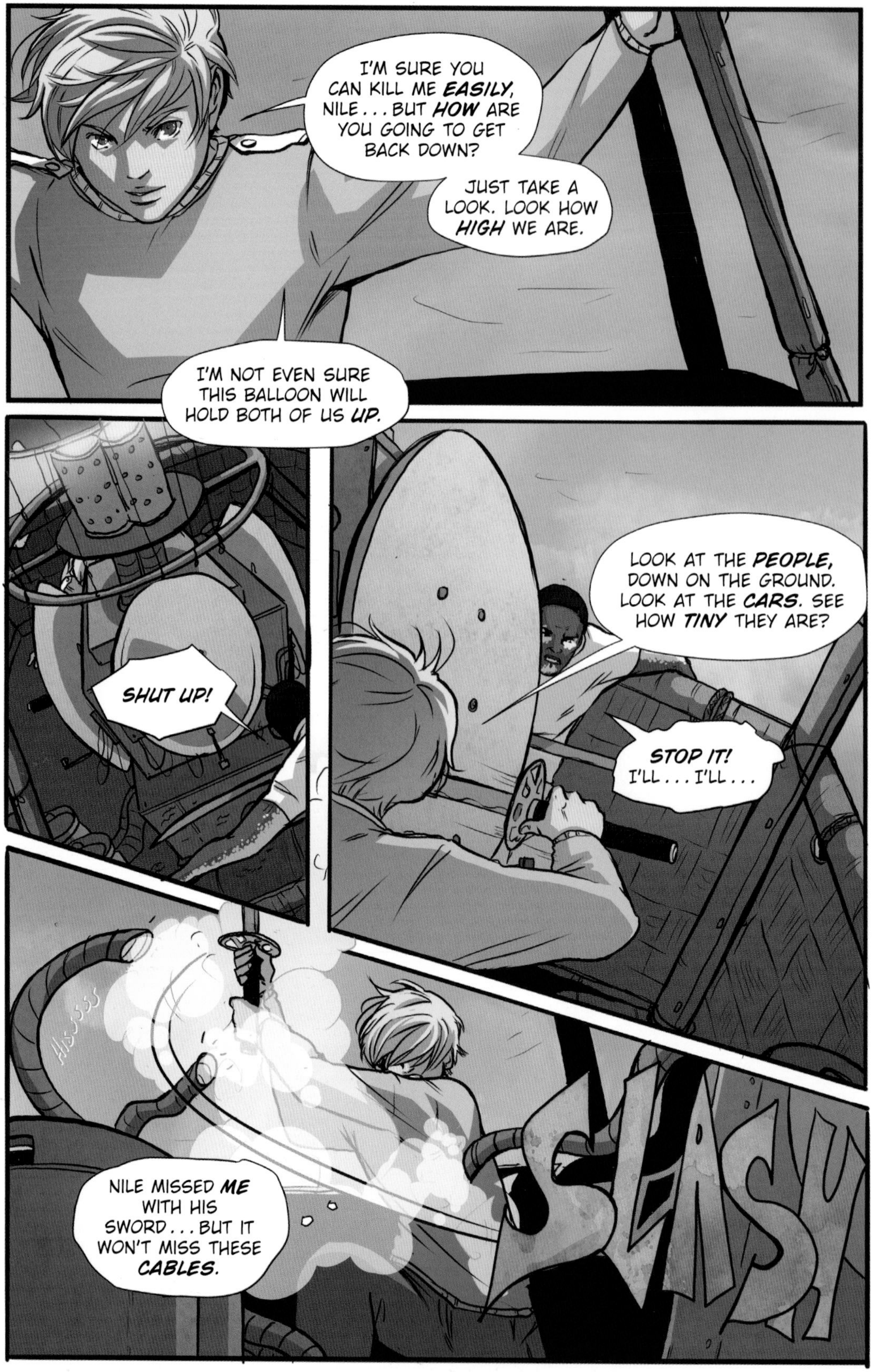
I'M SURE YOU CAN KILL ME EASILY, NILE . . . BUT HOW ARE YOU GOING TO GET BACK DOWN?
JUST TAKE A LOOK. LOOK HOW HIGH WE ARE.
I'M NOT EVEN SURE THIS BALLOON WILL HOLD BOTH OF US UP.
SHUT UP!
LOOK AT THE PEOPLE, DOWN ON THE GROUND. LOOK AT THE CARS. SEE HOW TINY THEY ARE?
STOP IT! I'LL . . . I'LL . . .
NILE MISSED ME WITH HIS SWORD . . . BUT IT WON'T MISS THESE CABLES.

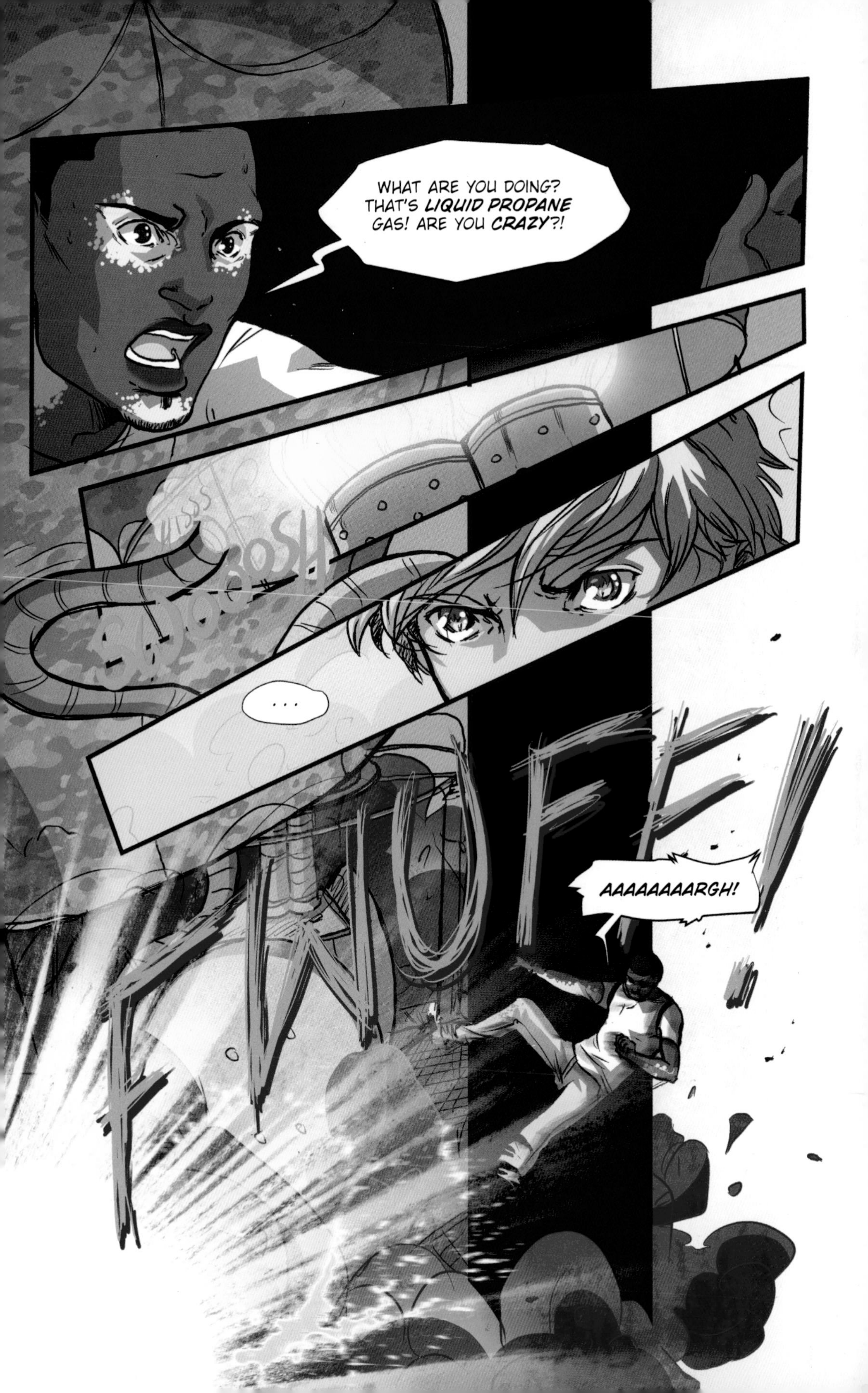
WHAT ARE YOU DOING? THAT'S LIQUID PROPANE GAS! ARE YOU CRAZY?!
SHOOOSH
. . .
FWUFF!
AAAAAAAARGH!

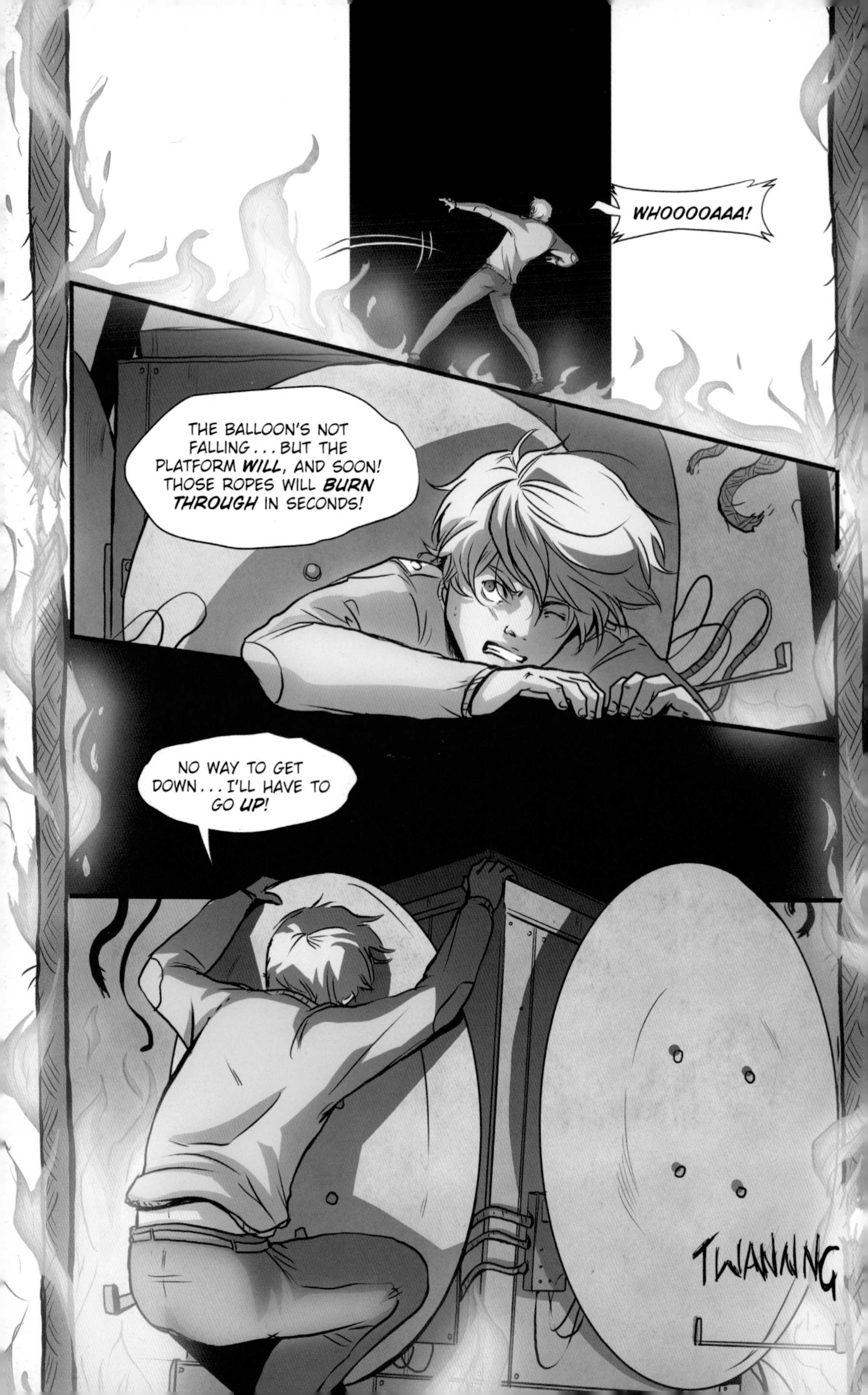
WHOOOOAAA!
THE BALLOON'S NOT FALLING . . . BUT THE PLATFORM WILL, AND SOON! THOSE ROPES WILL BURN THROUGH IN SECONDS!
NO WAY TO GET DOWN . . . I'LL HAVE TO GO UP!
TWANNNG

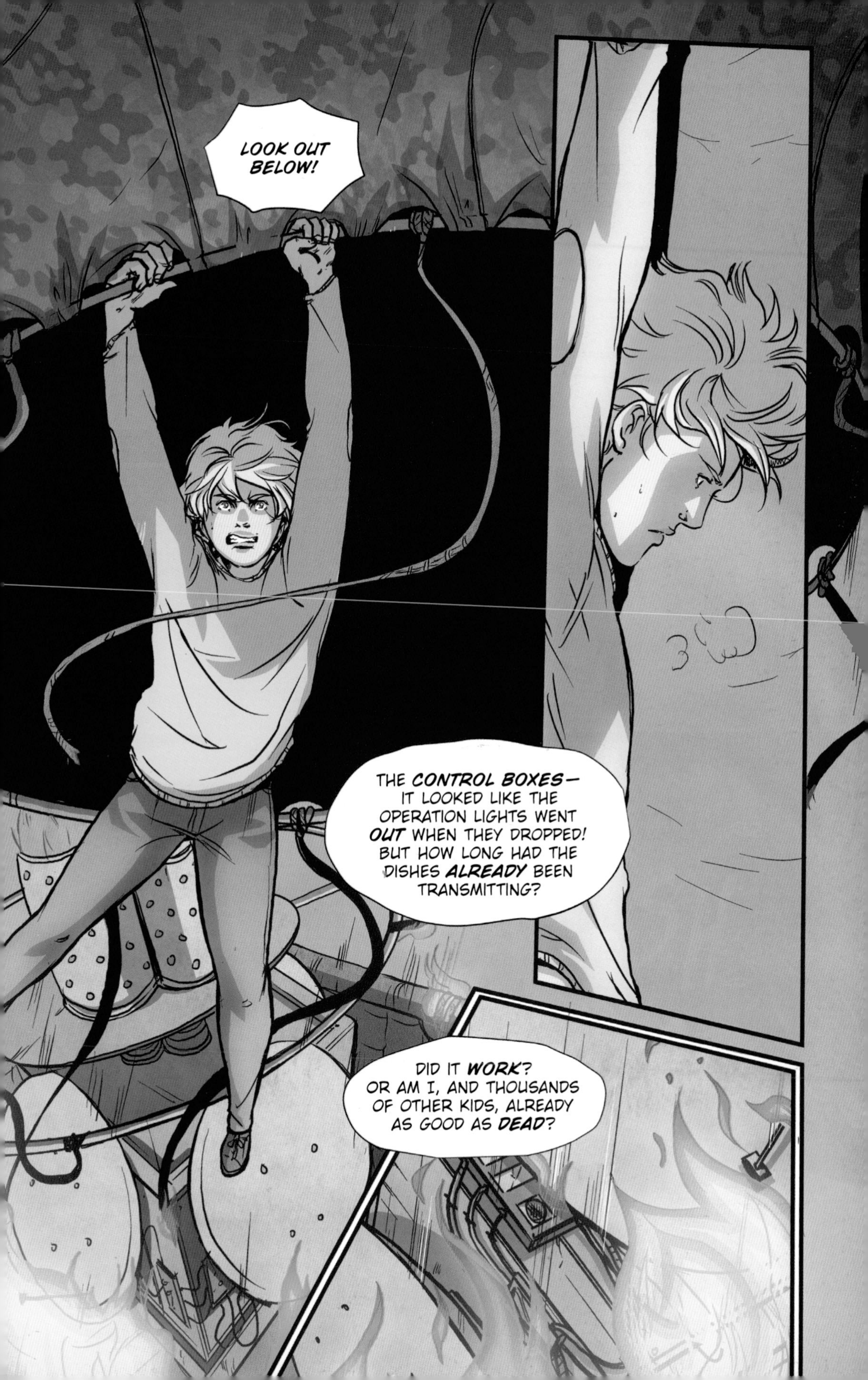
LOOK OUT BELOW!
THE CONTROL BOXES— IT LOOKED LIKE THE OPERATION LIGHTS WENT OUT WHEN THEY DROPPED! BUT HOW LONG HAD THE DISHES ALREADY BEEN TRANSMITTING?
DID IT WORK? OR AM I, AND THOUSANDS OF OTHER KIDS, ALREADY AS GOOD AS DEAD?

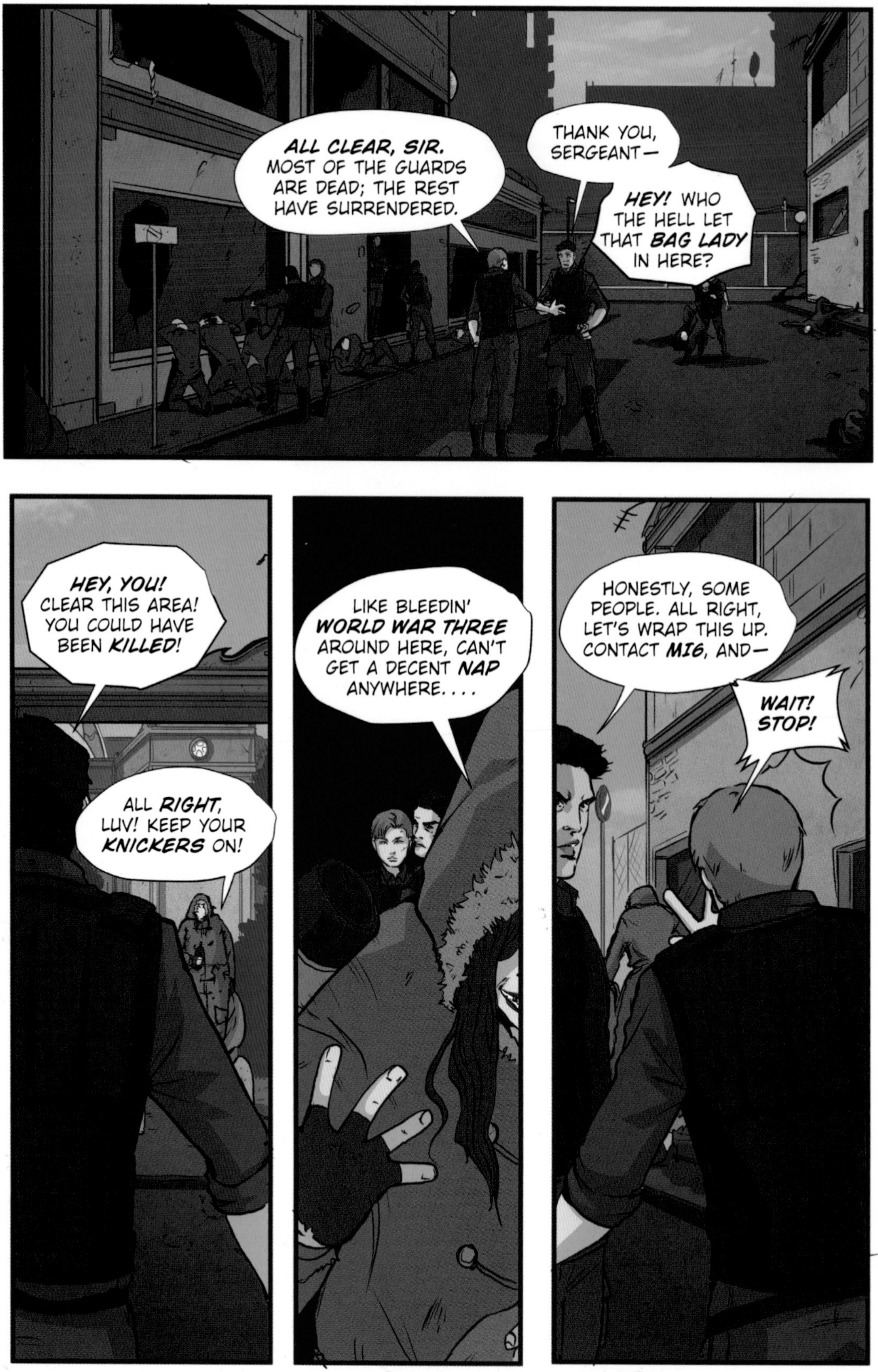
ALL CLEAR, SIR. MOST OF THE GUARDS ARE DEAD; THE REST HAVE SURRENDERED.
THANK YOU, SERGEANT—
HEY! WHO THE HELL LET THAT BAG LADY IN HERE?
HEY, YOU! CLEAR THIS AREA! YOU COULD HAVE BEEN KILLED!
ALL RIGHT, LUV! KEEP YOUR KNICKERS ON!
LIKE BLEEDIN' WORLD WAR THREE AROUND HERE, CAN'T GET A DECENT NAP ANYWHERE. . . .
HONESTLY, SOME PEOPLE. ALL RIGHT, LET'S WRAP THIS UP. CONTACT MI6, AND—
WAIT! STOP!

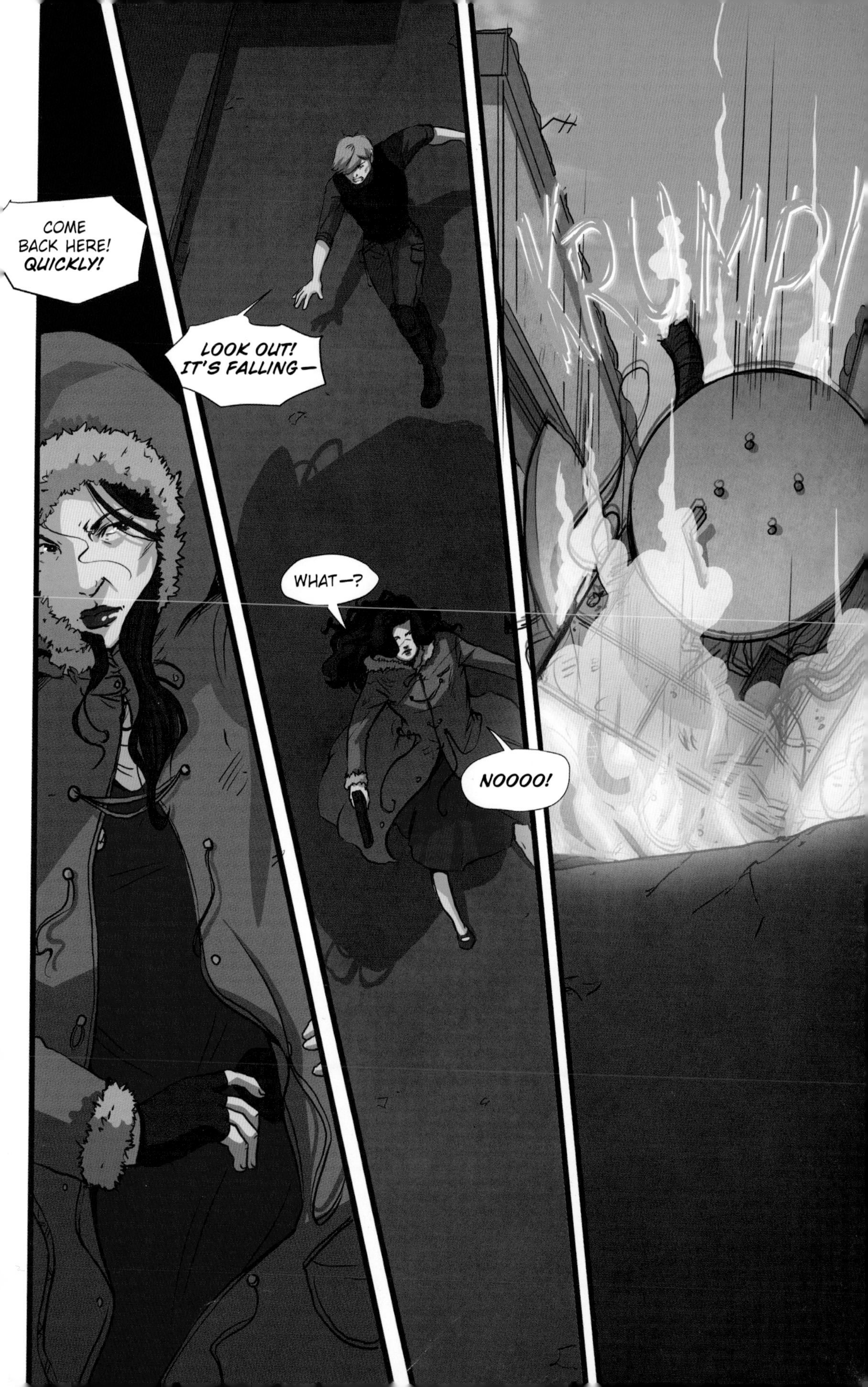

COME BACK HERE! QUICKLY!
LOOK OUT! IT'S FALLING—
WHAT—?
NOOOO!

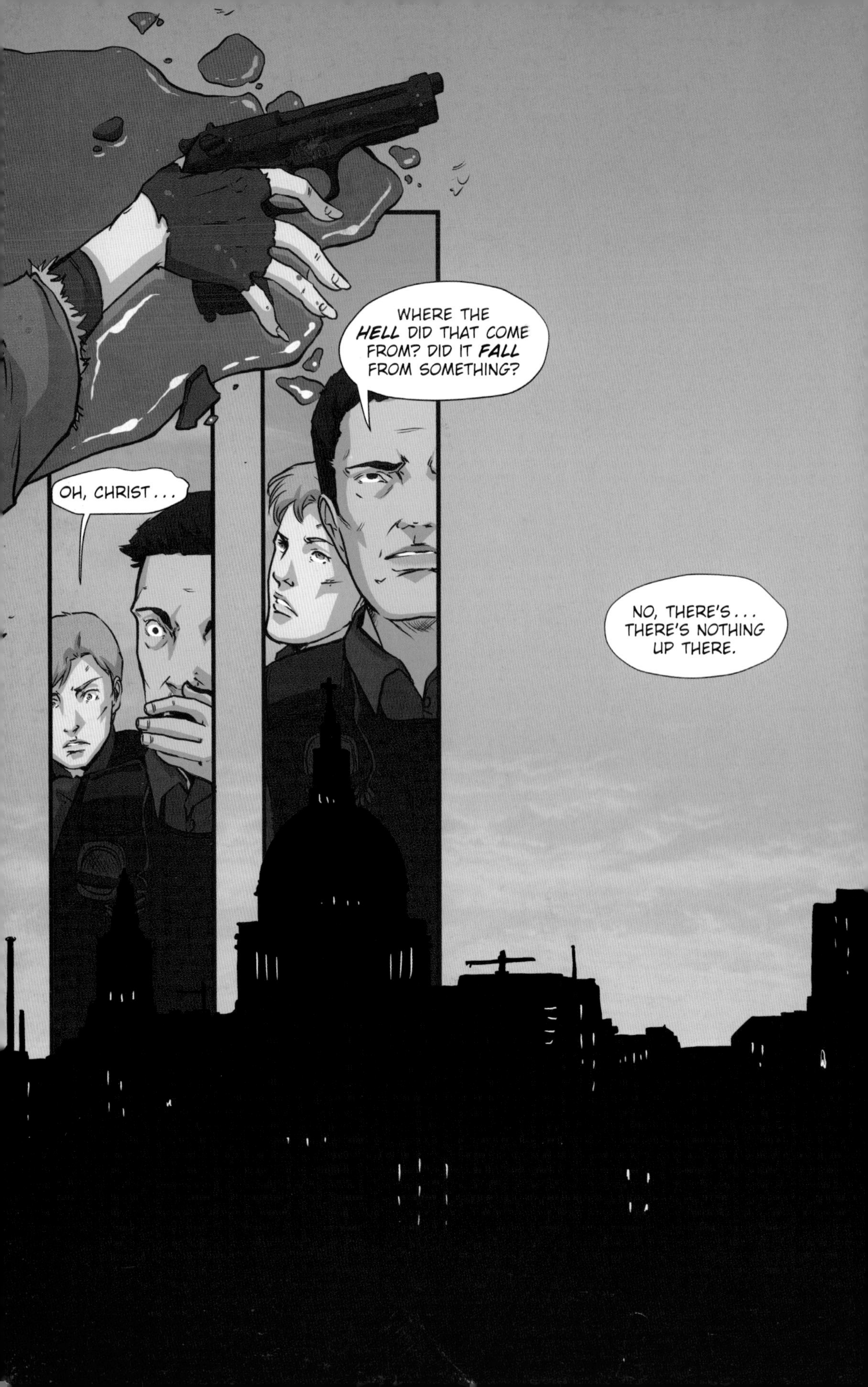
WHERE THE HELL DID THAT COME FROM? DID IT FALL FROM SOMETHING?
OH, CHRIST . . .
NO, THERE'S . . . THERE'S NOTHING UP THERE.

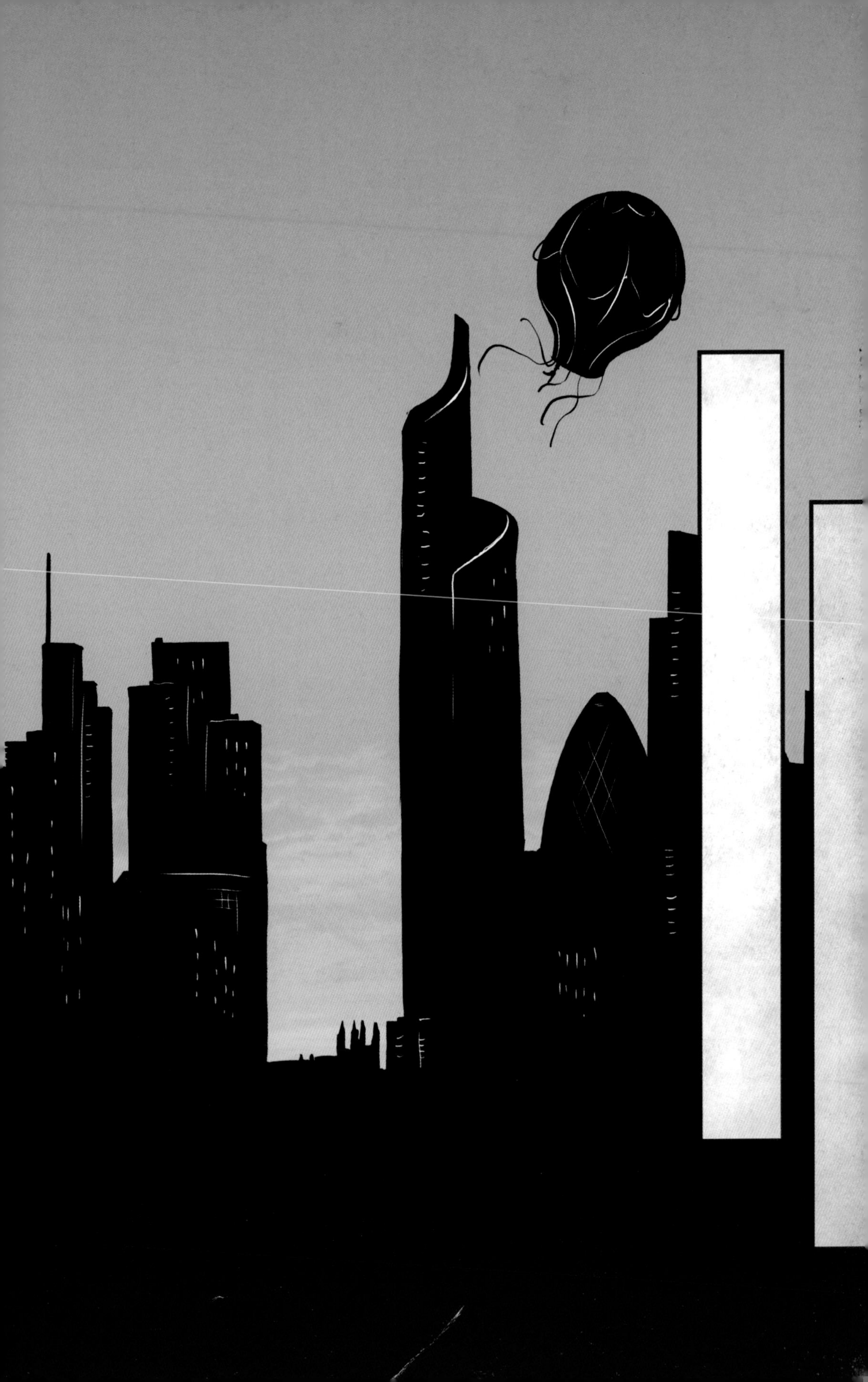

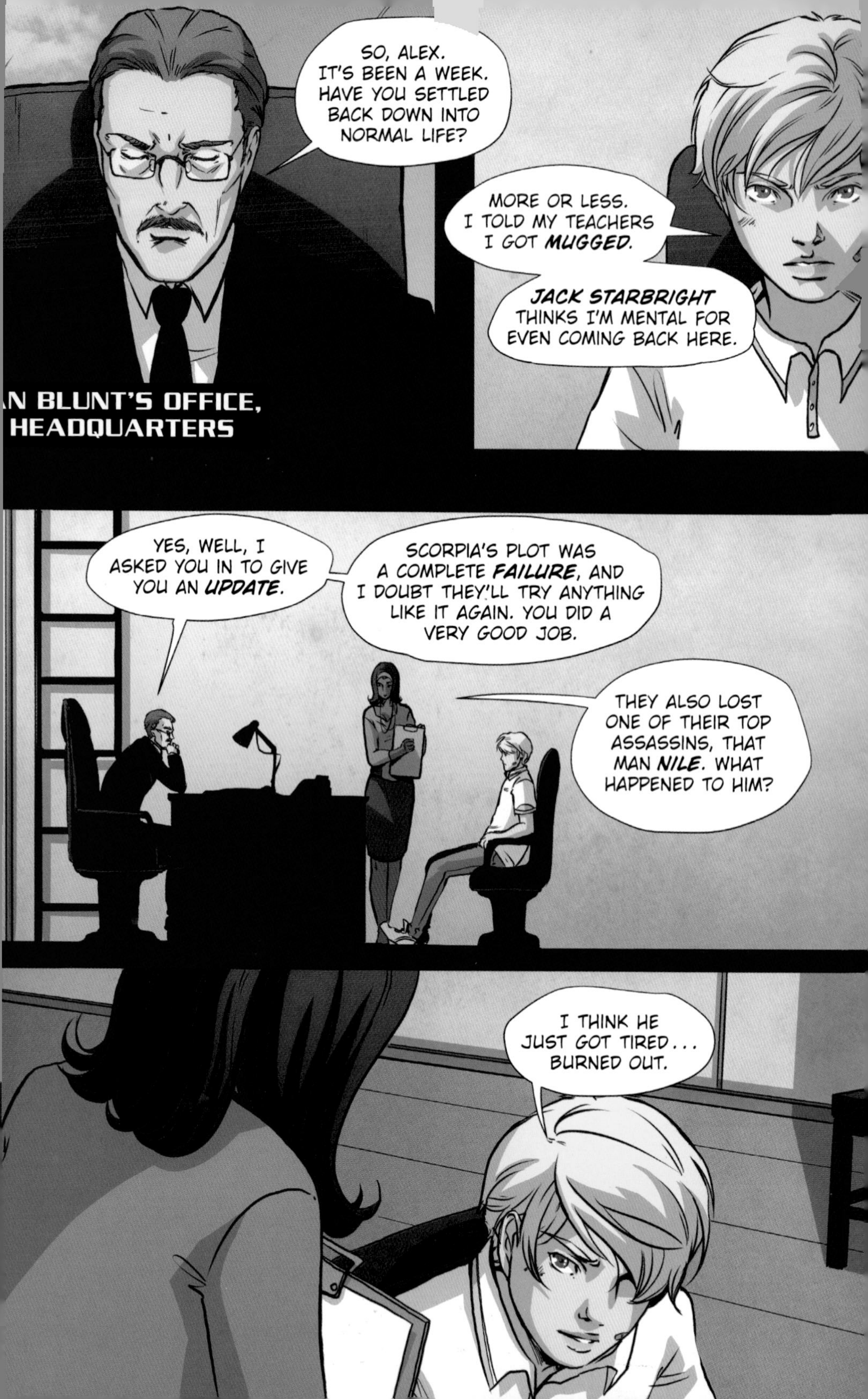
AN BLUNT'S OFFICE,
HEADQUARTERS
SO, ALEX. IT'S BEEN A WEEK. HAVE YOU SETTLED BACK DOWN INTO NORMAL LIFE?
MORE OR LESS. I TOLD MY TEACHERS I GOT MUGGED.
JACK STARBRIGHT THINKS I'M MENTAL FOR EVEN COMING BACK HERE.
YES, WELL, I ASKED YOU IN TO GIVE YOU AN UPDATE.
SCORPIA'S PLOT WAS A COMPLETE FAILURE, AND I DOUBT THEY'LL TRY ANYTHING LIKE IT AGAIN. YOU DID A VERY GOOD JOB.
THEY ALSO LOST ONE OF THEIR TOP ASSASSINS, THAT MAN NILE. WHAT HAPPENED TO HIM?
I THINK HE JUST GOT TIRED . . . BURNED OUT.

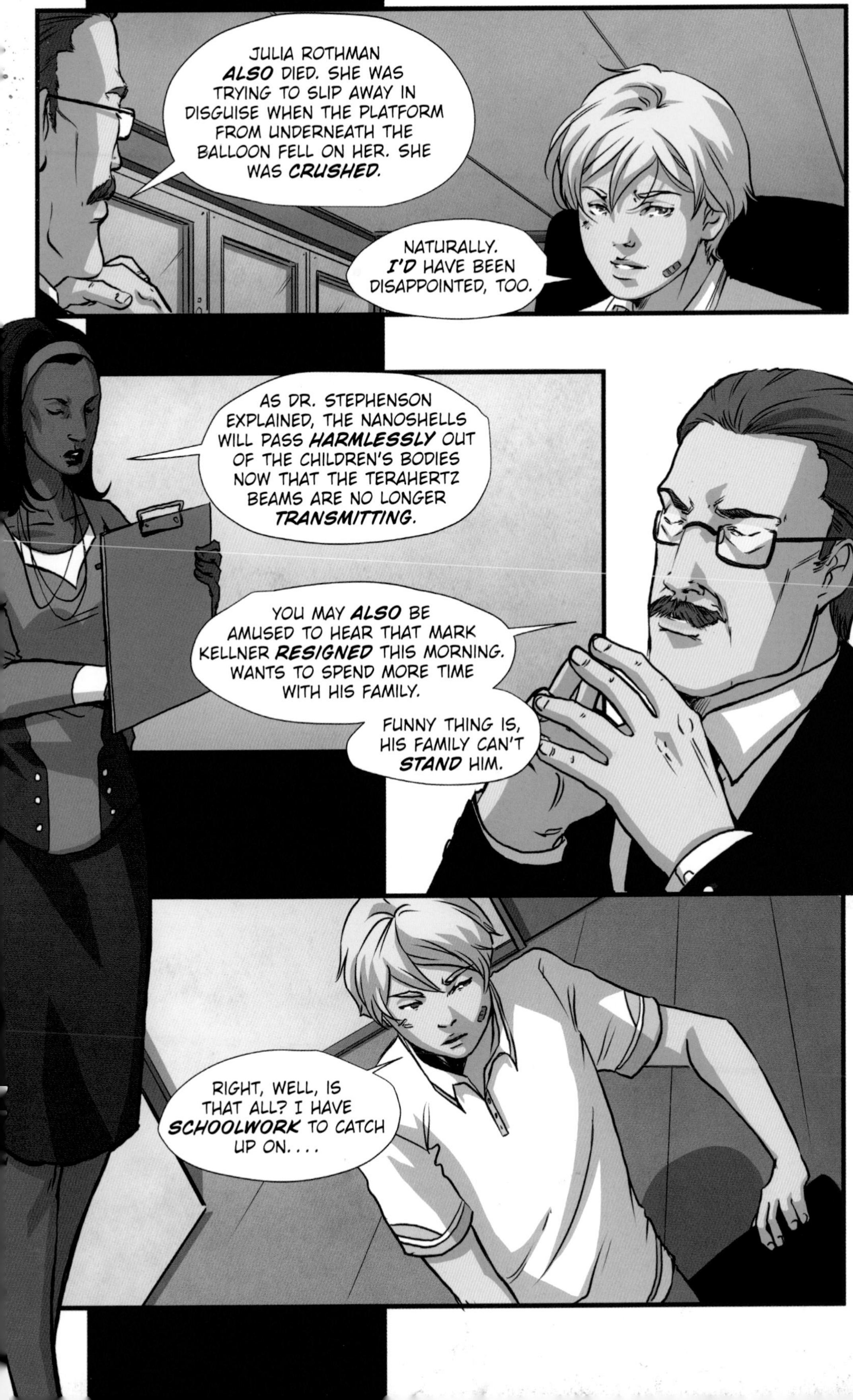
JULIA ROTHMAN ALSO DIED. SHE WAS TRYING TO SLIP AWAY IN DISGUISE WHEN THE PLATFORM FROM UNDERNEATH THE BALLOON FELL ON HER. SHE WAS CRUSHED.
NATURALLY. I'D HAVE BEEN DISAPPOINTED, TOO.
AS DR. STEPHENSON EXPLAINED, THE NANOSHELLS WILL PASS HARMLESSLY OUT OF THE CHILDREN'S BODIES NOW THAT THE TERAHERTZ BEAMS ARE NO LONGER TRANSMITTING.
YOU MAY ALSO BE AMUSED TO HEAR THAT MARK KELLNER RESIGNED THIS MORNING. WANTS TO SPEND MORE TIME WITH HIS FAMILY.
FUNNY THING IS, HIS FAMILY CAN'T STAND HIM.
RIGHT, WELL, IS THAT ALL? I HAVE SCHOOLWORK TO CATCH UP ON. . . .

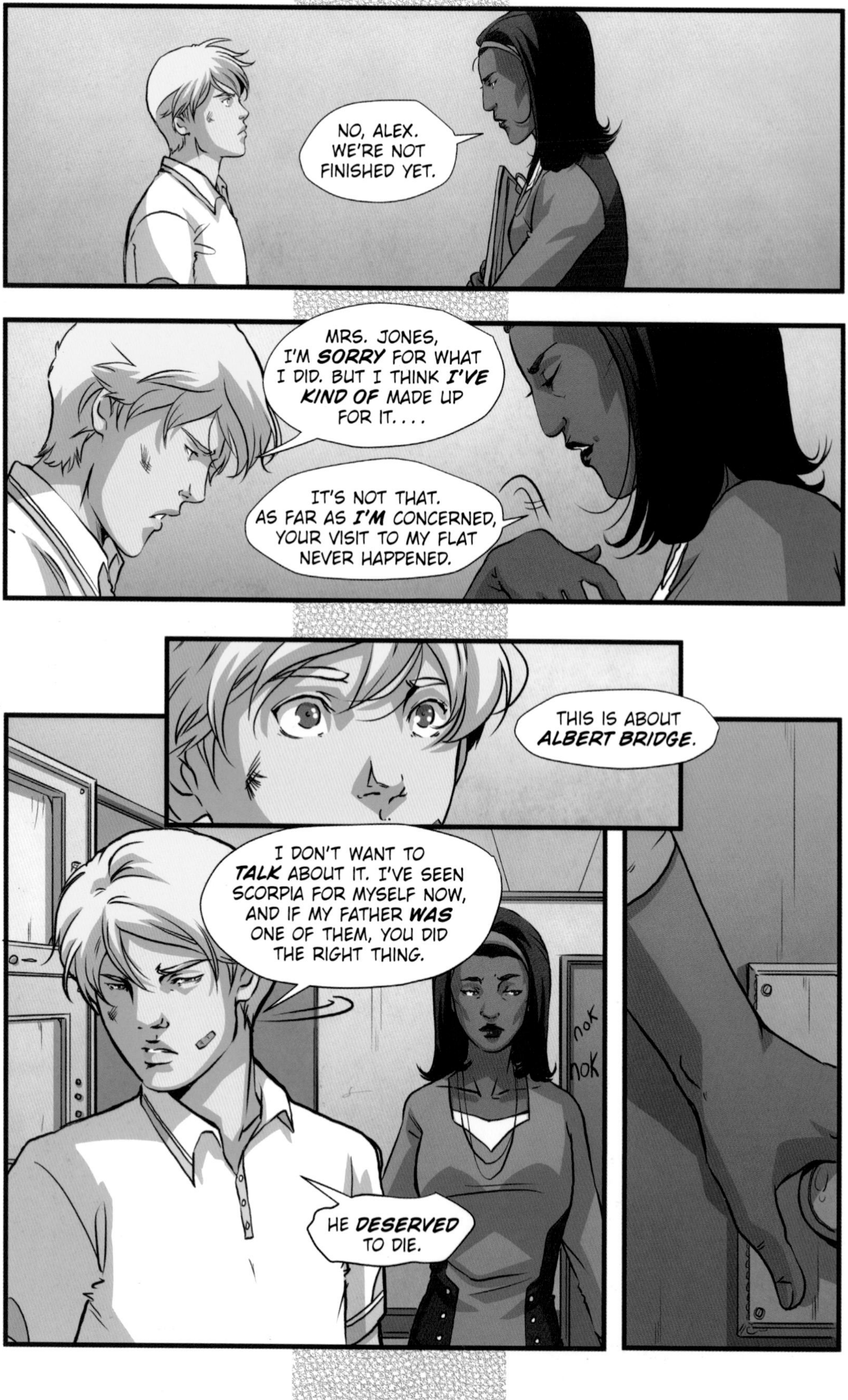
NO, ALEX. WE'RE NOT FINISHED YET.
MRS. JONES, I'M SORRY FOR WHAT I DID. BUT I THINK I'VE KIND OF MADE UP FOR IT. . . .
IT'S NOT THAT. AS FAR AS I'M CONCERNED, YOUR VISIT TO MY FLAT NEVER HAPPENED.
THIS IS ABOUT ALBERT BRIDGE.
I DON'T WANT TO TALK ABOUT IT. I'VE SEEN SCORPIA FOR MYSELF NOW, AND IF MY FATHER WAS ONE OF THEM, YOU DID THE RIGHT THING.
nok
nok
HE DESERVED TO DIE.

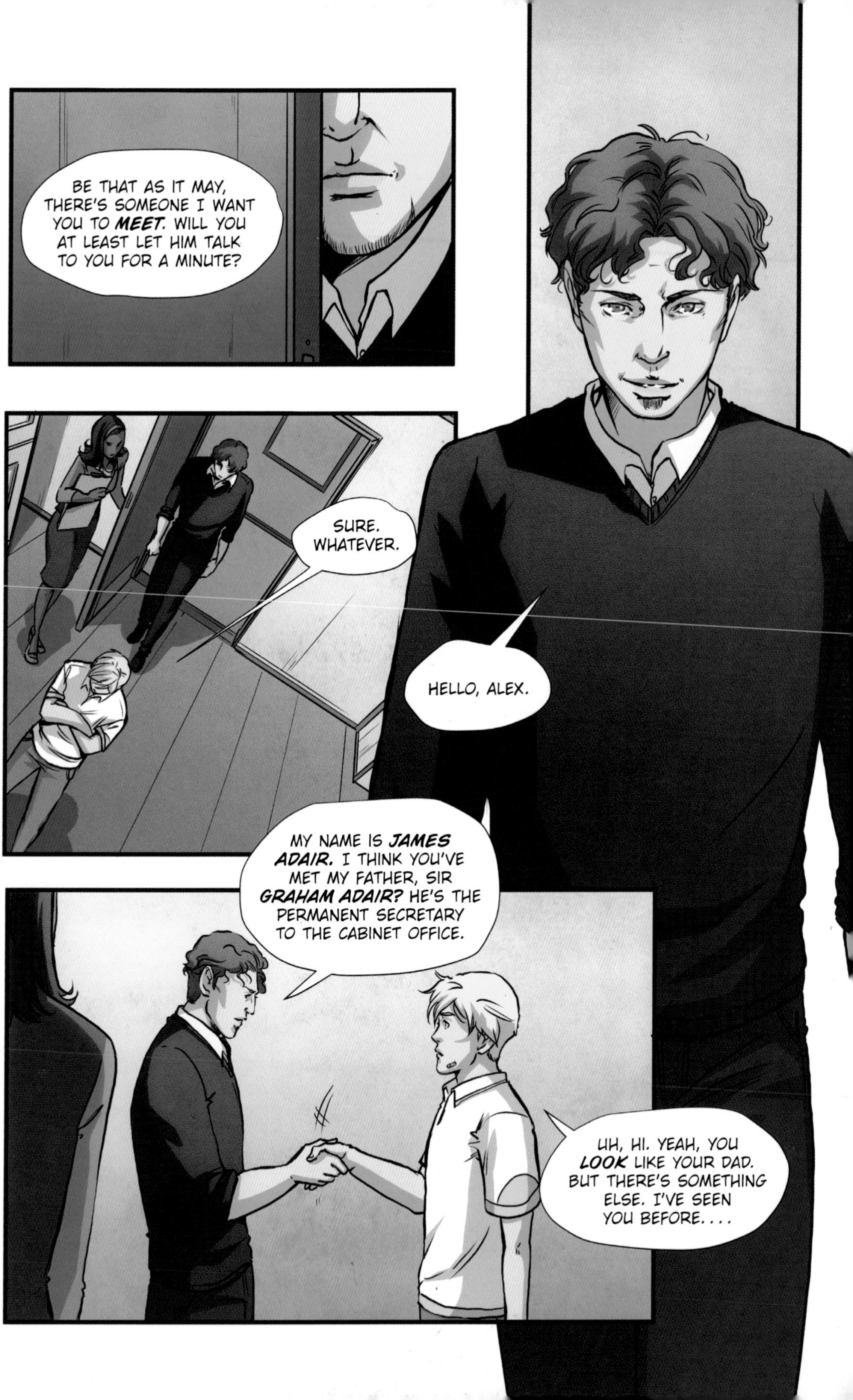
BE THAT AS IT MAY, THERE'S SOMEONE I WANT YOU TO MEET. WILL YOU AT LEAST LET HIM TALK TO YOU FOR A MINUTE?
SURE. WHATEVER.
HELLO, ALEX.
MY NAME IS JAMES ADAIR. I THINK YOU'VE MET MY FATHER, SIR GRAHAM ADAIR? HE'S THE PERMANENT SECRETARY TO THE CABINET OFFICE.
UH, HI. YEAH, YOU LOOK LIKE YOUR DAD. BUT THERE'S SOMETHING ELSE. I'VE SEEN YOU BEFORE. . . .

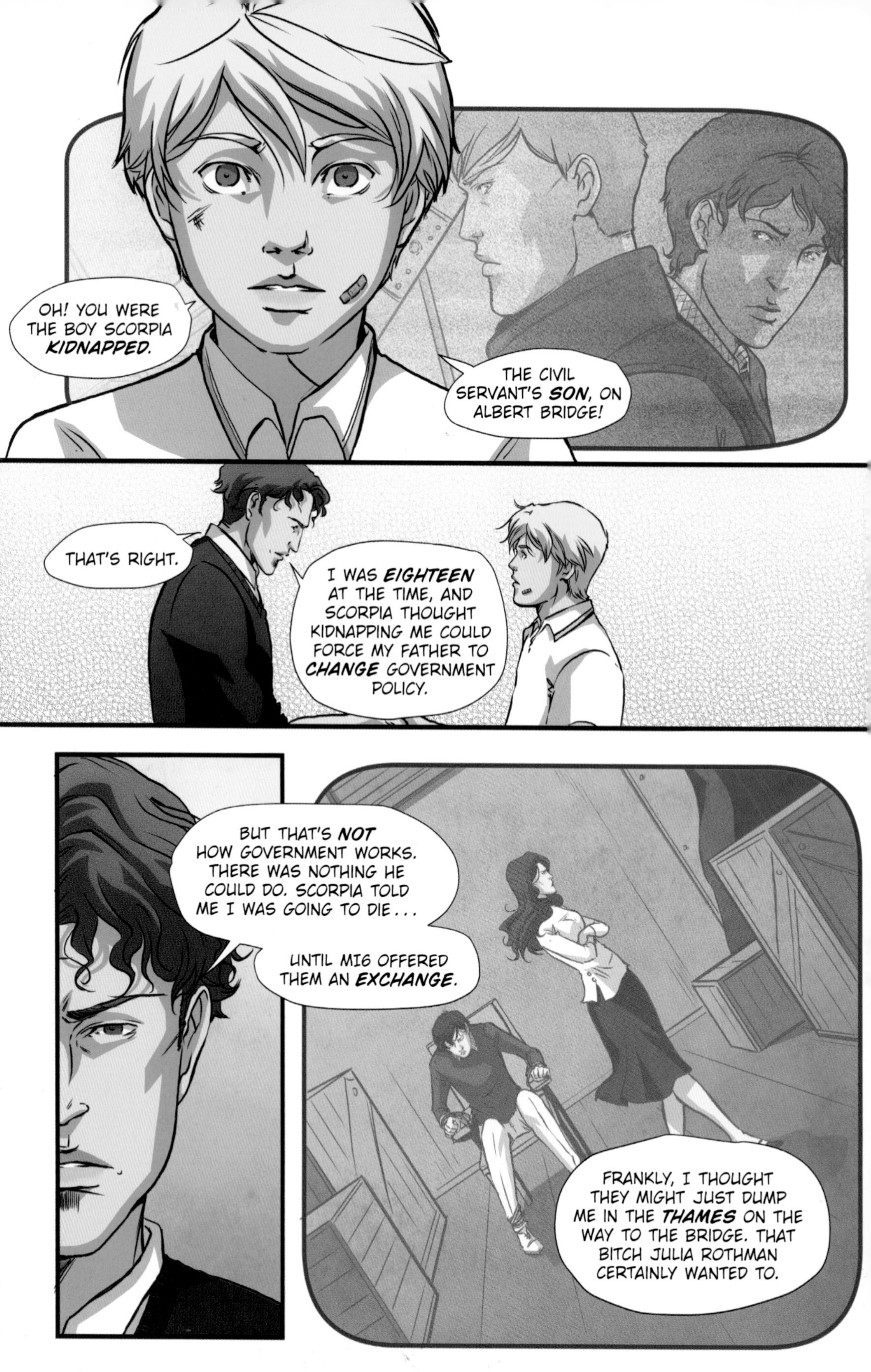

OH! YOU WERE THE BOY SCORPIA KIDNAPPED.
THE CIVIL SERVANT'S SON, ON ALBERT BRIDGE!
THAT'S RIGHT.
I WAS EIGHTEEN AT THE TIME, AND SCORPIA THOUGHT KIDNAPPING ME COULD FORCE MY FATHER TO CHANGE GOVERNMENT POLICY.
BUT THAT'S NOT HOW GOVERNMENT WORKS. THERE WAS NOTHING HE COULD DO. SCORPIA TOLD ME I WAS GOING TO DIE . . .
UNTIL MI6 OFFERED THEM AN EXCHANGE.
FRANKLY, I THOUGHT THEY MIGHT JUST DUMP ME IN THE THAMES ON THE WAY TO THE BRIDGE. THAT BITCH JULIA ROTHMAN CERTAINLY WANTED TO.

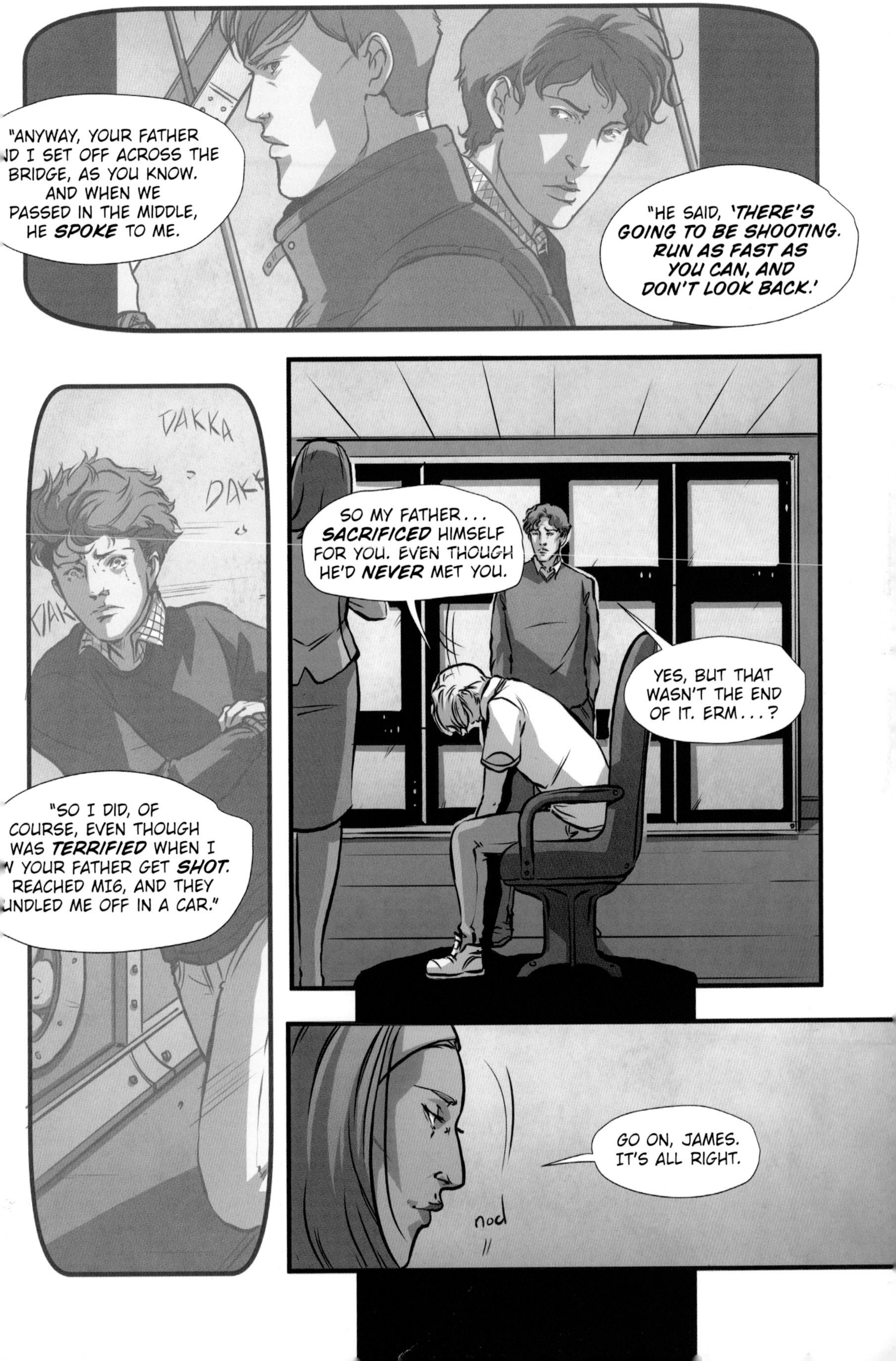
"ANYWAY, YOUR FATHER ND I SET OFF ACROSS THE BRIDGE, AS YOU KNOW. AND WHEN WE PASSED IN THE MIDDLE, HE **SPOKE** TO ME.
"HE SAID, **'THERE'S GOING TO BE SHOOTING. RUN AS FAST AS YOU CAN, AND DON'T LOOK BACK.'**
DAKKA
DAKK
"SO I DID, OF COURSE, EVEN THOUGH WAS **TERRIFIED** WHEN I W YOUR FATHER GET **SHOT**. REACHED MI6, AND THEY UNDLED ME OFF IN A CAR."
SO MY FATHER... **SACRIFICED** HIMSELF FOR YOU. EVEN THOUGH HE'D **NEVER** MET YOU.
YES, BUT THAT WASN'T THE END OF IT. ERM...?
GO ON, JAMES. IT'S ALL RIGHT.
nod

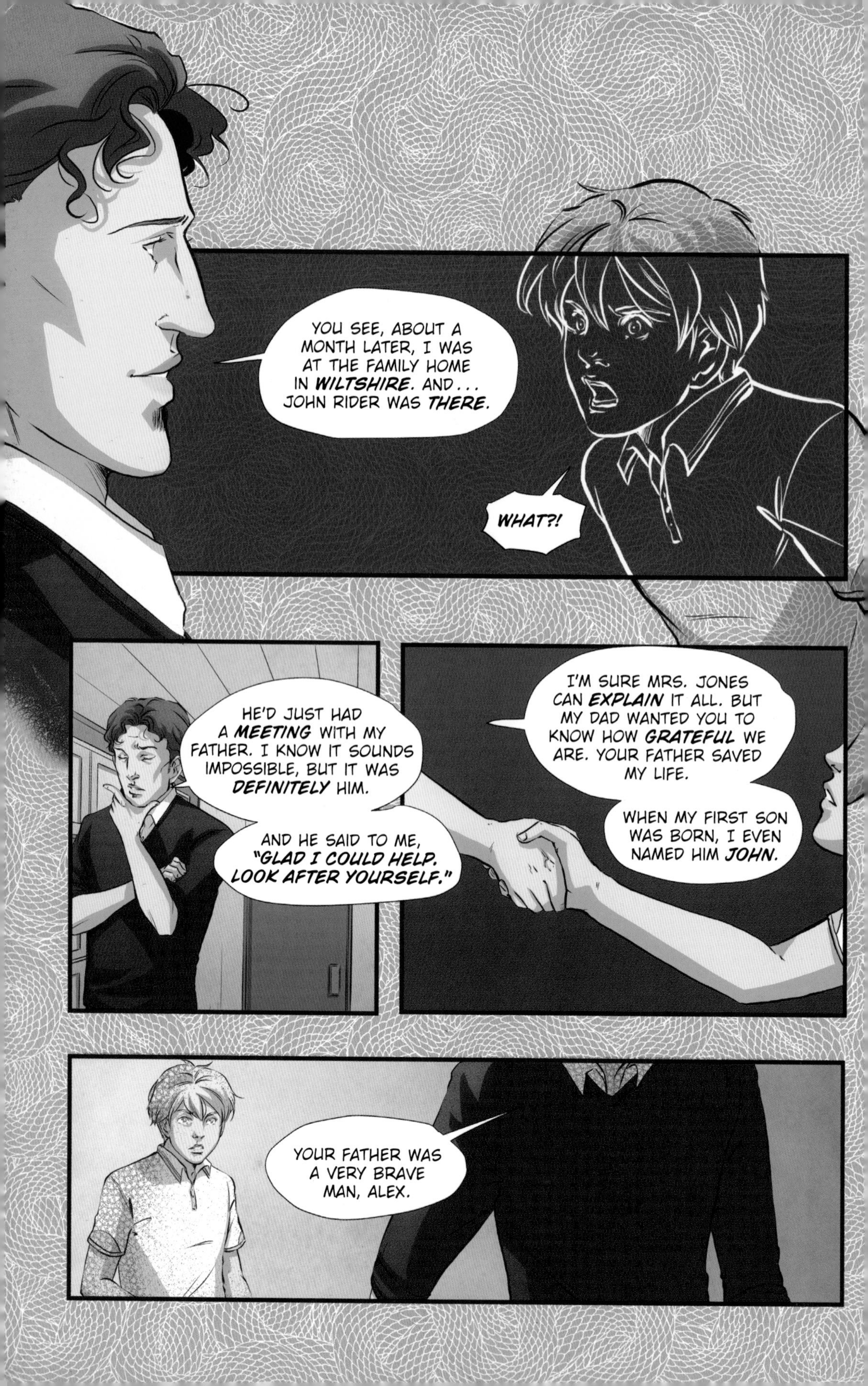
YOU SEE, ABOUT A MONTH LATER, I WAS AT THE FAMILY HOME IN WILTSHIRE. AND . . . JOHN RIDER WAS THERE.
WHAT?!
HE'D JUST HAD A MEETING WITH MY FATHER. I KNOW IT SOUNDS IMPOSSIBLE, BUT IT WAS DEFINITELY HIM.
AND HE SAID TO ME, "GLAD I COULD HELP. LOOK AFTER YOURSELF."
I'M SURE MRS. JONES CAN EXPLAIN IT ALL. BUT MY DAD WANTED YOU TO KNOW HOW GRATEFUL WE ARE. YOUR FATHER SAVED MY LIFE.
WHEN MY FIRST SON WAS BORN, I EVEN NAMED HIM JOHN.
YOUR FATHER WAS A VERY BRAVE MAN, ALEX.

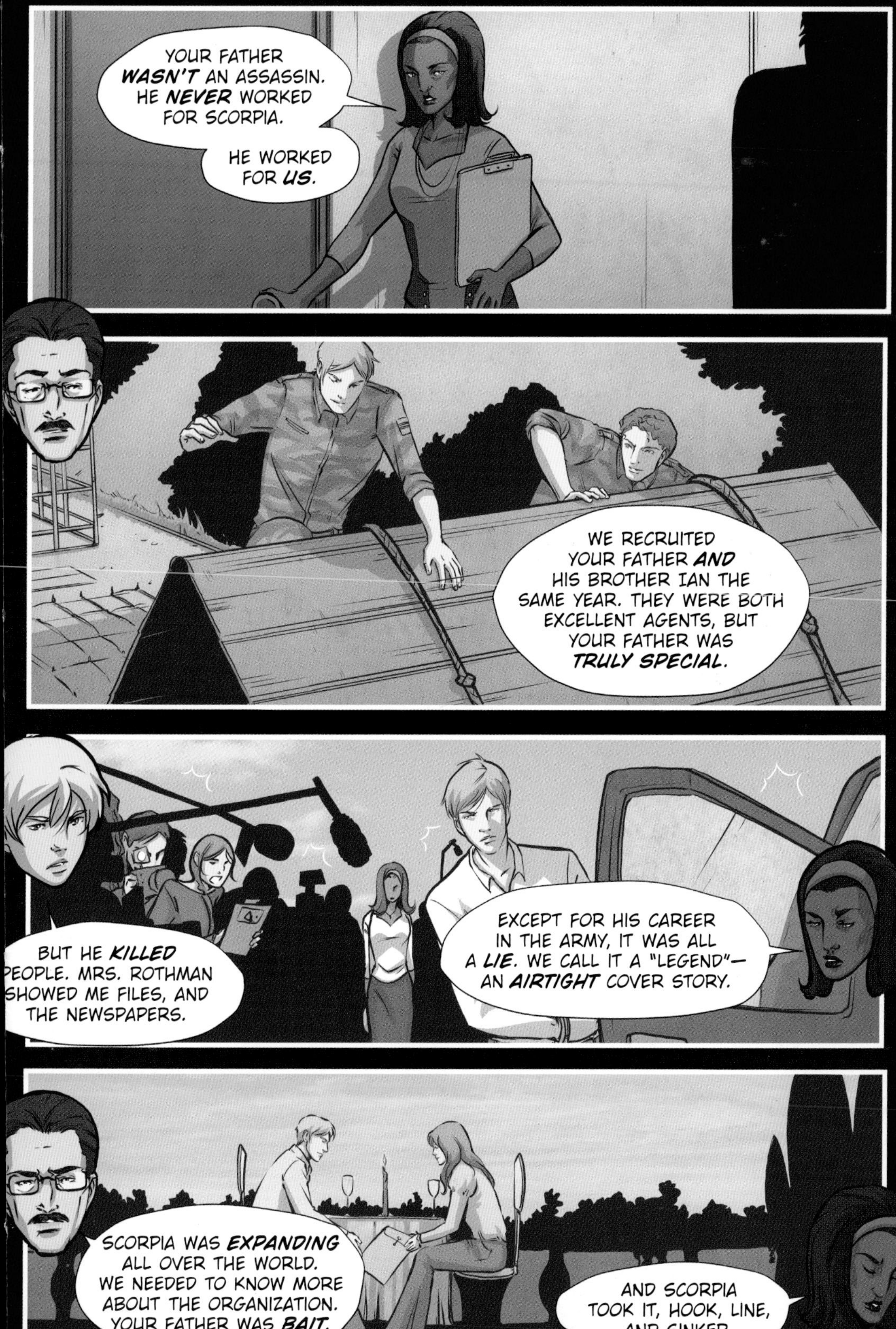
YOUR FATHER WASN'T AN ASSASSIN. HE NEVER WORKED FOR SCORPIA.
HE WORKED FOR US.
WE RECRUITED YOUR FATHER AND HIS BROTHER IAN THE SAME YEAR. THEY WERE BOTH EXCELLENT AGENTS, BUT YOUR FATHER WAS TRULY SPECIAL.
BUT HE KILLED PEOPLE. MRS. ROTHMAN SHOWED ME FILES, AND THE NEWSPAPERS.
EXCEPT FOR HIS CAREER IN THE ARMY, IT WAS ALL A LIE. WE CALL IT A "LEGEND"— AN AIRTIGHT COVER STORY.
SCORPIA WAS EXPANDING ALL OVER THE WORLD. WE NEEDED TO KNOW MORE ABOUT THE ORGANIZATION. YOUR FATHER WAS BAIT.
AND SCORPIA TOOK IT, HOOK, LINE, AND SINKER.

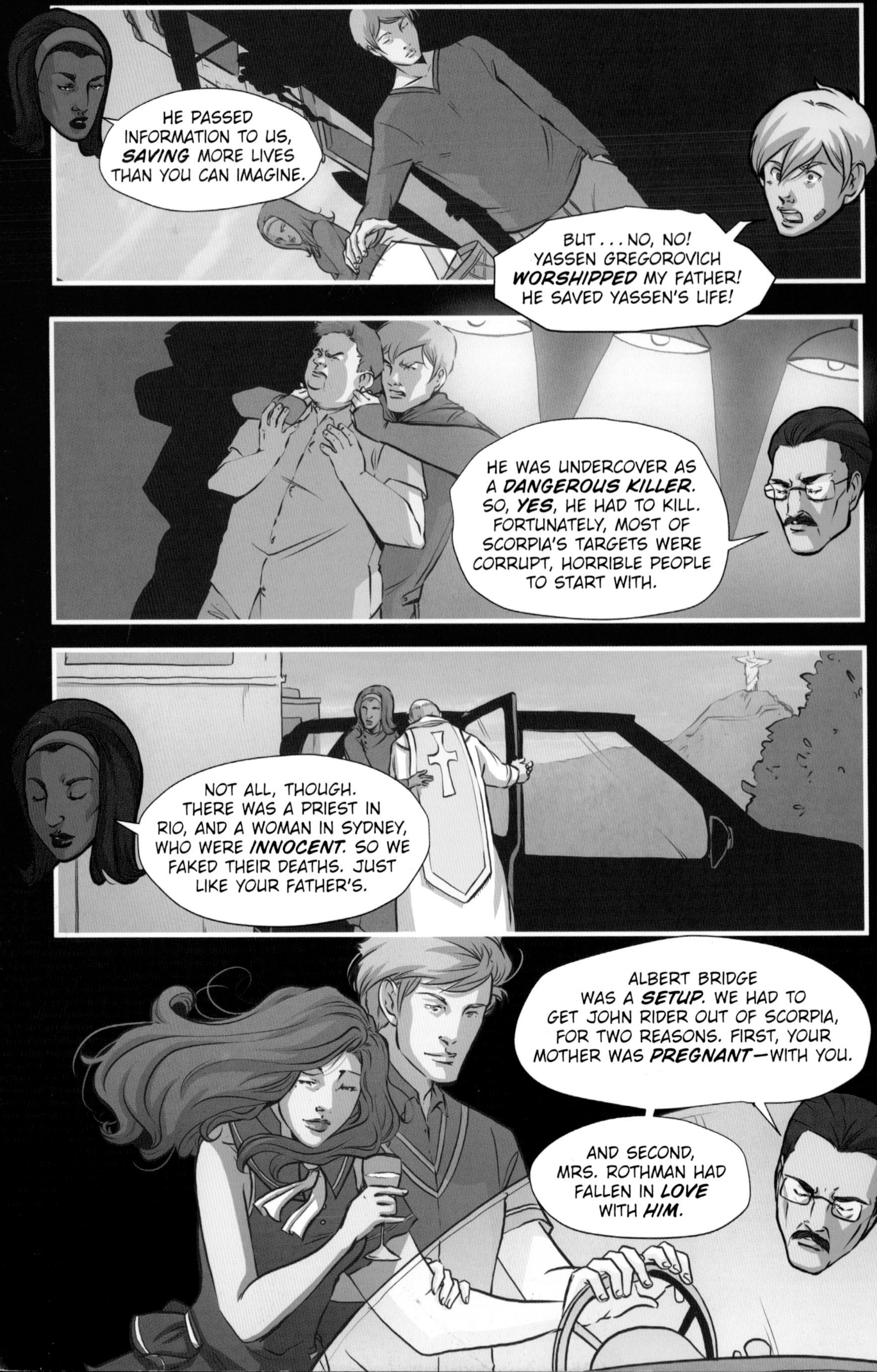
HE PASSED INFORMATION TO US, SAVING MORE LIVES THAN YOU CAN IMAGINE.
BUT . . . NO, NO! YASSEN GREGOROVICH WORSHIPPED MY FATHER! HE SAVED YASSEN'S LIFE!
HE WAS UNDERCOVER AS A DANGEROUS KILLER. SO, YES, HE HAD TO KILL. FORTUNATELY, MOST OF SCORPIA'S TARGETS WERE CORRUPT, HORRIBLE PEOPLE TO START WITH.
NOT ALL, THOUGH. THERE WAS A PRIEST IN RIO, AND A WOMAN IN SYDNEY, WHO WERE INNOCENT. SO WE FAKED THEIR DEATHS. JUST LIKE YOUR FATHER'S.
ALBERT BRIDGE WAS A SETUP. WE HAD TO GET JOHN RIDER OUT OF SCORPIA, FOR TWO REASONS. FIRST, YOUR MOTHER WAS PREGNANT—WITH YOU.
AND SECOND, MRS. ROTHMAN HAD FALLEN IN LOVE WITH HIM.

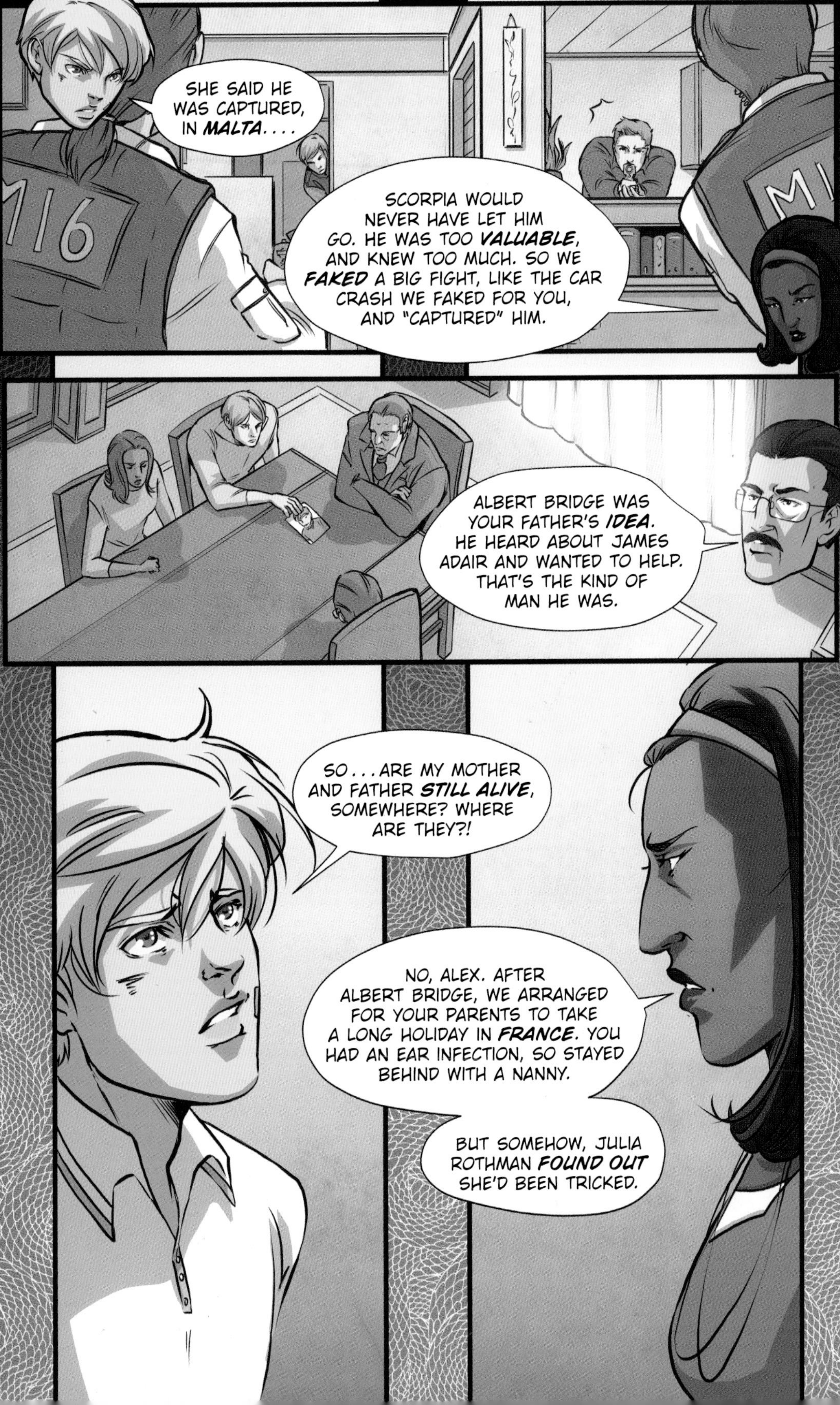
SHE SAID HE WAS CAPTURED, IN MALTA. . . .
SCORPIA WOULD NEVER HAVE LET HIM GO. HE WAS TOO VALUABLE, AND KNEW TOO MUCH. SO WE FAKED A BIG FIGHT, LIKE THE CAR CRASH WE FAKED FOR YOU, AND "CAPTURED" HIM.
ALBERT BRIDGE WAS YOUR FATHER'S IDEA. HE HEARD ABOUT JAMES ADAIR AND WANTED TO HELP. THAT'S THE KIND OF MAN HE WAS.
SO . . . ARE MY MOTHER AND FATHER STILL ALIVE, SOMEWHERE? WHERE ARE THEY?!
NO, ALEX. AFTER ALBERT BRIDGE, WE ARRANGED FOR YOUR PARENTS TO TAKE A LONG HOLIDAY IN FRANCE. YOU HAD AN EAR INFECTION, SO STAYED BEHIND WITH A NANNY.
BUT SOMEHOW, JULIA ROTHMAN FOUND OUT SHE'D BEEN TRICKED.

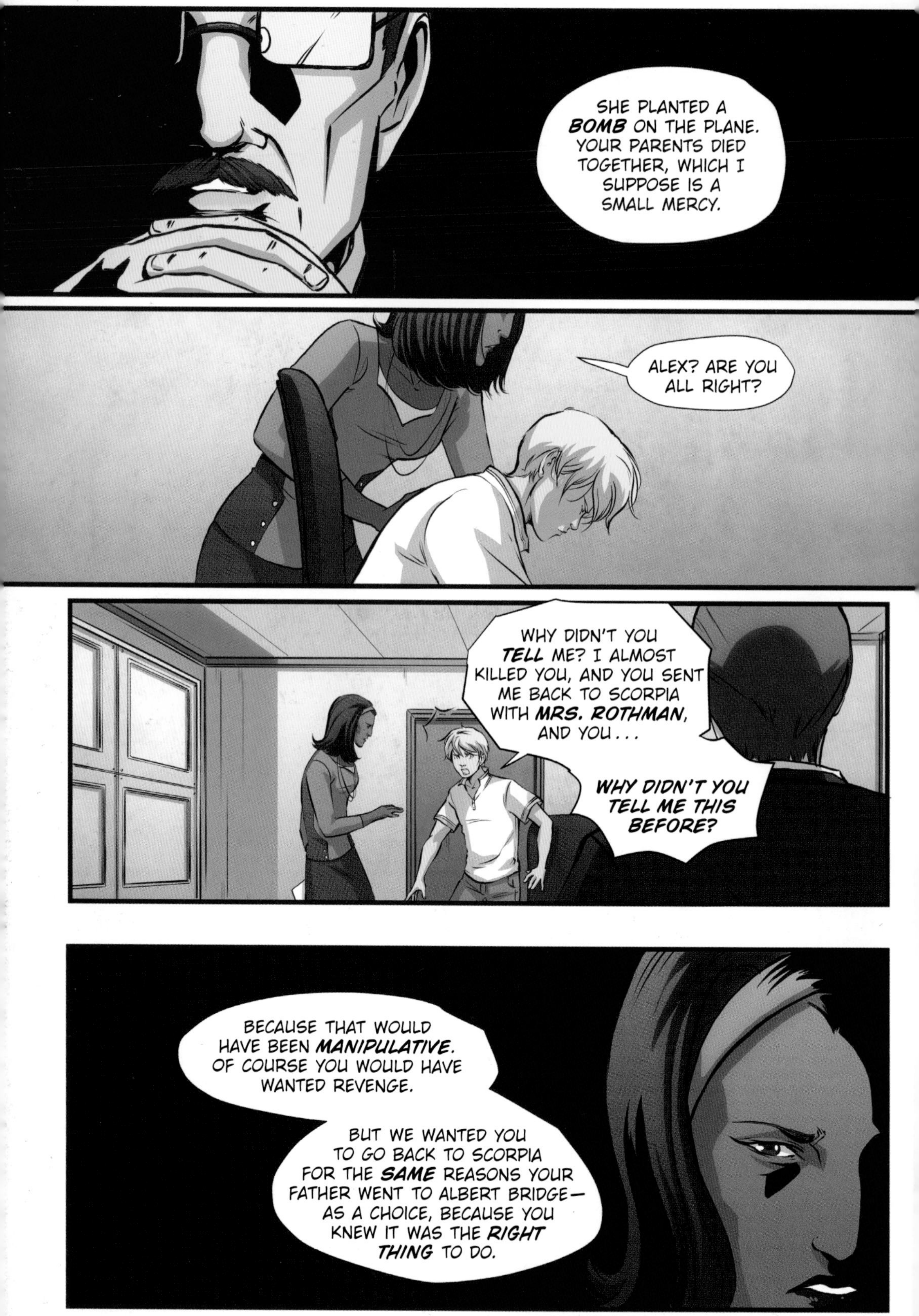
SHE PLANTED A BOMB ON THE PLANE. YOUR PARENTS DIED TOGETHER, WHICH I SUPPOSE IS A SMALL MERCY.
ALEX? ARE YOU ALL RIGHT?
WHY DIDN'T YOU TELL ME? I ALMOST KILLED YOU, AND YOU SENT ME BACK TO SCORPIA WITH MRS. ROTHMAN, AND YOU . . .
WHY DIDN'T YOU TELL ME THIS BEFORE?
BECAUSE THAT WOULD HAVE BEEN MANIPULATIVE. OF COURSE YOU WOULD HAVE WANTED REVENGE.
BUT WE WANTED YOU TO GO BACK TO SCORPIA FOR THE SAME REASONS YOUR FATHER WENT TO ALBERT BRIDGE— AS A CHOICE, BECAUSE YOU KNEW IT WAS THE RIGHT THING TO DO.

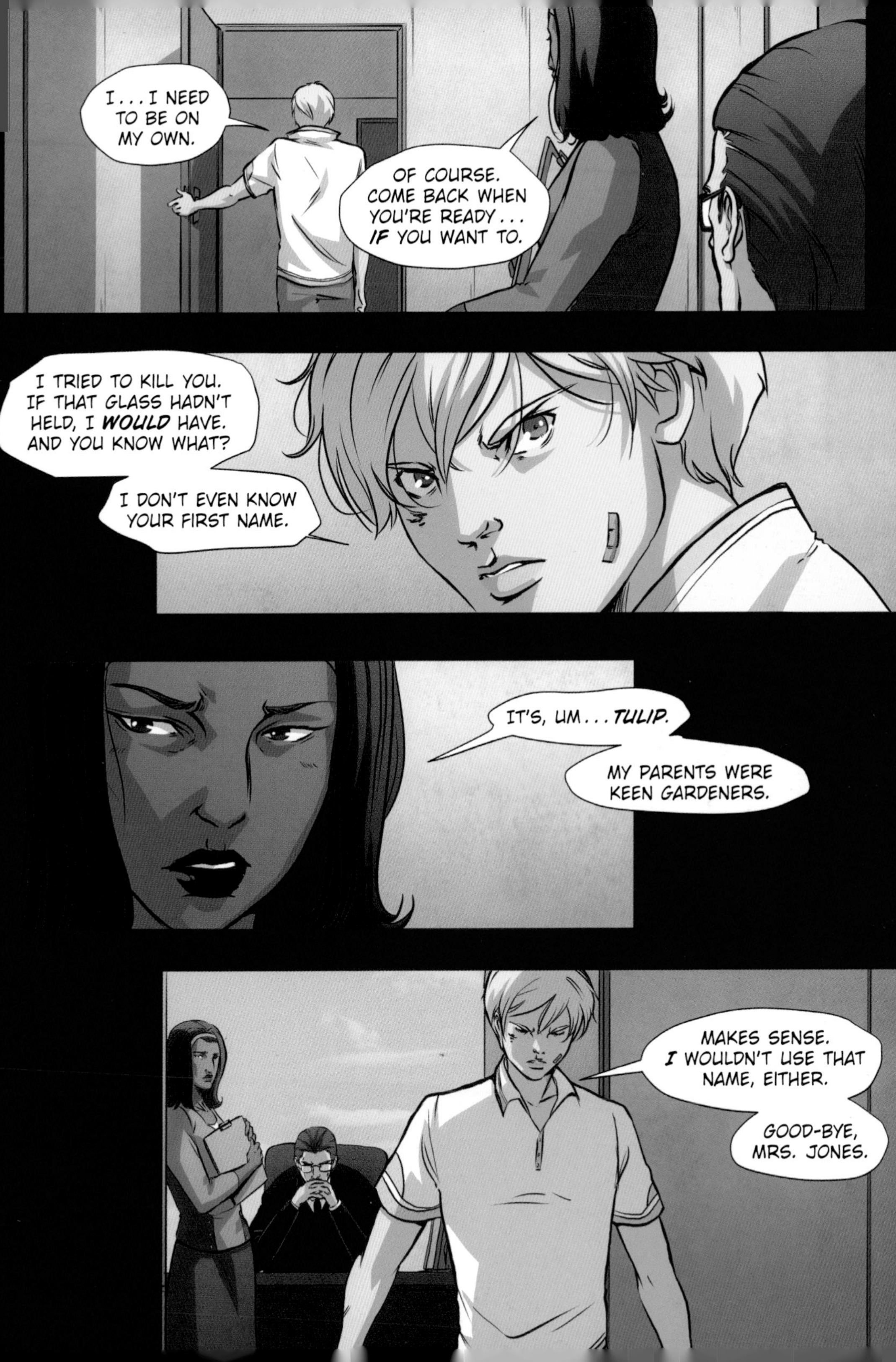
I . . . I NEED TO BE ON MY OWN.
OF COURSE. COME BACK WHEN YOU'RE READY . . . *IF* YOU WANT TO.
I TRIED TO KILL YOU. IF THAT GLASS HADN'T HELD, I *WOULD* HAVE. AND YOU KNOW WHAT?
I DON'T EVEN KNOW YOUR FIRST NAME.
IT'S, UM . . . *TULIP*.
MY PARENTS WERE KEEN GARDENERS.
MAKES SENSE. *I* WOULDN'T USE THAT NAME, EITHER.
GOOD-BYE, MRS. JONES.

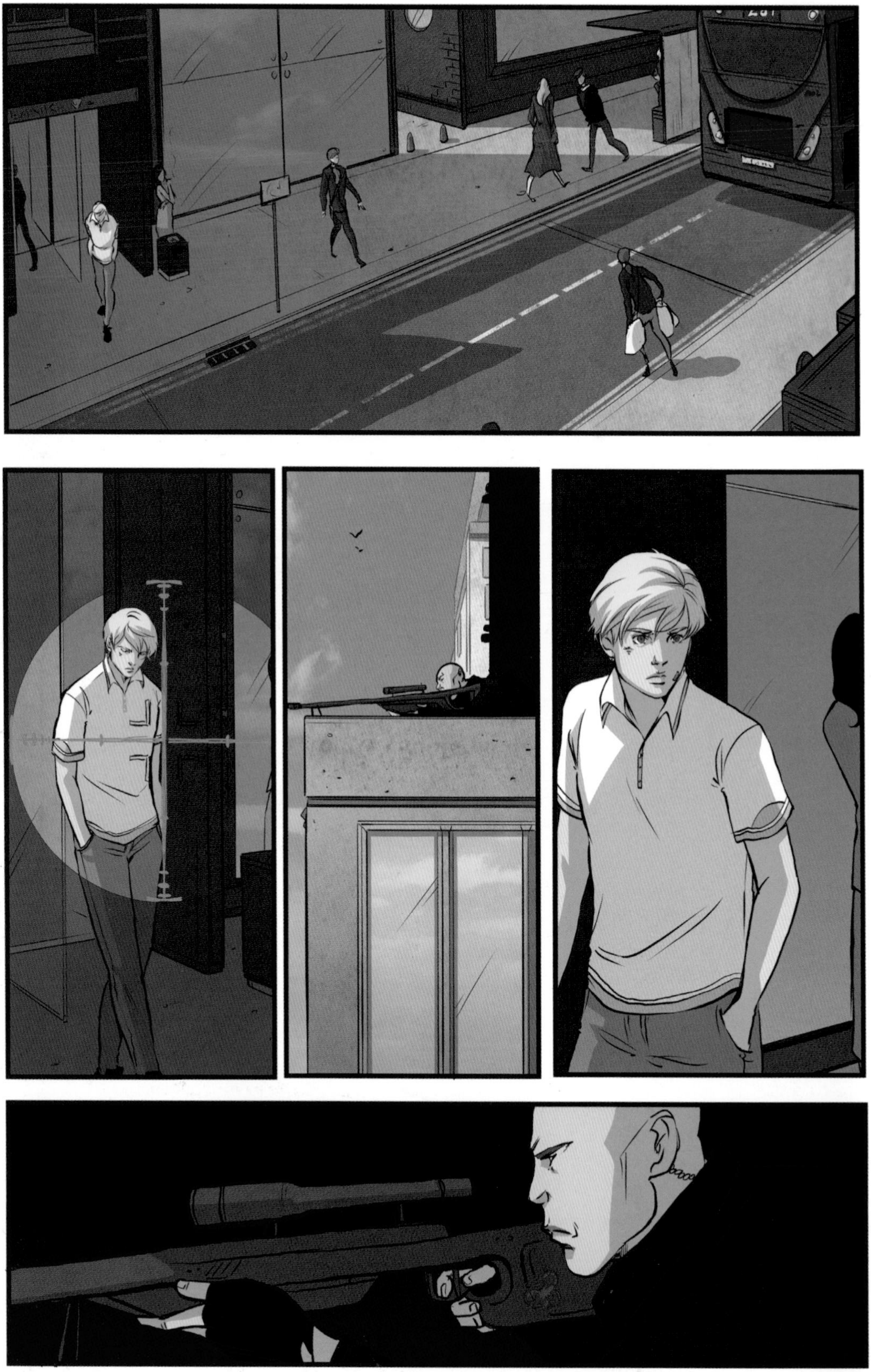

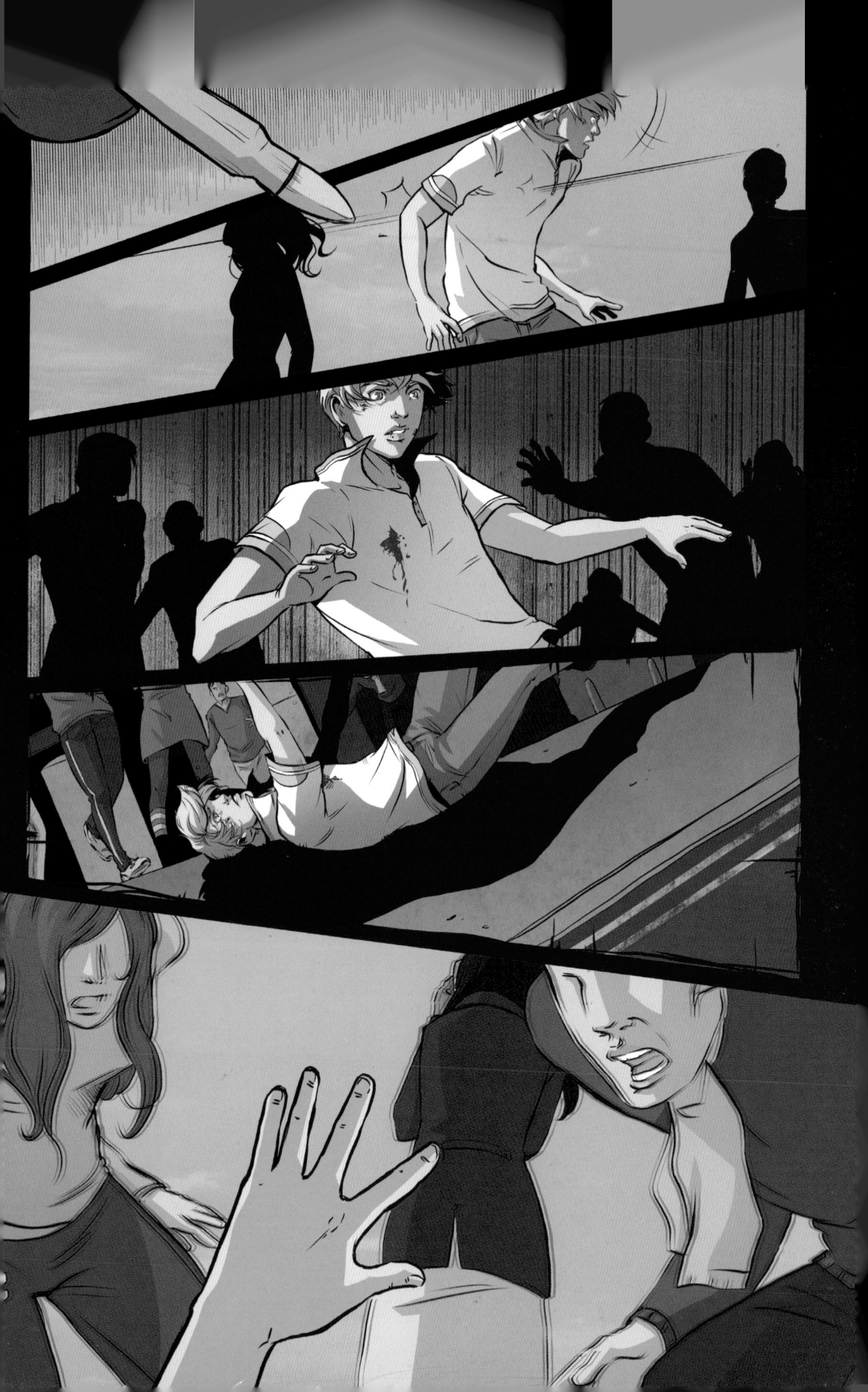

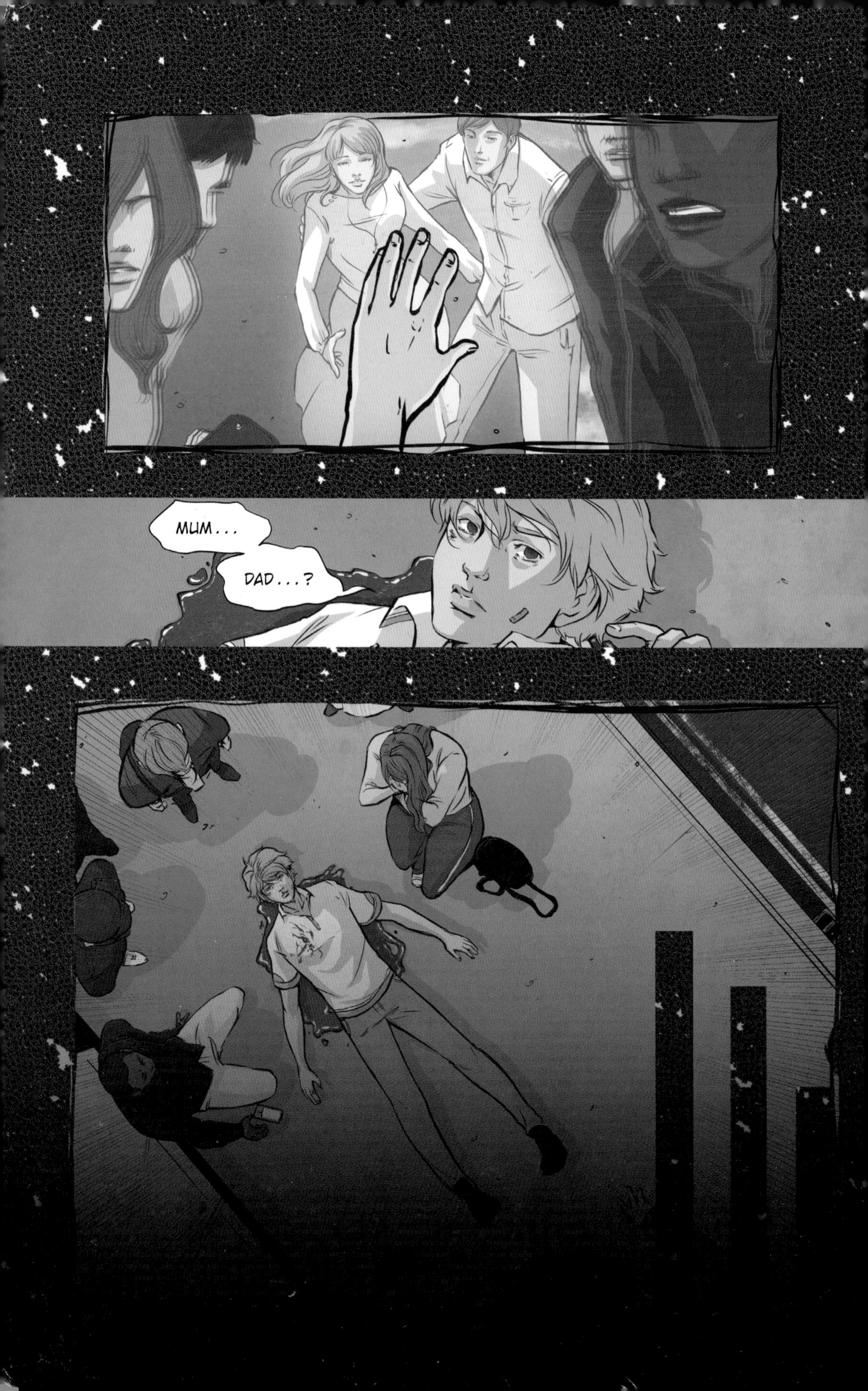
MUM...
DAD...?